D1765805

THE KING'S DAUGHTERS

THE TENTH CENTURY

MJ PORTER

Copyright notice
Porter, M J
The King's Daughters
Copyright ©2019, Porter, M.J, Amazon edition
All characters and events in this publication, other than those clearly in the public domain, are
fictitious and any resemblance to actual persons, living or dead, is purely coincidental.

ALL RIGHTS RESERVED. No part of this publication may be reproduced, stored in a retrieval
system or transmitted in any form or by any means without the prior written permission of the
author, nor be otherwise circulated in any form of binding or cover other than that in which it is
published and without a similar condition being imposed on the subsequent buyer.

Cover design by Flintlock Covers

❦ Created with Vellum

CONTENTS

AD923

Eadgifu clutched the child's head tightly to her chest as the horse she was mounted on thundered through the darkness.

She had no idea how long she'd been riding, but knew it was long enough for the night to have settled and to have wound itself almost back to dawn. The grey edges on the horizon were a testament to the fact that day would soon arrive once more.

While her son slept, it was reasonably easy going, or rather, as tranquil as it could be with a three-year-old strapped to her chest, but already she'd felt Louis stir twice and knew her luck would soon be at an end.

And what would she do then?

While ten men surrounded Eadgifu, only five of them were Wessex warriors. Only those five did she wholly trust, and yet, she trusted none of them enough to hand over her son to their care while she rested her aching back.

Louis was too precious, and he was all she had left now. And the future of her husband's kingdom was nestled within his small frame.

Eadgifu bit back a sob of despair. She'd vowed not to cry, not in front of these hard-faced men, their loyalty to her safety unquestioned. Yet, while darkness had sheeted the land, she'd allowed tears to fall freely down her face, drowning her son's fair hair in the sorrows of all her lost dreams.

Never before had she ridden so fast, and for so long. Eadgifu feared being followed, captured and taken before the bastard Count Heribert of Vermandois, her husband's traitorous gaoler, and one-time greatest supporter.

Heribert had promised sanctuary to King Charles, in light of what had happened after the Battle of Soissons. The usurper of Charles' kingdom and his enemy, King Robert, had been killed, but it had only plunged West Frankia into a higher state of unease. Charles lacked the support to rule West Frankia alone, but there was no valid alternative immediately evident.

But Heribert had seen too much potential in keeping Charles as a captive. This was why she dashed toward the coastline, in a desperate effort to return to Wessex, to her father, and the protection he would offer her son, and herself.

King Edward would be pleased to shield the heir of West Frankia until Charles could win his freedom and rule West Frankia once more. It would only add to her father's growing renown. He was the son of King Alfred, the mighty king who had kept the kingdom of Wessex whole against the ravages of the Viking Raiders.

Eadgifu strained to hear any sound of pursuit, too fearful to glance behind and catch a glow of lanterns and brands lighting the path of any pursuers. She told herself the risk of tumbling from her horse was too great but knew it for a lie.

Eadgifu's heart beat too fast, and between her arms and the reins of the horse, Louis began to struggle.

"Mama," his words were muffled, as she bent her chin to place a kiss on his damp hair.

"You must be still," Eadgifu urged her son in her native tongue, and not the dialect of West Frankia. She worried that the smooth gait of her animal might convince Louis that they were not on horseback.

"It will not be much longer," Eadgifu spoke the words, desperate to believe them herself, but fearing that she lied.

A good boy, Louis subsided against her, his small body keeping her warm where the cold night air tried to drive all feeling from her hands, feet and nose. His small hands wrapped themselves partway around her chest, two bright spots on the side of her back warming her more than all the cloaks and furs ever could.

On the path in front it was possible to now see enough that when the horse before her stumbled, she gasped in horror. The animal quickly recovered, and continue to race, but the warrior on the back of the animal, turned to meet her eyes, his gaze bleak beneath the hood of his cloak, before he swept his head back to the path they followed.

The roads had been kind to them so far, well maintained, and easy to follow, but as they came ever closer to the coast, Eadgifu could feel them beginning to disintegrate. Here, the roads were used often, and they were starting to perish from the heavy traffic. Perhaps, she considered, if there were less in-fighting in West Frankia, the roads would be better, and no one would fear for their lives when they rode on them.

There was an irony there that made her smirk with annoyance.

"Mama, I'm hungry," her son's soft voice permeated her thoughts.

"I am too," she tried to console, before adding. "We'll stop soon, and then there'll be bread, and something to drink." Eadgifu abruptly realised that her son spoke in the Wessex dialect too. How quickly they'd both abandoned their West Frankish ways.

Once more, Louis settled against her as daybreak finally bathed the horizon in a dazzling array of winter mauve and cerise. The sun glowed dully crimson, still mostly hidden, behind a bank of cloud that seemed to glow as though the horizon were on fire. There was nothing like a winter sunrise.

But still, Eadgifu could see nothing of the much longed-for coastline. How much further could it possibly be?

Only then her heart stilled, her ears straining to hear.

"Is that horses?" she called, hoping one of her escorts would hear her.

The man whose horse had stumbled pulled back and rode beside her, head cocked to listen before he nodded mutely, his head sweeping from side to side, as he tried to determine where their company came from.

"I don't know where they are," he called. "Keep riding. I'm sure I saw a glimpse of the sea."

Eadgifu's eyes strained, desperate to see the deep blue of the ocean and to know that they'd finally reached Boulogne Sur Mer. From there she'd be able to take a ship back to Wessex.

Yet, as much as Eadgifu squinted against the steadily rising sun, the clouds seeming to evaporate before the glowing orb, she could see nothing but shadow. Even her ears failed to pick up the distinct sound of the sea hitting the coastline.

"There," and Eadgifu followed the pointing hand of the warrior, hoping he'd spotted the coast, but instead he'd found the horsemen, half shadows, obscured by the slow sunrise, that no doubt illuminated them but still held the land before them in the grey of dawn, as they seemed to thunder toward them.

Fear beat inside Eadgifu like a drum skin, pulled too tight, the sound deep and foreboding. For a moment, her breath left her, as she spurred her horse onwards, her legs protesting the movement. Her gasp of pain was bitten back by her cold lips, her teeth snagging on them so that the taste of blood flooded her mouth.

Perhaps they would merely be able to ride straight past them. Surely no one would have heard of her plan to escape, not from Boulogne, and it was from there that the horses seemed to race.

In front of her, three of her warriors rode their horses directly at those coming toward her. How many were there? She squinted, counting to distract herself, trying to be rational, trying to excuse their evident haste as somehow not related to her.

"My Lady Queen," Beornstan, horror on his face.

"There are twenty of them," Beornstan announced, his voice high with disbelief. "If we must, we'll protect you, and you must ride on, with your son, and the baggage animal."

Next to Eadgifu rode an animal devoid of a rider, but laden down with all she'd been able to claim from her royal lifestyle. Inside the tightly laced saddlebags, was a fortune in gold and silver, jewels and gems, as well as three ceremonial dresses and a cloak of deepest, imperial purple, the proof that she was a queen, all be it, one without a kingdom for the foreseeable future.

"I understand," Eadgifu agreed hastily, her arms tightening around her son, as he fidgeted once more, his demands for food becoming more urgent.

She couldn't do this. Eadgifu felt her back hunch. This was too much. She would never escape but would end up a prisoner like her husband, and her son used in the political games that the nobility of West Frankia was so keen to play.

Only then did Eadgifu sit upright, settle her son once more, shushing him with another kiss, and gazing at her advancing enemy. If that was what they were.

"Behind us," the words from the rearmost rider almost deflated her again. But there was something about those racing toward her that made her heart leap with hope.

Was that? Was it even possible?

She fixed her gaze on the flickering banner racing toward them, the colours of the embroidery seeming to entice with promises of warmth and wealth, the shimmering of the gold thread drawing her eye.

"Is that the Wessex wyvern?" Eadgifu gasped the question, trying not to hope but doing so all the time.

Beornstan focused on the lead horse, and then he yelped.

"It's men from Wessex," Beornstan almost exploded. "They've come to rescue us."

Eadgifu almost sobbed with relief, only for the man at the back of their small company to dampen her relief.

"They're gaining on us," he called, his voice stark with the realisation that they might not reach the men coming toward them, before those behind caught up.

"Stay firm," Eadgifu commanded, her voice filled with the iron of command. She had determined who led the men of Wessex, and she could hardly believe it, and yet knew that she was safe now, all at the same time.

Before her eyes, ten of the warriors racing toward them spurred their animals on, exhorting them to ride even faster, ever more recklessly with the use of heels and reins. They rushed to come between them and the enemy who followed those who fled.

That her half-brother was one of those reckless men didn't surprise her, and equally made her appreciate that while the charge appeared irresponsible, it would succeed. It was far more under control than was immediately evident. It was not the wild dash for victory it seemed.

Trying to focus on going forward, and not on what was happening behind her, Eadgifu cried with relief as a force of fifteen men surrounded them. They turned smartly so that they rode with them, and not toward them, the other ten horses thundering on into the half-light of the new day.

Not that any slowed. If anything, the horses somehow knowing the end was in sight, rode faster. Eadgifu almost wished she could close her eyes, as the sun rose ever higher, lifting many of the shadows of night, but leaving just enough to fear the horse would stumble on the poorly maintained roadway.

Belatedly, Eadgifu heard the rumble of more horses' hooves and panicked, before a voice shouted in her native tongue.

"Nearly there," Athelstan gasped, somehow beside her, although Eadgifu had watched him ride beyond her and confront those chasing her. Surely enough time hadn't gone by for the enemy to be dead?

"They won't worry us now," Athelstan added, his sharp eyes on the coastline that abruptly formed in front of their charge.

"We'll soon have you both safe." As Athelstan spoke, he drew back, just a little, and Eadgifu had no idea what he did, until she heard his soft voice once more, coaxing the packhorse to slow. Of course, Eadgifu thought, with no rider, and at such speed, it could easily just keep racing ever forwards.

"Slow," Athelstan commanded his voice firm and filled with the resolve that comes from knowing the instruction would be immediately obeyed.

Eadgifu gazed down at her son where he once more slept, bored of waiting to be replied to. She hiccupped a sob, as the mast of a ship, ready and waiting in a narrow harbour, came into view, bobbing on the morning tide.

Eadgifu now allowed one glance behind her, and nothing more. She was determined to remember as much as she could of West Frankia, not to tell her son, but so the last four years wouldn't appear as a dream when she tried to recall them.

Only then did Eadgifu's horse finally grind to a total halt, the sound of crashing waves reaching her ears even over her erratic heartbeat and gasping breaths. Safety meant going into those waves, boarding the waiting ship, its outline coming ever more into focus with each wave crashing onto the harbour.

"Come, hand him to me. I'll keep him safe." Athelstan's voice was rich with the command, the sound so reminiscent of her father that she almost obeyed without even considering the words.

Eadgifu realised that everyone was already dismounted, some groaning and complaining as they tried to walk on legs grown cold and unresponsive after a night in the saddle. Others hastened to grab weapons and guard against any unexpected attack.

Eadgifu clutched Louis but knew she couldn't dismount and hold her son safe. Not after so long in the saddle.

Still, she hesitated, peering at Athelstan.

Her half-brother. How she loathed him. Athelstan looked so like her father, it was impossible to ignore his parentage, and yet she would if she could. Blue eyes met her own, a challenge in them. Her feelings toward him were no secret. And neither were his toward her. Or rather, his lack of them.

Athelstan seemed to think nothing of his father's family after his own mother's death.

Yet Athelstan was here, now, rescuing her.

Neither of her full-brothers were. No doubt Ælfweard and Edwin were warming their arses in a Wessex palace somewhere, safe from all harm.

And neither was her father.

"He's heavy," the words croaked from Eadgifu's mouth, her arms uncoiling from around her burden. The horse beneath her blew as heavily as she did, no doubt relieved to know the journey was finally at an end.

"Oof," the sound from Athelstan's mouth as he took the full weight of Louis from Eadgifu's arms forced a smile to her face, against all her desires to resent her brother, even though he'd saved her.

Yet Athelstan held Louis close, cradling her son with such fondness that a lump formed in her throat. Eadgifu looked away, handed her reins to the waiting Beornstan, his face red with cold, and labouriously forced her left leg over the horse's saddle, before releasing the right and landing with a soft sound of pain on the white sand.

Eadgifu groaned as her feet tingled painfully, her thighs chafing from the unusual activity of riding for so long.

"Hurry," Athelstan called softly, turning to lead her to the ship. "The initial enemy is dead, but more may come."

As Eadgifu walked around the front of her animal, patting the nose in thanks, for the animal had undoubtedly saved her and her son from a fate worse than death, her eyes focused on the busy work around her rather than her half-brother.

The Wessex warriors had stripped the pack animal, and her possessions were being carefully carried on board the bobbing ship. The animal, head down, looked as exhausted as all the others, as it pawed at the ground beneath, sandy and yet grassy all at the same time.

"What of the horses?" she thought to ask of no one in particular.

"A man from Boulogne will come for them, as soon as we're gone," Athelstan assured her, standing and waiting courteously beside the ship for her. Louis was still in his arms, for all it was clear from his curt tone that Athelstan wanted fewer questions and more moving.

"Good, they shouldn't suffer."

"They won't," Athelstan offered his arm to assist her on the uneven surface, but Eadgifu pretended not to see the movement, stepping around him, wincing with the actions as it felt as though small seax's stabbed at her toes.

Head high, Eadgifu walked with all the dignity she could muster to the ship.

It was neither the largest or smallest she'd ever seen, and it seemed too small to her to hold all of her belongings, and those of the warriors who'd escorted her, and those Athelstan had brought with him.

The sail was slack, the oars on the right-hand side out and ready, those on the left stowed away, as the ship dipped up and down in time to the waves.

Eadgifu swallowed her nerves. She didn't like being onboard a ship. The motion upset her stomach, and in her haste, she had no mint to chew.

Raising her skirt, she stepped into the hull of the craft, reaching out to claim a steadying hand, assured by the strength in the forearm of the sailor, someone she didn't know, but who seemed to command her rescue ship.

"My Lady, Queen Eadgifu," his voice was gruff but pleasant, his black hair and beard well-groomed. Perhaps a wealthy merchant.

"Come, there's a place beneath the canvas. For you and your son."

Eadgifu looked where the finger pointed and saw a crude structure erected near the central mast. While she quaked at the flimsy shelter, she could acknowledge that it was more than everyone else had.

Behind her, the ship shifted again, as Athelstan stepped onboard, his gait steady, his careful bundle of her son clasped in his arms. A look of wonder crossed his face, as he and Louis took the measure of each other, her son seeming to realise that this was a monumental moment in his short life.

Eadgifu wished she could snatch her son back, but knew it was impossible while she stood and braced herself against the waves that suddenly seemed far fiercer than before boarding.

"I'll bring him to you," Athelstan offered, his eyes far from her, as he looked behind. There were only two more yet to board the ship. She was holding everyone up.

"My thanks," Eadgifu forced, her chin high, walking to the offered canvas, and settling on one of her wooden chests, the lid now covered with a fur, and blessedly flat.

While she'd thought sitting again after so long in the saddle was the last thing she wanted, the relief was intense, her legs trembling even from the few steps she'd taken from her horse.

She was amongst men, warriors and merchants, and yet they were trying to make her comfortable. Athelstan settled Louis in her arms gently, peeling back the boy's cloak, to meet Louis' eyes with his own. Eadgifu looked away then, wishing she hadn't seen the sudden joy on Athelstan's face, the flicker of instant love for his nephew that had suffused his usual taciturn expression. She had little-seen him before but had always detested him all the same.

Athelstan may have rescued her, but Athelstan was just as much her enemy as King Robert and his bloody son, Count Hugh.

Decisively, Athelstan stepped away from his nephew and his half-sister, and Eadgifu was pleased to see him go. Athelstan settled himself on one of the many benches used by the shipmen, as though he were ready to row.

And then everyone was on board. With three oars pushed out against the stone side of the harbour, those on the right side of the ship forced a gap between the stone wall and the vessel. A coil of rope was being wound up by the ship's commander, thrown to him by a small face, almost no older than Louis, a gleam in the eyes, as the youth fingered the shimmering coin in his hand that the ship's commander tossed to him over the waves in payment.

Eadgifu focused on that face. It might be the last from West Frankia that she saw for some time.

As the ship pulled deeper and deeper into the current, the oars from both sides of the boat now dipping in and out of the waves, she thought to take a breath of relief, only for the ship's captain to douse all her hopes.

"There's a ship out there," he called, pointing behind Eadgifu. Although she turned, her canvas shelter shielded the ship from her view.

"It must just be Count Rollo?" Athelstan replied in a firm voice, never letting up from his rowing. Eadgifu was still amazed that her half-brother was taking his turn at rowing the ship. She'd not have expected it from him.

"Count Rollo?" While Eadgifu had meant to speak softly, the ship's captain had overheard her words. He'd made his way to her, to peer out beyond the creaking frame of the vessel.

"Count Rollo promised his assistance," the man confirmed, his words respectful enough, although his gaze was far away, his eyes narrowed against the glare of the sun.

Behind them, Eadgifu's eyes alighted on a gathering of people on the beach where they'd left the horses. She was sure that the horses had been quickly led away by a few figures that'd crawled around the animals, but now it appeared that they'd returned, which made no sense to her.

With the sun a halo of brightening yellow, half of the beach was thrown into shadow and half too bright to truly focus on, and yet she could still just about make out the horses all the same.

"Who's that?" she asked, her finger pointing back the way they'd come, wondering why none of the rowers had yet seen them.

"King Robert's men," the captain told her as he followed her finger. "Good job they have no ship waiting for them." Eadgifu nodded. No matter how much she screwed up her eyes, she could make out no discerning details about the horses and the men they carried. The ship's captain was clearly possessed of clear sight.

"It's Count Rollo's ship," the ship's captain announced, the tension easing out of the shoulders of all the rowers, Eadgifu's as well.

"He said he'd send ships, but not horses. Good man," Athelstan announced to his force of men, never ceasing in his rowing efforts. "He will escort us to Wessex."

"Once we get beyond his ship, we'll raise the sail," the captain announced. "It's windy enough that we could be in Wessex before nightfall. God willing."

The news thrilled Eadgifu. The thought of being still after the night of non-stop movement was an enticing one.

As the ship rode the waves, the oars pushing her ever further away from West Frankia, Eadgifu's eyes settled, not on the men and horses the ship's captain assured her were on the beach, but instead on the outline of West Frankia. She felt her breath hitch, the finality of her actions becoming a reality.

Her husband had lost his kingdom, but more importantly, so had she, and Eadgifu had no idea if she would see her husband, or her kingdom again.

AD924

Eadgifu could feel eyes on her and knew there could only be one person interested in her at that moment in time.

"What?" she demanded to know, her voice filled with annoyance.

Sisters could be so infuriating.

"Nothing," Eadhild replied, her tone smug all the same. She was pleased that already she had irritated her sister.

"Then go away," Eadgifu commanded, wishing her sister anywhere but close to her.

Bad enough her father was dead, her husband imprisoned and King Rodolphus claiming her husband's kingdom. She really didn't wish to contend with her infuriating sister as well. Not now. If she was honest with herself, perhaps never.

Hastily, Eadgifu smoothed her hands over her ceremonial dress, one of the few that she'd manage to leave West Frankia with, desperate to ensure she looked the part. Her father was dead, the king of Wessex. By rights, as the queen of West Frankia, she should have been accorded equal status to her father, and his bloody wife. But of course, she was an exile, and so too her son. Even her father had only been able to show so much pity for his broken plans in extending the reach of his family into the most potent monarchy on the Continent, that of West Frankia.

Not that he'd given up hope of restoring her husband to his kingdom, but Edward had been too easily distracted by events in Mercia since her return to have laid any firm plans for Charles' restoration.

"The colour suits you," Eadhild complimented her, and yet Eadgifu knew it was still a criticism.

"I've nothing in a darker shade," Eadgifu commented, her voice high with indignation. How could her sister think there would be time for a new dress to be made? Her father had only been dead a week.

But Eadgifu turned away from worrying about her dress, cloak, jewels and brooches, and turned to view her sister. Of course, Eadhild had a dress in a suitable colour for mourning, an expense, but one she seemed prepared to have taken to ensure she had the correct shade when the time came.

"Mother warned me before she died, and I took her advice." Eadhild's voice was high and smug, and Eadgifu bit down hard on her tongue to stop a tetchy response. "She said father would wear himself out with his obsession in Mercia, and of course, she wished me to wear suitable mourning for her own funeral."

Eadhild had been assiduous in visiting their mother in her nunnery, at Wilton. Eadgifu had found it to be more of a chore. Her mother was bitter and twisted, each and every comment a complaint aimed at her father, or her son, her imprisoned husband, or herself. Visits were far from pleasant. Eadgifu, other than knowing the annulment of her mother's marriage to the king was a contentious issue just waiting to be exploited when it was politically expedient to do so, had very little time for her mother while she'd lived. Even after she'd returned from West Frankia.

Lady Ælfflæd, or Sister Ælfflæd as she'd been called for the last few years of her life, was little use to her exiled daughter, and then she had compounded the issue by dying.

It seemed though that Eadhild had far fewer criticisms regarding her mother. Perhaps she'd even shared Sister Ælfflæd's complaints about King Edward. In the time that Eadgifu had been a wife and queen in West Frankia, her sister had become a woman, and one adept at keeping her own counsel.

Eadgifu's own thoughts about her father were far more mixed. He'd willingly married her to a man as old as he was to further his dynasty. That had never seemed like the action of a father who loved his daughter. And yet in doing so, King Edward had ensured she would be a queen in her own right, and the mother of her husband's heirs, for Charles' first wife had never produced a male child for him, despite their many years of marriage, and six daughters.

There'd been no legitimate heir for West Frankia until Louis' birth four years ago, and that had made Eadgifu a powerful force in West Frankia.

But then, while Eadgifu was fulfilling her wifely obligations, her husband had been put aside, another ruling in his place. Eadgifu was now a queen with no kingdom, and worse, her father was dead as well.

King Edward had not stinted to ensure that Eadgifu and her young son were treated with respect and well provided for at the Wessex court, but that didn't make it any more palatable.

And now he'd bloody died, fighting some rebels in Mercia, and that left Eadgifu once more uncertain of the future.

Her brother, Ælfweard, would succeed as King of Wessex, her despised older, half-brother, as King of Mercia, and just where that left her hopes of restoring her husband's kingdom to him, she didn't know.

The only advantage was that her brother, Ælfweard, was her firm ally. He always had been. As to Athelstan's thoughts about her, she preferred not to think about them, ascribing his rescue of her as down to duty and nothing else. Athelstan would never allow anything to impinge on his honour. He was a prickly man. He always had been. So she was told.

Yes, she'd thanked him for rescuing her and Louis when they'd arrived in Wessex, but Athelstan had merely bowed and having escorted her to Winchester, left without speaking to their father.

Athelstan had never been welcome in Wessex, and he knew it only too well.

"I understand our dear step-mother told you the news herself, and that you allowed her to leave the palace of Winchester." This was another grievance and one that Eadgifu didn't wish to hear. She was still furious at the tone her younger step-mother had used when informing her that her father was dead. The bitch.

That she'd then had the temerity to slip from the palace and claim sanctuary at the Nunnaminster was being laid entirely at Eadgifu's feet. What did her brothers and sisters expect her to have done? Apprehended her father's wife? Have her young step-brothers taken prisoner?

In the same situation, she knew they'd have failed to accurately predict the queen dowager's actions. All the same, Eadgifu was being blamed for the embarrassment, no matter the illogical sentiment.

"The bitch-mother told me of my father's death, yes. And then I made my way to the king's hall, to commiserate and congratulate my brother. Whatever the queen dowager chose to do, I was gone by then. Like the rest of us, I was with Ælfweard."

A smug expression lifted Eadhild's face. Eadgifu thought she might be pretty if it weren't for the constant arrogant expression on her young face.

Well, perhaps she would be.

Eadgifu knew it was said that all of her full sisters looked similar to her. She happened to disagree, but she kept the observation to herself. Eadhild shared the same high forehead and blue eyes, but her nose was far too narrow, and her mouth too pinched, in Eadgifu's opinion. As young as Eadhild was, she appeared much older, as though life had treated her harshly, and each fresh upset had marred her face.

"They say she will attend the funeral." Eadhild had leaned forward, over Eadgifu's shoulder, her eyes on Eadgifu's selection of jewels. There might not be a horde of them, rescued from West Frankia, but they were all beautiful pieces. Eadgifu bit back her annoyance. There was a reason she rarely showed her treasures, even to her sisters. She didn't want to be judged on her queenship by her jewels, and of them all, Eadhild was the one most likely to do so.

"She was his wife," Eadgifu exclaimed. "Of course, she'll attend the funeral." Eadgifu was still fiddling with her dress brooches, the damn pins refusing to fasten, as they should. While she worked on them, Eadgifu also kept glancing over her other shoulder, wondering just where her son had got to now.

At four years old, Louis was far too headstrong, and would no doubt be getting into mischief. At least he'd be alone, and not with his half-uncles. Her father's most recent children, both younger than her Louis, were not the type of children she wanted her son to associate with. They were far too much like their mother. The bitch-mother was flaccid until the opportunity presented itself to cause problems.

"Ælfweard will order her back to Winchester palace as soon as the funeral has finished," Eadhild continued to infuriate, and Eadgifu sucked down her annoyance.

"Ælfweard can do what he wants with her. She's no longer important. Ælfweard will rule, and he'll reclaim Mercia from our half-brother, and then Ælfweard will marry, and his sons will inherit from him." While Eadgifu spoke the litany, she admitted that she hardly cared. Provided Wessex had a strong king, who would support her husband and her son's claim to West Frankia, she didn't wholly mind who it was, although it would help that it was Ælfweard.

They had quickly rekindled their friendship on her return to Wessex, almost as though she'd never been gone.

But it was West Frankia that occupied her every thought from waking to sleeping, and often, in her dreams as well.

She would reclaim Charles' kingdom for him. She just needed time, and the right family member to help her.

Eadhild laughed then. The sound harsh and abrasive.

"Of course, she's important. She's a valuable widow, a woman with a great deal of influence in Kent, and she and Ælfweard have little liked each other. She refused to assist him with that land grant in Kent. She is, as you say, a bitch, but not an unimportant one. She and her sons, if they were older, would have a legitimate claim to rule the kingdom."

Eadgifu finally finished with her fiddling and swept her eyes around to look at her sister, unbalancing Eadhild with the force of the movement. Eadgifu could admit that she appraised her sister without annoyance for the first time since her exile from West Frankia. It seemed Eadhild had a good understanding of current affairs, even if Eadgifu still saw her as an annoying child, as she had been before her marriage five years before.

Eadhild's blue eyes glimmered with delight, and Eadgifu appreciated her careful choice of clothing once more. Eadhild's dress was a modest dark colour, not quite black. Black was almost as priceless as the imperial purple Eadgifu preferred herself. Instead, Eadhild dress was a dark blue, stitched in a flattering shape to enhance her burgeoning womanly curves. Eadhild was certainly no longer a child.

Like all of the children of Edward and his second wife, Eadhild shared the same blue eyes and thick chestnut hair of their mother, before it had turned grey and been hidden beneath the nun's wimple she professed to prefer. Eadgifu grimaced at the thought of her mother, almost pleased that she was dead, and her meddling ways were at an end.

"Who does Ælfweard intend to marry her to?"

"I hardly know that," Eadhild complained. "After all, you are his 'special' sister. The one he tells everything to."

Eadgifu held back her exasperation with her sister. Perhaps Eadhild was trying to help her, despite all evidence to the contrary.

"I'll have to ask him, perhaps tonight, at the funeral feast."

Eadhild grimaced.

"Why must we feast and drink to remember our father? It's unseemly."

Eadgifu shrugged a shoulder, the feel of the soft fabric on her shoulders recalling her to the fact that whether it was suitable for a funeral or not, her dress was impeccably well made, and weighed down with priceless jewels and embroidery.

"It's how it's done. I hardly think to worry about why. We can weep, if we wish, during the funeral service, and then we can begin helping Ælfweard with all he must accomplish."

Eadhild grimaced once more.

"Show your face, and then leave. I'm sure no one will expect you to sit and cry before them all." Eadgifu wondered why she was offering her sister advice. There was no real chance of her heeding it. There never had been.

Only now did Louis appear, his smart blue tunic already awry, his face half smeared with something. Behind him, his nursemaid hurried. Her hair was askew, and she looked as flustered as Eadgifu felt.

"Where has he been?" Eadgifu snapped. She was not about to share any sympathy with the woman, no matter her personal thoughts.

"In the stables, and the palace grounds, and in the hen house." The litany of outrages, spoken with the accent of West Frankia, almost brought a smile to Eadgifu's tight lips. Louis was a challenging child. Eadgifu thought it nearly a miracle that Matilde remained in Wessex. But then, Matilde probably had as little choice as Eadgifu did. Certainly, when Matilde had unexpectedly arrived, bedraggled, and tossed about by the sea having escaped West Frankia after Eadgifu, Eadgifu hadn't wanted to turn her away. Matilde and Louis had a special bond, even if most of it was born from exasperation.

"And you didn't stop him?" The nursemaid was far too used to Eadgifu to react to the taunt. Her face remained passive, only one fair eyebrow arching to show the impossibility of such a task. She was only a few years older than Eadgifu, but she had a gravitas about her that Eadgifu envied, and had envied, even when the queen of West Frankia.

"I'll leave him in your care," Matilde announced, and without waiting for an answer stalked from the chamber, her head high. Eadgifu swore softly. She didn't want to have to contend with her son during the funeral of her father. She should have minded her tongue. As much as she loved her son, he could be a trial, and Matilde had ensured she was adequately punished for her previous waspish tone.

"Ah, now that was well done," Eadhild chided her in her condescending tone, but already she was reaching out to grab hold of Louis' shoulders from where he was attempting to dive beneath the seats and roll in the dust that littered the floor after weeks and weeks of leaving the door open to absorb both the heat of summer and allow any cool breezes to enter the room. Although the door was firmly shut now.

Eadhild forced Louis to stand tall and ready for the funeral, as she dusted him down with hands that were gentler than they appeared.

Despite Eadgifu's annoyance with her sister, she couldn't deny that Eadhild was more able to engage Louis than she was. If she could be grateful, Eadgifu might have said as much, but instead, she turned her mind back to her brother.

"Does Edwin know of Ælfweard's plans?" She'd only been speaking to Edwin last evening. If he knew, he could have bloody well told her, Eadgifu thought with annoyance.

"I assume so. If even *I* know, then everyone must know."

Eadgifu sighed. Her sister was difficult and overly aware that as one of the younger sisters, her older brothers and sister too often overlooked her when they were deep in their plotting's.

"Apart from me?" Eadgifu challenged, determined that this didn't descend once more into a sulky argument about being ignored.

"Well, yes, apart from you. But is Ælfweard even speaking to you, after what happened with our father's bitch-wife?"

Eadgifu paused for a count of ten before responding.

"Ælfweard and I have had no cross words about our father's wife. He knows I was with him, mourning with him, and raising a toast to our father's long life and his many accomplishments."

As an afterthought, Eadgifu added.

"I didn't see you there. Where were you?"

Mutiny crossed Eadhild's face. Eadgifu smirked in triumph. Even now, such an achievement was to be savoured.

"Come," Eadgifu said, looking at her son, where he stood patiently holding his aunt's hand, something he never did for her, his face bright with alertness, and only a small smudge of muck remaining on his nose. "It's time to leave. We don't want to miss anything else."

For once, Eadhild didn't respond, and Eadgifu detected a slight ripple along her shoulders, Eadhild's back turned to her as she fiddled with something on the table. It was possible that Eadhild would genuinely mourn their father. Eadgifu hadn't yet decided on her own thoughts regarding her father's death other than the inconvenience of the thing. There was too much else to occupy her mind, her thoughts often turning to her husband, and more, to the rescue attempt she'd been assured by her father was due to take place shortly.

Eadgifu only hoped it happened before news of Edward's death reached Isaac of Cambrai, or it would never go ahead. Not without Edward's explicit agreement. For a moment, tears threatened her eyes, but Eadgifu squared her shoulders. Now was not the time for such thoughts.

As soon as the door on the chamber was forced open into the blistering summer's day, Eadgifu cursed her father once more. Why had he died during the worst of the summer heat? Funerals were for winter, not the summer.

Immediately, Eadgifu began to feel a trickle of sweat working its way down her back. She was not dressed for the summer, her ceremonial robes heavy and cumbersome, not to mention, stiff with embroidery. It would be difficult to hold her poise when her face was bright red, and her dress stuck to her in all the wrong places. It was hard enough to look regal in such garb in the winter, let alone the hottest summer she'd known for some years.

Surely the funeral could have been held earlier in the day? Why had they insisted on waiting until beyond noon?

Looking towards the busy stables, she caught a glimpse of her father's ealdormen in a tight knot. She grimaced. Her father's four ealdormen were not her allies. They, like her father, had agreed to her marriage. It little mattered to her that they'd also supported her return to Wessex, and voiced agreement when Edward had asked if an attempt should be made to rescue Charles from captivity. She still held them accountable for her marriage in the first place, just as she had her father.

"Come on," a brighter voice filled the air, and Eadgifu turned to meet the hectic gaze of her youngest sister, Ælfgifu. She was barely older than Louis and had only been a baby when her father had set aside their mother. Even now, Ælfgifu little understood the real deceit their father had practised on them all. She even, and Eadgifu didn't like to admit this, was quite enamoured of her step-mother.

"Ælfweard and Edwin are waiting for us."

"Where's Eadgyth?" Eadgifu looked around, aware she'd not seen her other sister for some time.

"She's already at the New Minister. She has been all morning. And so have I, but I thought I should come back, and ride in the procession. As you asked." Ælfgifu was always too happy to please others.

Shaking her head in annoyance, Eadgifu took the few wooden steps down to the ground and began to walk toward the stables.

"Not that way," Ælfgifu called in annoyance. "They're waiting, in front of the king's hall."

Wonderful, Eadgifu thought. She was not the most elegant of horsewomen and had tried to avoid the animals as much as possible since her return to Wessex. She would have much preferred to mount her steed out of the watchful eyes of everyone. But she supposed it was too late to complain now.

As their small party made their way to the king's hall, a hush fell amongst the servants and other courtiers.

A royal funeral was a time for sorrow. Or so she supposed. But really, Eadgifu thought, everyone simply watched everyone else to determine who would hold the reins of power going forward. The funeral was just part of the flux taking place between the death of one king, and the coronation of another. It was a necessary part of the process.

While Ælfweard would be King of Wessex, she was still Queen of West Frankia, although her husband was, admittedly imprisoned. Her status was, if she was honest, higher than Ælfweard's at the moment, as she had been crowned queen of West Frankia, but she was trying not to stress that point. Not while there was still so much to decide, and she needed her brother's support.

West Frankia was not the sweeping kingdom it had been before Charles treaty with Count Rollo had settled Normandy upon the

Viking Raiders in a bid to make allies of them, not enemies. Yet, it was West Frankia, once a part of Charlemagne's vast empire. Perhaps, she hoped, Charles and Louis might one day rebuild that empire. Then she would be an empress. No one in her family would be able to make such a claim.

The horses, laid on for the royal family, and the ealdormen, and other royal family members, were all waiting patiently, festooned in their garb of the House of Wessex, the Wessex wyvern in abundance on saddles and banners that the household warriors would ride with. Eadgifu searched for her horse amongst them all.

Pleased, her eye settled on the pie-bald stallion, and with Louis before her, Eadgifu made her way to the animal. The waiting stable-hand eyed her respectfully and pulled a wooden step to her preferred side of the animal.

With a gentle welcome on the animal's nose, Eadgifu steeled herself and then mounted the animal. The horse barely moved, while the stablehand spoke words of encouragement to the animal. She then had Louis lifted up before her by a waiting servant and then tried to settle the pair of them.

Louis was yet too young to ride alone, but it hadn't been necessary to have him beside her. Indeed, she should really have allowed Eadhild the honour. She was much better at riding, and of keeping Louis amused.

"Comfortable?" It was Edwin, her other full-brother, who taunted her, and stubbornness settling over her, Eadgifu nodded curtly in response. She eyed him critically. Almost a mirror image of Ælfweard in looks, Edwin only lacked Ælfweard's rounded cheeks. In fact, Edwin was gaunt all over. Eadgifu knew the cause of it far too well.

"Always. It's my honour to have my son before me."

Of all eight of Edward's children with his second wife, Lady Ælfflæd, she was the only one to have birthed a child. At times like this, it was good to have something to laud over them all.

"As you will," Edwin commented, his disbelieving face showing just what he thought of his sister's feeble attempts to ride with her son. "But you might still have a son at the end of it if you allow me to have him?"

Edwin, of course, was a competent horseman, for all he was not much of a warrior. And Eadgifu couldn't deny that Louis had grown a great deal since their last ride together. As Louis' complaints escalated, Eadgifu reluctantly nodded.

"Take him, please, and be careful with him. He's precious to me." While the servant enacted the exchange between the two horses, Edwin rolled his eyes at Eadgifu for making the whole operation so tricky. She just stopped from demanding Louis back. This was not the time for such petulance.

That would come soon enough when they arrived at the New Minster.

But Edwin, for all his shortcomings, managed his horse well, and Louis delighted in being with his uncle. Eadgifu tried to ignore the near incessant chatter, as their horses took them through the gateway of Winchester palace and out onto the road that led to the New Minster, but when Eadhild joined Edwin, and Louis' laughter came ever louder, Eadgifu found her attention drawn to the three of them.

How happy they all were. How little they knew or could even understand what she'd lost, and how difficult it was proving to get it all back, and still sweat trickled down her back. Eadgifu would have liked nothing better than to turn her horse around and return to the palace and divest herself of the too heavy clothing.

Ælfweard directed his horse to her side, his expression difficult to read. Ælfweard was another one of her siblings whose true feelings toward their father's death were unfathomable. Ælfweard had long wanted to rule, and their father had given way only in small matters, toying with his oldest son from his second marriage.

Ælfweard had spent time in Mercia, when their cousin, Lady Ælfwynn had succeeded to the kingdom after the death of her mother, Lady Æthelflæd, Edward's sister. But he had been pushed out in favour of bloody Athelstan, raised in Mercia, and a favourite of all the nobility there. Ælfweard had refused to return there since, saying the place stank like a pig sty and that he had nothing in common with the half wild-Mercian population.

Now, Eadgifu steeled herself for whatever tongue lashing Ælfweard intended to direct her way, as she watched his hooded eyes and gleaming forehead. It seemed that the heat was getting to her brother.

Yet Ælfweard remained silent, and Eadgifu was forced to begin the conversation.

"Eadhild informs me you will make our step-mother remarry."

If Ælfweard was surprised that Eadgifu knew this, he didn't show it, although his nostrils flared slightly. Eadgifu knew this was more because his thoughts had been recalled to their father's third wife.

"She's too valuable to lose to a nunnery. All those lands she holds in her own name. Our father might have thought he gained Kent through his marriage to her, but really, she gained the most. It's about time she had a husband more suited to her, and one who'll keep those bloody brats from Wessex and from thinking they have any right to my kingdom."

Eadgifu held her frustration in check. Ælfweard was likely to complain about anything if he thought he could get away with it and had a willing ear. Eadgifu was not minded to be that willing ear today. Especially not when the argument was far from a fresh one.

"What will you do? Have her abducted from the nunnery?" Eadgifu laughed as she spoke. It sounded ludicrous to her, but it wasn't. Many a king had 'stolen' himself a bride from a nunnery. It infuriated her, even though she would have no problem with it happening to her step-mother, provided it never happened to her, or her full-sisters.

Ælfweard's gaze was steady as he turned to look at her.

"What if I did? What would it be to you?" Eadgifu felt her mouth drop open in shock at Ælfweard's intimation, and she held his eyes until he was the one forced to look away. How dare he?

"You are ready for what will happen in the New Minster?" Ælfweard's voice was quieter now, his voice filled with wheedling.

"Yes, I'm ready for what will happen in the New Minster."

"Good," was the short response she got, and then Ælfweard forced his horse forward, and she was left to ride alone.

In front, she watched her brothers with jaundiced eyes. Ælfweard would be king. The thought was not quite as appealing as it should be, and Eadgifu tried to dismiss the worry gnawing away at her. As she'd learned with Charles, even weak kings could still accomplish a great deal, provided you were the one directing their actions.

She could already tell that Ælfweard would need a great deal of direction.

As Winchester appeared before her, Eadgifu settled to her horse's gait, keen to look comfortable and commanding before the men and women of Wessex. While internally she might grimace and wish not to be seen, Eadgifu knew just how important it was to give the correct impression, and this was the first time she'd been called upon to do so since her return from West Frankia.

While it might be imperative to have the support of the king, she knew it was also good to cultivate the more general population. The goodwill of the merchants and farmers could sometimes go a long way to helping an action that others might disapprove of.

Eadgifu dropped from her horse as they neared the grounds of the New Minster. Here, crowds had gathered to watch the procession of nobility making their way inside. She paused, straightening her skirts, and realising, under the harsh glare of the summer sun, that her dress was far from as sedately coloured as she'd thought when choosing it.

A murmur ran through the crowd, and she knew it would be directed at her and her siblings. While Eadhild had chosen a muted dress, Ælfweard and Edwin gleamed like peacocks in their bright green tunics, and her own imperial purple suddenly seemed too bright, and unsuitable.

Still, holding her head high, her chin jutting out, she strode to join Ælfweard and Edwin, taking hold of Louis' hand. Her son watched her with mutinous eyes, as Eadhild also joined them, but Eadgifu refused to allow Louis to leave her side.

He was hers, and he would walk with her to honour his grandfather.

Only then did Eadgifu actually hear Ælfweard and Edwin's discussion, and her heart sank just as much as it soared, for her brothers were discussing, in overly loud voices, how they would aid her return to West Frankia.

"We'll send ten ships, and over a thousand warriors," Ælfweard was announcing, "under your command, Edwin, and you will free Charles from his captivity."

Eadgifu pasted a haughty expression onto her face, frozen in shock at her brother's stupidity, and tried to rush past them, only for her gaze to fasten on someone she truly didn't want to interact with, her step-mother. Cornered, Eadgifu was forced to hover with her brothers, nodding along as though she agreed with their too-loud conversation when really, she didn't. But, now was not the time to bring her brother, the new king of Wessex, bar his election by the witan, and coronation, to order.

Luckily, Eadgifu noticed then that her step-mother had fallen back, and she took the opportunity to hurry into the New Minster, sweat beading her face, and her hair, making her curse her father for dying in the heat of summer all over again.

The interior of the New Minster was blessedly cool in comparison to the outdoors, and Eadgifu paused. She was aware of many eyes on her from those who had already made their way inside.

It was only a handful of days since her father's death, but he had been travelling with many of his favoured ealdormen and bishops, and so almost all had been able to follow the king's coffin to Winchester from Edward's place of death at Farndon.

Eadgifu supposed she should be pleased that her father was so honoured as it also meant there were more people here to see the humiliation of her step-mother.

With Louis quiet beside her, the echoing expanse of stone above his head seeming to render him speechless, Eadgifu allowed Eadhild to walk beside Louis, his hand in hers, as they made their way to the front of the New Minster.

The gold and silver on display dazzled her eyes as sunlight

streamed through a high window, devoid of glass. But she kept her head low, unwilling to actually view her father's coffin.

Until now, she'd stayed as far away from it as possible, too consumed with frustration at the actions of her step-mother, and keen to stay close to Ælfweard in the short run-up to him being proclaimed as king. Seeing it now, even out of the corner of her eyes, forced Eadgifu to realise that her father was truly gone, and his death was more than just an annoyance.

She felt her lip tremble with grief, and sucked it, hard, to force herself to focus on what was about to happen, and not on her true feelings on the matter.

A row of chairs had been arranged for the children of the king. As Eadhild led Louis into the row, Eadgifu risked looking behind her to make sure the rest of her brothers and sisters were close.

They needed to arrive all together, or their intentions would be impossible to fulfil.

Ælfgifu came next, her eyes filled with tears as she looked at their father's coffin, covered with his war banner, depicting the wyvern of Wessex. Eadgifu eyed it with contempt. The banner was too old and tatty, and she wished Ælfweard had been less keen to use it. A new banner, bright with golden thread would have looked far more magnificent than the fabric that looked as though a thousand horses had stepped over it, all of them with mud on their hooves.

Ælfgifu quickly settled beside Eadgifu, and then Eadgyth was joining her, and so too were Edwin, Æthelhild and Eadflæd, allowed to sit with the other royal siblings, although their place should have been with the nuns of Wilton, come to pray for their king's soul.

Eadgifu met the eyes of her two religious sisters, noting that they wore the dull dresses of their order, with only a few hints at their royal heritage. Eadgifu tutted loudly, meeting the eyes of her sisters quickly. Surely, she thought, it shouldn't have been necessary to ensure they dressed correctly.

Annoyance warred with stubbornness on Æthelhild's face, whereas Eadflæd simply raised an arch-eyebrow at Eadgifu's own outfit, the criticism easy to decipher.

Before Eadgifu could speak, Ælfweard and Edwin arrived, and quickly behind them came their step-mother, her two young sons, and Lord Osferth.

Eadgifu sighed heavily. Lord Osferth was an unacknowledged bastard son of her grandfather, she was sure of it, but none ever spoke of it, although Osferth was accepted into the nobility of Wessex, and accorded a great deal of prestige because of it.

He had the look of her father about him, and if no one ever said it aloud, it was only because the politics of the court demanded no one ever voice what everyone knew. It would have been unseemly to accord a bastard son to her overtly religious grandfather.

Osferth could always be relied upon to staunchly support the king, but today he'd made his loyalties clear, and Eadgifu huffed in annoyance, only for it to be replaced with a smirk of delight, as a young voice reached her ears.

"Where's father?" it was her second youngest half-brother who spoke, and immediately every single person in the New Minster fell silent. Eadgifu sought out Edmund, turning where she stood, only for another voice to ring out.

"Come, young lord. Your father will be buried today. He sleeps, forever, in the coffin, there." Eadgifu sighed once more. Was there no awkward situation that Lord Osferth wouldn't try and ease?

Only then, Eadgifu caught sight of her step-mother's young face as she came to an abrupt stop at the front of the New Minster, realising there were no seats for her. Eadgifu had always resented her father taking a younger wife. Even now, her step-mother was effortlessly graceful, while Eadgifu felt sweat once more flowing down her back.

Still, Eadgifu held her face straight, not wanting her step-mother to realise that even such a small act could make her feel so triumphant. Would it always be like this now? Could Eadgifu finally make up for the years she'd felt slighted by her step-mother?

"We need more seats," it was Lord Osferth who spoke, his voice calm and yet carrying into the vast space of the New Minster. Eadgifu felt the shift amongst those in the congregation, and imagined, but didn't turn to see, curious eyes leaning any way they could to see what was happening with the royal family.

When Eadgifu did allow her gaze to flicker to Ælfweard it was to see fury flashing in his brown eyes. And then she heard it, and exhaled as well, schooling her expression so that when a bench was placed before her seat, no one would see her pure rage.

Bloody Æthelwine and Ælfwine, Eadgifu thought of her cousins, as she took in their appearance. They could always be relied upon for their loyalty to Lord Osferth, for all they were not his children.

Again, her gaze swept over her cousins, noticing just how like her father and Lord Osferth they were in appearance. It was impossible to deny anything about Lord Osferth when the proof was before them all, daily.

Only then did her step-mother settle before Eadgifu, with her two young sons, and Lord Osferth, making use of the wooden bench provided for them. Yet, as Eadgifu mused on this unexpected turn of events, while Ælfweard whispered too-loudly to Edwin of just what he would have done to his cousins when he was king, Lord Osferth, who'd stayed standing, continued to look down the aisle, as though waiting for someone else.

Instantly, Eadgifu knew whom Lord Osferth waited for. And she was not disappointed, as her other half-brother and half-sister made their delayed arrival.

Lord Athelstan, she knew, of course, but Lady Ecgwynn was even now a mystery to her.

Lady Ecgwynn had refused to step foot in Wessex since their father had remarried Eadgifu's mother, and of course, Eadgifu had never been to Mercia either. To her, Mercia was a place of war and death and battles, riddled with Viking Raiders, attacking wherever and whenever there was an opportunity. When Ælfweard had tried to explain to her that Mercia was much more than that, Eadgifu had refused to listen. How, she'd thought, could he lecture her about Mercia when his feelings were the same?

Eadgifu couldn't believe that Lady Ecgwynn had actually made the journey to honour their father in his death. Yet, more than that, she watched the older woman with interest.

It would be impossible to deny who her father was, for Ecgwynn looked very much like Eadgifu and her other sisters, the only notable difference was that she had auburn hair, just like young Louis. Eadgifu reached out, to run her hand over Louis' head, only to feel him turn away from her, no doubt distracted by his young uncles, who sat before them, now, and who Louis hadn't seen for nearly a week.

Louis and his younger uncles were sometimes friends, but Eadgifu had always tried to prevent Louis from playing with Edmund and Eadred. But she hadn't failed to notice that Louis dominated his uncles, and of that, she did approve.

Now that the intention to humiliate her step-mother had back-fired, spectacularly, Eadgifu realised she'd have to endure the funeral mass while her half-sister and brothers, sat in front of her. They blocked her view and were impossible to remove from her eye line, no matter how much she tilted her head. Well, Eadgifu reconsidered, apart from young Eadburh.

This gave Eadgifu pause for thought. Her full sisters, nuns in Wilton, sat with the rest of the family, but it seemed that Eadgifu, only just older than Louis, had determined to sit with her religious community of Nunnaminster.

Eadgifu ground her teeth in frustration.

The girl was barely even five years old, and yet she'd upset the careful plans of her half-brother, and new king, and it seemed, that Eadgifu's step-mother had also given her consent to the arrangement for her daughter.

Eadgifu almost wished she could walk from the New Minster and return to Winchester palace without witnessing her father's burial. It might be scandalous, but it would be far better than sitting here, out-played by all of her half-sisters and brothers, aided by her hated step-mother and before the whole court.

Eadgifu dared not look at Ælfweard as the holy men made their way to the front of the New Minster, led by Bishop Frithestan, in his finest robes of white, gleaming with jewels. Ælfweard would be furious, and he had good reason to be. After all, he was now king of Wessex, bar the official vote by the witan of Wessex.

Athelstan had given no indication of his decision to come to Wessex. While he might be the son of Edward as well as the rest of them, he had also been proclaimed king of Mercia by the Mercian witan, who had acted far more quickly than the witan in Wessex upon hearing of Edward's death. But then, as she knew, Mercia was a frontier kingdom. It needed a king. It couldn't sit and wait for the witan to be convened, and it was irrelevant when their king had opted to be buried in Wessex rather than Mercia.

Eadgifu felt her foot tapping as she wondered if it would be possible to treat Athelstan's arrival at the funeral as an invasion by a foreign force? And in the end, it was the delicious thought of suddenly apprehending Athelstan and holding him against his will that allowed her to endure the funeral with mingled fury and twisted delight.

Her father was dead, and her brother would be king of Wessex, her half-brother would be king of Mercia. Unless something happened to Athelstan. If only, she thought to herself, that could somehow be arranged.

AD924

E adgifu sat before the muted assembly, picking at her food, her thoughts elsewhere.

There was a space at the head table where her step-mother should have been sitting, but the bitch-mother had refused to attend her husband's funeral feast, and now Ælfweard and Edwin, so drunk that they could barely support their own heads, toasted to their father, and rather than drinking the almost priceless wine, seemed to throw it over their shoulders.

Eadgifu could feel her body tensing at the ridiculous behaviour of her brothers. Her sisters sat murmuring beside her, all of them arranged in descending age order, apart from her brothers, who'd been placed together. Eadgifu wished they hadn't been. It would have been far better for the brothers to be kept apart. At least then she wouldn't feel the appraising eyes of so many on her.

As if she could recall her brother to himself! What control did she have over Ælfweard?

To the far side of her drunken brothers, Lord Osferth sat beside Bishop Frithestan. Eadgifu observed the conversation was as stilted as her own with Eadhild, who tried to speak to her. Eadgifu had responded once or twice, single-word answers, and yet Eadhild still prattled in her ear.

Eadgifu sighed heavily. The day had been an utter disappointment. Now her brothers were going to embarrass her even more than she had already been.

Did they not realise what they did?

For what felt like the entire evening now, Eadgifu had held her tongue, bided her time. She was aware that soon the feast would be over, and she could withdraw either to her chamber or to the women's hall. Either option would be better than being here, now.

Eadhild's words finally caught her attention, and Eadgifu felt her head swoop to her sister's face.

"What did you just say?" Eadgifu demanded to know. If Eadhild was surprised by the sudden attention of her sister, she didn't show it.

"I said, Ælfweard has instructed Bishop Frithestan to have our step-mother removed from the Nunnaminster. He intends to take command of Edmund and Eadred."

"And has the bishop told her of Ælfweard's intentions to force her to remarry?"

Eadgifu smirked as she spoke. How quickly she could adopt the attitude of being on the 'winning' side and take actions as necessary. In West Frankia, her control had abruptly withered away. But in Wessex, she might perhaps begin to exercise some power, and if not, then she could certainly be seen as being close to Ælfweard.

"I imagine so. The damn fool. Surely secrecy would have been better?"

Eadgifu snorted in surprise at Eadhild's words.

"It little matters whether he uses surprise or not. It's not as though our step-mother has any option but to obey, now that our father is dead." Eadhild held her tongue, but Eadgifu could tell that she had some firm ideas on the matter.

Behind her, a loud roar of drunken laughter erupted from her brothers. Eadgifu felt her face flush maroon as she turned to see the pair of them draped over each other. Both were incapable of stand-ing, or drinking, or doing anything but laughing as though they'd said the funniest thing ever. Eadgifu knew that couldn't possibly be the case.

Fury guiding her actions, Eadgifu stood abruptly, her chair tumbling backwards behind her with a crash, as she gathered her dress and strode from the hall. She was not about to be made a fool of by being forced to endure any more of their behaviour.

BUT TWO DAYS LATER, Eadgifu had cause to regret her decision, and it was Eadhild who alerted her, once more, of events beyond the walls of the palace of Winchester.

"Our step-mother has fled Wessex, taking her sons and daughter with her, and travelling to Mercia with King Athelstan."

"What?" Eadgifu glared, her discarded embroidery forgotten about in her hands. She'd only picked the work up to make it appear as though she did something. Really, she'd been determining the best choice of husband for her step-mother, or rather, the worst option. The man, she'd decided, needed to be a close ally of Ælfweard with no compassion for the widow, and even less for her children. Now it seemed, her plans would come to nothing.

"When did this happen? Has Ælfweard sent men to track her down?"

"There's little point. It happened during the night. She's gone. Safe in Mercia."

Eadgifu stood, her intention to seek out her brother.

"I wouldn't," Eadhild cautioned, settling to her own chair, and sipping delicately from Eadgifu's abandoned wine goblet. "Ælfweard is blaming you for it all. After all, you let her leave the palace first. What happened after that must also be your fault."

Eadgifu felt her face flush at yet another reminder of her step-mother's deceit, only enhanced by her sister's smug-looking expression.

"You're not very high in the king's favour at the moment, dear sister. I would stay away from him, for now at least."

Eadgifu could already feel her body turning toward the door, determined once and for all to explain to Ælfweard that she hadn't 'allowed' her step-mother to leave the palace. She was determined to ignore Eadhild's warning, only for the door to open as Eadgyth stepped inside.

"Sisters," Eadgyth spoke to them both, and then paused, clearly detecting the tension in the air.

"What have I missed now?" Eadgyth all but sighed, while Eadhild shrugged one shoulder carelessly.

"Little of importance. Our step-mother has fled to Mercia with our young brothers and sister."

Eadgyth's eyes flickered from Eadhild's face to Eadgifu's, as though looking for confirmation. Eadgifu was surprised she seemed unconcerned by the development.

"Ælfweard should have acted, rather than threatened if he wanted our step-mother to remain in Wessex. It was obvious she would not stay here or seek sanctuary in Kent. There are too many men there who would take her as their wife, forcefully if necessary. She hasn't been the damn queen for all these years not to understand how everything works."

"You almost sound as though you approve," Eadgifu found herself complaining.

"Who's to say I don't. She has no husband now, and her children are too young. Our step-mother must look after her own interests. Certainly, King Athelstan will treat her kindlier than our own brother will."

Eadgyth stalked past Eadgifu and settled beside Eadhild, although the two didn't look at each other. Eadgifu had detected some unease in the relationship between her two younger sisters. It seemed she was right to think so.

"Where are you going?" Eadgyth asked Eadgifu when she still stood unmoving before the door. "I wouldn't think to speak with Ælfweard. He's still nursing his head from all the wine and ale he's consumed. I hope he rules as well as he drinks," the comment brought a small smile to Eadhild's face, which Eadgifu noticed with surprise.

Perhaps they weren't quite so uneasy with each other as she'd begun to think.

"Ælfweard is trying to organise his coronation, amongst all this," Eadhild explained. The witan had convened the day before, and of course, Ælfweard had been nominated as the king of Wessex. Now, he needed the ceremony to be conducted as soon as possible, and Eadgifu had been trying to make alterations to one of her dresses so that she would appear regal enough for her brother. The work was tedious, though. She'd far rather be helping Ælfweard, but of course, couldn't in light of the news of their step-mother's departure from Wessex.

"If he wasn't already annoyed and angry, now he's furious and incoherent. I've never known his temper to be so short, and he stinks of sweat and wine both." As she spoke, Eadhild screwed her nose up in disgust, and Eadgifu thought better of seeking out her brother and returned to her sewing.

An uneasy silence settled between the three sisters, outdoor sounds muted through the thick wooden walls.

Horses came and went, while carts creaked in and out of the fore-court. Arguments erupted every so often, only to fade away, as though the opponents had simply decided they'd won by walking away from the other.

Through it all, Eadgifu strained to hear the clipped footsteps of her brother, knowing that despite it all, Ælfweard would seek her out at some point that day. His complaints would fall more abundantly than rain, in his anger at the embarrassing spectacle of losing control of his step-mother, and youngest brothers and sister.

It was not the most auspicious start to Ælfweard's kingship.

"Here, give me that," it was Eadgyth who broke the silence, her hands reaching for Eadgifu's all but cast-off dress, where it lay untouched on her lap. "You'll never get it finished in time, and the stitches you have done are ragged."

Eadgyth had the dress transferred to her own lap before Eadgifu could refuse, and Eadgifu settled her gaze on her sister's gifted hands and nibble fingers. Eadgifu couldn't deny that Eadgyth was a much better embroiderer than she was.

It was almost a relief to see the work given to someone else.

In West Frankia, Eadgifu had employed a woman to make her clothes for her. In Wessex, she simply didn't have the money required, even as the sister of the new king. She thought longingly of the territories she'd held in West Frankia, and of the coins and wealth that had come her way from those properties. Then, she'd been able to purchase anything she'd wanted to, and hadn't needed to worry about the expense of new clothes and vibrant threads.

Eadgifu sighed with frustration.

If the rescue attempt on her husband failed, as somehow she knew it would, if it even happened, she would have to force her brother to give her more property to support her. As the king's sister she'd be able to claim something from him. After all, her wealth was all in West Frankia, and she couldn't foresee returning there, not anytime soon.

To begin with, Eadgifu had hoped her fleeing to Wessex would be a temporary solution to her husband's imprisonment. But with the passing of each and every week, her hopes of a quick return had faded, as had her hopes that Charles would be released.

No, Eadgifu was coming to realise that she might well be stuck in Wessex until Louis had grown to manhood and could take his kingdom for himself. It was not a pleasant thought.

If Ælfweard's failure to berate her that day surprised her, it was in a good way. Perhaps, she hoped, Ælfweard had realised that what had happened since their father's death was not her fault after all.

Yet, when she was woken two days later, by urgent hands on her arm, Eadgifu felt her heart sinking.

"What is it?" she demanded to know of her sister, who tried to drag her from her bed.

"Ælfweard is ill."

"From too much drinking?" Eadgifu asked, thinking to return to her sleep, forgetting that Ælfweard had left Winchester the morning before, without even saying goodbye to her.

"No, not from too much drinking. I don't know all the details. We must ride to Oxford. They're saying he might die." Eadhild's voice ended almost on a shriek, and Eadgifu was startled to wakefulness and found herself rushing from her bed.

"Die? From what? He was well yesterday."

"I don't know. Stop asking questions and hurry up. Edwin went with Ælfweard, but Eadgyth is dressing, Ælfgifu as well. We must make it to Oxford and find out what's happening."

Eadgifu dressed quickly, her mind a swirl of possibilities. Their father had died, they said from some sort of sickness. Was it possible that Ælfweard had succumbed to the same thing? Fear made her clumsy. By the time she was dressed, all three of her sisters were waiting for her in the doorway. Louis with them, complaining that he'd had no food and what were they doing, and why did he have to go?

Eadgifu looked around, hoping to see Louis' nurse, but wherever Matilde had gone since their argument before her father's funeral, the woman had not yet returned. It was frustrating and also to be expected. Matilde had been challenging to manage when Eadgifu had been the queen of West Frankia. Now that the title was worthless, it was only Matilde's love for Louis that kept her close, and when Louis misbehaved, and Eadgifu blamed her for it, Matilde often took herself away for a few days.

Eadgifu could do with her now but appreciated Eadhild's fore-thought in including Louis in their journey to Oxford. Only then she stopped, so abruptly, that her sisters didn't realise what she'd done. If Ælfweard had a sickness, should any of them go near him? Should Louis?

"What now?" Eadhild called with annoyance, from some distance away, when she'd realised her sister was not actually following her.

"If it's a sickness, we shouldn't be there. Louis shouldn't be there."

"If it's a sickness, Louis won't go near his uncle. But we must still go to Oxford. It's the only way we'll learn the truth of what's happening." It was Eadgyth who spoke, and Eadgifu found herself agreeing to the rational words.

"Fine," Eadgifu agreed, rushing to catch up with her sister. Outside, there were horses and an escort of the king's household warriors. Eadgifu took the time to consider just when Eadhild had learned the news about their brother. She certainly seemed to have taken the time to organise their departure well.

Mounting her horse, Eadgifu's eyes settled on Louis. She didn't wish to ride with her son, not even the short distance to Oxford. She looked around, trying to decide if she knew any of the household warriors well enough to have them take Louis, but these men all seemed to be strangers to her. Beornstan could be relied upon, but it appeared he'd gone to Oxford with her brother.

In the end, the decision was taken from her. Eadhild settled in her saddle and instructed Eadgyth to hand Louis to her, taking the time to flash a look of triumph at her sister. Eadgifu held back her sharp comment. She didn't wish to ride with Louis and could hardly berate her sister for taking responsibility for him.

Eadgifu noticed that as soon as Louis was settled, a servant reached up to hand him a small linen packet. Inside, Eadgifu imagined, would be bread and cheese for her growing son. Eadhild really did think of everything, Eadgifu thought with mild irritation.

"We'll ride as fast as we can," Eadhild instructed the escort. "Oxford is our destination." One of the men nodded smartly at the order, and quickly gave instructions. Ten of the men took to the front, another ten at the rear of their small party as they rode through the gates of the palace of Winchester, turning north to head toward Oxford.

Eadgifu felt a bead of sweat form on her forehead and grimaced.

It was going to be a long, hot day in the saddle, and at the end of it, there was no certainty of what they'd find.

If Ælfweard were genuinely ill and succumbed to his symptoms, then Edwin would have to be voted king in his place.

The thought of Edwin as the king of Wessex was almost laughable, and yet, Eadgifu realised, there would be little choice. At least, she decided as her horse settled into a fast gait beneath her, Edwin would be easier to command than Ælfweard. Hopefully, he wouldn't be as upset with her about their step-mother as Ælfweard was.

Yet, unbidden, tears began to streak down Eadgifu's face. It felt terrible to be thinking of a life her brother was absent from. Could it be true that he was so ill that he was dying? Annoyed with herself, she angled her horse closer to Eadhild's and called across the divide.

"How did you hear of Ælfweard's illness?"

"One of Bishop Frithestan's monks brought the news this morning. He was travelling to the New Minster, for a relic, I forget which one. They hoped it would cure Ælfweard." Eadhild's eyes glittered with conspiracy as she spoke, and Eadgifu glanced down to see her son looking at her with alert eyes. She hoped then that her earlier tears didn't show on her face.

If Bishop Frithestan had thought it necessary to send for some relic, no doubt something related to St Swithun, then it did seem that Ælfweard was mortally ill. She shivered, despite the sun beating above her head and the sweat that had formed on her forehead.

First her father, and now Ælfweard, in only a matter of weeks. Eadgifu looked upwards, a prayer forming on her lips as she gazed at the beauty of the day. She would not exhort her God to save her brother, but she would pray for his health, and for the future because she knew she wasn't alone in thinking that Edwin was not suited to rule.

A further shiver juddered down her spine.

If Edwin wasn't fit to rule, where did that leave her? Where did it leave the House of Wessex? Certainly, no one would think it suitable for a child of four to rule Wessex. Surely not?

Only then Eadgifu gasped, realising that the truth could be worse, for none would choose to have a four-year-old boy rule Wessex, and equally none might want her younger brother. Edwin was a foolish youth, too fond of his wine and ale. But there was someone, with far more experience than any of them, and Eadgifu felt her lips curl with distaste.

Athelstan.

She must do all she could to support Edwin's bid for the kingdom of Wessex. She couldn't even consider the calamity of having Athelstan as a ruler of both Wessex and Mercia.

Eadgifu vowed then that she could never let that happen.

WITHIN SIGHT OF OXFORD, the tower of the church just coming into view, a rider rushed toward them. The horse seemed out of control, but it abruptly stopped before, the rider's face coming into sharp focus.

"The king is dead," the man announced, his tone too sharp, his shock evident in his delivery of the news to the household warriors who rode in front. Not that any of them didn't hear the announcement. As they all gasped, the messenger glanced at them, comprehension slowly dawning on his face, as he realised he'd just told the royal sisters of their brother's death and far too brusquely.

Eadgifu felt ice sheet down her spine, her worse fears realised, as she kneed the animal forward.

"Where is the king?" she demanded imperiously, no sympathy for the shock on the man's face, or his wobbling lips.

"In the church," the man replied, pointing to the building coming into focus before them. "At the west gate. The church there. I am," but his words were lost on Eadgifu as she encouraged her horse to a quick gallop, desperate to see the truth.

Eadgifu forced her way through the escort of ten warriors, unheeding of those about their business on the road into Oxford. She angled her horse toward the gateway, feeling the rush of the wind in her hair, so fast did her animal abruptly race.

The yells and jeers of those she passed were lost in the thrum of the air. Only in view of the actual gates, thronged with people about their daily routine, did Eadgifu rein in the animal, bring her under control, before demanding to be allowed inside the walls.

By then, two of her escort had caught up, and Eadgifu waited impatiently for them to accomplish what had been beyond her.

A path opened up before her, and through it, she walked her horse, her eyes seeking out any she knew in the crowd, trying to determine if it was common knowledge that Ælfweard was dead.

But the looks she received, while respectful, were also blank. It seemed few knew.

Before the church, Eadgifu all but leapt from her horse, flinging the reins at one of the escorts, as she finally arrived at where she needed to be.

There was a hush surrounding the church, as though none dared speak. Her footsteps echoed too loudly on the stone floor, as she strode inside, pulling her leather riding gloves from fingers, and hunting for whoever was in charge.

What she didn't want to see, not yet, was Edwin, and yet it was he who strode toward her, his gait unsteady, face flushed from the heat, too much wine, and from his sorrow.

"Sister," Edwin called, his brown eyes glazed and struggling to focus. "You are here. Thank God," Edwin didn't seem to recall that he was even in a church as he spoke. "Brother Ælfweard, the king, it was so sudden. Gone, just like that," and with the pronouncement made, Edwin's shoulders shook, and a sob wrenched from his belly.

Eadgifu enveloped him in her embrace, desperate for none to see Edwin in such a state, wishing she'd not allowed her two brothers to travel to Oxford alone.

How was it even possible that so much could have happened in less space than a day?

Footsteps around her, alerted to the arrival of the rest of her sisters, young Louis as well, his face bewildered at rushing to arrive at just another church.

Edwin stepped away from her, his face anguished, content to tell his remaining sisters his story as Eadgifu bent down to her son, running her hand along his forehead where dirt marred his face.

"I'm afraid that I have sad news for you. Uncle Ælfweard has died. I'm truly sorry."

When Edward had died, Louis had little seemed to notice or indeed to understand who he was. Her father might well have fathered thirteen children, but he had been a distant man until his children were more interesting, and Louis had not yet fallen into that category. Edward had been a distant figure for Louis, but Ælfweard was someone he knew well.

Eadgifu watched Louis, reaching out to clutch his small hands in her own, as confusion on his face was swamped by understanding. His chin wobbled, a tear tracking its way down his smooth cheek, for all he didn't cry.

"Is there to be another funeral?" Louis asked, his chin sticking out, his voice showing what he thought of funerals.

"There will be, yes. In time."

Louis nodded with understanding, but twisted his hands, freeing them from her own, making his way to Eadhild. Eadgifu watched with mutiny in her heart as Louis allowed Eadhild to comfort him, rather than her.

Frustrated, Eadgifu turned to meet the eyes of her remaining sisters. Ælfgifu, young as she was, sobbed broken-heartedly. In contrast, Eadgyth was assessing the situation, her eyes bright in the gloom of the church.

Only then did Eadgifu's eyes settle on her brother's coffin, and for a moment she felt so weak it was impossible to move.

While her thoughts tried to direct her to consider the future, her heart demanded that she take the time to mourn Ælfweard.

With Louis under the care of Eadhild, Eadgifu walked to the front of the church, noticing for the first time the monks who prayed for her brother. There were also bent backs of other men, no doubt the nobility who'd been attending upon Ælfweard when he'd met his death, including some of his ealdormen.

Just as at her father's funeral, the coffin of her brother was covered with a banner depicting the wyvern of Wessex, only this one was too fresh. It was clearly unused. The contrast between the two men couldn't have been greater.

Her father had died as an old warrior, too old to fight his own battles any more, but respected enough to command the warriors of Wessex and Mercia. Her brother had barely had time to do anything, including arranging his own coronation. Eadgifu reached out her hand, feeling the smoothness of the embroidery and cloth beneath her fingers.

Her brother lay in the coffin, covered by the banner, and yet she wished to see him, to look on his face one final time. Only now was not the time.

With a choked sob, Eadgifu curtsied to the coffin and then took to her knees, shaking with the horror of it all.

Ælfweard had been no more than a boy, really, or at least to her. He had been little more than an annoying brother, although one who in recent weeks had grown in stature with their father's death, if not in skill. All that potential, gone, just like that.

Tears poured from her eyes, settling on her dress where it strained over her thighs.

Ælfweard would have been a terrible king. She knew that. But he had been her brother, and in that capacity, he'd been far from awful, if also far from caring and attentive. Ælfweard had not come to rescue her and Louis from West Frankia. Ælfweard had not even tried to convince their father that Eadgifu needed to live in more magnificent splendour than she could afford. Indeed, Ælfweard had done almost nothing to further her cause, although, he had promised to, once he was king.

Now all that was as nothing.

Wessex once more had no king, and Eadgifu feared what would happen next, as her sisters and brother joined her at the front of the church. Louis was not with them, which forced Eadgifu to look around her, only noticing then that Lord Osferth was leading Louis from the church.

Bloody Lord Osferth, always in the right places at the right time, as though he could perceive such significant changes before they occurred.

Without Ælfweard, the stable House of Wessex suddenly looked fragile. There was Edwin, who would become king now, and there were Eadgifu's young half-brothers as well, but until Edwin married and fathered a son, there was too much that was unknown. And when the future became unknown and clouded with possibilities, Eadgifu knew that ambitious men would work quickly to exploit any potential gain. Her time in West Frankia had shown that to her, in dazzling clarity.

Her thoughts flickered to King Athelstan, in Mercia. Would he know of Ælfweard's death? Would he even care? Or would he be too consumed with ensuring Mercia remained peaceful, holding onto the lands that had only just been reclaimed from the Viking Raiders through the building of the burhs.

Eadgifu knew that time was suddenly pressing. If King Athelstan were to remain as King of Mercia, then the Wessex witan would need to move quickly to select Edwin as their new king. It had to be done before King Athelstan even knew of his half-brother's death.

Eadgifu's head remained bowed, but in her mind, she formulated a plan for the future, a way to ensure that Wessex became Edwin's, and then, she would be able to manipulate him into helping her husband. And her son, and herself.

THE PROCESSION back to Winchester was accomplished with far less haste, but with no less purposefulness.

Eadgifu rode beside Edwin, trying to rouse him from yet another drunken stupor. The coffin of their dead brother was laid on a cart and pulled by four of the strongest horses to be found in Oxford.

While Ælfweard had died suddenly, too quickly for a will to be transcribed, Eadgifu had insisted on Ælfweard being buried in the New Minster. It might not have been Ælfweard's choice of burial place, but Eadgifu was determined that he be buried with all the honours accorded their father only a few days before.

Ælfweard might never have been crowned king of Wessex, but the witan had elected him, and as such, he needed to be buried as a king. If only for the good of their family.

Eadgifu had instructed that no word was sent to Mercia to inform either her step-mother or half-brother and sister of Ælfweard's death. Edwin needed to be elected as king sooner rather than later. With that in mind, Eadgifu had Edwin organise

Ælfweard's funeral for the following day, and for the witan to convene the day after that.

On the day that Ælfweard should have been ordained as king of Wessex, he was instead lowered into the ground beneath the New Minster, with his father, grandfather, grandmother, and uncle. Throughout the service Eadgifu's thoughts were consumed with the hope that while they buried Ælfweard, King Athelstan and her step-mother were at Kingston Upon Thames, waiting for the royal family to arrive for the coronation that would never happen.

Provided that was the case, there would be no time for King Athelstan to return to Winchester and disrupt her carefully laid plans.

Throughout the funeral mass, Eadgifu's ears strained, fully expecting to hear the clipped footsteps of King Athelstan on the stone floor. She was relieved to leave the church, alongside her brother and sisters, and return to Winchester palace without King Athelstan appearing.

The people of Winchester had turned out for Ælfweard's funeral, just as they had for their father's, but there had been uneasy looks, and some complaints loudly voiced about what would happen next. The break in the hot summer weather had not helped matters either. Rain had tumbled from the sky, as though determined to cover them all and flood Winchester itself. Eadgifu was pleased to return to the palace, change from her funeral clothes once more, and preside over the funeral feast for Ælfweard beside Edwin.

Edwin disappointed her. She knew he must be riddled with shock at what had happened to Ælfweard, and the new expectation that he would be king. But Edwin had done nothing but drink for the last few days, his words constantly slurred, with no thought for winning support from the nobility of Wessex.

Eadgifu had discussed the problem with her sisters. While none of them liked the thought, it had been decided that during the feast they would need to mingle with the nobility. They could assure them all that Edwin would be well in a few days and that it was all just the trauma of the last four weeks that had made him appear so unstable and difficult.

It had been decided that the loyal ealdormen who'd served her father would be keen to see Edwin as their king. They were to promise continuity from their father's reign, and assure the three men that all would be as it was before. Ealdorman Osferth might prove both more difficult and more manageable. It all depended on whether or not he had taken the time to consider that King Athelstan could become King of Wessex as well as the King of Mercia, in light of this new tragedy.

Dressing with care, Eadgifu turned to her jewellery box, looking for her queenly rings, bracelets, and necklaces, her head briefly hovering over the small crown she'd been able to bring away with her. Could she wear it? Should she wear it?

"I don't think it would do to remind the old men that you're a queen when we have no king." Eadhild's voice rang with conviction, and Eadgifu was only annoyed because she agreed with her sister, for once.

"I had no intention of wearing such a treasure. Not here," Eadgifu winced as the words left her mouth, for they were too sharp when she wanted her sister's help.

"Then, that is good. Now, hurry. Eadgyth is not as good at handling Edwin as you are."

Once more, the words were infuriating merely because they were true.

With a final check on her jewellery, Eadgifu strode to the king's hall, from which enticing smells erupted. Along the way, she navigated around the outdoor cooking areas that had been erected to deal with the significant number of guests.

The weather had caused problems, and temporary structures had been built over the smoking pits to try and keep the food from spoiling. Eadgifu was forced to watch where she placed her feet, not wishing to ruin her priceless shoes. She grimaced.

The heat had been unbearable, but the rain was just as annoying, causing the air to steam in between each steady downpour. It was just the sort of weather that could spoil the harvest and also any food already in storage. She would need to take the time to ensure the palace store was free from all pests and dry as well.

In the forecourt, other men and women were hastening inside, the sky turning black with heavy rainclouds and Eadgifu heaved a sigh of annoyance. It seemed the weather was not done playing tricks on them yet.

At the doorway she paused, squinting into the murkier interior, unsurprised to find the hall was far less densely packed than for her father's funeral feast. Ælfweard might have been elected as king, but he had been unpopular with everyone. She said a swift prayer that Ælfweard was not here to see the desultory attendance. As much as he'd been a poor judge of his popularity, it would still have upset him to see his death so poorly mourned.

Louis, she'd excused from the feast, because Matilde had finally reappeared, all smiles and treats for Louis. Eadgifu was more pleased than she wanted to be. Matilde needed even more careful handling than the nobility of Wessex, but her bond with Louis couldn't be denied.

Eadgifu made her way to the raised dais at the front of the hall. Edwin was already there, with Eadgyth, neither of them looked pleased with the other, and Eadgifu braced herself.

Edwin, it was clear, had already drunk too much. His eyes were hooded, his hand clasped so tightly around a tankard that Eadgifu could see where his fingers had turned white.

The funeral had been a trial for Edwin, his tears falling without ceasing down his young face. But, at least without wine to hand, he'd been able to keep some hold on his emotions. That was going to be impossible now.

"You took your time," Eadgyth complained as Eadgifu curtsied before her brother, and then sat beside him, her hand resting over his.

Eadgifu tried to ignore the harsh words of her sister, and instead bowed her head in apology. Not at all mollified Eadgyth flounced to her own chair, and Eadgifu heard wine being poured and then drunk just as quickly. She almost turned to berate her sister, but there was no need. Eadhild had arrived as well and spoke harshly with Eadgyth.

"Brother," Eadgifu kept her voice low, as she tried not to wince from the rancid wine fumes pouring from her brother's open mouth. "You must try and retain your dignity. This is a funeral feast, not a brothel."

The words were sharp if delivered quietly, and Edwin's eyes seemed to focus on her face, his mouth opening and closing as though he worked to decipher the meaning behind them.

"Wessex cannot have a drunk king," Eadgifu continued. "You must preside over this feast and speak to your ealdormen and nobility, and assure everyone, that when they vote for you at the witan tomorrow, it is for the good of Wessex."

"Why would they not vote for me?" Edwin asked abruptly, the statement permeating his mind.

"There are others with better claims," Eadgifu stated, meeting her brother's eyes and seeing all his hurt and anger reflected in the gaze.

"I am the king's son, and I am the king's brother. I will be king. There is no other." Edwin retorted, his head swinging as he tried to lift his tankard, only for Eadgifu to stay his hand.

"There are other sons of the king. Some of them have the reputation of being warriors, and are already elected as a king in their own right."

Fury flickered in Edwin's eyes, although whether because she spoke of problems with the succession, or whether it was because she refused to allow him access to his tankard, Eadgifu didn't know.

"The men will be loyal to the House of Wessex. They always have been in the past."

"Your brother is a member of the House of Wessex," Eadgifu stated, wondering why she was bothering to have the argument with her brother.

"He is a bastard, and our father never acknowledged him."

Eadgifu laughed at the absurd statement. She couldn't help it.

"Our father named him King of Mercia. How much more acknowledgement do you want?"

Edwin's eyes clouded in thought, and Eadgifu hoped she'd made an impact on him.

"Our father told me that Mercia was a backwater, only good for keeping the Viking Raiders from Wessex. It was not an honour that he bestowed on Athelstan when he made him King of Mercia, but a punishment."

"Anyway, why do you champion him? Is it because he rescued you from West Frankia? Would you rather he was king?" Edwin's voice had risen higher and higher with indignation as he spoke, and Eadgifu wished she could slap her brother, and restore his sensibility but it would be construed as an attack on the king, and those in the hall would all witness it.

"I do not champion King Athelstan, but I appreciate a threat when I see one. You have nothing to offer the men and women of the witan. King Athelstan has everything to offer."

"He will not be made the King of Wessex. Our father would never have allowed it."

"But our father is dead. How will you stop it?"

"There's no need to stop it. It won't even be a problem. I have the family line. I am a member of the House of Wessex. My father and my brother were kings before me, and I will be king after them."

Edwin's expression had turned mutinous, and Eadgifu realised there was no point talking to him further.

"I only hope you are right brother, for I doubt it," Eadgifu complained, standing so that she could sit in her own chair, far from her brother. Edwin would have the ear of Bishop Frithestan and Ealdorman Wulfgar throughout the feast.

Eadgifu wished them luck, for Edwin was so drunk, the conversation would be just about impossible.

She settled to worry and fear for the events of the next day, for she couldn't help thinking that no matter their haste, the funeral and witan would not have been done quickly enough.

King Athelstan was a threat, as were her step-mother and half-brothers.

Damn her father.

And damn Ælfweard.

AD924

W hile the men and women of the witan settled, Eadgifu felt her gaze drawn time and time again to her brother. Edwin sat at the front of the king's hall, on the raised dais, the usual long table cleared away.

It seemed that not only had Edwin not taken her advice the previous evening, but he had also done so with a will that surprised her. His face was ashen, his hand around his wine goblet stretched white with the pressure of keeping the vessel upright in his hand, and he looked ancient.

While she tried to block the voices of the nobility as they discussed her brother's visible state of distress, the voices of her sisters were far harder to ignore.

"Bloody fool," Eadhild stated the obvious, shaking her dress as she settled in the chair that had been laid in place for her, next to Eadgifu. The weather had turned during the night, a welcome return to the heat of the earlier summer, and yet it had only served to make the air smell dank and damp. Eadgifu wrinkled her nose, and so too did Eadhild as she examined her shoe.

"Bloody ruined," Eadhild complained, the damp patches clear to see on the coloured leather. Eadhild had chosen not to wear her dress of mourning, but rather one with brighter colours, but not too bright. Eadgifu was beginning to realise that Eadhild was not a great fan of being the centre of attention. It probably got in the way of her sneaking around so that she always knew what was happening to the king.

"You should have looked where you were going," Eadgyth offered without any sympathy. In contrast, Ælfgifu looked about ready to cry at the desecration of the shoe.

It was better to discuss shoes than Edwin. That much was sure.

"Is there news of King Athelstan?"

Eadhild asked the question that Eadgifu had been trying not to consider, and she turned heated eyes on her younger sister.

"What do you know?" Eadgifu demanded, but Eadhild, a glint in her eyes, and her shoes forgotten, merely chuckled low in her throat.

"Nothing, I assure you. If I had, I would have shared that news with you. Rest assured."

Eadgifu exhaled heavily with relief. Still, it didn't work loose the kinks in her shoulders from a night of relentless tossing and turning. When sleep had finally come, it had been as dawn was making itself known, so it had been too short, and too hard to wake from.

Not for the first time that summer, Eadgifu considered when she'd last enjoyed a full night's sleep. Certainly, it had been a great many months ago.

"Edwin has made an effort," this time it was Eadgyth who criticised in a gentle whisper, and Eadgifu felt her face grow tight with distress. If even her sisters were commenting on Edwin's attire, then what would others be thinking?

Not that she honestly had time to consider it, for while Edwin was seated on the dais with three of the ealdormen, a commotion was occurring behind them all. Eadgifu's heart sank. She knew who it would be, and what it would mean, and she was not to be disappointed.

King Athelstan's summer cloak was flung over one shoulder, his eyes bright and fierce, as he made his way to the front of the hall. But it was the woman walking alongside him that made Eadgifu hiss violently. Her bitch-mother. Really, Eadgifu considered, she had realised that this might happen. Still, there was a difference in thinking something and seeing it happen before her eyes.

Together, her half-brother and bitch-mother made their way to the raised dais, before the nobility of Wessex. Eadgifu knew then that her hopes for the future had been extinguished.

The only comfort Eadgifu received in those few moments was the look on Edwin's face. She'd warned him. He'd failed to heed her advice, and now a man swept into Wessex who had the required gravitas that Edwin so lacked to lead their father's kingdom.

Eadgifu consider that her bitch-mother walked like the haughty cow she'd always been, her young sons forced to skip to keep up with King Athelstan. Athelstan walked as though he had a war to win, and perhaps he did, although Eadgifu thought he'd probably won it, just by turning up.

While King Athelstan and her bitch-mother settled beside Edwin, but far enough away for all to know they were not of one mind, Eadgifu's eyes rounded on Archbishop Athelm. Suddenly he seemed keen to begin the proceedings, although he'd been dallying before. Had he known? Eadgifu thought it likely.

"My lords and ladies, Queen Eadgifu." The Archbishop's voice was rich with the tones expected of all churchmen. Eadgifu sorrowed that the queen Eadgifu he mentioned was not her, but rather her father's third wife, and hated step-mother.

"Much sorrow brings us together, now, to discuss the future. Much lamentation, and much loss and while our time for mourning is far from over, Wessex must have a ruler, and that is what we are here to discuss and decide."

"Why is he here?" Eadgifu felt her eyes close in distress. Bad enough that King Athelstan had shown her brother up just in appearance, there was no need for Edwin to make it worse.

"I'm my father's son," King Athelstan stated flatly so that all could hear his words. Eadgifu was reminded of his voice from when he'd come to West Frankia, to rescue her, and Louis. It was not a memory she much liked.

"My father made me his heir in Mercia, and the ealdormen there have acclaimed me as their rightful lord and king. With the unexpected passing of my brother, I must remedy this new division of Mercia and Wessex and unite the two kingdoms to the glory of my father's name, and that of my grandfather before him. The future lies in unity. Our strength lies in that singular purpose." The words King Athelstan spoke were those of a man who knew how to rule. Eadgifu realised then that even her own husband had never sounded quite as regal as her half-brother.

"The future of Wessex doesn't concern you," Edwin leered, his pointing finger visibly trembling. Eadgifu knew she was barely breathing. Her entire body was tight, too tight. She dared not move for fear of breaking the tense atmosphere between her brother and his rival.

"I'm King of Mercia. I would also be the King of Wessex. I have a great deal to offer Wessex, and I'm not alone in believing such." King Athelstan spoke with such confidence that even Eadgifu found herself almost believing his words. Only then her bitch-mother stood and added her own words, and broke the illusion.

"I'd have it known, and recorded that I, Eadgifu, Queen of the Anglo-Saxons, support the claim of King Athelstan, oldest acknowledged son of King Edward and his first wife, Lady Ecgwynn. He's the warrior king the two kingdoms need to remain united as one and to thwart the Viking Raider attacks."

"The king's youngest children, Edmund, Eadred and Eadburh also support their older brother in this."

"She is but our father's whore," Edwin chortled as their bitch-mother finished speaking. Eadgifu felt her sisters all inhale at the same time. These were words only ever meant to be spoken behind closed doors and amongst themselves. Yes, they could allude to it, but none of them had ever openly spoken against their father. It would not have been agreeable, to any of them.

"Lady Eadgifu is a queen of the Anglo-Saxons, her coronation above dispute, and more, she was our father's wife, and the mother of our young brothers and sister."

"There was no impediment to the marriage, was there, Archbishop Athelm?" The Archbishop, anticipating King Athelstan's question, showed no hesitation in answering.

"My lords and ladies, there was nothing to prevent the king's third marriage, or call it into question."

"None here would dare deny the family likeness?" King Athelstan queried, and Eadgifu knew that no one would dare gainsay him. The similarity was too great. Her two half-brothers were so like young Louis it was almost painful. Just like Lord Osferth and his resemblance to King Edward, only that resemblance had never been overly spoken about. But this was different. There was a kingdom to win.

Eadgifu hoped her brother would show some sense in his dealings with King Athelstan, and yet she also knew he wouldn't.

"No reason to call the marriage into question," Edwin spluttered, wine sloshing from his goblet. "Then what of my mother's survival? A living wife, and then a new, younger one. I hardly see," Edwin's words slurred into silence, and yet Eadgifu heard them clearly, and she was sure that everyone in the king's hall would have done so as well.

"I believe that such an argument would bring your own birth and claim into question." Archbishop Athelm spoke the words that Eadgifu wished her brother's thoughtless comments hadn't forced. Her hands folded too tightly in her lap, Eadgifu could do nothing but watch her brother make matters worse by lunging toward the Archbishop on unsteady legs.

Eadgifu watched as King Athelstan inserted himself between the two men, his face serious, his intention clear.

"Stop him," it was Eadhild who whispered the words, but Eadgifu couldn't stand. Her body welded in place as Edwin, too drunk to hold himself upright unaided crashed to the floor, with none to rescue him but his half-brother.

Driven by vehemence, Edwin spluttered and gesticulated wildly, fighting free from his brother. Eadgifu realised that the men and women of the witan were actually standing to get a better view of her brother's antics.

She swallowed her horror, turning to face Eadhild, knowing her own expression was as shocked as her sisters. Edwin had called into question the legality all of their births.

"What can I do?" she asked, but her sister's eyes were only on their brother.

"You'll never doubt the legitimacy of my father's and mother's marriage again," Edwin managed to speak clearly, his words directed at Archbishop Athelm.

Athelm wisely acknowledged Edwin's words while offering nothing in return. Eadgifu couldn't wrench her eyes away from her brother.

She felt powerless to do anything. Her brother said things that should never have been spoken aloud before the witan of Wessex, while other men, more sober men, easily countered each and every argument. As was right.

"The king's marriages were all legal, and have long been held as such," King Athelstan stated, coming to the aid of them all. Not that Eadgifu could ever thank him for accepting the children of their father's third marriage.

Edwin's already murderous face was contorted with ever more rage. It only increased when King Athelstan held up his hand, the clatter of gold and silver meeting more gold and silver, an attestation to the military glories King Athelstan had enjoyed. Few wore such Viking jewellery, unless they were tried, and tested, warriors.

A smug expression touched Edwin's lips as Ealdorman Ordgar, with his skinny build and hawk-like nose, stood from his place on the dais to whisper in Edwin's ear. It was not long before Edwin spoke again, triumph on his face.

"I'll acknowledge that my father's marriage to Lady Eadgifu was lawfully carried out. My mother happily divorced my father to spend the remainder of her days in prayer and quiet contemplation. And further, both of these marriages were enacted when my father was already King of Wessex, and so the children born, are, indeed throne worthy."

Eadgifu was unsurprised when it was Ealdorman Osferth who stood next, speaking into the shocked silence.

"My Lords and Ladies, as a member of the House of Wessex, I believe I'm an expert on who is, and who isn't eligible to claim the throne."

Ealdorman Osferth paused before he began to speak. "I was there when King Alfred declared who would rule after Edward." Eadgifu's eyes were downcast at the words. She knew precisely what Lord Osferth was about to say.

"I was there," Lord Osferth reiterated, his voice filled with conviction. "While I would never criticise My Lord Edward and his choice of Ælfweard, God rest his soul, as our king, I feel that the decision was not the correct one."

"And now there is the opportunity to put wrong the error, and I would gladly do so. As King Alfred, who saved our great kingdom from the Viking Raiders proclaimed, it is Athelstan who will be our king. The King of Wessex and of Mercia. The future of the Anglo-Saxon race will only be assured by making Athelstan our ruler. And neither am I alone in my belief."

Eadgifu realised quickly that it was now that the other men of the women who supported King Athelstan over her brother would make that known.

And indeed, the people she turned to face, standing from their seats, were not that great a surprise to Eadgifu, although each one felt like a fresh betrayal.

First, Archbishop Athelm, obviously. Then the Bishops of Worcester and Crediton, and the Abbess of the Nunnaminster and then the Abbess of Wilton. Eadgifu turned to meet the confused eyes of Eadgyth. Why had their sisters not told them of this possibility? Wilton was a royal nunnery. It should have supported Edwin without even considering King Athelstan as a potential candidate for the kingship of Wessex.

That King Athelstan's cousins added their support as well was again no surprise to Eadgifu.

Men that Eadgifu didn't know also stood to support King Athelstan. These, she assumed, would be his allies from Mercia. They shared his warrior look and stance. As did yet others, with blonde hair and beards, all wearing arm rings. They must be King Athelstan's Viking allies, Eadgifu decided. Eadgifu had seen similar men before. In fact, Rollo, a Viking Raider settled in and around Normandy, had helped King Athelstan rescue her and Louis. Eadgifu had never had a problem with allying with such men, and it seemed she shared that with King Athelstan. It was not a pleasant realisation.

Eadgifu gasped. She'd known that Edwin would lack sincere support. Still, she'd not appreciated just how much backing King Athelstan would have in Wessex.

Eadgifu turned and gazed at her sisters. All of them looked back at her, their expressions just as confused if resigned as Eadgifu's own. They all knew that Edwin had lost the fight, but it seemed that Edwin had not realised. Not yet

With his face pulsing with rage, his body thrumming with outrage, Edwin's bellowing laughter was a surprise. Eadgifu felt the tension all the way to the tip of her hair at the strange sound emanating from her brother. Could he not just stop now? Was it not already embarrassing enough?

"I'll banish all men of Wessex who refuse to follow me, especially those men and women of the church who owe their position to my father."

No one moved after the extraordinary announcement, all waiting to see what Edwin would do next.

"These people are not even of Wessex," Edwin's hand was raised in derision, gesticulating to the warriors, Mercian or Viking, who stood to pledge support for King Athelstan. Eadgifu couldn't rip her eyes away from Edwin, for all she wished she could.

"Byrhthelm stands with King Athelstan," it was Eadhild who whispered the words to Eadgifu, her head twirled all the way around, while Eadgifu kept her gaze on Edwin. This was an even more significant blow for Edwin. Byrhthelm had long supported King Edward, and they had all assumed he would transfer his allegiance to Edwin. After all, he had supported Ælfweard.

"Everyone is standing," it was Eadgyth who informed Eadgifu of this new development. Eadgifu keeps her gaze on Edwin, and finally, his eyes flickered to her own. For a moment, Eadgifu felt as though she looked at Louis, all the hurt and confusion reflected back at her. Still, she shook her head, trying to dissuade his from speaking further. From causing more damage.

King Athelstan moved to the front of the dais, and it was this movement that drew Eadgifu's attention away from her brother. As such, the next words shocked her, even though they didn't fall from Edwin's mouth.

"And yet you will rule Mercia when the kingdom belongs to Lady Ælfwynn?" Bishop Frithestan, so close to Edwin the previous night, speaks aloud the words.

It seemed that Edwin was not yet done as he chuckled maliciously at the outburst from the Bishop of Winchester.

Eadgifu dropped her gaze to her hands in her lap. Her father's treatment of Lady Ælfwynn had been far from his finest moment, and this reminder was unnecessary, especially when it seemed that Lady Ælfwynn was long dead.

"My father locked Lady Ælfwynn in a nunnery on the death of her mother. My father plotted to remove her from ruling Mercia, and claimed it in her name." King Athelstan's voice was calm, as though even this announcement had been expected.

"I've never approved of those actions. But now I have the influence and power to reverse that action, and I have."

"Lady Ælfwynn is here," the words rushed from Eadhild, but Eadgifu didn't look up, instead listening as her cousin joined King Athelstan on the dais. The tread of such strident footsteps on the wooden floor was enough for Eadgifu to know that Lady Ælfwynn was very much alive, despite her father's assurance that she wasn't. A soft conversation took place on the dais, only Eadgifu couldn't hear the words spoken between her cousin and the children of her step-mother.

What else had her father lied to her about?

"I relinquish my rights to Mercia in favour of King Athelstan. I've had a great deal of my life stolen from me, and I intend to make up for that. I'll marry, as I choose, and I will support King Athelstan in all he does."

"Long live King Athelstan," the voice that bellowed the words was young and unafraid of upsetting Edwin. Eadgifu wondered who it was, but decided it just might be the man that Lady Ælfwynn meant to marry.

"There's no further impediment to Athelstan being declared the King of Wessex, as well as Mercia." Archbishop Athelm had returned to the dais, and Eadgifu knew the final vote was imminent and prayed for it to hurry up. She wanted to be gone from here. There was too much to think about.

"The Witan of Wessex will elect Athelstan as their king. Is everyone in agreement?" A chorus of 'ayes' greeted the question, some muted, others exuberant but it was clear that Athelstan has been over-whelmingly accepted as King of Wessex.

"Then we declare Athelstan, son of King Edward, as King of Wessex, and Mercia. Long live the king." Archbishop Athelm made the final pronouncement. Perhaps of everyone there, it was only Eadgifu and her sisters who were silent, not even daring to meet the eye of Edwin, or that of Athelstan, the new King of Mercia and Wessex.

Eadgifu allowed the tears to fall down her cheeks, unheeding of who saw. King Athelstan had rescued her from West Frankia when she needed saving, but his thoughts toward her were and always had been enigmatic.

What this meant for her future, and for the future of her husband, and her son, she didn't know, but she feared in her heart that she knew King Athelstan would never help her. Why would he even consider it?

ANGLO SAXON CHRONICLE FOR AD924

This year King Edward died among the Mercians at Farndon; and very shortly, about sixteen days after this, Ælfweard his son died at Oxford; and their bodies lie at Winchester. And Athelstan was chosen king by the Mercians, and consecrated at Kingston.

AD926

E adgifu tried to settle the deep unease that coursed through her body, but it was impossible.

King Athelstan, garbed as the king of the English, watched as Count Adelolf bowed before his cousin. King Athelstan wore his crown on the crop of blond hair that fell almost to his shoulders, the shimmer of the crown all but blinding.

Adelolf spoke to the king, his voice loud enough for all to hear within the hall. He said he visited England at the behest of Count Hugh, although it was also a family visit of one cousin to another.

Count Hugh. Just the mention of his name set Eadgifu's stomach rolling.

Count Hugh was the son of the man who'd stolen her husband's crown. He was not to be trusted, she was sure of that, and yet, it seemed that Count Hugh had forgotten that Eadgifu even lived at the court of the English king as his representative spoke to King Athelstan, and that angered her.

With each gift, presented by an array of men and women from West Frankia, Count Hugh was making an impassioned plea to be granted leave to marry one of Eadgifu's sisters. She would be taken to West Frankia, become his countess, while he ruled the kingdom alongside his brother by marriage, the current king of West Frankia, King Rodolphus. And all the while Eadgifu's own husband, the rightful king, festered in a prison of Count Heribert of Vermandois' devising.

That fact had not been mentioned. Eadgifu imagined they'd forgotten about the English king's tie to their imprisoned king. What she didn't know, was what King Athelstan would do about it, if anything.

Since the failure of Isaac of Cambrai's attempt to free her husband, the year her father and brother died, Eadgifu had heard nothing about her husband. Not a single word. And neither had King Athelstan mentioned him to her. In fact, she and King Athelstan had barely said more than three words to each other.

Eadgifu's eyes narrowed, wondering just what her half-brother was thinking.

King Athelstan had rescued her and Louis from West Frankia, perhaps from the clutches of Count Hugh. Would he genuinely allow a new marriage to take place?

Eadgifu didn't know, and that angered her as well. By rights, she should know her half-brother's thoughts, but they were virtual strangers, nothing else. They just happened to share a father.

"My Lord King, these gifts, from Count Hugh, are magnificent, and I know you will understand their great importance," Count Adelolf's voice rose and fell with excitement. Eadgifu found herself digging her nails into her hands to stop herself from crying out in anguish.

"Here, is the sword of Constantine, the great emperor, in which one of the nails of the Passion has been mounted." King Athelstan, with his known love of holy relics, the more obscure, the better, had the grace to lean forward in his chair, beckoning for the sword to be brought before him.

The West Frankish man lowered his head, handing the ceremonial blade to Count Adelolf. The king's cousin then stepped forward with the gift so that King Athelstan could truly see it.

Eadgifu tried not to strain, not to look, for she knew only too well just what this sword was. She had seen it before. It had belonged to her husband, before his imprisonment. She now knew who'd stolen so much of Charles' wealth since his incarceration.

Rage burned beneath her skin at King Athelstan's evident delight. He reverently took the sword from Count Adelolf's hands and held the blade first one way, and then the other, allowing the light to play over the dulled edge. His eye immediately picked out the nail from Christ's cross, where it was embedded in the hilt of the sword.

King Athelstan's face lifted in a rare smile, and Eadgifu grumbled under her breath.

"Careful sister," Edwin, at her side, seemed to be enjoying her anger, and yet his words were coolly offered. "Careful, now is not the place for this."

Whether Edwin was right or not, Eadgifu thought to dismiss his words, laced as they were with the wine her brother seemed to drink continuously from morning until night. She never saw him without a goblet or his servant without a wine jug close to hand.

Damn him. He should have been king, not bloody Athelstan. And certainly, Edwin would not have entertained this embassy from Count Hugh. No matter that it was led by Count Adelolf and his mother, the Lady Ælfthryth of Flanders, their father's sister.

Lady Ælfthryth had been treated with great respect by King Athelstan, although Eadgifu was sure that the two could never have met before. Was it just all part of King Athelstan's performance, or were he and his aunt closer allies than she thought? Certainly, Flanders had been an uneasy ally of her husband's.

Eadgifu could not remember ever meeting her aunt before, but there had been many people surrounding King Charles. She might have had, but equally plausible that she had not. It was a conundrum, and one she'd faced when first meeting Lady Ælfthryth in a more intimate setting.

"And, My Lord King," still Count Adelolf spoke. "This is the holy lance with which Charlemagne won the war against the Saracens." As Adelolf spoke, King Athelstan looked up from his perusal of the holy sword. His eyes feasted on the elongated lance, crafted of dark black wood, burnished to a high sheen, and with all the marks of a weapon intended for show, and not for war. Eadgifu tutted under her breath, while King Athelstan's eyes lit even further.

Again, the weapon was presented to King Athelstan via Count Adelolf. Eadgifu watched on, her rage, and position forcing her to remain seated, for all she would far sooner have stormed from the room. She did not need to witness this bribing of her despised half-brother by a man she hated even more.

Yet another of King Charles' treasures. Had Count Hugh taken all from her husband? Was there nothing left for Charles to reclaim when he was finally free? No, she couldn't believe that, wouldn't let herself think that.

Trying to steady her rapid breathing, Eadgifu focused on Count Adelolf. Certainly, she had met Adelolf before. He had long been an ally of Count Hugh, along with his brother, Count Arnulf. His place here, at the English court in Wessex, was a testament to just how much Count Hugh trusted her cousin.

But she couldn't find it in herself to trust him. Not now. Not ever, even if the family resemblance was impossible to ignore.

Adelolf, like the other males in the House of Wessex, was a reflection of her father, and her two full-brothers. He shared the same brown, hooded eyes, and high forehead with cheeks that should have been angular, but which puffed out too far, seeming to drag the forehead lower, and cast his eyes beneath his nose. Adelolf was far from an attractive man, and not just because he was Count Hugh's ally.

"Quiet sister," beside her, Eadhild sat forward, her hands clasped tightly in her lap. Eadgifu turned away, unsure where to look to retain her slight hold on decorum. Before her Count Adelolf bartered for Eadhild's hand in marriage, an agreement tentatively made before the death of their father two years before. Yet Eadgifu had managed to convince herself that it would never happen. She had been sure that King Athelstan would never let it happen. Not after what Count Hugh's father had done to Eadgifu's husband, and the father of young Louis. If nothing else could be said about Eadgifu's relationship with her half-brother, there was at least sincere regard for Louis.

Eadgifu just couldn't see how King Athelstan would be able to reconcile honouring the agreement drawn up before he was king, with the current status quo.

It was beyond her, and so she chaffed, held in place by the dictates of who she was, and yet couldn't look away and spare herself from each new dagger to the heart.

"And, My Lord King," and now two members of the embassy stepped forward, unfurling something between them, and Eadgifu knew what it was even before Count Adelolf spoke.

"This is the standard of St Maurice, which Emperor Charlemagne brought back from his endeavours in Spain."

Again, King Athelstan gazed at the gift with hungry eyes. It was so uncharacteristic of King Athelstan to allow his emotion to show, that Eadgifu wanted to stand, shout at her despised half-brother, and recall him to himself.

"Such gifts," Eadhild's voice was filled with wonder at her side, and Eadgifu stifled the urge to inform her sister of just who Count Hugh was, and what sort of husband he would likely make. He'd already had one wife, and one marriage, ending without children on the death of Countess Judith.

But that wasn't what concerned Eadgifu. No, it was his perfidy for committing treason against an anointed king. With Count Hugh for a husband, her sister, who she despised almost as much as King Athelstan at this moment, would never know who her husband's allies and enemies were. Count Hugh seemed to change sides more often than the damn Viking Raiders, and she'd not thought that was possible.

"Such treasures," Eadhild continued to extol, speaking to Ælfgifu, and the only one of the sisters who watched with as much wonder as Eadhild did herself. Eadflæd sat to the side of Edwin, was silent, and yet Eadgifu was sure she knew her mind. But not so much Eadhild's. Or rather, she did and wished she didn't.

"Count Hugh is too generous," Edwin slurred, his only complaint.

"Too desperate," Eadgifu confirmed, her tone filled with revulsion, only to feel the eyes of Eadhild searing into her.

"Just because our father sold you too cheaply, don't think that I'll allow the same for myself." The whisper was too harsh and too loud. More eyes were watching them than Eadgifu would have liked.

Yet Eadgifu laughed, she couldn't help it, even though the sound was alien to her ears. It spoke of her experiences and disbelief that Eadhild would so easily disregard them.

"What, Count Hugh sends spices and perfumes, onyx, emeralds, a gold crown for King Athelstan, so heavy it is almost too much to lift, let alone wear around his head, and still you think the marriage unworthy of me." Eadhild's colour was high, her face contorted with rage and frustration at her intractable sister.

Eadgifu wondered how Eadhild could welcome the proposal, especially when Louis was so much a favourite of his aunt's.

"Yes, I do. Anything from count Hugh is not good enough for you. You should be a queen, not a countess. And remember, this is me telling you that. And I don't even like you." Eadgifu hissed her words, uncaring of who heard, refusing to be distracted by Edwin's censorious expression.

Eadhild's eyes opened wild with fury. Before more could be said, Eadgifu felt the eyes of others on their family argument. She shook her shoulders, trying to dispel the tension in her body, and present the image of unity that King Athelstan would expect from them all.

She was unsurprised, when a moment had passed, to catch the intrigued eyes of Lady Ælfthryth watching her. Of course, Ælfthryth would be judging them all, just as much as King Athelstan would.

"Look, the king is beckoning for you."

It was Ælfgifu who was most attentive to King Athelstan's commands, as always. Carefully, Eadhild stood, smoothing her expensive dress, before Edwin stood abruptly, baring her way, holding out his hand to escort his sister to the side of the king.

Eadgifu watched her full-brother with loathing. It was always the same. No matter the words of hatred that erupted from his mouth when King Athelstan was discussed, Edwin could never allow an opportunity to pass him, to take advantage of his melee of sisters and the opportunities they promised for him to finally make something of his position, and his life.

While Eadhild curtsied before King Athelstan, Edwin bowing smartly, Eadgifu's gaze skimmed those who sat opposite her. There was her bitch-mother. Whereas before her step-mother had been watching the king, now her eyes settled on Eadgifu, a challenge in the mocking look.

Eadgifu tried to meet the gaze but was forced to turn away, the heat too much for her to endure. Her bitch-mother, she could admit to herself, knew the dark forces that swirled through Eadgifu's thoughts far too well. It only made Eadgifu hate her even more.

"They say that Count Hugh is the most powerful and independent of all the West Frankish nobility." It was Eadgyth who finally spoke, her words seeming to ground Eadgifu from flying into a fury.

"It's not hard when your brother by marriage is the king, and you own more land than anyone else, and, your own father usurped the rightful king." Scorn dripped from Eadgifu's mouth as she spoke.

"It might be a means for you to have Charles' restored to his kingdom."

The words came from Ælfgifu, and Eadgifu swept a hate-filled look toward her youngest sister. She was growing into a fine looking woman, and yet Eadgifu only ever saw the child, not the woman before her

"If King Athelstan consents to the marriage, as he clearly will do, there will be no need to ever release King Charles. King Athelstan will be consigning my son to never knowing his father, and never being able to rule his own kingdom. If Count Hugh has a bride from the House of Wessex, why ever would they need to restore the one they already have?"

The words exhausted Eadgifu all at once, and she felt her chest deflating, her cheeks turning from red to white as she realised the truth of the words. It was this that truly lay as the root course of all her anger.

There'd been only one attempt to release King Charles from his imprisonment under Count Heribert, and it had failed. If this wedding went ahead, there would be even less talk about it. Indeed, in all honesty, Charles would be quietly forgotten about by all but herself, and Louis. And, Louis' recollections of his father were only hers, told him enough times that he thought them his own.

The thought was depressing and utterly sincere.

None of her sisters had ever met Charles. Only Matilde shared any recollection of Eadgifu's husband, and the two women were more likely to argue than find common ground. Why Matilde stayed in Wessex, Eadgifu didn't know. Sometimes she wished Matilde gone, but other times, she cursed the woman for even considering leaving.

"Eadhild would not allow them to take Louis' kingdom from him." Again, it was Eadgyth who spoke, her words clearly meant to endear her to Eadgifu. Eadgifu wondered why Eadgyth of all people was speaking in support of the match. Did she hate Eadhild so much that she wanted her gone from Wessex, no matter where she went?

"What, you believe Eadhild would risk all for my son, her nephew?"

"Eadhild loves Louis, she always has. I've heard her speak to him, of times in the future when he'll be king of West Frankia. If she can help him, then she will."

"'If' is a very big word," Eadgifu dismissed, frustrated by Eadgyth's caution. It was no secret that Louis and Eadhild, despite all Eadgifu's efforts, were close. Eadhild was often to be found entertaining her son, giving in to all his whims, tolerating his foul temper and grumpy attitude.

Of all his aunts, it was Eadhild that understood Louis the best, even better than his mother.

"Count Hugh wants a wife to give him sons, not a wife interested in having her nephew restored to his kingdom. Eadhild will never have any influence over her husband concerning West Frankia. It's merely a surprise that Count Hugh didn't make himself king after his father's death."

"Is it a surprise, or is it a realisation that King Rodolphus had the support that Count Hugh lacked? They might well be brothers by marriage, but King Rodolphus has always been more acceptable to the other lords of West Frankia than Count Hugh. After all, King Rodolphus offered continuity from his father by marriage. Count Hugh offered only more war."

"You speak as though you're an expert on events in West Frankia. Have you been there, sister dear? Do you know the truth of which you speak, or do you merely recite what others tell you?" Eadgifu couldn't keep the bite from her mouth, no matter that she and Eadgyth could usually be relied upon to have a unity of purpose.

"I, I," Eadgyth faltered, and then turned her blue eyes on Eadgifu, a warning flickering in them. "I'm listening and learning all the time, my decision is not yet made, either one way or another. I suggest you do the same sister, listen, rather than just pronounce."

Eadgyth turned away then, her gaze seemingly absorbed by the continuing prancing of Count Adelolf. Eadgifu fumed. She wanted to be gone from the king's hall at Abingdon, but knew, that if King Athelstan had failed to invite her, that she'd have seethed at that over-sight as well.

Frustrated, Eadgifu held her left hand tight with her right, trying to still her vehemence and powerlessness. King Edward should have sent support to King Charles after the Battle of Soissons, and certainly when he'd been imprisoned by Count Heribert. She knew that, and still hated her father for his failure to truly appreciate the peril Charles was in.

Her father had brushed aside her concerns, content to hold her son under his command, while the great nobility of West Frankia tore itself apart. Even his support for Isaac of Cambrai's rescue attempt had been tepid, a purse of coin, a band of twenty Wessex men to support the effort. It had all been worthless.

"Your husband will be released, when the nobility realise that King Rodolphus is no better than your husband at managing the kingdom. Once Count Rollo and his people attempt to claim more of West Frankia, which they will, the nobility will appreciate that Charles had no choice but to come to terms with him. Until then, count yourself lucky to be returned to Wessex, knowing that you're safe and will be honoured as Charles' wife and the mother of his son."

Her father's words incensed her, even now. Her father had been wrong, and three years later, Charles was still a prisoner. No one, not one single member of the West Frankish nobility had made any attempt to contact Eadgifu during her exile. It was as though she had been forgotten about, just as Louis had been.

Until now.

Only the embassy was not even here for her, or her son, but rather for a bride for Count Hugh, of all people.

No longer able to take it, Eadgifu stood and sweeping from the king's hall, unheeding of whose eyes followed her, or who noted her outrage. If King Athelstan wished to call her to account for such rudeness, then he was welcome to try.

Outside the king's hall, she paused, breathing deeply of the fresh air, pleased to feel the sheen of sweat that had clung to her skin, begin to dissipate.

She was a queen without a kingdom, and at the moment, the only person that seemed to understand that was herself.

Sighing, she strode toward the women's hall. At least it would be quiet there, and she would be pleased to think her own thoughts. It was little consolation, but Eadgifu knew that no matter her thoughts, her sister would marry Count Hugh. As much as she did not much like her sister, Eadhild, she knew that her life with the most obnoxious of the West Frankish nobility would not be to Eadhild's liking.

No matter what she might think.

But Eadhild must make her own mistakes, just as Eadgifu could admit, she had done in the past.

AD926

E adgifu angrily brushed stray tears from her eyes, cursing as she did so.

The surge of emotion that rushed through her body was so powerful, she almost feared she'd not be able to step outside her room.

With longing, Eadgifu thought back to the day, all those years ago, that she'd left her father's court, bound for a new husband and a new life.

Her nerves then had ensured the colour in her cheeks had been high. Yet she'd been excited as well as nervous. For all of Eadgifu's life, her mother, and to some extent, her father had been adamant that their oldest daughter was destined for a marriage far more superior to anything that had gone before. Her father had been filled with self-importance that his daughter was to marry the King of the West Franks. And she'd been even more conceited about the entire arrangement.

The day before she'd left Winchester, Eadgifu had visited her mother in Wilton Nunnery. The stain of her setting aside had made Lady Ælfflæd bitter, and yet she'd crowned with delight on seeing her daughter before her marriage.

"A marriage to a king," her mother had smiled, the movement forcing the customary wrinkles, and anger from her face. Eadgifu had offered a small grin in reply. Her mother had enveloped her in an embrace that had carried with it the reminders of a happy childhood, and a gentle mother.

Her mother might have become all angles and harsh words in the final years of her marriage to her father, but in the beginning, Eadgifu knew it had been a happy marriage and a good place for children to grow up. How else could anyone explain the eight children that her father and mother had produced between them?

"Come, I have much to tell you," her mother had beckoned Eadgifu to sit before her. Sister Ælfflæd had adopted the poise of a King's wife, although the position had been taken from her, and given to a woman half her age.

"I know what to expect," Eadgifu had responded, keener to share words with her mother that weren't laced with ambition.

"Hah," her mother had laughed. "You think you know everything, but all the women about to be married know nothing. You do not know how to please your husband beneath the furs because you've never had a man before. And believe me, he will know what he's doing. How many children does he have?"

Eadgifu had grimaced at the reminder that her husband was not a young man, that he had a bevy of daughters to his name, and that he was as old as her father.

"Six daughters, and an illegitimate son."

"You'll want to entice him enough that he never goes near the court whores again." The words had fairly dripped with scorn, and it had been all Eadgifu could do not to chastise her mother. Eight pregnancies had given Edward all the opportunity he needed to dally with the women of the court. If her mother thought she was oblivious of that, then it showed just how little she knew the true nature of her husband.

"Don't just open your legs for the man. Make him work for it." As her mother rubbed her hands, one over the other, resting them on her lap, Eadgifu was forced to look away from the raw need on her mother's face. The thought of her parents in bed together was bad enough but to realise that even now, and after all he'd done, her mother still desired her father was a horrific realisation.

Did her father still visit with her mother? Did they yet bed each other even now? The thought had horrified Eadgifu, and she'd hoped it to be caused only by her own worries.

"Now, people will say that there's no sure way to ensure a male child. I agree with them. Believe me, I tried everything to beget Ælfweard and Edwin. Don't let anyone entice you into anything dangerous. Your ability to birth an heir is your most precious commodity. Guard it well, and keep your husband away from the wine before you let him part your legs."

Eadgifu had shivered into her cloak, for all the day outside had been warm.

Her mother had cackled once more at her daughter's evident unease.

"Such things should not disgust you. It is only right."

"It is only right between a husband and a wife, and you, mother, are a nun, and should be thinking of anything but the relations that occur between a man and a woman."

Swift fury had smothered her mother's face, highlighting all the dips and hollows that the dim candlelight had covered until now. Eadgifu could only hope that she'd never look as dried up and consumed as her mother did.

"We will see what you think after your marriage," and the words had been far from kind. "When your body is on fire from the touch of a man, you will desire that touch more than you can ever imagine."

Eadgifu touched her own cheeks now, running soft hands over the gentle curves, teasing out the skin, trying to determine if it lay flat or wrinkled. The candlelight was too dim in her chamber to truly take advantage of the looking glass. Rather than new lines on her face, she felt the tracks of her earlier tears and shook her head in frustration. Her earrings swung from side to side, the jangle of the precious metals and gems, reminding her of all that was lost.

She'd escaped from her kingdom with some of her jewels, and

more importantly, her young son. But her husband was still beyond her, and she feared, in the darkest of nights, that she'd never see Charles again, and would certainly never feel the warmth of his body beside her. She hated to admit that she desired his touch, just as her mother had warned her she would.

Angrily, Eadgifu stood, her arms tense, her fists clenched, and into the silence came a banging on the door.

"My Lady, the cavalcade is about to leave."

"I am ready," Eadgifu replied, hoping the words were no lie.

Outside, in the forecourt before the King's hall at Winchester, there was peaceful chaos. Many of those about to escort Eadhild to take ship to West Frankia had long been ready, spilling through the open gates, and waiting, some distance down the road, where the people of Winchester lingered, to catch a final glimpse of the princess before she went over the narrow sea.

But in the forecourt, there was a hush of expectation, as Eadgifu strode to stand beside her half-brother. Eadhild had decided to ride, rather than settle in a cart. Her favourite animal sat ready, saddle and harness shined to rich mahogany, the animal's black and white dappling brushed so well that Eadgifu had to blink away the brightness from her dancing eyes.

Her younger sisters waited, the pair of them pressed tightly together, as everyone waited for the King, his half-sister, and the accompanying nobility, to exit the King's hall.

Eadgifu sighed softly, reminded of her own departure from Winchester, at the same time realising that she'd never see Eadhild again, not in this life. It was one good result of this royal marriage.

Eadhild and she had never been friends, or allies, but rather enemies and combatants. Even now, Eadgifu wilted away from witnessing her sister's triumph.

The doors of the King's hall were flung wide open by the attendant door wardens. In the abrupt silence, Eadgifu had eyes only for her exultant sister, led into the courtyard by King Athelstan.

Eadhild was dressed in clothes suitable for riding beneath her cloak, but the cloak itself was a thing of exquisite beauty. It might well be the summer, but the thick furs that formed the basis of the cloak were brushed to an even higher sheen than her horse's coat, and it glittered with gold, silver and other precious gems.

Eadgifu swallowed down the spike of jealousy. Her father had never provided such an item. Had it come from Count Hugh or from King Athelstan? She determined not to discover its origin. Either answer would only upset her. Enough to know that her sister went to her husband far better supplied than she had been for her own marriage.

Eadgifu knew it was because her father had been King of Wessex, whereas her half-brother was King of the English, but that little settled her resentment.

The 'oohs' of delight that spilt from her younger sisters admiring mouths were enough for Eadgifu to appreciate she wasn't the only one jealous of such good fortune.

Neither could she tear her eyes away from Eadhild's self-satisfied expression, as she progressed to her waiting horse, accompanied by King Athelstan, who had his arm linked through her own, and more, who rested his hand over Eadhild's gloved one.

The gesture was strangely intimate, and Eadgifu looked away, her breath coming too fast as she fought for composure.

She was sure she'd never been so smug at the time of her own marriage. She was convinced that the thoughts of her sisters had been paramount in her mind. She was sure of it, or so she convinced herself.

"My Lord King," Eadgifu curtsied as King Athelstan neared her. She was aware of her sisters doing the same. So too were the wives of the noblemen, who would be left behind while Eadhild travelled to the coast in the company of their husbands. Eadhild would then move on to West Frankia, her journey only ending in Paris, where Count Hugh awaited his new bride.

"Queen Eadgifu," King Athelstan was never one to forget her correct title. The use of it now was a gentle caress in the tense atmosphere allowing Eadgifu to stand with her back a little straighter, her chin far higher, as Athelstan greeted his other half-sisters and half-brother.

All the while, Eadhild's eyes, the same colour as her own, blue as the ocean, settled on Eadgifu, defiance in the tilt of her chin.

"Sister," the lack of her title grated, and yet Eadgifu held her poise.

"Sister," the reply carried the snap of stretched cloth.

"Do you have any advice for me," the taunt was softly given, and yet Eadgifu knew there was more to come.

"Please your husband in the marriage bed, but keep him faithful." The words, not quite as crudely given as Eadgifu had heard from her own mother, resulted in a smirk of delight on Eadhild's face.

"He had better please me, and not vice versa," Eadhild retorted, no sense of embarrassment on her face, for all they spoke of such a personal matter.

"Then I would advise you to watch the count's enemies just as carefully as you do his allies."

Eadhild's eyes penetrated her own, as though seeking to discover the truth of the words. Her mouth opened and then closed again, a firmness settling around her mouth. Eadgifu gloated internally. Her sister had tried to embarrass her, in reply Eadgifu had reminded her of the dangers her marriage presented. If her own sister could be forced to flee West Frankia for her life, then there was no guarantee that it wouldn't happen to Eadhild as well.

"Count Hugh is favoured by the West Frankish nobility. He might not be the King, but that is better. None shall seek his downfall. None are powerful enough." The disdain in Eadhild's voice filled Eadgifu with loathing. That Eadhild was right only heightened her dismay. Yet, Eadgifu needed to send her sister away with more than just angry words, and bitter retorts.

Steeping herself for this unpalatable moment, Eadgifu leaned in close to her sister so that her words would reach only Eadhild's ears.

"I beg you to encourage your husband to free my husband, to restore Charles to his throne and to enable Louis to know his father."

Eadhild jerked back, as though the words had singed her ear, swift fury filling her eyes. Eadgifu abruptly knew that Eadhild would do nothing for Charles, even if she could have done.

But before further angry words could erupt between them, Eadgifu felt a small hand slip into her own, and looking down, she struggled to keep moisture from her eyes.

Louis.

If there had ever been anything that could have united the two sisters, it was Louis. Now he stood between them, his eyes alight with mischief, a smudge of mud on one cheek, a puppy encircling his filthy boots, as he held his mother's hand in his right hand, and his aunt's in his left.

His gap-toothed grin gazed up at them both.

"I'll miss you, Aunt Eadhild." The voice was high, a wobble to his voice, and regardless of her beautiful cloak, Eadhild sank to her knees, her eyes on Louis, as Eadgifu looked on. The two of them had long been allies. Eadgifu had never quite had the heart to force Louis to choose between the two of them. Not when Eadhild had proved to be a more natural parental figure than Eadgifu could ever be.

"I'll miss you as well," Eadhild confirmed, reaching out with her free hand to rub at the mud on Louis' cheek, seeming not to care when the equally muddy puppy leapt up to lick her face. Eadgifu grimaced, knowing she'd have never allowed such to happen to her. But Eadhild chuckled.

"I don't wish to leave Mond behind, but I will, because you and he are such good friends. In years to come, you can send me one of his puppies. Agreed?" Louis' face split with delight at the words, his eyes brightening, and Eadgifu knew that even in leaving, Eadhild had won her son's heart one more time.

"Of course, Aunt Eadhild. I'll only send you the best of the litter. But, it'll be a few years." Louis offered the final sentence with worry on his face, as though forced to remind Eadhild of the fact, even if it might sway her to take the pup with her.

"I know, and that's fine with me. He might not like it in West Frankia, not now he's used to Wessex," Eadhild continued. "Better to have a younger pup who can get used to living somewhere new."

Louis nodded vigorously, as he leant forward to offer his aunt a kiss on her cheek, so similar to the dog's lick, that Eadgifu chuckled without meaning to at the similarity between the two. Hearing the sound, Eadhild glared up at Eadgifu, and hastily made her way back to her feet, the pup circling in an out of her legs.

Her eyebrow arched at her sister, and Eadgifu fumbled for the right words to say. She didn't wish to part on bad terms with her sister, but neither did she feel like explaining herself.

Eadhild surprised Eadgifu by leaning forwards, her words intended only for Eadgifu's ears.

"Anything I do will be for the child, not for his mother, and not for his father."

Without leaving time for a reply, Eadhild moved on, Louis following in her wake, as she bid goodbye to her sisters and brother. Eadgifu fought for composure, aware of Edwin's mocking eyes on her.

Her damn brother. With Ælfweard dead, Edwin should have been King. But Edwin was a fool. Just like Eadhild, Athelstan was enamoured of her son, but not her. Her lips curled as she considered that. She didn't find Louis an easy child, certainly not all of the time, but it was he, and not her husband, that she knew held the keys to the future.

Her younger sisters cried softly as they made their goodbyes to Eadhild, while Edwin sighed and looked bored. Eadhild's escort was busy mounting up, and Eadgifu's lips curled once more as her gaze settled on Lord Osferth. It was he who'd supported Athelstan over Edwin. Eadgifu found it beyond herself to forgive him, even if, in the darkest reaches of her heart, she knew he'd been right to prevent Edwin from becoming King of Wessex.

Osferth would ride to Sandwich with Eadhild, accompanied by the West Frankish embassy, that included Count Adelolf and Lady Ælfthryth. As soon as Eadhild boarded the ship that would take her to West Frankia, she'd be left with few men and women of Wessex to support her and would be almost entirely under the control of the West Frankish embassy.

Eadgifu paused, reminded of her own journey into the unknown, and for the first time felt a flicker of unease. There was much she could have told Eadhild, a great deal she could have warned her about, only her underlying jealousy and hatred of her superior sister had prevented her. Perhaps there was still time to make amends?

Turning to one of her servants, she beckoned them close.

"Run to the kitchen. Ask for mint. Quickly."

The servant bobbed, turning in her haste, feet fleeing through the melee and somehow still managing to make her way to the open door of the King's hall without injury. Still, Eadgifu tapped her foot urgently. Even now Eadhild had finished with her farewells, curt-seying one final time before King Athelstan, and turning to mount her horse.

Louis stood beside her, unwilling to let Eadhild out of her sight.

King Athelstan, a soft smile on his face, bent down, and hoisted Louis onto his shoulders, a touching moment so that Louis could see more easily what was happening. As Eadhild settled in her saddle, ensuring reins and harness were tight, she turned and ran her hand over Louis' face before leaning forward, and leaving a kiss on his muddy forehead.

Louis' enraged disgust at such an action made Eadhild laugh, the sound high and a little out of control. Eadgifu watched on, envy curdling her heart, as the servant reappeared, handing a bundle of tied linen into her hand.

Without so much as a thank you, Eadgifu took the softly rustling packet and weighed it in her hand. Should she? Could she?

Swallowing down her own better judgment, Eadgifu walked to where King Athelstan and Louis were sharing final words with Eadhild. Unsure how to intrude on their private moment, Eadgifu hovered to the side, the smell of mint enveloping her, as her heartbeat ever faster in her chest.

It was Eadhild who noticed her first, her forehead furrowing at the sight of her sister once more.

Eadhild opened her mouth, as though to defend her actions toward Louis, but Eadgifu stepped forward, her hand outstretched.

"For the sea voyage. It will settle your stomach."

Eadhild reached out to take the linen wrapping, a perplexed expression on her face, as Louis continued to babble on about his puppy, and the wall of sound around them grew and grew until it suddenly faded, and there were just the two of them.

"My thanks, Queen Eadgifu," without waiting for a reply, Eadhild encouraged her horse forward, never turning, not even to wave to Louis, and Eadgifu was left astonished.

Her sister had never used her title. Never.

AD926

E adgifu would rather have been far from the scrutiny of so
many than sat beside King Athelstan, but her half-brother
was keen to celebrate the treaty with Count Hugh, and
Eadgifu knew her attendance at the feast was compulsory.

It little helped that she was forced to sit in the middle of Edwin
and King Athelstan, while her two sisters were sat to the left-hand
side of Athelstan. Eadgyth and Ælfgifu had a far easier role to
perform. They could chatter amongst themselves and ignore both
their brother and half-brother. Eadgifu was unable to do either.

At least the food was excellent, or so she consoled herself, eating
well of the baked fish, savouring the soft centre and crunchy exterior.
The wine was excellent as well, a gift from the West Frankish delegation that Athelstan favoured.

To the far side of Edwin, sat her father's third wife. And that was
the only part of the feast that Eadgifu could allow herself to enjoy, for
her bitch-mother was not enamoured of Edwin.

Her younger half-brothers were seated with Louis, under the
watchful eye of ealdorman Ælfwold. Ealdorman Ordgar and Wulfgar
had begged King Athelstan to excuse them from the feast. Athelstan
had done so gracelessly, but Eadgifu had witnessed his hesitation.

Neither man looked well, and Eadgifu appreciated why the king was pensive.

A king without allies could fall. The same had happened to her husband and had led to his imprisonment at the hands of over-mighty subjects.

Eadgifu was busy trying to think of something to say to King Athelstan or Edwin when she noticed a commotion at the doorway to the king's hall.

King Athelstan, alert as ever, was already aware of the problem when Eadgifu turned her eyes from the doorway to glance at her half-brother.

His brow, as so often, was deeply furrowed, his eyes piercing, as though he could determine what was happening, just by staring for long enough.

Quickly, Lord Ælfstan was allowed to approach the king. A flicker of both unease and pleasure punctuated Athelstan's face as Ælfstan took to his knee before the king.

"Rise, my lord," King Athelstan's voice was loud enough for all to hear. He stood abruptly, bowing to his half-sisters and his step-mother, and making his way from the hall. Lord Ælfstan followed him, without speaking, into King Athelstan's private study.

"I wonder what that's all about?" Edwin's voice was heavily slurred from too much wine, as Eadgifu watched King Athelstan and Lord Ælfstan. Only when the pair had entered King Athelstan's small chamber inside the hall, did Eadgifu turn to stare at her brother.

Edwin was younger than her, by a handful of years, but she knew he looked older, even older than Athelstan. Edwin was a source of disappointment to her.

"I'm sure King Athelstan will share what news he deems fit."

She spoke to try and forestall her brother's tendency to complain constantly about his half-brother whenever they were alone. Eadgifu was bored with the tediousness of listening to the same old and tired complaints. It was becoming an effort even to make the conciliatory noises that Edwin expected from her.

"Lord what's his name is from Mercia. I imagine something's happened to his precious Tamworth or Chester."

Edwin spoke derisively, his wine goblet swaying before him, as he vaguely indicated the area north of Wessex. Eadgifu hissed angrily at him as wine sloshed down her expensive gown.

"Apologies, dear sister," Edwin exclaimed too loudly, drawing the eyes of more and more people in the hall to both his behaviour and what he'd done.

Eadgifu was tempted to storm from the hall and was forced to bite down on her tongue hard enough that she tasted blood to stop her hasty action. She might thoroughly detest Edwin's whining and drunk behaviour, but she'd never show it to others within the hall. She and her brother and sisters needed to maintain the charade that they were united in all they did. No matter how much her brother humiliated them.

A servant rushed to her side, a clean rag in her hand, and Eadgifu eased her ragged breathing as she felt the comforting stroke of someone trying to erase the stain of the blood-red wine.

"A little vinegar, My Lady Eadgifu, and you'll never know the stain was there." The voice was soft and insistent but filled with respect. Eadgifu nodded without turning to meet the eyes of her servant.

"My thanks," Eadgifu managed to spit through clenched teeth. Edwin continued to sway his goblet of wine from side to side. Thankfully, there seemed to be little left inside the container, with half of it staining her dress.

Her eyes were trained on the sturdy wooden door that led to Athelstan's private space. She hadn't been inside the room since the death of her brother Ælfweard. But even before that, she'd been an irregular visitor to the office. Her father had only allowed her access to discuss her marriage. And then, once, on her return from West Frankia, to assure her that he'd do all he could for Louis and her husband.

Her father's promises had come to nothing, but she still hoped it would be different with King Athelstan. King Athelstan had a genuine affection for his nephew. He also cared for his foster-children, as well as the sons of his father's third marriage. That affection was missing from his relationship with the children from his father's second wife.

Eadgifu knew much of it was because of age.

The smaller children were all enamoured of their older half-brother. While King Athelstan spent little time with them, that which he chose to share with them was always filled with laughter and joy. Not like the sullen silences that settled over such tense affairs as this feast. Not for the first time, Eadgifu considered why King Athelstan put himself through the awkwardness of entertaining his half-siblings. Or, she considered, perhaps he felt none of it.

It was a conundrum and one she'd never yet managed to solve. Certainly, she felt the strain of all such occasions dearly.

At her side, Edwin had lapsed into near silence, soft snores showing that he'd fallen asleep in his chair once more. To the side of him, Eadgifu heard her step-mother's soft sigh of annoyance, but before she leapt to her brother's defence, the door to Athelstan's door opened once more, and Lord Ælfstan strode out, his destination the door of the hall, while her half-brother wound his way back to the dais, stopping here and there to whisper to men who stood and followed Lord Ælfstan.

It was so inconspicuously done, that Eadgifu was sure none noticed but her.

As King Athelstan settled beside her, she watched him covertly, her focus, to all intents and purposes, on her meal, and not the king.

As the last of the men King Athelstan had spoken to exited the king's hall, Eadgifu almost imagined she'd witnessed the entire thing. But then the king sighed softly.

"My Lord King, all is well?" Eadgifu wished she'd held her tongue when King Athelstan didn't reply immediately. It had become some-thing of a test for her. Just how long could she maintain her lack of interest in the affairs of the king's court? She never wanted King Athelstan to know just how much it riled her to be a mere hanger-on in a court where her opinion was rarely if ever sought.

Yet, for once the king turned to her, a look of suppressed anguish in his deep-set eyes.

"It seems I've lost a sister to marriage today, only to regain one."

For a moment, Eadgifu had no idea of what Athelstan spoke. After all, she was sat beside the king, Eadhild was making her way to Sandwich, whereas Eadgyth and Ælfgifu flanked King Athelstan to the far side. Of the remaining sisters, Æthelhild and Eadflæd were both safe in Wilton Nunnery, and young Eadburh was in the Nunnaminster.

King Athelstan, as though sensing her confusion, allowed a flicker of distaste to cross his face. Then Eadgifu remembered and wished she'd never spoken. Of course, Athelstan had a full sister, Lady Ecgwynn, and she was married to Sihtric, King of York, and had been since January.

Eadgifu held her half-brother's gaze. She'd offer no apology for forgetting the half-sister she'd only met once.

"What has befallen King Sihtric?" Eadgifu demanded, keen to know more, even if King Athelstan was unhappy with her.

"A case of mistaken faith and unruly followers. Lady Ecgwynn will remain in Mercia for the time being."

Eadgifu gasped at the implication in the words.

"He has divorced her?"

"No, she has divorced him. She'll not stay wed to a man who doesn't share her faith." So spoken, King Athelstan turned to face the men and women arranged before him. The feast was reasonably calm, for all that some had clearly drunk just as much as Edwin. They now sang loudly, proclaiming their battle glory for all to hear.

"The men will ensure her safety as she returns to Tamworth."

Eadgifu held her tongue. There was much at play here, and gloatingly she thought of King Athelstan's grand plan, and how it had faltered after only half a year. Beside her, Edwin snorted loudly in his sleep, and she leaned across and nudged him heavily in the chest.

"Wake up you bloody fool," she whispered harshly, unheeding that her step-mother heard her words and the desperation in them.

If King Athelstan should be proved to have made a false step in marrying his allegedly beloved full-sister to Sihtric of York, then there was the smallest hope that his supporters would grow uneasy with his decisions. They could call him to account for his actions. Until now,

Athelstan had ruled with the firm support of his Mercian allies, and the growing grudging respect of the Wessex witan. One false step and Eadgifu was sure that there might just be the potential for her brother to claim the crown of England for himself.

She thrilled, eating more heartily of her meal, and making an effort to speak to Athelstan of her sister's impending marriage to Count Hugh. Perhaps it was time he was reminded that she was skilled in the politics of the court.

King Athelstan watched her, his blue eyes blazing with a modicum of respect that thrilled her more than it should the longer she spoke with him.

While Edwin might be a drunkard, she wasn't, and she was just as much her father's daughter, as Athelstan was his son.

The following day Eadgifu called her two younger sisters to her side in the women's hall. She was keen to know what they had discovered about Lady Ecgwynn.

Ælfgifu was much in favour with both their step-mother and with King Athelstan. Too young to take great offence when Athelstan became king in place of Edwin, no amount of discussion could convince her that Edwin was the rightful king. Eadgifu had long since given up, the knowledge that it was a lie an unpalatable truth.

"Sister," Ælfgifu offered, a bob of a curtsey before she tumbled to the floor, and embroiled herself in a game with Louis and his young uncles. Eadgyth, an arched eyebrow showing what she thought of her younger sister's behaviour, carefully held her dress to one side and settled in the chair that Eadgifu indicated.

"Sister dearest," Eadgyth had an infuriating habit of expressing too much familial regard between the sisters. Eadgifu had long since realised it was done merely to annoy, and yet it still irritated.

"Sweet sister," Eadgifu replied her tone sickly sweet.

"Urgh," Eadgyth's immediate response brought a smile to Eadgifu's lips as she watched her sister's face turn nauseous.

"You should hear yourself if you don't like that."

Eadgyth looked about to argue, but Ælfgifu flounced upwards, settled on a chair, and looked between her sisters, an expectant look on her face.

"What do you want?" Ælfgifu asked, seemingly unhappy to be stuck with her older sisters.

"I thought we should just, you know, say hello to each other, now that Eadhild is gone."

"But she only left yesterday. I doubt she's even in Sandwich yet. I'm sure we didn't need to meet quite so urgently. I was busy."

Eadgifu flicked a censorious gaze at her youngest sister.

"You should never be too busy for your family."

"Urgh," now Ælfgifu complained, her hands high before her in frustration, before dropping them into her lap.

"We both know you want to know all about Lady Ecgwynn, but I have nothing to report." Trust Eadgyth to speak so bluntly.

"Oh well if that's what you want, you should have said. King Athelstan tells me that she'll return to Tamworth and that Lord Ælfstan is to escort her. The king intends to recall Sihtric to his religion, and to his wife."

"But they're divorced?"

"Yes, for now. But, they could always reconcile. Lord Ælfstan and his brothers are to gather a force on the border with York, ensure King Sihtric knows that the king will retaliate if the alliance is repudiated."

"But what of Lady Ecgwynn?"

"I'm sure she'll be fine," Eadgyth dismissed, watching Louis, Edmund and Eadred. Her mind seemed to be on matters that were not concerned with their little lamented half-sister. "She'll probably be pleased to return to Mercia. I wouldn't wish to be married to a Viking Raider. And a heathen one at that."

"But what if she has a child, a half-Viking child, with Sihtric."

"Then she'll have a child. It's no different to what happened with you and Charles."

"Of course it's different," Eadgifu felt her temper fraying. "I was his queen and the mother of his only legitimate son. Lady Ecgwynn is just a discarded wife of a blood-thirsty Viking."

Eadgifu realised that her youngest sister was scrutinising her carefully, a look of utter disbelief on her face.

"Do you not know that Lady Ecgwynn suggested the match? It was never King Athelstan's intention to force Ecgwynn to marry. He adores his sister."

Eadgifu felt her pulse once more beat too fast. She didn't know this. Had King Athelstan truly given his sister so much freedom?

"I take it from your silence that you didn't know. I'm aware that Edwin argued against the match, but Lady Ecgwynn had no problems with it. She's spent more time with Viking men than she has the men of Wessex."

Eadgifu was surprised at her sister's insight into Lady Ecgwynn.

"How do you know all this?"

"I listen, sister, and I'm quiet, and that means that sometimes I hear things I probably shouldn't because people don't even realise I'm there." Ælfgifu looked proud of her accomplishments if a little surprised that Eadgifu was unaware.

"While you haunt the women's hall, dreaming of returning to West Frankia, I concern myself with England. It would benefit you to do the same."

Eadgifu lifted her hand, as though to slap her sister, but thought better of it. Perhaps she was the one that needed the slap, to awaken herself to what was happening in England. Ælfgifu smirked, possibly reading her thoughts.

"Will you tell me all that you hear," Eadgifu tried instead. "I'm not in King Athelstan's confidence. I'd like to know more."

"I'm sure you would," Eadgyth interjected. "Perhaps walking around with your nose out of the clouds would help. We all know you were once Queen of West Frankia. But you never will be again, and you need to accept that and make the best of what you do have. Athelstan, as much as I hate to admit it, is far more reliable than your husband."

While Eadgyth's words stung, Eadgifu held her angry reply. It seemed she was learning a great many unpalatable truths.

"Will Lady Ecgwynn come to Wessex?" she instead asked her youngest sister.

"No. She will not."

"Are you so sure of that."

"I am," Ælfgifu maintained. "Athelstan might want his full-sister close, but Ecgwynn has only ever had a concern for Mercia, especially now she's fled from York."

"Why are you so interested?" Eadgyth taunted. "Are you worried she'll take your non-existent place at Athelstan's side?" The laughter was cruel, and yet Eadgifu allowed it, her lips turning down as she realised she was perhaps her own worst enemy.

"I'd just prefer to know before everyone else does," Eadgifu confirmed, her voice low, her eyes switching between her two sisters.

"Then you should ask nicely, sister dearest, and I'll run to you with every rumour I hear." Eadgyth still spoke to rile, but Eadgifu was suddenly too tired to argue further.

"And I'll inform you of all I know as well. Provided you are a little kinder to us. We, as you said, are your sisters, not your enemies." Eadgifu, chastised by her youngest sister, bowed her head in acknowledgement.

Her sisters had yet to find husbands, or make the decision to enter a nunnery. Eadgifu could well understand why they were so interested in King Athelstan's policies, yet she had far more at stake.

King Athelstan had made no move to bring about the release of her husband. She knew, although admitting it was too painful, that Charles would never walk free from his imprisonment.

That meant the future rested on Louis' shoulders.

At least, Eadgifu thought, King Athelstan, adored her son. If not for her, then maybe he would act to assist his nephew.

ANGLO SAXON CHRONICLE
ENTRY FOR AD926

This year king Athelstan and Sihtric king of the Northumbrians came together at Tamworth, on the 3d before the Kalends of February ; and Athelstan gave him his sister.

Eadgifu paced around the women's hall. Her emotions were a riot.

King Athelstan had ridden to war a month ago, and news was expected any day soon, and still, she didn't know how or what to feel.

The past year had been awkward. Eadgyth had arrived in West Frankia and married Count Hugh, but Eadgifu knew little more than that.

And now, well King Athelstan had ridden to make war on the kingdom of York following the breakdown of Lady Ecgwynn and Sihtric's marriage, and Sihtric's subsequent unexpected death.

Should King Athelstan die in battle, then Edwin would have to be named king in his place. Her half-brothers, Edmund and Eadred, were far too young to become king, no matter what King Athelstan or their mother thought.

But, and this was the cause of her anxiety, and the very thing that forced her to fling the door wide open and stride through the woodland that occupied the far end of the enclosure at Winchester, did she want King Athelstan's death now that it was actually a possibility?

There had been a time when Ælfweard had first died that she'd thought Edwin should be king. But while Edwin drank himself insensible each and every day, King Athelstan worked hard to secure the kingship, making both allies and enemies as he saw fit. And as much as she hated to admit it, he had won her respect.

Did she really want a drunk on the throne? How would Edwin ever ensure her son reclaimed his kingdom?

Outside, the air was warm, the rain of earlier leaving the odd puddle along the woodland path she pitched herself along. More than once, she wished she was as old as her son, and able to stomp into the puddles, allowing the muddy water to dirty her dress and drench her expensive shoes.

She'd not slept well the day before, somehow knowing that today there would be news. But the day had dragged, and now she feared that no announcement would arrive. That would mean another sleepless night.

Eadgifu sighed. She just needed to know, one way or another, whether her half-brother lived or was dead.

Being the king's sister gave her no privileges to know information before anyone else. In fact, despite her best efforts with her two younger sisters, Eadgifu was sure they colluded to keep her ignorant of affairs.

"My Lady Eadgifu," the voice was soft and yet iron-hard at the same time. Eadgifu sighed. Right now, the last person she wanted to see was her bitch-mother.

"Lady Mother," Eadgifu dipped a curtsey, all the same, taking the opportunity to work her face into a more pleasant expression.

"The waiting is hard, isn't it?"

A sympathetic, if perplexed expression touched the younger woman's face. Eadgifu struggled for some sense of balance and the right reply. She'd not thought any would know what upset her so much.

"Yes, it's been a long time since we had news."

Her bitch-mother dared to laugh, the sound a little too sharp.

"The king has been sending messages on an almost daily basis. Have you not been told?"

Swift fury descended over Eadgifu. She preferred to stay away from the king's hall. It was too humiliating to watch her brother drink and drink until he could barely hold his tankard to his lips. She'd thought she could rely on her sisters. Clearly not.

"The king is well, that is what's most important to know." Her bitch-mother arched an eyebrow as though daring her to disagree, but Eadgifu found her tense shoulders settling, the anxiety in her stomach dissipating.

"Then I'm pleased, and would thank you for settling my worries."

Her step-mother inclined her head, eyes busy as she scoured the woodlands for her sons.

"Then I bid you a good day." Eadgifu stopped to watch her step-mother stride off. She swallowed the bitter knowledge that her younger sisters would rather work against her than with her. While Edwin was no use to anyone, with his ridiculous plans and ideas, no more than the drunken myths, he told himself, Eadgyth and Ælfgifu clearly saw their older sister as just such an annoyance to be tolerated.

Allowing her fury full-head, Eadgifu strode off, not in the direction of her step-mother, but rather deeper and deeper into the woodlands, until the sun faded overhead, obscured by the tall canopy of the surrounding trees, and she felt herself alone for the first time in many years.

A handy tree stump provided a welcome seat, and while Eadgifu puffed and pulled her dress tidy before her, dark thoughts clouded her brow.

What, she considered was it that she genuinely wanted?

Was it her husband, or her son, or just some sign of respect from her brothers and sisters?

Traitor tears began to fall down her cheeks, as Eadgifu realised that she was never likely to have what she wanted. Who could give her back her kingdom and her crown, when her husband wasn't even able to escape his captivity if he still lived at all?

. . .

WHEN THE SERVANT sidled up to her in the women's hall, Eadgifu felt exhausted and on edge. Despite her step-mother's assurance that King Athelstan was well, a niggling doubt worried at her. She could remember when her husband had been apart from her, how everyone had assured her that all was fine, and yet it hadn't been, and she'd not seen him since.

"My Lady Eadgifu," the servant, not her usual one, bowed deferentially and waited to be acknowledged.

"Yes," Eadgifu croaked, her voice still husky from the despair that had gripped her earlier.

"The Queen Dowager has asked me to inform you that the king, Lord Athelstan, is well. York has been claimed, and even now, he seeks peace with the men from the Kingdom of the Scots, Strathclyde and Bamburgh."

Eadgifu could barely comprehend the words.

"The king is well?" she reiterated, just to be sure, and the servant, a perplexed expression on her face, nodded, and bowed once more. Eadgifu could feel curious eyes on her but ignored them.

"Then please send my thanks to the Queen Dowager," she managed to gabble, more relieved than she'd thought possible to know that Athelstan yet lived, and remained as king.

The servant walked smartly away, and immediately Eadgifu turned to meet the too curious eyes of both Eadgyth and Ælfgifu. While Ælfgifu smiled, clearly having heard the message, Eadgyth looked more thoughtful.

"I didn't realise you and the bitch-mother were such good allies," Eadgyth eventually spat.

"And I didn't realise that my sisters were so vindictive as to keep information from me."

"If you didn't seclude yourself in the woman's hall, you'd know a damn sight more," Eadgyth growled. Ælfgifu watched on, her mouth parted a little, as her gaze switched from one of her sisters to another.

"I'm not welcome in the king's hall," Eadgifu tried, but Eadgyth shook her head.

"You're just as welcome as the rest of us, only you won't endure the humiliation of having a brother such as Edwin." Eadgifu opened her mouth to protest, only to shut it again.

"The Queen Dowager was kind enough to send word. There's no need for any of us to attend the king's hall."

"That's how you'd like it, isn't it? Pining away for a lost husband, and a lost kingdom. Away from the eyes of the rest of the court, blaming everyone but yourself for what happened, and equally what hasn't happened."

Rage turned Eadgyth's face puce, and Eadgifu watched in horror as her younger sister stood, body thrumming with anger.

"You, sister dearest, are our oldest sister, our sister." Eadgyth beat her chest as she spoke.

"You, sister dearest, shouldn't be hiding but fighting for our positions, and fighting for your son's future." With a swirl of linen, Eadgyth swept from her place beside the hearth and stalked to the door. Eadgifu was not alone in watching her sister with her jaw dropped wide open.

All eyes in the room, every servant and noble lady, including her son, watched Eadgyth's progress. Yet none spoke as the door banged closed on Eadgyth's back. And then Ælfgifu muttered.

"Well, that went well," dropping her eyes down to the embroidery in her hand, Ælfgifu settled to silence with those few words spoken.

Struggling to control her emotions, Eadgifu looked for something to focus on and settled on the flames in the hearth. They burnt yellow, not blue, the fire more for light than heat, and yet she could feel her tears streaming down her face.

Eadgifu wanted to be angry, furious, outraged that her sister should speak to her in such a way, and yet she couldn't help but think her sister might well be right.

AD927

Not that Eadgifu could immediately do anything to better her sisters' positions, and yet she resolved to.

The news from King Athelstan continued to be good. A peace treaty was signed with the King of the Scots, the King of Strathclyde, and the Earl of Bamburgh at Eamont.

A further agreement was reached near Hereford with the Welsh Kings, Hywel Dda, Idwal and Owain.

While such good news flooded in, Eadgifu thought long and hard about the last few years.

Was Eadgyth correct? Had she simply decided that sulking was a better way of explaining her continued presence in England, rather than trying to return to her husband?

If nothing else, Eadgifu realised she needed to force King Athelstan to provide for his two remaining sisters. It was clear to Eadgifu that Ælfgifu was unsuited to life in a nunnery. She also imagined that Eadgyth would much rather have a husband than a prayer to warm her bed each night.

The problem remained, as always, of just who would make a suitable husband for her sisters.

So far, of her father's three daughters to wed, two of them had married kings, and Eadhild had married a man who thought himself almost a king. That the first two of those marriages had stalled and then faltered was irrelevant. Eadgifu realised that her sisters would need kings as husbands, and that meant looking beyond England's shores, and indeed the shores of her island.

It would be impossible to marry her sisters to the kings of the other kingdoms in Britain, and not just because the men were all married, and with children already.

No, King Athelstan would never allow it. After all, he'd used Ecgwynn's marriage to King Sihtric as a basis for claiming York after Sihtric's death. It would not be impossible for others to do the same, with the English crown as the prize.

Eadgifu could see sense in the decision. While women, any children born of a union would think they had a claim to England's throne. Far better to ensure the children born to his sisters could claim a crown that wasn't England's.

Put simply, just like Eadhild, Eadgifu and Ælfgifu needed to marry into a monarchy on the Continent. And here, Eadgifu thought she might be the best person to offer suggestions. After all, as Queen of West Frankia, she'd come into contact with many of the royal families. And if she'd not met them, then she had much more knowledge than King Athelstan could lay claim to.

While Eadgyth and Ælfgifu watched her with angry eyes over the coming weeks, Eadgifu considered just how she could present her decision to the King. After all, they rarely spoke with one another than with remarks about Louis' progress. Would the King listen to her and take her suggestions seriously if she made some?

At one point, Eadgifu considered enlisting the support of her step-mother, but while they'd had some sort of brief understanding on that day in the woodlands, Eadgifu was unsure that she wished to continue with any form of cooperation with her.

Her step-mother was almost as ignored as she was. Yet, her step-mother had strong allies, Lady Ælfwynn amongst them, Athelstan's favoured cousin. And of course, her step-mother was also the mother of Athelstan's favoured younger, half-brothers. If even she could hold no sway over King Athelstan, then how was Eadgifu to do so?

In all the celebrations of King Athelstan's return to Winchester after concluding both of England's treaties with her neighbours, Eadgifu wavered in her resolve. King Athelstan was supreme, confident, measured and assured of all that he'd accomplished and hope to do in the future.

There were few voices raised against him, and even Edwin seemed to have reconciled himself to his despised older half-brother. Even Eadgyth and Ælfgifu seemed swept up in the jubilation of the royal court. Eadgifu thought she should leave the matter alone, but eventually realised that her sisters would never demand their brother find them husbands, and time was advancing.

While Ælfgifu was the youngest of them all, Eadgyth needed to be wed to ensure she could have children. It was that knowledge that drove Eadgifu to seek out King Athelstan one day when he was in his stables.

If he looked dismayed to see her, his blond hair holding a stray piece of hay as he groomed his own horse, Athelstan had the decency to quickly correct his expression.

"My Lord King," Eadgifu wrinkled her nose as she curtseyed. She was not a fan of the royal stables and far from understood the obsession with the huge hulking beasts.

"Lady Sister," Eadgifu stood with a rigid smile on the face at the acknowledgement of their shared father. "Have you some concern about Louis? I had hoped that with the new tutor, he and his young uncles had become friendlier. I would like it if they were allies, not enemies."

Not expecting to discuss Louis, Eadgifu felt her thoughts scatter, struggling for the right answer to his question.

"No, I'm happy with Louis' tutor, and of course, Edmund and Eadred are delightful." Eadgifu held back that she found Eadred an annoyance, and Edmund too timid. She was pleased that Louis was more dominant. It boded well for the future.

"Ah, then I'm pleased you are happy with the arrangements." A silence fell between them, into which king Athelstan turned back to his black warhorse, continuing his interrupted grooming, seemingly content with the uneasy atmosphere.

Eadgifu found her eyes drawn to her brother.

She couldn't deny that he was undoubtedly her father's son. If she narrowed her eyes just slightly or added a few lines to his smooth face, Athelstan could have been Edward. The main difference between the two men had always been Athelstan's physical build. He'd made his reputation as a warrior in Mercia, and he was still just as robustly built. Each sweep of the rough horse comb was accomplished with a restrained movement.

Eadgifu fought for calm, and for the will to say the words she'd been rehearsing since the summer months.

"My Lord King," she'd decided during her considerations, that the use of the King's title was best.

"Lady Sister," King Athelstan replied, in a repeat of their initial greeting.

Eadgifu swallowed down her unease.

"I should like to discuss with you the future of my dear sisters, Eadgyth and Ælfgifu."

"Ah," a flicker of respect crossed King Athelstan's face. "You have no need to concern yourself with them. I'll take the matter in hand when it's the right time," he continued.

"I," again Eadgifu stumbled over her words. She'd not expected King Athelstan to make such a non-committal response.

"I believe the time is close. While Ælfgifu is the youngest of us all, I believe that Eadgyth would welcome a marriage."

King Athelstan paused in his actions and turned his fierce blue eyes her way.

"I welcome your feeling of duty toward your sisters. But really, I assure you, when the time is right, husbands will be found for my dear sisters, or, if they wish, I will allow them to remove themselves to a nunnery."

Eadgifu winced at the hope in his voice. How much easier it would be for everyone concerned if Eadgyth and Ælfgifu did become nuns.

"After all," and here King Athelstan's face was filled with compassion. "To date, these marriages have been far from successful. We have young Louis from your own marriage, but Lady Ecgwynn has nothing but a dead husband. As of yet, there is no news that Eadhild's union with Count Hugh has proved to be fruitful."

"It's only been a short time," Eadgifu immediately defended, wondering why she would think to speak in favour of her absent sister, but feeling a fierce loyalty to her all the same.

"I'm aware of that," King Athelstan gently chuckled. "I pray for the marriage to be fruitful. And I pray for your husband to gain his freedom as well." The knowledge that the King did have some concern for her husband was a shock.

Eadgifu had thought that Athelstan had forgotten long ago that she'd even ever had a husband. It was always a surprise to realise just how fervent King Athelstan's faith was. Certainly, she didn't share his love of learning and collecting the relics of holy saints.

"I had hoped that Eadgyth may have sent news of how Charles fares, but as you say, she's only been with her husband for just over a year. I'm sure it takes time to learn who will be her allies, and who not." The King's voice soured as he continued, and Eadgifu realised that he spoke from his experiences when he'd first come to Wessex as her King.

"I would have some suggestions of eligible bachelors," Eadgifu pressed on, determined to say what she'd come to share. She turned away from the flicker of fury on King Athelstan's face.

Only then he sighed, and ran his hand over his face, shaking his head from side to side. Eadgifu watched him unsure of what he'd do next.

"Perhaps you could speak to Lord Osferth on the matter. He is family as well and has the best of intentions toward all of us. He'll be able to help you to root out those who would be suitable husbands and those who would not. When that has been done, I will consider your suggestions."

With that, the King turned to place his saddle over his horse, and

Eadgifu thought the conversation was finished. She even turned to walk away only for soft words to reach her ears.

"My thanks sister, for speaking with me. It would be good if we could always be allies, although I doubt that will ever happen." Unsure whether to respond or not, Eadgifu continued walking away from her half-brother and King.

She had no real answer to give him.

It was too difficult to put into words her feelings toward him. She hadn't realised that she had any sentiments towards him until he'd ridden to war, and the fear that he wouldn't return had tormented her. But now, with peace seemingly assured, she could feel old resentments beginning to fester once more.

"Perhaps not," she whispered under her breath pleased to make her exit from the stables and have fresher air to inhale. She heard King Athelstan murmuring to his horse, encouraging the animal, and then Athelstan rode past her, his eyes on where he wanted to go, as though she didn't exist at all.

Maybe it would be easier for him if he didn't have so many sisters.

It would certainly be easier for her if there were fewer brothers.

LORD OSFERTH SOUGHT her out three days later. Eadgifu eyed him thoughtfully.

It was impossible not to know that he shared some of their heritage. While Athelstan looked like her father in the right light, and with a tilt of the head, Osferth was almost her father, only a little older, and a little wirier. She smiled at him as he bowed before her, his grey hair still lying thick on top of his head, his physique that of an active man.

"Queen Eadgifu," Osferth even sounded like her father, although he'd always been more deferential in his interplays with her.

"Lord Osferth," she inclined her head gracefully, looking up from her game of tafl.

"The king has asked me to seek out your advice, on a personal matter." Eadgifu appreciated him then for the faithful courtier he was. She would have felt embarrassed if Ælfgifu, her tafl competitor, had known that she wished to speak of potential marriages. Knowing Ælfgifu, she would misinterpret the matter, perhaps thinking that her older sister was keen to be free of her.

"Shall we walk outside?" graciously, Eadgifu nodded her head, a smile of apology to Ælfgifu.

"You were winning anyway," Ælfgifu grimaced, relief on her face at being able to walk away from the board with some of her pieces still in play.

"I never win this game," Ælfgifu complained to Lord Osferth, watching her sister with a flicker of interest on her face.

Calling for her cloak, Eadgifu hunkered inside the warmth. It was a bitterly cold day, frost lacing the ground, and turning any stray grass, flowers or herb, rigid in its grip.

Lord Osferth held the door open for her, and she breathed deeply of the chill air. Better to get it over and done with. Still, they walked in silence until away from the prying eyes of those busy about the King's business, and keen to make rumours of anything unusual they saw.

"The king is aware you have some concerns for your sisters' futures and would like to find them husbands." There was warmth to Lord Osferth's voice. There always had been whenever he'd spoken to her in the past. He'd managed to keep close to King Athelstan on his accession. Eadgifu envied him the freedom he enjoyed with her half-brother, and before his reign, with her father.

"I merely feel that time moves quickly. With Eadhild's marriage to Count Hugh last year, it feels right that Eadgyth and Ælfgifu should have the same opportunities."

Lord Osferth laughed. The sound unexpected and rich with understanding.

"Your father had many daughters. You're right to champion your sisters' causes. I'm sure they don't wish to become nuns. They would no doubt have already made their intentions clear."

Eadgifu felt her tense shoulders relaxing. Unlike King Athelstan,

Lord Osferth seemed keen to speak with her, and far more understanding of what she was trying to accomplish.

"I imagine you appreciate that husbands from amongst the English nobility would be difficult. I know Athelstan made no argument against Lady Ælfwynn's marriage to Lord Athelstan, but it was the least he could do after she surrendered her claim to Mercia in his favour. And, of course, the brothers have always been Athelstan's firm supporters."

"I'm more than aware of the difficulties, and of course, I imagine that a king from one of England's close neighbours would be unacceptable. King Athelstan has enough brothers to succeed him, even if he doesn't wish to marry. No, I'd been considering eligible men from close to West Frankia."

"Excellent, I hoped you'd understand the necessity of such an approach. It will make our discussion much easier."

"Have you heard from dear Eadhild?" Lord Osferth murmured his thoughts following Eadgifu's all the way to her lost kingdom of West Frankia.

"Little, I'm afraid. We were not the closest when she lived in Winchester."

"No, but she was so fond of young Louis, and of course, you were kind enough to stave off her seasickness with the gift of mint leaves to chew."

Eadgifu abruptly stopped walking. She was unaware that any knew of that, but of course, Lord Osferth had journeyed to Sandwich with Eadhild.

Lord Osferth stayed quiet, although she glanced at his face to determine if he teased her.

"King Athelstan has contact with Count Hugh. The King has reminded Count Hugh of his responsibilities to his wife's family, but I fear Count Hugh is not quite as influential as he led Athelstan to believe with all those gifts he sent to Abingdon. No doubt, it's easier for him to allow his brother by marriage to remain as King, even though he has no right to the position."

Eadgifu nodded, amazed to discover someone in Winchester who understood the affairs of her lost kingdom as well as she did. The remove, both in time and distance, sometimes made her think she'd imagined her marriage after all. Only Louis' existence proved to her that she had been a wife, and a queen, even if only for a short amount of time.

"Your husband is the captive of Herbert, Count of Vermandois. Regrettably, Herbert sees too much advantage to keeping your husband as his prisoner. I'm afraid, I don't think he'll ever be released, and you reunited, but I know Athelstan hoped that Count Hugh would intervene on his behalf to enable you access to him."

Eadgifu gasped at hearing such a stark account from Lord Osferth, and for a moment, she felt tears in her eyes, before she blinked them away. It was not something she hadn't long realised herself.

"And into that hot-bed of Frankia, you would seek to wed your sisters?" The question in Lord Osferth's voice forced Eadgifu to reconsider her decisions.

"I can't," Eadgifu eventually admitted, "think of more suitable places to search for husbands for them. Yes, there is often war and upheaval, but I would sooner look to West Frankia and her neighbours than to the Viking Raiders." As she spoke, Eadgifu knew she was right to make the distinction. Charles had married one of his daughters to Rollo of Normandy. While Charles had done so to protect his kingdom, and to give his sanction to Rollo's acquisition of Normandy, Eadgifu shuddered at the thought of doing the same for her sister.

While Lady Ecgwynn might have chosen to wed Sihtric, the Viking King of York, Eadgifu didn't want her sisters to be forced to such a match.

"You are, no doubt correct. And, I understand there are many unmarried men. I would hope that someone there would be a husband for Eadgyth and Ælfgifu."

For a moment, Eadgifu imagined she was being humoured, only Lord Osferth looked and sounded genuine.

"Of course, there is some history of finding husbands in West Frankia. Your aunt, of course, married the Count of Flanders. I've spoken to the King's administrators who have the most knowledge of the area. They've suggested several names. But, before we take the matter further, I would like to be assured that your sisters are as keen to marry as you believe. As you're aware, leaving England is no small undertaking."

The sentiment was softly given, and once more, Eadgifu felt tears mar her vision. She had been terrified to leave England, scared to marry a man she'd never met, in a kingdom she knew only fragments of information about. The fact that she'd learned to speak their language so quickly had been a considerable advantage.

Now she laughed shakily.

"I confess I've not spoken to my sisters of the matter. I simply realised that, as their oldest sister, I should ensure they weren't forgotten about."

"I don't believe the king would ever forget about his sisters, but," and Lord Osferth held out his hand to prevent Eadgifu from interrupting him. "I believe you're correct to speak to the King. Matters of family are close to his heart."

The words astonished Eadgifu but then, King Athelstan and she didn't honestly know each other. Their father had made sure of that.

"And your husband's daughters. Do you know if they're married?"

A slight grimace touched Eadgifu's face. If her relationship with her sisters was strained, the few years she'd been Charles' wife had undoubtedly ensured that she was hated by his daughters.

"I'm afraid that they and I were never friendly."

"Ah, of course. My apologies," Lord Osferth demurred. Eadgifu couldn't help thinking that her intentions of acting for her sisters were beginning to come under too intense scrutiny. She swallowed down her unease.

"My sisters and I are very different," Eadgifu determined to explain. "They became women while I was in West Frankia." Eadgifu snapped her mouth shut on the torrent of excuses she wished to present. If Lord Osferth thought her merely trying to rid herself of unwanted women in her life, then he was wrong. But she was not prepared to offer more than she had.

"And of course, you're the only one with a child. I am aware that motherhood changes much." Osferth's calming words soothed Eadgifu's fluster, but still, she was aware they'd not discussed a great deal.

"Would it distress you should more of your sisters be married to your husband's enemies?" Such a question immediately dispelled her moment of serenity. Truly, how would she feel? Eadgifu had cautioned Eadhild about marrying Count Hugh, but in all honesty, Eadgifu had never much like Eadhild and had realised quickly that her lone voice would not stop the marriage.

"These men change their allegiances too quickly to keep track of everything," Eadgifu tried to laugh off the question. Still, it hurt, all the same, and coming to a stop, she turned to face Lord Osferth, searching his face as she spoke.

"I wish my sisters to have the joy of a happy union, and children, in the future. I would not wish on any of them the disruption of my own marriage. The men must be powerful or assured of such a position. I would not wish them to endure, such as I have."

"Very well, My Lady, Queen Eadgifu. I will take your words under advisement, and when I have suggestions of suitable men, I'll ensure you that both you, and your sisters, are informed. The King shares your concerns and worries. Be assured of that. No sister of his is ever to suffer the ignominy of losing a husband, as you and sweet Lady Ecgwynn have been forced to do."

Eadgifu nodded, unable to trust her voice.

She hadn't expected such sympathy from Lord Osferth, and certainly none at all from King Athelstan. Eadgifu had always thought her father disappointed in her when she returned from West Frankia. Not that he'd ever said anything to her face. Her mother had been less polite. She'd made it clear that Eadgifu had failed her. Eadgifu almost wished her mother had lived long enough to be disappointed by her sons, as well as her daughter.

Together, they made their way back to the women's hall, where Lord Osferth paused.

"Louis is a delightful child. I'm sure his father would have been proud of him."

Without pausing for an answer, Lord Osferth turned to walk to the King's hall, and Eadgifu watched him go with emotion clogging her throat.

AD929

For over a year, Eadgifu heard nothing further from Lord Osferth about her sister's marriages.

She grew disappointed and then despondent. Her relationship with Eadgyth and Ælfgifu didn't improve any further, and neither did the bitch-mother make any further overtures of friendship. Yet Eadgifu was unsurprised by that.

King Athelstan was safe. While he busied himself with the problems of governing such a vast kingdom, there was no threat of war.

The only real problem seemed to come from Edwin and his drunken ways, and persistence in plotting against the king. Eadgifu kept as far from Edwin's counsels as it was possible to be. She had no intention of being caught up in something she didn't even desire anymore.

Not that King Athelstan was always at Winchester, indeed he travelled extensively in Wessex and Cornwall, taking with him the men of the household but never the women.

Riddled with boredom, Eadgifu often journeyed to Wilton to visit with Æthelhild and Eadflæd.

Eadgifu found the conversion of her sisters from the young girls they had been to the modest nuns they now professed to be, strange to witness.

Of all her sisters, she'd been closest to Æthelhild before her marriage to Charles. But while she'd been in West Frankia, Æthelhild had travelled no further than to Wilton.

Not that the nunnery was particularly strict in its adherence to the holy rules. Still, Eadgifu didn't think she could ever have given up her luxurious and wide bed for the narrow cots her sisters made do.

"Sister, it is good to see you. I hope all is well with the king and our family."

As ever, Æthelhild's greeting just about bordered on polite. But the words were always said a little hopefully. As the sister who'd not taken her holy vows, but instead adopted the lifestyle of a lay sister, Eadgifu often got the impression that Æthelhild was just waiting for the right opportunity to escape from her life of good works and contemplation.

"Indeed yes, the king is well, as are our brothers and sisters, although it has been some time since news reached me of Eadhild."

A soft sigh of acceptance was all Eadgifu heard as she gazed at her sister. For all that Æthelhild professed to be an active member of the community, the fact that her hands remained soft and subtle, if demurely clasped on her dress of simple grey linen, belied the sentiment.

Why were her nails never cracked or her hands roughed by soil, if she was such a busy person? Not that Eadgifu had yet been tempted to ask. She was sure that if the subject were broached, Æthelhild would have her own cutting response. Going on childhood arguments, Eadgifu would rather not know her sister's true thoughts about her.

"Then I will offer God my thanks this evening," Æthelhild intoned, for all that Eadgifu detected the derision in her voice.

"What brings you to Wilton?" By now, Eadflæd had joined the two sisters, her wimple firm around her face, making it appear more severe than her youthful beauty would have allowed. Eadgifu was far from surprised that Eadflæd had demanded to take her vows and become a nun. She'd always been pious and also outraged by their father's multiple marriages.

"Can a sister not simply come and say hello," Eadgifu tried to laugh, but both of her sisters shook their heads at her, although they said nothing.

"Really? I simply came to see how my sisters were. King Athelstan is once more away from Winchester, and it allows me more time to follow my own pursuits." The bark of laughter from Æthelhild that accompanied her words was so loud it caused disapproving glances to be cast their way.

"I'm sure that Athelstan keeps you busy, sister," Eadflæd tried to console, while Eadgifu found her temper igniting at Æthelhild. It was difficult enough to accept that she had no real position in the king's select band of allies. Even worse that Æthelhild, who had never even attended King Athelstan's court, was also aware.

"You must excuse Æthelhild," Eadflæd tried to mollify. "Brother Edwin has visited dripping his poison into her ears and making wild statements he can't support."

The realisation that Edwin no doubt ridiculed her as much as she thought of him as ridiculous, brought bile to Eadgifu's mouth.

"Edwin is a bloody fool, and his only enjoyment in life is to upset the king." The words flowed like molten rock from her mouth, and yet she refused to retract them when four shocked blue eyes looked her way.

"He plots with other disaffected people, but none of them has any following. If he's not careful the king will be forced to take action against him."

"Would Athelstan do such a thing?" It was Eadflæd who asked the question.

"If Edwin leaves him no choice, then he'll have to."

"And what of Eadgyth and Ælfgifu?" Æthelhild spoke as though Edwin hadn't been mentioned at all, although Eadgifu detected unease in her sharp eyes.

"What of them? I know they visit you more often than I do."

"But when will they marry?"

"Do you know that they want to marry?" Eadgifu asked, curious as to what was said when she wasn't around.

"Of course they do," Æthelhild reprimanded. "There's been more than enough time for them to become nuns if they wanted to. Even Ælfgifu is old enough to know what she wants."

"Then, I don't know. I had spoken to King Athelstan about it, but it was some time ago. I've heard nothing since."

"Ah, then you should remind him," Æthelhild ordered Eadgifu.

"It's not my place to meddle. If my sisters wish to marry, then they should let the king know themselves."

A wry smirk greeted her statement.

"And what of your husband then? Eadhild tells me that he's not been seen for nearly a year."

"What?" Eadgifu glared at Æthelhild. "You've heard from Eadhild?"

"Yes, every two months. Why, when did you last hear from her?"

Eadgifu didn't want to admit it had been over a year, and that she'd failed to reply to her sister's letter. It had been filled with wild stories of her life as Hugh's wife, and Eadgifu had felt the jealousy that coursed through her body as physical pain.

"Well anyway, Eadhild says that Charles hasn't been seen for over a year, but that she had asked Count Hugh to ensure all was well. More than that, I can't say."

"And does she have a child yet?"

"Sadly no, that is why she wrote to us, to send some relics to her, that might facilitate her attempts. She doesn't say as much, but I'm sure that Count Hugh is eager for sons to follow in his footsteps."

"Yes, I'm sure he's just as ambitious as his father before him." Eadgifu felt her lips lengthen and turn down. Hugh's father, Robert, had fathered many sons and daughters, and even though he was not dead, his reach was almost as long and far as the Dublin Vikings.

"Then I shall pray for her," Eadgifu answered mildly, trying not to consider the potential reasons for her husband's disappearance. His captor had been using him as leverage to advance his own family for the last few years. If Charles were dead, which was the implication, then it would soon become apparent.

Eadgifu considered how she would feel if Charles was dead? They'd only been married for a short time before Charles defeat at the

Battle of Soissons, and her return to Wessex. She's known her son for longer than she had her husband.

The thought of seeing Charles once more no longer tormented her.

It would have been much easier if Charles had died, rather than being captured. At least then she could have publicly mourned instead of having to do so in secrecy.

"I hear that our bitch-mother is highly regarded by the king." Æthelhild pulled Eadgifu back to the warmth of the hall, food and wine being offered by Eadflæd.

"I wouldn't know. I have as little to do with her as possible." Once more, Æthelhild's response of high eyebrows almost incited Eadgifu to anger. But, as she helped herself to wine and sipped deeply, she remembered that it had always been Æthelhild's primary purpose to upset her sister.

"Then I think you should keep a close eye on her. Edwin thinks that King Athelstan and she have some sort of agreement regarding the succession. He wishes to know if Edmund will succeed King Athelstan and not himself."

Now it was Eadgifu's turn to answer with incredulity on her face.

"Does Edwin truly believe that King Athelstan would ever make him king? It has been clear from the beginning that King Athelstan would never accept Edwin as king. Why else did King Athelstan convince the Wessex witan to vote for him to be king?" Eadgifu shook her head from side to side, a wry smirk on her face at her brother's blindness.

"Edwin truly is delusional," Eadgifu continued, unprepared for the look of shock on Æthelhild's face at her words.

"What has Edwin been telling you?"

"That Athelstan had named him as his heir, and that he would soon be given an ealdordom." Æthelhild's voice was filled with censure.

Eadgifu spluttered drinking her wine, just managing to keep the fluid in her mouth.

"Edwin might sit in the king's hall, and pretend to his heritage, but King Athelstan tolerates him, nothing more. It is on Louis, Edmund and Eadred, as well as the other foster-sons that he pins all his hopes for the future. King Athelstan has engaged a tutor for all of them. They attend lessons and are taught more than I imagine Edwin knows, and all of them, apart from Alain of Brittany, are children."

"But Edwin said, he assured me, when he said," Æthelhild seemed to be struggling to form a sentence.

"I assure you, even from my limited contact with the business of the kingdom, that Edwin has no position with the king. He is simply kept close because it's best to know what an enemy is doing, rather than worrying about it. If Edwin has made promises to you, then you must forget them. They'll come to nothing."

"You speak harshly of our brother," Æthelhild complained, her face white with disbelief.

"I speak as I find. Edwin is not even half the man that Ælfweard was, and even Ælfweard probably saved us all by dying when he did."

Saying the words out loud was exhilarating, and Eadgifu faced her sisters with no hint of apology in her voice. In fact, she almost enjoyed seeing the dismay on Æthelhild and Eadflæd's face. Only then Æthelhild started to laugh, a low sound that Eadgifu hardly recognised as coming from a woman, let alone her sister.

"And here," Æthelhild gasped, "I thought you a fool and too vision-less to ever realise."

The shock Eadgifu felt forced her mouth open, while her eyes flickered between her two sisters.

"What? You share my opinions?"

"Yes, and so did mother," Eadflæd explained, and now Eadgifu sat back in her chair, feeling deflated and unsure of all that she thought she'd ever known.

"Father knew as well. Why else do you think he remarried?" Æthelhild's comment sparked fury from Eadgifu, and she stood, intending to stride from the room, only to feel the warm hand of Eadflæd on her arm.

"Don't leave sister," Eadflæd implored, contrition on her face. "We knew it was not our place to cast dispersions on our brother, not when you seemed to care for him so much."

"So, you let me believe that you all thought he should be king, and not Athelstan, rather than telling me the truth."

It was Æthelhild who answered. "Would you have listened to us, sister? You have never been one to listen to those who had opposing views to your own."

"But father, really, he told our mother that?"

"Not at the time, no. He simply advised her that more children were needed. Our dear father never explained to our mother why. Only just before his death did he come to our mother and explain his plans for the future. It was she who begged our father to allow Ælfweard to rule Wessex after him. He would sooner have left it all to Athelstan."

"But he never even liked King Athelstan."

"I imagine," Eadflæd stated, "that there's no need to like someone to recognise that they might be better equipped to rule."

Eadgifu shook her head in shock, shaking her dress and settling beside her sisters' once more, aware that curious if deferential eyes were looking their way.

"I, I," and still Eadgifu paused, her eyes settling first on Æthelhild and then on Eadflæd as though trying to determine whether they teased her or not.

"I assure you," Æthelhild spoke first. "It is the truth. We would not lie to you about this. Father was reluctant to allow Ælfweard to rule. He was adamant that Edwin never should."

"Then, our father should have made his opinions well known. It would have saved a lot of problems. Edwin is always plotting to overthrow King Athelstan."

"One day, he'll force the king to act against him. It would be better, certainly more convenient if Edwin simply disappeared, but I can't see that King Athelstan has the palate for it."

This time, Eadgifu managed to withhold her shock better at hearing her own thoughts spoken aloud.

"There is more than one reason why I chose the life of a lay sister," Æthelhild spoke softly. "It's much easier to be outside of the control of Edwin."

"Edwin doesn't control me," Eadgifu retaliated hotly.

"No, he doesn't because you are a queen and he is not a king. But if he ever had even the semblance of influence at his fingertips, he would try to, and don't deny it." It was Eadflæd who spoke in support of her sister.

Eadgifu lifted her goblet to her lips, keen to delay any form of an answer. Again, it seemed that her sisters were far more politically astute than they pretended to be. With a trace of sorrow, Eadgifu considered just how much she and her sisters could have accomplished if Edwin had not been a constant problem to circumnavigate.

"I admit, you are probably correct," Eadgifu eventually acknowledged, cradling her goblet between her two hands to stop them from shaking. This had been a conversation of shocking revelations and not at all the meeting she'd envisaged.

"The knowledge, while too long in coming to you, should open your eyes to Edwin, and you must be the one to support our youngest sisters," Æthelhild confirmed. "You are the only one remotely equal in stature to King Athelstan."

Eadgifu nodded, absently, replaying all those times she'd been forced to avoid the king's hall to stay away from her brother. It would be difficult for her to suddenly move her usual residence from the women's hall to the king's hall without anyone noticing, least of all Edwin. And yet, only then would she have the constant contact with King Athelstan that she felt she needed.

Sinking into silence, Eadgifu felt her sisters' attention drift away, as they picked up prayer books and embroidery. She had much to think about. Not all of it pleasant, but perhaps she would now have the assistance of her two sisters, even from their seclusion in Wilton Nunnery.

AD929

The letter felt heavy in her hand, as though her sister had sent far more than words to her.

Eadgifu almost feared to open it. Indeed, she could feel the curious gaze of Ælfgifu as she simply held the sealed parchment in her hand. She had been doing so since it had been pressed into her hand by one of King Athelstan's servants earlier in the evening.

What would it say? She worried that the news would be poor. After over a year of hearing nothing about her husband, Eadgifu had thought herself reconciled to his inevitable death. But now it seemed she'd held out some small hope that Charles still lived.

The seal, bloody-red wax, was unbroken beneath her fingers. The letter was addressed to her, and although it appeared to have first been delivered to King Athelstan, he seemed to have made no effort to break the seal and read the contents.

For the first time, she wished that King Athelstan were a little less honourable. If he'd read her letter, and it contained terrible news, then he could have come to her himself, and perhaps softened the blow. Now she was all alone, and she didn't wish to be.

Frustrated with herself, Eadgifu stood, and clutching the letter in her hand, and swung her cloak around her shoulders, before venturing outside. If the news was poor, she wished to read it alone.

Hastily, Eadgifu made her way to her chamber. Finding the room deserted, she settled on the edge of her bed, feeling its reassuring creek underneath her. This room had been hers when she was small, and not yet a bride. While it hadn't been hers immediately on returning to England, it was now hers, and here she felt able to hide away from all prying eyes.

A single candle burnt on the table, and she pulled it toward her, examining the seal one final time.

It seemed her sister, Countess Eadhild, had influence and power at her fingertips, for the seal carried her own name.

With a sharp fingernail, Eadgifu sliced open the seal and rolled out the stiff parchment. It had been well-cared for on its journey to Winchester. For the first time, Eadgifu realised that the letter had probably not arrived alone. Rather it would have been carried with a collection of such messages, addressed to the king, his ealdormen or even the bishops and archbishops of England. But who, she considered, had brought it here?

"Dearest sister," the words were elaborately written, and immediately Eadgifu recognised Eadhild's hand. She'd always enjoyed learning to write rather too much. Eadgifu had thought it a trial to endure. Her father had insisted that the grandchildren of the learned King Alfred could not possibly go through life unable to read and write for themselves. Eadgifu had grumbled at the work. Eadhild had not, and even Eadgifu could admit that the endeavour had proven worthwhile, time and time again.

"I send my warmest regards to your son, and to yourself. I have recently spoken with a member of the king's circle, who happened to see Louis only six months ago. He assured me that Louis was fit and well, and growing to be a fine young man. I am pleased to know as much.

As to my own attempts to become a mother. I am, sadly, not yet able to announce a son or daughter, but I am assured it will happen soon."

Eadgifu's eyes quickly scanned line after line as Eadhild spoke of her day to day life and small matters that were not Eadgifu's prime concern. Not now.

Only at the end of the letter did Eadhild mention her husband. And the news was too brief and general to be of any use.

"As to your husband. I have no news to offer. He has not been seen since I last wrote to you."

Eadgifu reread the line, as though hoping more would be revealed from such bland words, but there was nothing, and abruptly she began to sob. Her shoulders shook, and the letter trembled in her hands. She was unable to stop her stream of tears, although she did have the presence of mind to slide the parchment away from her wet face.

After all the care taken by those responsible for bringing news to her, she didn't wish to damage it before she'd truly had time to absorb all that her sister wanted to tell her.

For what felt like a long time, Eadgifu sobbed, the sound harsh in her own ears, and although she felt the door open to her chamber, in a swirl of wind, no one interrupted her, or came to comfort her. She was pleased. Unable to stop sobbing, she wanted no one to see her like this. No one.

Eventually, Eadgifu curled into a ball, her hands beneath her head as she lay on her bed, inhaling the comforting aroma of her own clothes, and bedding. She could take solace in the knowledge that she was safe from all harm.

THE FOLLOWING DAY, hollow from the grief of not knowing, Eadgifu sought peace amongst the woodlands behind the walls of Winchester Palace. She'd briefly considered riding to Wilton Nunnery but had dismissed the idea. She wanted no one to see her while feeling so distraught and wrung out. While her servants had made no comments about her appearance, and even her sisters had held their tongue on seeing her, Eadgifu knew she looked awful.

The last person she expected to see in the woodlands was Lord Osferth, and yet it seemed he'd been searching for her.

Hailing her as she meandered along the trampled down paths, Eadgifu had briefly considered ignoring him. The thought of seeing sympathy and compassion on his face, the face of her father, was almost too much to bear.

"My Lady, Queen Dowager," as ever, Lord Osferth's manners were impeccable. If his smart bow was slower than usual, Eadgifu determined not to notice.

"My Lord," her voice sounded cracked and broken, as Eadgifu realised she'd not spoken since her outburst of yesterday. She coughed, apologetically, and tried again.

"Good morning, Lord Osferth," where Osferth's face had shown concern for her greeting, a tight smile now played along the planes of his face.

"It is a pleasure to see you. There's much to discuss, and Athelstan is keen to have your opinion on the matters."

The words were wholly unexpected. Just how long had it been since she'd first spoken to King Athelstan about her sisters' marriages? She was sure her advice wouldn't be needed on any other matters.

"Come, I will tell you all as we walk to the king's hall. Athelstan was speaking to the messengers, determining all he could from them, but still, he is perplexed."

"About what, My Lord?"

"Ah, apologies, I'm so pleased to find you, I've forgotten to tell you what so excites me. The king has received an overture of friendship from Henry, King of East Frankia. Henry wishes a marriage alliance with the House of Wessex."

The news stunned Eadgifu, for all she had once thought Henry might have made a good husband for one of her sisters.

"Has Henry's wife died? I've heard nothing of such," Eadgifu exclaimed.

"No, no, it is for his son."

Frantically, Eadgifu tried to place an age for Henry's son.

What was it that she knew about Henry, known as the Fowler, for his love of hunting?

"Is this for his legitimate son or his illegitimate one?" Immediately she felt on edge. Henry had been briefly married to a woman who'd taken her vows as a nun. While she had been labouring to birth Henry's first son, the Papacy had announced the union invalid. The good lady's vow made the marriage illegal. Whether she'd wanted to or not, she'd been forced back to her nunnery, while Henry had married again.

"His legitimate heir, Otto, is his name."

Once more, Eadgifu tried to recall what she knew about Otto.

"He is but a youth," Eadgifu exclaimed.

"Otto is near enough seventeen years old, or so the letter states."

"Seventeen. Then he's untried in battle and ruling." What Eadgifu didn't add was, 'and probably young and handsome.' She'd been forced to marry an old man. How typical that Eadgyth would manage to marry a man younger than her.

"Why does the king wish my advice?" they were rapidly clearing the woodlands. In the distance, the king's hall was shimmering under the gentle glow of an early summer's day.

"Well. No, I shall let the king explain that to you himself. Be assured, King Athelstan is keen to hear all you can offer him about East Frankia."

Eadgifu imagined she should be pleased to be considered such an asset by the king. Still, coming so close to her letter from Eadhild, she would far rather have not been talking about husbands for her sisters.

On entering the king's hall, Eadgifu stalled in the doorway. Mirroring Lord Osferth's hurry, she'd been expecting the king's hall to be busy with men and women, discussing the news, but instead she found it almost deserted, King Athelstan drinking quietly on the raised dais, her brother slumped on a chair close to Athelstan. But other than the servants, there were few others in attendance.

At Lord Osferth's insistence, she resumed her steps and mounting the dais, curtsied to her half-brother, and king.

A smile of welcome suffused King Athelstan's face as he spotted her, and bounded to his feet, his hair light from being in the sun a great deal, his skin starting to shade with the warmth of the summer.

"Sister dearest, be welcome. It's good to see you. I see too much of young Louis, and not nearly enough of you." The exuberant welcome froze her greeting on her face. If King Athelstan never saw her, then it was because he so rarely invited her to his many feasts, when he was in attendance.

"My Lord King, brother," the words didn't flow naturally. "I hope Louis pleases you. Certainly, I believe he attends his lessons well and learns as much as possible from the monks."

"I'm well pleased with your son's progress, but please be seated."

King Athelstan indicated the chair next to Edwin's and yet closer to him. While Eadgifu would rather not have made eye contact with her brother, she knew it would only lead to difficulties if she didn't acknowledge him.

Even as early in the day as it was, Eadgifu could see Edwin's eyes were bloodshot, his smug expression ruddy from too much wine.

"Sister dearest," Edwin's voice grated, copying as it did, King Athelstan's words.

"Brother dearest," Eadgifu managed to mutter through tight lips, wrinkling her nose slightly at the rank odour that emanated from him.

Quickly, she settled in the chair, and turned to King Athelstan, noting as she did so, that Lord Osferth sat opposite her, his back to the room. She would have preferred such a position. Then only her brothers would have been able to read her expression.

"Brother, sister, Lord Osferth." Athelstan shunted his chair closer to the table, the wood of the chair legs protesting as it ground over the floor, as he called their small meeting to order.

"I've received a letter from King Henry of East Frankia, asking permission to send an embassy to England to find a bride for his oldest son, and legitimate heir, Otto."

It seemed that Edwin was unaware of this, as a shocked exhalation followed the statement. King Athelstan's eyes looked beyond Eadgifu to meet Edwin's but Eadgifu kept her focus on Athelstan.

"I'll not send another of my sisters to some far-off country I've never heard of. It's a bloody outrage." Edwin's response was immediate and shouted, rather than spoken. Eadgifu winced, wishing Edwin hadn't been included in the meeting,

For a moment, King Athelstan appeared to be perplexed, his forehead furrowing, his eyes glancing down at the parchment in his tapping fingers. King Athelstan was a man of action. Even just the act of sitting was difficult for him.

"I should like to hear more," Lord Osferth said into the strained silence. "What else does the letter say?"

For a moment longer, Athelstan stared at Edwin, or so Eadgifu assumed before he cast his eyes to the text he held.

"They offer to send an embassy, to consist of one of Henry's allies and several members of his extended family, although not the boy himself. They would wish to meet my sisters and then discuss terms with us. They promise fabulous riches and life as a queen for one of my unmarried sisters."

"Hah," the grumble from Edwin echoed too loudly. "It's not exactly gone well in the past has it? I would think it unwise to risk another failed union." While Eadgifu had been anticipating her brother's stance, it still shocked her to speak so openly of her husband's exile, Lady Ecgwynn's divorce, and Eadhild's continuing childlessness.

"Your sisters can't marry anyone from England. Would you constrain them to live as unmarried women? I would rather give them the chance to find a husband and become mothers if they so desired it."

"Hah," Edwin's cry was filled with derision. "You would simply rather have them all gone from England. I know you've asked them to consider a life in a nunnery and that they both refused. I'm aware that ambitious men would hope to marry them."

"I've never wished my sisters anything but a happy life," King Athelstan's retort was tight with outrage, a glint in his blue eyes. Perhaps, as much as Eadgifu hated to admit it, Edwin was correct in his interpretation of King Athelstan's actions.

"If," Eadgifu spoke into the silence, "my sisters are happy to marry, as I understand it, then I see no reason why they shouldn't be informed of the proposal and the embassy allowed entry to England. I would, however, prefer it if one of my sisters was chosen before the embassy arrived. I would not wish them to argue with each other. After all, there is only one proposal of marriage."

Unwilling to see the look on Edwin's face at her words, Eadgifu kept her gaze firmly on Athelstan.

"I would agree with Lady Eadgifu. There is no harm in the embassy visiting England, and it would be an honourable marriage for a sister of the king of England. I believe the King of East Frankia rules over people not too dissimilar to the English, and that the language is almost identical."

While King Athelstan absorbed the advice he'd asked for, his eyes remained focused on Edwin. Eadgifu was surprised by the lack of dismay on Athelstan's face. She'd always assumed that King Athelstan despised Edwin, but that didn't seem to be the case.

"Then that is what will be done," King Athelstan announced, already rolling the letter tightly in his hand. "Sister, I would ask you to speak to my sisters. Inform them of the proposal and ensure they're both amenable to the idea. As to who should be chosen, I would suggest Ælfgifu. She might be the youngest, but she is the closest in age to Otto. I imagine that Eadgyth would sooner have a husband more similar to her in age."

Eadgifu bowed her head to acknowledge the words, but behind her cold façade rage boiled. Her father had never had such compassion for his daughters' welfare.

With the decision made, King Athelstan bounded to his feet, Lord Osferth struggling to follow him just as quickly. As the king bowed to Eadgifu, she attempted to rise, as she should when the king stood, but he waved her back to her seat.

"Don't stand. We are family."

With that, King Athelstan strode to the doorway and into the bright daylight beyond which temporarily illuminated the hall as the door wardens flung open the doors.

All the same, Eadgifu tried to rise hastily. She didn't wish to be left alone with Edwin. Not now.

But a clammy hand on her left hand stalled her attempts.

"Come sister dearest. Sit with me. I would know why you're so keen to sell your sister's cheaply. Are you as tired of them as Athelstan?" While Edwin seemed to speak in jest, there was a hard edge to his voice that Eadgifu groaned to hear. Indeed, as she turned to face him, Edwin was already instructing a servant to refill his wine goblet.

"I'm not keen to see my sisters 'sold' off, as you so inelegantly state. If they are to have husbands, they must come from East or West Frankia. I would not have them married to a Norse bastard, or to one of the ealdormen of England."

"You would simply sooner have them gone so that you can play queen without them laughing at you."

Eadgifu barked a laugh in response. She couldn't help herself.

"You think I play at queen? I can assure you that my influence and actions are as nothing compared to when I was Queen of West Frankia in more than just name. You would do well to remember that when you make your jibes at my expense. At least I have earned the name of queen, you have barely even earned the name of lord, let alone king."

Fury turned Edwin's already puce face darker than the juiciest of plums. Eadgifu almost wished she'd not let her ill-humour condition her words.

"You there, fetch my sisters. I would speak to them." The words were shouted at the servant closest to the door, a long finger trembling as Edwin pointed.

Eadgifu held her poise despite her brother's despicable behaviour. She had no idea what her sisters would say but determined the discussion may as well include Edwin, as not.

Eadgifu caught the eye of one of the waiting servants, and when they bent before her, she asked for warmed wine to be placed on the table, along with two more wine goblets. She would show her brother had queens should truly conduct themselves.

As her sisters came within the king's hall, eyes full and unsure, she eyed them critically.

She and her sisters were all similar in appearance. In the wrong light, she often thought she glimpsed her mother and not her sisters at all. They all shared the same blue eyes and blond hair, neatly braided and tied back from their faces. But whereas Eadgifu believed she wore her position with grace and poise, Ælfgifu was far more exuberant with her choice of colours and gems. In contrast, Eadgyth was more assured in her selection of clothes.

Eadgyth often tried strange new ways of wearing her hair, and even now, a shimmer of rubies and emeralds glittered amongst it. Eadgifu was not sure the arrangement really added to the glamour of her already rich and luxurious blond hair.

At their looks, Eadgifu beckoned them forwards, to join her and Edwin. If she thought disappointment flickered on their faces that the brother who'd summoned them was not the king, she believed Edwin was oblivious. How would he even consider it, when the feeling was not one he shared?

"Brother," Eadgyth curtsied to Edwin, before taking the seat that Lord Osferth had only just vacated.

Ælfgifu followed suit, sitting opposite Edwin. Both of them glanced at Athelstan's empty chair, as though he sat there still.

"Sisters," Edwin was expansive in his greeting although Eadgifu was not alone in wincing at his loud voice. "It's good to see you. But now is not the time to pass the time of day with you, but rather to discuss Athelstan's letter from the King of East Frankia."

At the mention of the word king, both sisters appreciated precisely what they were about to be asked. Both sat straighter although Eadgifu was busy filling their goblets with wine.

Eadgifu would have preferred to be the one having the conversation with her sisters. Still, Edwin had spoken first, before she could even form a 'hello' and seemed oblivious that he monopolised the conversation.

"King Henry of East Frankia has asked for permission to send an embassy to England for the intention of finding his son and heir a fine wife."

Eadgyth immediately seemed to grasp that only one wife was needed, while there were two sisters. Ælfgifu simply looked stunned at the thought of a husband.

"I have, of course, spoken to the king, as your brother, and made it clear that I find the idea of sending you to some stranger's court abhorrent."

Eadgyth's eyes sought out my own, a question in them, perhaps wondering if Edwin spoke for them both. Eadgifu shook her head, just a little, and Eadgyth's eyes lit with understanding. Ælfgifu, however, looked rebelliously at her brother.

"Brother, you would think not to allow me to marry?" Ælfgifu's words were spoken in an exhalation of surprise. Even now, she had somehow managed to retain an almost childish naivety about how Athelstan's court operated, and her brother's place in it.

"Of course not, sister," Edwin slurred. "But it would be acceptable for you to marry much closer to home."

Ælfgifu's next words proved that she did have a modicum of political astuteness.

"But that would never work brother. It would unbalance King Athelstan's careful governance of England. All well and good if Athelstan chose to wed an English woman, but not for his sisters to do so. I should not like my children to be treated as poorly as Lady Ælfwynn was by our father."

Eadgifu started at the words, a splash of wine staining the wooden table. She had never been sure that Ælfgifu fully understood their father's actions when he'd secluded Ælfwynn in a nunnery. It seemed that she had. Perhaps better than even Edwin had.

"What?" the response flustered Edwin, while Ælfgifu sought out Eadgifu's agreement with her eyes. Eadgifu nodded confidently in reassurance.

"What does the king inform us of this?" Eadgyth asked, her question aimed at Eadgifu although her eyes raked her brother's red face.

"The king is keen to know that you're pleased with the idea and to have it known that of course, only one of you will be needed. He thinks it best if we know who would prefer the position."

Understanding flashed in Eadgyth's eyes.

"What do you know of this man?" Eadgyth asked as Eadgifu realised Edwin had failed to mention the son's name, only the father.

"Otto. A young man. He was born in 912. He's Henry's first legitimate heir, although he does have an older, and acknowledged son. The papacy declared the earlier union unlawful and the child illegitimate and so unable to rule after his father."

"And what is he like?" Already Eadgifu could sense that Ælfgifu was caught up in the thought of a young husband. Neither did she miss the grimace on Eadgyth's face at the realisation that Otto was nearly ten years younger than her. Eadgifu could already sense that Eadgyth was keen for Ælfgifu to put herself forward as the potential bride.

"Well," Ælfgifu muttered, flushed with excitement. "Surely it is Eadgyth who should be next to marry. After all, she's older than me, if not by much." Ælfgifu's voice had flooded with disappointment at the realisation, and yet Eadgifu admired her for considering her sister first.

"But, sister, you would be the same age, with the opportunity for a long and happy life together. I do believe any young man would be keen to wed you."

At Eadgyth's words, Ælfgifu's mouth opened into a wide 'O' of surprise. If possible, she flushed an even deeper shade of burgundy.

"Then it is arranged," Eadgyth said, already preparing to leave the king's hall. "Ælfgifu would welcome the idea of a husband, and will be the better suited."

Without pausing to hear more, Eadgyth strode from the hall, and Eadgifu couldn't help but think that her step was lighter than on arrival. Perhaps Eadgyth genuinely did wish her sister to marry Otto.

Ælfgifu looked to Eadgifu, her mouth still open, as Eadgifu leaned across to touch her hand in reassurance.

"There will be an embassy, at some point soon. We have time to arrange everything and for you to prepare. I'll teach you all that I knew before I left for West Frankia, and also many things that I wish I'd known."

Only now did Eadgifu's eyes glance to catch sight of her brother, as Ælfgifu's gaze kept wavering uncertainly toward him. Edwin's eyes were hard as iron, his disapproval etched into every line of his being.

"Come sister," Eadgifu distracted her. "We'll drink to your good fortune, and then we will ensure King Athelstan is informed of the decision made here."

A small giggle escaped Ælfgifu's mouth as Eadgifu pressed the warmed wine into her hand, and drank deeply.

The scent of the wine reminded Eadgifu of her marriage, and with it, myriad memories flooded her mind. Eadgifu pushed them all aside, determined not to sob in front of her delighted sister.

Eadgifu and Ælfgifu both ignored the sullen silence of Edwin. Eadgifu tried to feel some empathy for his situation, but it defied her. Her brother was a disappointment, and it seemed he knew it only too well.

THE FOLLOWING weeks were filled with activity that had not been encountered since Eadhild's marriage to Count Hugh.

Athelstan made no comment on the decision that Ælfgifu was the preferred bride. It seemed he was content provided his sisters were.

Eadgifu found Ælfgifu was often in her company as they busied themselves with ensuring Ælfgifu had all she needed. Every so often, Eadgifu was minded to caution Ælfgifu from getting too excited. No marriage had been formally agreed, and it was always possible that the embassy may not agree to King Athelstan's terms. Eadgifu was sure, from conversations she'd had with Lord Osferth, that King Athelstan would not sell his sister cheaply. The knowledge both reassured and worried Eadgifu in equal measure.

But when the embassy was continually delayed, even Ælfgifu became withdrawn, the delay proving interminable, until their bitch-mother stepped into the women's hall.

As always, Eadgifu couldn't help but admire her step-mother's poise and calmness. The relationship was not one of closeness. It wasn't with any of Edward's daughters, apart from Lady Ecgwynn.

Still, Eadgifu admired the bitch-mother for never stinting in her duties toward her husband's daughters, who mostly despised her.

As she'd been in the situation in West Frankia, Eadgifu knew how hard it was to continually feel such hatred.

"There is good news. The embassy from East Frankia has arrived. Even now they're guests of the king, and he's keen for you to join him at Abingdon."

Eadgifu watched with amusement as Ælfgifu's face flushed first with pleasure, and then with fear, her hands gripping the arms of her chair tightly.

"Then we must be ready to leave, as soon as possible," Ælfgifu stammered, looking at Eadgifu for confirmation.

"Yes, the king has asked you to leave as soon as possible but not to rush. The king is content to enjoy the negotiations with the ambassadors."

Ælfgifu nodded, while Eadgifu sought out Eadgyth in the women's hall. Her other sister had been kind in the last few weeks but also reserved. Eadgifu worried that she might well have come to rue the decision that Ælfgifu be offered as a prospective wife.

"Are we all to attend?" Eadgifu asked of her step-mother, unsure even of her own position.

"Yes, yes, the king is keen for his sisters and his foster-sons, and younger brothers to attend. Even Edwin is welcome. After all, you are all one family." Eadgifu's step-mother spoke brightly, and yet there was an edge to the words. Eadgifu was hardly surprised. While King Athelstan might hope his family was united, the truth was starkly different.

"We'll leave tomorrow, provided all is well." With the words spoken, Eadgifu's step-mother turned and left the women's hall. Eadgifu paused for only a moment and then began issuing stringent orders and instructions to the servants.

On her own marriage, Eadgifu had only had her father to assist her, and he had been little use. She was determined to ensure that Ælfgifu's marriage was far better arranged.

. . .

Two days later Eadgifu, flanked by her step-mother, and two younger sisters entered the hall of Abingdon Abbey, in which King Athelstan was already seated.

While the journey had been simple enough, the start had been fractious, with too many people following the conflicting orders of others. In the end, it had been Eadgifu's step-mother who'd managed to resolve everything and ensure the cavalcade left Winchester in a timely fashion.

Not that Eadgifu had thanked her, but had rather fumed that she didn't hold the required position to do so.

Abingdon Abbey itself was ancient, although the wooden hall was a recent build, and Eadgifu scented the smell of fresh-cut wood with pleasure.

Winchester Palace was a reasonably new build, no older than twenty years. Yet, it felt ancient compared to the new hall at Abingdon.

On arrival, Eadgifu's step-mother ordered everyone to dismount and only when she was happy that people looked their best, did she allow them to enter the hall.

If Eadgifu noticed a sheen of triumph on her step-mother's face, she resolved to ignore it. She was keen to see the ambassadors and determine what had already happened, and what the king thought of the men and women sent from East Frankia.

"Sisters, brothers," King Athelstan, his blond hair hanging too long, although his moustache and beard were neatly groomed, leapt to his feet on seeing his family and rushed to greet them all.

A soft kiss of welcome on Eadgifu's cheek surprised her, as did King Athelstan's equally warm greeting for Edwin. Eadgifu imagined this meant that her half-brother was pleased with the way events were unfolding.

"Now that you're here," King Athelstan waved expansively, "I'll arrange a grand feast, and the ambassadors will be invited as well. Then we can all get to know each other." King Athelstan spoke with a rare, wide grin, although his eyes were more for his foster-sons than his half-sisters. Eadgifu caught a look pass between her step-mother and half-brother that she was unsure how to interpret. No doubt it was merely a silent plea for her assistance with the planned feast.

While Eadgifu had no end of experience in such matters, it was always his step-mother that King Athelstan relied on in such cases. To begin with, the oversight had burned, but now Eadgifu ignored it. Rather her step-mother shoulder the onerous task, than herself.

Edwin grunted a suitable reply, and quickly seated himself and called for wine and food. Eadgifu hesitated to do the same, and indeed, Ælfgifu hovered at her side, just as unsure.

"Come, come, wine and cheese. You must be hungry from your journey. When you're refreshed, I'll speak to you about what you can expect."

With those words, King Athelstan bounded for the door, leaving them seemingly alone. Yet, they were not left but a moment before Lord Osferth appeared. From his slow approach, Eadgifu surmised that Lord Osferth had been attempting to greet them all since their arrival. That his actions seemed to slow every time she saw him unexpectedly saddened her. Eadgifu would not enjoy it when there was no longer anyone who resembled her father so closely at court. It would be like losing her father all over again.

"Welcome, My Ladies, My Lords," for all that Lord Osferth bowed as smartly as ever, as Eadgifu and her sisters' curtsied, alongside her step-mother, Edwin declined to rise from his seat.

"The king is about his business, but I'll answer all your questions and ensure you have all you need."

True to his word, Lord Osferth ensured Eadgifu had a room to share with her sisters and bowed before hurrying away, leaving them with a handful of their servants.

Just for a moment, no one moved, just pleased the journey was at an end, and then Eadgifu took command.

"We will need our clothes airing, and water to bathe in, please."

She pulled her riding gloves from her hands and wrinkled her nose.

"I stink," Eadgifu complained, while Ælfgifu dropped to a chair, and sighed extravagantly. Eadgyth surprised Eadgifu by laughing.

"Well, it seems the king is finally pleased to see us all. I never thought that would happen."

Eadgifu found her mouth curving in reply.

"I believe you're correct," Eadgifu grinned. "Let's see if we can stay in his good graces."

While they were summoned to eat with the king that evening, it was not an elaborate affair. The king called for his foster-sons to sit with him, while Eadgifu and her sisters sat further away.

Eadgifu scanned the hall. She was sure that strangers attended upon the king, but she'd spent too little time in the king's hall at Winchester to know for sure, and settled to watch, aware she was under just as much scrutiny.

"Are the ambassadors here?" It was Ælfgifu who asked the question, as she fidgeted in her seat. None of the sisters wore their most exquisite dresses or jewels, thinking it a muted, family event. Eadgifu could tell that Ælfgifu was ruing the decision, although Eadgyth seemed not to mind as she ate heartily and drank sparingly from her glass goblet.

"I'm sure the king would have informed us if we were under observation. Now eat, and stop worrying. We'll formally meet the men and women tomorrow."

Yet while Ælfgifu settled, Eadgifu grew increasingly uneasy and knew she was right to be when Athelstan's priest, Cenwald sought her out just before she left the hall.

"My Lady Eadgifu," she was never sure what to think of Cenwald. He was one of Athelstan's companions, never far from his side, and yet she also knew him to be ambitious.

"My Lord, Cenwald," Eadgifu inclined her head. He was dressed in a priest's garb, and yet she caught a glimpse of an expensive golden cross hidden beneath his robes.

"The king has asked me to assure you that all is proceeding well. And, he's given me the honour of accompanying your sister to Saxony, and with it, the position of bishop of Worcester."

Eadgifu swallowed heavily. She remembered the churchmen who'd travelled with her to West Frankia. They'd all been ambitious men, expendable at the time, but assured of her father's favour if they served him well while away from England. It was just another reminder of how politically motivated the entire endeavour was.

"King Athelstan has also given me permission to seek out news of King Charles while I'm away. It's to be hoped that those with loose lips will speak more openly than your dear sister can do."

Eadgifu startled at the mention of her husband, the words dragging her from trying to absorb all that Cenwald was telling her.

As so often was the case with the men of the church, Cenwald was a tall and sparse man, his hair a mess where it grew beyond his tonsure. Cenwald was also earnest and keen. The combination was perhaps not the best.

"Then I'm pleased to hear as much. I know my brother wouldn't lightly lose one of his most dedicated churchmen on a journey to Saxony."

"My thanks, My Lady Eadgifu. The ambassadors, there are six of them, led by a Duke Gilbert of Lotharingia, are an intelligent collection of men and women. They're much admired by King Henry, and Duke Gilbert is his son by marriage. There is a keenness to ensure the union is agreed as smoothly as possible."

"Although, well, before I burden you with my worries, we'll simply see what tomorrow brings. Until then." With such ambiguous words, Cenwald bowed his way out of Eadgifu's presence, but she watched him pensively. Surely there was not a problem already? She resolved to speak to the king as soon as she could.

Yet Eadgifu had no opportunity that evening, the king retiring early so that she was forced to ask her servant to wake her at daybreak. She needed to speak with her half-brother before the business of the day began.

Only when she was dressed and leaving her chamber the following morning, her two sisters still snoring softly, did her servant rush to her.

"The king is making ready to ride on a hunt. He's in the stables." With a cry of frustration, Eadgifu bunched her skirts together.

"Take me to him, and rush." It was early enough, or so she hoped, that no one would see the Queen of West Frankia running through the abbey buildings and wonder what was on fire.

Only as the sound of men calling one to another reached her ears, did Eadgifu pause, and collect herself. The servant turned to gaze at her, a critical look on her face.

"You should straighten your hair," the servant offered, before leading the way into the stables, as Eadgifu patted her hair into some semblance of normality.

Eadgifu carefully wound her way through the mass of horses, and men, all talking far too loudly, until she caught sight of King Athelstan's horse, and then a fair head bending low beside the animal.

"My Lord King," despite her slower steps, Eadgifu puffed as she spoke, and the king's head shot up, his surprise evident to see in his wrinkled forehead.

"Sister dearest, do you wish to hunt?" his voice was perplexed, and she shook her head angrily.

"No, I do not, but I must speak to you, urgently."

With only a soft sigh, the king beckoned her closer, his gaze sweeping the immediate area to make sure they wouldn't be overheard.

"Did Bishop Cenwald speak to you last night? I told him to wait until today or tomorrow, in the hope the matter would resolve itself."

Eadgifu floundered. How to answer? Yes, Bishop Cenwald had spoken to her, but only in tantalising snippets. She paused and luckily, the king spoke into the silence.

"The possibility of the alliance is too significant to dismiss the request although I think it unacceptable. In good conscience, I don't believe I should send away both of my sisters for the son to choose from, but they seem committed to the idea."

Eadgifu's could feel her face whiten as the king spoke. If it was true, then it seemed that Ælfgifu might not have the husband she hoped to gain, and equally, that Eadgyth might be chosen, even though she didn't want to be. And how would it be explained to them both? She could not believe that the king even thought it an acceptable question for the East Frankish ambassadors to have made.

"I'll not allow both of my sisters to be sent to Saxony as though they're cattle to barter over. You must put a stop to the ridiculous idea." The rage in her voice startled the king so much that he stopped what he was doing and gazed at Eadgifu in shock.

"If the decision is made, to send both of my sisters," King Athelstan spoke slowly. "It would not be your place to tell me no. I am the king."

"And I am a queen, and more, I've taken responsibility for my sisters' future. King Henry seeks to show that England is so desperate for a union, her king will risk two women, and not just one, at a stranger's court. It's reprehensible."

"Now sister dearest," King Athelstan's face had lost its exuberance in the wake of her fury. "Now is not the time for harsh words. As I said, I'm sure that once they see Lady Ælfgifu, they'll know that she's the correct wife for Lord Otto. They're the same age, and while I know little about such matters, I believe it will mean she can have children for longer than Eadgyth. I'd ask you not to speak of the matter to either of them. At least not yet."

"I can't keep such information to myself. My sisters must be made aware that all is not as clear as we were led to believe."

"As your king, I command you to silence." Eadgifu shivered at the vehemence in her half-brother's words.

"You're not just a king, you're a brother as well. You must protect your sisters." Eadgifu's voice was shrill as she spoke as loudly as she dared, hoping no one eavesdropped on her clash with the king.

"I'm fully aware of my duties and responsibilities to every member of my damn family, Queen Eadgifu." The formality in the king's voice surprised Eadgifu, the use of her title as a sign he was masking his true feelings.

"I'll do what must be done, and so, I hope, will you." With that, the king mounted his horse and rode through the stables. Into the sudden silence, Eadgifu panted.

The very idea her half-brother had just spoken about outraged her. It threatened to undo her, there and then. Somehow, Eadgifu had allowed herself to believe that King Athelstan would ensure her sisters' futures. It seemed she'd been very wrong to think so. As the sound of hooves over the hard road faded, she stumbled from the stables, determined to seek out her sisters, and leave Abingdon all together.

Whatever the king thought he was about to accomplish, Eadgifu was determined to thwart it.

Hastily, she strode back toward her chamber, kicking hay and straw from her boots as she went, but when Eadgifu arrived, the room was empty.

With a sigh of annoyance, Eadgifu made her way to the main hall, relieved to find her sisters sitting and eating, the rest of the hall relatively deserted. She didn't wish their conversation to be seen by too many people.

"Sister, where have you been?" Eadgyth spoke first, the surprise at seeing Eadgifu easy to hear in her voice.

"I've been speaking to the king."

"Oh, about the feast and meeting the ambassadors?" Ælfgifu asked, her cheeks flushing at the thought.

"Somewhat yes, but I must speak with you both, and neither of you is to allow others to know your true thoughts. Not everything is as we believed it."

"How so?" Eadgyth asked, while Eadgifu settled on a chair close to her sisters, and moved closer to them. She wanted this to be a private discussion.

"You must both promise me to stay calm, allow no one to know what we speak about, or its effect on you."

"I promise," Eadgyth immediately announced, her tone making it clear she wasn't sure that her sister had anything to say that might unduly worry her.

Ælfgifu paused before adding her own promise. Eadgifu had the overwhelming desire to reach out and clasp her younger sister's hand. But she didn't. Instead, she fixed Ælfgifu with a cautionary stare.

"Do not react, not at all."

Eadgyth sighed heavily, but Eadgifu ignored her. No doubt she thought the matter was of little concern.

"The ambassadors are here to arrange a marriage, but there'll be no decision on who Lord Otto weds until he has met both of you, in Saxony."

Eadgifu looked at Ælfgifu as she spoke, unsurprised to find heavy tears settling in her eyes, but it was the response of Eadgyth that surprised her most. Immediately Eadgyth stiffened, her face turning as white as Eadgifu's own at the news.

"I'm not a cow to be haggled over," Eadgyth hissed, while Eadgifu nodded.

"I'm aware of that. I'm fuming. I think we should leave Abingdon and return to Winchester. King Henry can look for a bride elsewhere."

"But, but," it was Ælfgifu who spoke the words. "Surely it would not be so bad?"

"Really," Eadgyth hissed, her lips tight with disgust. "You'd sooner be paraded before some stuck-up prince in the hopes that he might choose you. Have you no self-respect?"

Eadgifu expected Ælfgifu to wilt under such an onslaught, surprised when she didn't.

"I'd sooner have the opportunity of a husband and a kingdom in the future, than none at all. It's not as though there've been other suit-ors. East Frankia is large. Whichever of us doesn't marry Otto might have the chance to meet another husband. Surely that will be possible?"

The pleading in Ælfgifu's voice almost forced Eadgifu to capitu-late. But she didn't.

"I'm the wife of a king, our half-brother is the king. We can't parade my two unmarried sisters before a party who might, or might not decide to take one of you as a wife."

"Well," Ælfgifu snapped, leaning back, her arms folded over her heaving chest. "I'm happy to do whatever the king asks me to do. I'd sooner run the risk of a powerful husband than remain here as an unwanted sister." With her statement made, Ælfgifu leapt to her feet, marching from the abbey hall. Eadgifu watched her younger sister go with her mouth open in shock.

"Well, I didn't expect that sort of response. Not at all." Eadgifu turned to meet the flashing eyes of Eadgyth, her rage seeming to pour from her, hotter than a blacksmith's forge.

"Stupid girl," Eadgyth managed to state, her lips tight. Her shoulders were so rigid beneath her embroidered dress and elaborate dress brooches that Eadgifu worried that she might simply snap in two.

"When did you learn of this?" Eadgyth demanded to know when they'd both lapsed into an uncomfortable silence for a few moments.

"Just. The king asked me not to tell you. He hopes that the ambassadors will meet Ælfgifu and determine she's the right choice."

"Always so good at reading his enemies and allies, but terrible at seeing how his family will react. Our half-brother is not as wise as some might have us believe."

"Shall we return to Winchester? I'm prepared for the king's wrath."

Eadgyth sighed heavily, her young face lined with worry.

"No, I need to think about this. You're right to be furious, but Ælfgifu might also be right to say at least travelling to East Frankia will give us both the chance of finding a good husband. Certainly, there are none to be found in England."

Eadgyth stood then, inclined her head toward Eadgyth and left the hall, with far less flounce than Ælfgifu. Eadgifu watched her walk away, uneasily.

Eadgifu was prepared to do anything to protect her sisters but had no idea if she was ready to let them leave England without the firm promise of a husband.

Eadgifu called for her servant to bring her embroidery, and by the light of the hearth and the candles, she took up the work she so despised. Louis had outgrown his ceremonial tunic, and she knew it was her place as his mother to ensure he was clothed adequately for the impending feast.

As she stitched, the thread flashing in the glint of the candles, Eadgifu watched her step-mother enter the hall, and begin giving instructions to Athelstan's servants. Trying not to ruin the attempts at thinking clearly about this new conundrum, Eadgifu turned back to her sewing. She ignored the bustle around her until she heard the rustle of fabric and looked up to meet her step-mother's eyes.

Eadgifu could never forgive her father for marrying someone younger than his daughter. But, as Charles' wife, she'd too often been on the receiving end of harsh treatment from his daughters. She tried to remember that when faced with her step-mother. It was never easy.

"There's a great deal to organise," her step-mother offered, sipping delicately of her warm wine, handed to her by a hovering servant. "Such a lot to deal with, and all to ensure this meeting runs smoothly. I shall miss young Ælfgifu, I can't deny that she and my sons are friends."

Eadgifu startled at the words. But of course, why would King Athelstan tell her step-mother of the problems when it seemed he'd deemed the news too incendiary to even tell her? The only person he'd trusted seemed to be Bishop Cenwald. That didn't surprise Eadgifu.

"You're doing a magnificent job," Eadgifu tried to comfort, her mind firmly focused on the conundrum of her sisters.

"I didn't seek praise, but you have my thanks all the same. I saw Eadgyth earlier. She seemed unhappy."

Eadgifu laid down her sewing and looked to her step-mother, determining just what she wanted to say to the woman who'd replaced her mother in Edward's affections. They were not allies, but her step-mother had proved her worth in the past, as little as she liked to admit it.

"She's unhappy, and Ælfgifu is angry with me because I want to return to Winchester and forget that King Henry ever approached the king."

A spark of indignation flashed in her step-mother's eyes, and Eadgifu wished she'd explained better.

"No, not through spite, but King Henry has told his advisors that Lord Otto will need to choose the best out of Eadgyth and Ælfgifu, in person. They must both travel to Saxony, but only one of them will find a husband."

Eadgifu watched her step-mother's rapidly changing expression with a modicum of enjoyment. It was good to know that her anger was justified.

"The king would never do such a thing? Surely?"

"I believe he will. King Athelstan hopes that the ambassadors will see Ælfgifu and change their mind, but I'm not convinced. I wished to leave, but Ælfgifu is determined to stay, and I've no idea how Eadgyth truly feels. She's considering it now."

Eadgifu lifted her hands and dropped them in dejection.

"We're not here for him to barter with. We are his sisters, and we deserve the respect of our half-brother both because we are family and because he's our king."

"I imagine Edwin has taken the news poorly."

Eadgifu felt a judder of unease at the statement.

"I've not yet spoken to him about it. I truly don't wish to be the one to do so."

"I'm not surprised. It'll be another complaint against the king, and already Edwin stacks them up as though hoping they'll eventually topple over, burying the king, but they will not. King Athelstan is the king that England needs. Unfortunately, Edwin would simply return England to the state it rested in under King Edward."

Eadgifu felt hot rage at the criticism of her father, but then she subsided. It was nothing that Eadgifu hadn't already come to realise for herself.

"You greatly respect my half-brother?" Eadgifu probed. Of them all, she would have thought that her step-mother would have resented King Athelstan the most.

"The king and I reached an accord early on. It's not a secret to anyone. Ælfweard would have forced me to remarry, taken my sons from me. King Athelstan did neither of those things."

Eadgifu nodded. It was true. It was also true that he'd never forced her to remarry or taken Louis' upbringing from her. Occasionally he did ask her permission only after arrangements had been put in place.

"The marriages that have already been contracted by you and your sisters have done much for England. They reinforce the respect the House of Wessex is held in. Yes, you are devoid of a husband, and father for your son. And yes, Countess Eadhild has done little to make that situation better, and yes, Lady Ecgwynn divorced her husband.

But Ecgwynn allowed King Athelstan to claim York. Now, the exalted marriages you and Eadhild made have other men keen to ally themselves with the House of Wessex as well."

"You might think yourself in an unhappy situation, cast aside as you are, but if you'd not birthed a son for King Charles, then I doubt there would have been much interest from other royal and noble families. Certainly, I believe that King Sihtric consented to the marriage because of the ties it brought him with the families of West Frankia. It legitimised his dynasty, just as Charles did by marrying his daughter to Count Rollo of Normandy."

"So, you say it's my fault for being fertile that my sisters are so keenly fought over."

"It's not your fault," her step-mother commented, her lips in a flat line as she spoke, searching for the correct words.

Her step-mother started again.

"King Athelstan has many sisters, and while three of them are in royal nunneries, that still leaves many more to find good husbands for, and they should all have expectations of a kingdom to rule."

"After all, you are the daughters of a king and the granddaughters of King Alfred. The House of Wessex is the oldest dynasty in all of our kingdoms, England, West Frankia and East Frankia."

"It just so happens that all of these potentials have come together at the same time. You and your sisters have great advantages, and King Athelstan can't squander them. Neither should he give in to every noble family who looks for an alliance with his own."

Eadgifu nodded her head, seeing the wisdom in her step-mother's words.

"If my father had only taken one wife, he would have had but one daughter and a son to marry."

"Yes, he would, and then the House of Wessex would not be where it is now. Yes, Athelstan would have become king as a matter of course. Still, I don't believe that Lady Ecgwynn would have been wasted on a Viking Raider, and then allowed to retire to a nunnery, even if it was all her own choice."

"So," Eadgifu smiled sadly. "We're in this predicament because my mother was too fertile, and my father too keen to claim his marriage rights."

"You could say that," her step-mother confirmed, a shrug to one of her shoulders.

"So all this is because of sex?" Eadgifu taunted, keen to see how her step-mother would respond.

Her step-mother chuckled softly. "Yes, it is. Let us be grateful, as we can be, that we need never endure that again," her step-mother spoke with a sparkle to her eye, and Eadgifu found laughter gurgling from her mouth. She'd never allowed any sentiment or understanding to warm the strained relationship with her step-mother. Perhaps she should have done.

"Speak with the king, your brother. Inform him that he can't damage Louis' potential claim to West Frankia in marrying your sisters. King Athelstan loves your son, as he does my own. He'll listen to that caution, as he might not to anything else."

Eadgifu nodded, surprised to discover the advice was sound.

"Perhaps, but what can he do? Can he demand Lord Otto comes to England?"

"I doubt that, but he can include the provision that both of your sisters must be royally married, irrelevant of which one Otto choices. We can't have either Eadgyth or Ælfgifu returning to England unmarried, cast aside, and with no prospects. It will be the same as locking them in a nunnery."

Her step-mother sighed, her expression bleak.

"And soon, we must both begin this game for our own sons, for they'll have to marry, and we must find the right women for them, even as young as they are." The thought shocked Eadgifu, and she startled. Louis was still a child, how could her step-mother think of his marriage? But if Louis were to be a king, he'd need a dynasty to follow on in his footsteps.

"It never stops, does it?" Eadgifu complained, but she felt better for venting her frustration and hoped that she'd be able to help her sisters now with a cooler head. She'd not thought that her step-mother would be able to provide an insight into the character of her own half-brother. But then, as her step-mother had said, she and King Athelstan had long ago reached an agreement when he became king.

Not for the first time, Eadgifu wished she'd done the same, rather than supporting Edwin.

That path had always been doomed to failure. If only she'd known.

EADGIFU ENSURED it was made known that she wished to speak to the king as soon as possible. She was surprised when the summons came almost immediately upon his return from the hunt.

"My Lady, Queen Eadgifu." The formal tone of King Athelstan's greeting alerted her to the fact that he was prepared to speak with her, but only in the most official of ways.

Eadgifu was content with such an agreement. It would allow her to speak without the heat of her fury.

"My Lord King," she curtsied before him and stayed standing as he surveyed her.

"You may speak openly to me," the king eventually conceded, his bright eyes seeming to approve of what he saw.

"I'm pleased that our relationship allows as such," Eadgifu stated, thinking quickly of what she wanted to say.

"This arrangement, with the embassy from Saxony, it concerns me, as you know. I don't believe the House of Wessex should so easily succumb to what amounts to a demand for our sisters to be presented before their king and his son so that he can decide which to marry."

King Athelstan's gaze was steady, no trace of annoyance showing, and yet his constant movement had stilled.

"I've been reminded today that I am, as you say, Queen of West Frankia, anointed as such and raised above others by that holy touch. My son should, and will, one day be king of West Frankia. Countess Eadhild is married to one of the great noblemen in West Frankia, even if he is an enemy of my son." Eadgifu couldn't stop the comment from pouring from her voice, although she noticed that King Athelstan did have the decency to flinch slightly at the reminder.

"It would be unbecoming for the King of England's sisters, and the

Prince of West Frankia to have his aunts paraded before the East Frankish court as though trophies to be haggled over."

"The authority of the House of Wessex must be maintained, the honour that our house would bestow upon the East Frankish king by consenting to the match must be appreciated. If both of my sisters are to travel to East Frankia, it must be done with the absolute understanding that a union as good as, if not better than this first proposal, must be arranged for my other sister."

"I'll not have one of them returned here as though surplus to requirements. As the head of our family, and King of England, our own ambassadors, must be sent to East Frankia. They must have your full support to arrange a marriage of suitable stature, and with a suitable dowry for both."

"If this is not done, the value of our family will fall in the eyes of all our neighbours. We might well open England up to attack from a resurgent Viking force as well as undervaluing my son, the future King of West Frankia."

Respect flickered in the king's eyes as Eadgifu spoke, and yet she felt it best not to labour the points she was making. King Athelstan was a man of action, of deep thought and understanding. She was reminding him of that, on this one occasion that he seemed to have overlooked what was self-evident to her.

"But no other kingdom has sent a delegation," the king commented.

"No, they haven't, but I could name many territories where I suspect a marriage proposal could come from. I'm also sure that if King Henry were tasked with such, he'd endeavour to find a suitable bride for my sister. After all, he would not want the stock of our family to fall either. Even if he's not quite realised that yet."

A wry smirk split the king's face, as he considered Eadgifu's arguments.

"I'd thank you for such bold advice, and for not being afraid to question my decisions. When I meet with the ambassadors, I'll ensure that this is all understood. There will be provisions made for whichever of our dear sisters is not married to Lord Otto. But, will Eadgyth consent, with that provision?"

"I'm sure she would rather be wed than unwed," Eadgifu confirmed. "Merely the thought of the closeness in age between Ælfgifu and Lord Otto made Eadgyth suggest her sister."

The king nodded in understanding.

"Then assure both Eadgyth and Ælfgifu of this new development, and I'll begin fresh negotiations with the ambassadors. You're right to remind me that my sisters are of great value not just to England, but to their family as well."

Eadgyth nodded, just once, pleased to know that she'd succeeded in this, if in nothing else in the five years since she'd fled to Wessex.

"As to young Louis. I'd hope that this might change things for him. I'm always hopeful that his claim will be recognised, and it will be a benefit to him to have the future King of East Frankia as his uncle."

"It will, yes. Louis is rich in uncles. All he needs now is a kingdom."

Eadgifu surprised herself with the words, and yet admiration flashed in the king's eyes, as Eadgifu turned to leave. Only then the king spoke once more.

"Our step-mother is a worthy woman. If you choose to absorb what she has learnt as Queen Dowager of England, I'm sure it will assist you once you return to West Frankia." Eadgifu stilled, for a moment furious that her step-mother had spoken to the king before she did.

"Our step-mother didn't tell me anything," the king hastened to add. "But I recognise the logic of the argument, and the desire to speak out. As I said, our step-mother is a woman who understands the worth of her position, and that of her sons. I can only recommend her to you."

Eadgifu pursed her lips, but then dipped into a curtsey. She didn't wish to discuss her step-mother with the king. But neither could she deny his entreaty. Certainly, Eadgifu had found wisdom in her step-mother's words, and it appeared, that the king was not above heeding the advice given by her step-mother.

That was worth remembering.

AD929

Eadgifu sought out Bishop Cenwald in the king's hall. He was, as expected, surrounded by his clerics and seemed focused on some task at hand. Eadgifu almost reconsidered and left him to whatever task the king had set him, but shook her head and dismissed her worry.

"My Lady, Queen Eadgifu," Bishop Cenwald saved her from having to gain his attention, by noticing her himself.

"Bishop Cenwald, I would speak with you. If you have the time." While she couched it as a question, both knew he would not put her off.

Hastening to her side, Eadgifu tried to decide how to phrase her question. She had an assurance from King Athelstan, but she wanted more.

"I am curious about the men who lead the embassy from East Frankia." The question seemed to come as no surprise to Bishop Cenwald, and Eadgifu considered that the king had already warned his bishop of the probable request.

"My Lady, I would tell you all I know. Shall we sit or walk?"

Eadgifu admired the man's smooth acceptance of the change to his plans.

"We should sit, and perhaps drink. I imagine there's much I should know."

Bishop Cenwald nodded, his eyes bowed. Eadgifu realised his fingers were splattered with ink, and with long since healed wounds from where he, perhaps as a younger man, had splashed the ink over himself.

"It is both a curse and a blessing," Eadgifu offered, her eyes on his hands, and Bishop Cenwald allowed a wry smile to touch his lips.

"The trials of thinking you know best when a child."

With that, they sat together, close to the hearth. The heat was welcome, as the morning was still chilly.

"The embassy is led by a man called Duke Gilbert." Bishop Cenwald seemed keen to speak. Eadgifu resolved to listen and learn, while she indicated to her servant that food and drink were required. She'd not yet eaten, and her stomach felt empty and hollow.

"Duke Gilbert ruled Lotharingia. I believe you know of the territory." Eadgifu startled at the mention of the territory that had caused so much disharmony between East and West Frankia. However, it was King Rodolphus who'd finally lost his hold on the land, not King Charles, and for that, she was pleased.

"I know of the man," she agreed, unsure why Duke Gilbert should lead the embassy.

As though sensing her confusion, Bishop Cenwald explained.

"He married one of King Henry's daughter's last year. Duchess Gerberga. King Henry and Duke Gilbert are firm allies."

This made sense to Eadgifu.

"How many daughters does King Henry have?" she asked, although she'd determine not to interrupt the bishop.

"Just the two. Gerberga and Hadwig. Hadwig is younger."

"And sons. How many sons does King Henry have?"

"Four, I believe. Although the oldest son is illegitimate."

"Yes, I knew of that. But it is the oldest legitimate son who is to be married?"

"Yes, Lord Otto. I don't believe the other sons are ready to marry yet. And the youngest of them all is destined for the church anyway."

Eadgifu absorbed the information. She needed to know all she could.

"So none of the other children are married, other than Gerberga?"

"I believe not. I am unsure about the illegitimate son though. Of course, he has no claim to his father's kingdom."

"So Duke Gilbert is held in high esteem by King Henry?"

"He must be, My Lady."

"Or is he simply being kept on a tight leash. I believe he is not the most loyal of men." Here Bishop Cenwald looked shocked, his mouth dropping open just a little. Eadgifu would have smiled at his stance, but she was too busy trying to form an opinion of Duke Gilbert, and what he would, and wouldn't be able to promise on behalf of his father by marriage.

"Duke Gilbert was loyal to my husband, only then he invited King Henry to occupy Lotharingia. Then he changed his mind and offered his fealty to King Rodolphus. I am aware that a more cordial relationship with King Henry has since been reasserted."

Bishop Cenwald held his tongue, clearly unsure how to respond to Eadgifu's spoken thoughts.

Silence fell between them, and the bishop used the opportunity to eat the bread and cheese brought for them. Eadgifu nibbled absent-mindedly on a piece of hard cheese.

King Henry wanted an alliance with England. While it would appear that sending his son by marriage as his representative was an honour, Eadgifu knew too well the way the minds of the kings in East and West Frankia worked to think that was all it was.

Had King Henry sent Duke Gilbert so that he could take advantage of his absence? It was an intriguing thought.

"The Duke is already a father. He and his wife have a son. King Henry is pleased."

"I'm sure he is."

"Duke Gilbert is keen to represent his father by marriage's family, but he is also anxious to be gone from England as soon as possible. King Henry rides to war, against the Slavs. The Duke would rather be supporting his king."

Eadgifu nodded, chewing at the same time. Slowly, she was starting to understand the plans of King Henry.

Now that Duke Gilbert had a son and an heir, King Henry really had no use for him. Not if he was about to make a name for himself against an old enemy. Once that was done, would King Henry move to oust his son by marriage. Or, she considered, was she trying to make too much from a simple marriage proposal, and an alliance between two kingdoms.

Wives were always needed for sons who would one day be kings, and wives, as Eadgifu knew, were best when found from outside the kingdom in question.

"Duke Gilbert speaks with the full support of King Henry."

"I am sure he does," Eadgifu offered. "And do you believe that King Henry will honour any concessions that Duke Gilbert makes to bring about this union?"

Bishop Cenwald turned away, looking into the heart of the fire, and his silence told Eadgifu that she was correct to ask such a question. She settled to wait for an answer. Time was not pressing, not now that King Athelstan had listened to her and agreed that Eadgyth and Ælfgifu were too valuable to throw at the feet of the East Frankish.

"I believe that Duke Gilbert is a man not without influence. The union with Duchess Gerberga might have been enacted to ensure Lotharingia stays loyal to King Henry, for now. For the future, King Henry's grandson will rule there, but Duke Gilbert is no fool. I do not believe that he would make any concessions he couldn't guarantee."

Eadgifu absorbed the opinion. Really, she would have liked to ask more people, but it was Bishop Cenwald who'd spoken with Duke Gilbert.

"Then I will respect your judgement, and endeavour to speak with Duke Gilbert myself," Eadgifu confirmed. She was not going to mention the need for two marriages to Bishop Cenwald. Not yet. King Athelstan might well have already informed of such, but Eadgifu was determined to speak with Duke Gilbert herself. She would have the opportunity at the feast, being arranged for that evening.

. . .

EADGIFU DRESSED CAREFULLY, as did her two sisters. While they'd not spoken again of Eadgifu's desire to leave Abingdon and refuse all marriages for her sisters, there was an unspoken agreement between them all that it might still prove to be the only option.

Much depended on the evening, and Ælfgifu was all a flutter, her face bright with excitement. In contrast, Eadgyth was more sedate.

Eadgifu allowed Eadgyth to arrange her hair for her. Ælfgifu looked through Eadgifu's jewels, and found some she liked, a precious ruby to adorn her neck, and matching hair clips. Ælfgifu was a pretty young woman. The jewellery enhanced her youth, whereas Eadgyth's more sedate clothing accentuated her maturity.

Both of her sisters looked delightful, and even Louis seemed stunned when he came to greet them and escort them to the feast, in his guise as Lord Louis. Young he might be, but King Athelstan was ensuring his courtly education was not overlooked.

"My Ladies, My Lady Mother," Louis looked smart in his court tunic, and for once, he seemed devoid of all smatterings of mud. Eadgifu thought she must remember to thank Matilde for her attention to Louis.

As they walked through the gathering dusk to the king's hall, Eadgifu was aware of others streaming to the feast, all wearing their most elegant clothes. Inside the building, Eadgifu could immediately see that her step-mother had transformed the hall into a meeting place worthy of kings and dukes.

Grudgingly, Eadgifu accepted that the flowers and greenery used to decorate each of the four long tables was just enough not to overawe the guests and take up all the room.

Gold and silver platters were loaded with white bread, and the hearth burned merrily at the centre of it all, the smell of fresh herbs flung onto the flames, warming the room more than the heat.

Hastily, Louis escorted his mother and aunts to the table on the dais and bowed smartly as he helped them all find their seats, to the left of where King Athelstan would sit.

Louis then scrambled away, finding seats with his young uncles, and Eadgifu tried not to wince at the loud argument that immediately ensued. As always, Lord Osferth was on hand to solve the problem of the squabbling nephew and uncles. Eadgifu's eyes strayed to where the king was making his way into the hall, escorting a man who Eadgifu knew must be Duke Gilbert.

The Duke was older than Eadgifu had imagined. His hair was starting to turn to grey, and Eadgifu wondered why it had taken him so long to marry.

Perhaps his marriage to Duchess Gerberga was not his first?

Duke Gilbert wore clothes similar in style to King Athelstan. She didn't miss the flicker of gold and silver on his wrists, fingers and around his neck, or on the ceremonial seax he wore on a weapons belt.

The man gleamed with his wealth, and in comparison, King Athelstan suffered, other than in his physical attributes. King Athelstan walked like the assured warrior-king he had always been. Duke Gilbert distinctly lacked in comparison, and no amount of gold and silver could make up for it.

While Duke Gilbert seemed consumed with the conversation he was having with King Athelstan, she watched his flickering eyes as he evidently sought out the king's sisters amongst the mass. She knew the exact moment that Duke Gilbert's eyes settled on Ælfgifu and then on Eadgyth. There was no hesitation in his eyes, and a faint nod of his head showed his appreciation.

Eadgifu was far from surprised.

In their own way, both of her sisters were beautiful and vibrant. They would make any man a good wife. But of course, it was about finding the right man.

Everyone settled to their feast, eating, drinking, toasting, and listening to the skald. He regaled the guests with tales of ancient Britain, the story of the Gododdin, raising cheers from the warrior men King Athelstan surrounded himself with. Yet Eadgifu knew that the business of the evening would be conducted when everyone had drunk and eaten their fill.

She resolved to drink little, but eating well, while Ælfgifu spoke excitedly to Eadgyth, pointing out and discussing the other members of the embassy.

Bishop Cenwald to the far side of King Athelstan spoke with two bishops sent by King Henry, whereas one of the tables was seated with King Henry's other followers. There were young men, and women, no doubt the sons and daughters of his most loyal supporters, and also monks and scribes. They'd all been sent to do the business of recording all they found out about the King of England, and his sisters.

Eadgifu recognised some of the people from the night before. Her sisters had been under scrutiny for longer than they'd been led to believe.

Only when the wine and ale flowed more freely, the food cleared away, did King Athelstan stand and lead Duke Gilbert over to Eadgifu and her sisters.

Eadgifu quickly realised that Duke Gilbert had drunk as sparingly as she had. His stance was steady and his breath, when he bowed over her hand, was far from heady.

She found she approved of the man, even before he opened his mouth.

"Lord Gilbert, these are my sisters, Queen Eadgifu, Lady Eadgyth and Lady Ælfgifu." Duke Gilbert met the gaze of Eadgifu and her sisters in turn. King Athelstan spoke with warmth in his voice, and it surprised Eadgifu until the king looked directly at her.

No doubt this was a response to her earlier criticisms.

"My Ladies, I am honoured to meet you all," Duke Gilbert spoke their language but with a hard accent that reminded Eadgifu strongly of West Frankia.

"And we would welcome you to the English court," it was Eadgyth who spoke, which surprised Eadgifu. She had thought her sister might not wish to make herself known.

"England is a wonderful country, filled with fine roads, and fields of crops, and even more magnificent buildings and churches." Eadgifu held her tongue. She knew that Lotharingia was festooned with ancient buildings, far more magnificent than anything on offer in England, apart from at Canterbury and Winchester. Still, as the king seemed so pleased with the Duke's words, Eadgifu forbore to cause embarrassment.

King Athelstan moved to escort Duke Gilbert away, but Eadgifu stalled his request.

"Come, Duke Gilbert, come and sit with my sisters and I. Tell us of East Frankia." The request was a reasonable one, and King Athelstan seemed to find no harm in it, leaving the Duke in the hands of his sisters.

While Eadgyth and Ælfgifu listened eagerly as Gilbert described the riches of East Frankia, most notably Aachen, she waited for an opportunity to speak directly to him. It came, eventually, as Ælfgifu and Eadgyth eventually lost interest in the discussion, turning to talk amongst themselves.

"I have seen you before," Duke Gilbert's words were directed at Eadgifu.

"And I believe I have seen you before as well. But, that was another lifetime ago."

"Perhaps," Duke Gilbert mollified, "but you are little changed in the intervening time."

Eadgifu was not immune to flattery, and she found a blush working its way along her neck.

"I'm afraid that I can offer you no news of King Charles, but I'll endeavour to have anything delivered to him that you'd like to send." The kindness of the words surprised Eadgifu, and for a moment, her throat was too tight to speak.

"His son is growing fast."

Duke Gilbert lapsed into silence, seemingly comfortable to wait for her to recover from his words.

"You are kind to take such a risk."

"It's no risk for me. Not when I have the support of King Henry behind me."

Eadgifu absorbed the confidence in his words. This was what she needed to know.

"Your king thinks to choose between my sisters?"

Duke Gilbert had the good grace to show some unease.

"King Henry doesn't wish his son to be married to a woman who wouldn't please him."

"So why didn't Lord Otto come himself?"

"Lord Otto was unable to leave East Frankia, while his father rides to war."

The answer was a reasonable one, but still, it rankled.

"Then, perhaps King Henry should have waited for events to be more secure."

Duke Gilbert chuckled at the implied criticism.

"King Henry is a man who is keen to think something, and have it done, almost in the same heartbeat."

"King Henry is rude to think that my sisters can spend half a year travelling at his request."

Duke Gilbert's head tilted to one side.

"I am here to ensure their safety."

"And I am here to say that it is not only rude toward my sisters but when one is destined for heartbreak, it is also cruel. If the father is cruel, then no doubt the son is as well."

The gasp of surprise from Duke Gilbert assured Eadgifu that she was right to have this private conversation with him.

"My Lady, I assure you that neither the king nor his son thought to be cruel. I assure you, while Lord Otto might well be young, I believe him fully capable of pledging his heart to a wife."

"And what of his wife's sister? What will he do to her?"

"My Lady," Duke Gilbert fought to find the right words, but lapsed into silence, this time, Eadgifu enjoying it, rather than vice versa.

Eventually, the Duke spoke, his eyes meeting Eadgifu's own.

"I believe King Henry may have been thoughtless, but not cruel. I will pledge, on my honour, and that of my king, and his grandson, that should the arrangement be agreeable, I will personally ensure a suitable marriage for whichever of your sisters, my young lord, realises he cannot love. As we journey to Saxony, I will collect my wife, and my grandson from Lotharingia, and have them support your sisters, and myself, in ensuring that this is done."

"My wife is King Henry's favourite daughter. He will do nothing to upset her, especially not when she has just become a mother. And Lord Otto adores his sister. He will also ensure that all is seemly. I confess, the king's suggestion seemed acceptable to me, but now I realise it was more of an insult than an honour. I would thank you for alerting me to the potential difficulties."

Eadgifu inclined her head at the words.

"The way of men is not always to be admired," Eadgifu eventually offered, although inside she crowed with delight at accomplishing what was needed, quite so quickly and easily. It seemed that Duke Gilbert was a highly intelligent individual. That he was also susceptible to her suggestions, only made her esteem him even further.

"I believe it more to be the way of kings, but in this, I will agree to disagree with you, and hope that we can still work together. And, as I said, I will promise to ensure King Charles receive any message you may wish to send to him."

Eadgifu forced a tight smile to her face. Her small victory could never make up for what had happened to Charles, but if she could aid her sisters, then she would, and Duke Gilbert seemed to be a quick-thinking man. He would need to be.

THE DAY before Eadgyth and Ælfgifu were due to leave Winchester, on their journey to Saxony, escorted by Bishop Cenwald, Duke Gilbert and a whole host of English and East Frankish men and women, Eadgifu and her sisters all converged on Wilton.

Eadflæd and Æthelhild were all smiles for their departing sisters. Eadgifu felt the impending loss more keenly. After all, Eadflæd and Æthelhild had lived apart from the rest of them for many years now. While East Frankia was a long way away, it would be little different, or so Eadgifu decided, feeling sorry for herself.

"Well," it was Æthelhild who spoke, her voice high with delight. "It seems the prospect of a royal marriage suits you both." The teasing in her voice was light. Eadgifu realised that her sister was more than aware of how high emotions ran between them all.

Even Eadgyth grinned at the statement.

"Sooner that, than a life of praying. I don't know how you manage it." Again, there was no criticism, but rather a wistfulness from Eadgyth.

"I prefer to argue with myself, than anyone else," Æthelhild confirmed. "I always wish to win my arguments, and it's the only way. I wouldn't want a man to think he knew better than I did." Eadgyth giggled at the lofty words, while Eadflæd rolled her eyes.

"And who would want anyone to sanction you for owning so many pairs of shoes."

At this, all five of the sisters laughed, and Eadgifu felt tears running down her face, some from laughter, some from sadness.

"It will be a big change for you," Eadflæd offered later when Eadgifu was preparing to return to Winchester.

"It will be yes, but I am hopeful that my husband may yet be released from his captivity. Certainly, Duke Gilbert believes he will gain access to my husband without too many problems."

Sadness settled over Eadflæd's face at those words, but it was banished just as quickly.

"Then I hope for your sake, and for Louis' that Duke Gilbert can fulfil all of his ambitious claims to our family."

Eadgifu nodded, her throat too tight to make speaking possible, pleased when Eadflæd turned away to wish her sisters goodbye for the final time.

Much rested on Duke Gilbert, and Eadgifu could only share Eadflæd's hopes, as she journeyed back to Winchester with Eadgyth and Ælfgifu one final time.

The future stretched bleak in front of her, unlike for her sisters.

She truly needed something to change and found her thoughts turning time and time again to Charles, imprisoned in Peronne at the instigation of Count Heribert.

Perhaps, with the aid of King Henry, flush with his coming victory, and the royal marriage with England, Count Heribert would finally realise that he was not strong enough to keep an anointed king in captivity. Eadgifu could only hope that proved to be the case.

THE DAYS and weeks after Eadgyth and Ælfgifu's departure from Winchester were long and lonely. After the excitement of being allowed to meddle in the embassy from East Frankia, Eadgifu found her time increasingly empty of any demands. Time and time again, she journeyed to Wilton to see her sisters.

King Athelstan seemed to have dismissed his sisters from his thoughts once more, and while Eadgifu waited impatiently to know the fate of Eadgyth and Ælfgifu, it appeared that her half-brother did not.

At Winchester she had no one but Edwin as her ally, and being allied with Edwin was becoming increasingly dangerous. Her brother was a drunk, and an out of control one. Time and time again, he planned treason against King Athelstan, and none of it was done with any great secrecy.

Eadgifu despaired of her brother and moved to distance herself from him. But that only left her even more isolated. Lord Osferth was a welcome respite into her loneliness, but even he had much to do, at the king's bequest. Equally, Louis' time was taken up with his education, his puppies, and Matilde. Eadgifu considered that she needed to make her own allies or risk being even more marginalised.

For Charles, she had sent with Duke Gilbert, a lengthy letter, telling him all she could think about their son, alongside a letter written by Louis himself. She had also thought to send some small jewels. She had no idea of whether Charles had his own money to buy what he needed, or whether he was entirely dependent on the good wishes of Count Heribert.

The thought chilled her. She would never want to be entirely dependent on her captor.

When a messenger rode in for King Athelstan, Eadgifu thought little of it, until Lord Osferth sought her out in the woodlands behind the palace. His face was pale, his lips tight, and there was a rolled parchment in his hands.

"My Lady, Queen Eadgifu," for a moment Lord Osferth's voice had faltered, and Eadgifu glanced at him in surprise. She had never known Osferth to stagger in his fierce attention to titles.

"My Lord," she inclined her head. "Is that news from Lady Eadgyth or Ælfgifu?"

"I am afraid not, although, there is news that Lady Eadgyth will marry Lord Otto. Lady Ælfgifu has agreed on a match with a Lord Louis from one of the East Frankish kingdoms. He is not a duke, or a count, or a king, but he is the brother of one."

The news brought a smile to Eadgifu's face, and she exhaled softly. It was a relief to know her sisters were safe and married, and that Duke Gilbert had kept his word in that regard. She still waited for news about Charles.

"This was also sent, addressed for you. From Duke Gilbert." Lord Osferth held the parchment out to Eadgifu, and she stepped to claim it, but paused, her hand encircling it, while Osferth still also held it.

"I take it you know the contents?" she asked, her voice tight with worry.

"I'm afraid I do," Lord Osferth confirmed, and Eadgifu knew her husband was still a prisoner. A gentle tear slid down her cheek. What, she thought, had she honestly expected Duke Gilbert to accomplish.

"I am sorry for your loss, My Lady, Queen Dowager," and only then did Eadgifu realise that the news was far, far worse than anticipated.

"Queen Dowager," her chin wobbled as she spoke, and pity flooded Lord Osferth's eyes.

"I am truly sorry, My Lady," Lord Osferth confirmed, turning smartly, and leaving without saying anything further.

For a long time, Eadgifu just stood there, not even reading the parchment, tears falling down her face. Time and time again, she made to open the letter, to read aloud the truth that her husband was dead, but she couldn't make it real. Not yet. Not when she'd hoped for something so very different.

Only when she shivered, recalled to herself, did Eadgifu slice open the seal and read the stark words.

There were few of them, although the letter was signed as from the Duke and Duchess of Lotharingia.

"Regret to inform you of the death of King Charles, the third of his name, on 7th October at Peronne."

There was no mention of the cause, although it continued that he'd been buried at the monastery of Saint-Fursy.

Eadgifu's eyes blurred, the words swimming before her, and then she turned on her heel and marched to the king's hall.

Unheeding of any who called to her as she strode without seeing, Eadgifu barged through the half-open door, the door wardens too slow to act. Her eye settled on her despised half-brother. King Athelstan sat on the dais, surrounded by his monks and bishops, ealdorman and king's thegns, and he didn't even look at her as she marched before him.

"This," she waved the parchment at him. "This is all your bloody fault," she screeched into the soft murmur of conversation that stopped abruptly.

"This, dearest brother, is what your disinterest has done to me, and more importantly, to my son, a boy you profess to love and care for. This. This is all because of you."

Tears streamed down her face, yet she felt calmly assured, as she noted the horror on her half-brother's face, and her bitch-mother rushing to intervene.

"This is what our great king has done," Eadgifu continued to shout, her eyes seeking out every one's on that dais, and holding them firm.

"My son no longer has a father, and it is all your damn fault."

With the words spoken, Eadgifu stormed from the king's hall.

Her half-brother was just as selfish as her father had been, and she would never forgive him.

AD936

She eyed her half-brother with interest.

The years had been kind to King Athelstan, if not to her. Even now, she hid her hands amongst the folds of her delicately embroidered dress. She wished that it was so easy to hide the fine lines that dotted her face, pulling her lips taut, and making it impossible for her to smile with pure joy.

King Athelstan, with the luck of a man with a beard to cover the worst of the ravages of time, looked younger than her, not older, as she took in his beautiful clothes, athletic build, and piercing blue eyes.

Sometimes she believed that King Athelstan saw everything, even deep into a person's soul, and that had used to worry her, but not anymore.

Eadgifu was unused to her half-brother needing her for anything since she'd blamed him for her husband's death all those years ago, and yet it seemed that he did, on this singular occasion.

"Come closer, dear sister," his voice was soft, beguiling, and she allowed a flicker of irritation to cross her face. She was no frightened hound to be coaxed from a hiding place. She was a bloody queen, just as he was a king. If her husband was dead, and her kingdom under the command of another, it didn't stop her from being a queen. Certainly, it had never stopped her step-mother.

Again, a flicker of annoyance touched her face. It was not easy to like her step-mother, but it was impossible not to admire her.

"My Lord King," Eadgifu affected a small curtsey and followed his hand as he indicated she should sit before his large desk, in the wooden-backed chair. She took the time to gaze around her. Not since she was a young woman, about to be shipped off to her old husband, had she been inside this room.

It was the king's own space. None were allowed to enter without his express permission.

Back then, nearly half her life away it had been her father's room. It had been her half-brother's for the last twelve years.

"We should talk, and please, just call me Athelstan." Eadgifu was taken aback once more. Her half-brother had always insisted on the use of titles in the past. He was a stickler for protocol. She'd always assumed it was because of his upbringing, far from the hubbub of Wessex. But then, she was prickly about the use of her title as well.

Even now, he looked at her, as though waiting for her to say something. But she stayed her tongue. If she were to call him Athelstan, she would need to think the 'king' part first. She'd vowed never to address him with any greater familiarity.

King Athelstan gazed at her a moment longer, and then shrugged, looking down at where his hands were clasped before him, his elbows on the table.

There were vellums and books all over the desk. It was a mess, and Eadgifu was amazed to discover her meticulous brother could be so disorganised.

"I need to speak with you about your son, my nephew."

Barely settled in her chair, Eadgifu felt her spine stiffen, and she was pleased she merely perched on the offered seat.

"It's your half-brothers who cause the problems, not him."

Silence filled the room at her denial, and she winced at her strident tone. Again, King Athelstan fixed her with his eyes before turning aside.

"I have reports that I'm to be visited by an embassy from Count Hugh."

Eadgifu held her breath, unsure what this had to do with her son, already cursing her bloody sister and her damn fool husband.

King Athelstan gazed at her once more, holding her eyes with his own, and then looked down, a manuscript in his hand. She watched him as he squinted, feeling a flare of triumph as his eyes strained, wrinkles forming around them. Perhaps he wasn't quite so immune to ageing as it appeared on the first inspection.

So caught up in her triumph, it took her too long to realise that King Athelstan spoke, and she caught only the final words.

"Restored to his crown and kingdom."

King Athelstan's piercing gaze seemed to bore into her, expectant, and yet she'd heard nothing but those six words. Did they even relate to her son?

When the silence dragged on, King Athelstan shook his head.

"I expected a little, well, more from you," he admitted, when the silence becoming oppressive. Still unsure what she'd missed while thrilling over King Athelstan's signs of ageing, she groped for the right response.

"Sorry, could you repeat that. I, I can't believe what I'm hearing."

If King Athelstan sensed that she'd only heard a part of it, he gave no sign in the flicker of his eyes downwards.

"I didn't either," King Athelstan admitted, once more picking up the manuscript. This time he held it before him, and more importantly, Eadgifu turned her gaze from him, focusing instead on her hands, bunched in her lap.

"Greetings My Lord King Athelstan from His Lord, Count Hugh." She listened to him recite the letter once more, but the mention of her brother by marriage almost made her shut her ears.

"In the interests of our great friendship and family ties, it behoves me to send an emissary to your Court to discuss a matter that personally touches me greatly. The kingdom of the West Franks requires strong leadership, and I intend that Lord Louis be restored to his crown and his kingdom following the death of King Rodolphus in January."

Eadgifu allowed the words to sink in, trying to determine the correct response.

Yes, Count Hugh was her brother by marriage, but never before, in the span of that marriage, had Hugh made any such overtures toward her son. Certainly not while his brother by marriage had claimed the kingdom of West Frankia as his own.

In the heavy silence, King Athelstan lowered the manuscript once more, his gaze piercing on her, and Eadgifu felt unable to look away from the intensity of his eyes. His blue eyes had such great power. She only wished she could use her own to such effect.

"This is unexpected," Eadgifu faltered, entirely unsure how to react. While her heart had thrilled at the thought of Louis taking his rightful place as the ruler of West Frankia, the fact the impetuous behind the move came from Count Hugh, was unpalatable, if not unexpected. After all, he was related to both of the two previous kings. Count Hugh had a great deal to lose if he was not intimately linked to the new king.

"How old is Louis now?" King Athelstan spoke as though he were some forgetful uncle. Eadgifu knew the king was entirely aware of how old Louis was. After all, he'd gifted Louis with costly presents each and every year to celebrate his birth, but she played along all the same.

"Sixteen." Only a little younger than when she'd become Charles' second wife. It felt like a lifetime ago.

"Not yet old enough to rule alone, then," King Athelstan spoke with consideration.

"Still old enough to need a regent to act in his name," Eadgifu spoke with a bite of unease. Count Hugh was too powerful. Hugh's wife was too powerful. And worse, it was Eadhild. She and Eadhild had parted badly, all those years ago, and Eadgifu had never thought it worth the effort to even attempt reconciliation.

"Count Hugh has no children of his own."

Not a criticism, but rather a statement. Eadgifu, despite her unhappy relationship with her sister, restrained her desire to defend Eadhild. It was not always the fault of the woman if a marriage produced no children.

"No, he doesn't, from either of his two marriages. His first wife was barren as well." Eadgifu answered softly, unsettled. She'd been worried about Athelstan's intentions when he'd summoned her to his side. Now she was even more ruffled. What was going on?

"Should we allow the embassy?" King Athelstan asked her directly. This surprised her even more. The king never asked her for an opinion.

She hesitated, while King Athelstan watched her keenly.

"He is your son," the king gently probed. "As my nephew, I've always supported him and made no pretence of my desire to see him claim his rightful inheritance. But he is your son, not mine, and I'd do nothing without your agreement."

Eadgifu held her flash of temper in check at such a lie but then shook her head in frustration. The king didn't lie. Any decisions made in the past that had excluded her had been minor compared to this. What did it matter who was Louis' tutor as long as he learned? What did it matter who he trained with, provided he became a warrior in the same shape as his Uncle?

"I imagine it would be sensible to allow the embassy and to see what Count Hugh really offers Louis. Would I be involved in such discussions?"

"Of course," King Athelstan murmured. "Louis is your son," the repetition was spoken as though the king reminded himself of that fact.

"But I must travel to York. They must come to me there as I've business in the North. You'll accompany me to York. Louis will, as well. Perhaps my young brothers too. They're all old enough to need to learn how to negotiate successfully."

Eadgifu swallowed down her unease. York was too close to the kingdom of the Scots for her liking. While peace had been established at the treaty of Eamont in 927 between the Scots and the English, Athelstan had been forced to march into Constantin's kingdom only

three years ago. He'd had to reassert the peace terms, taking both his
men and his fleet to the land of the Scots. Young Edmund had travelled north then, fought with the rest of the king's household
warriors, and made his first kill. She wasn't sure that she was ready
for Louis to do the same.

Eadgifu thought furiously. What did she know about current
affairs in York? Was it peaceful? Was it safe, and did she even wish to
meet with Count Hugh's embassy?

"Who will he be sending as the lead negotiator?" It couldn't be
Count Adelolf, for he had sadly died three years previously. The same
year her brother Edwin had been executed for treason. But she
dismissed that thought quickly.

"Count Hugh has named none of the members of the embassy, but
I would be far from surprised to see Cousin Arnulf included this time.
I travel to York to meet with Haakon." Count Arnulf was Count
Adelolf's brother, and as such, still her cousin.

Eadgifu nodded, her thoughts distracted.

"Will Count Hugh come himself?" The thought of meeting the son
of the man who'd stolen her dead husband's kingdom was unsettling.
She knew Count Hugh. She'd met him many times while living in
West Frankia. He'd always been a superior individual, assured of
himself. Would she be able to speak politely with him, even if he now
offered the kingdom back to her son?

"I doubt it. Several holy men, perhaps a few bishops and archbishops, and someone who speaks with Hugh's full support, such as Count
Arnulf."

King Athelstan paused then, a thoughtful look on his face before
he continued.

"There's no need to fear Count Hugh. He needs your sister, and
your son too much to cause any difficulties now, no matter your
history with him. No doubt when Louis is restored to his kingdom,
Count Hugh will be his greatest servant, and then you and Eadhild
will be reunited. Should you like that?"

Half rising, mirroring Athelstan's actions behind his desk, Eadgifu
found her movements faltering. Should she like to see her sister

again? Would she like to see any of her absent sisters again? The question distracted her from the shock at finding her old argument to Athelstan about the honour of his family, and what that demanded from others, regurgitated to her.

King Athelstan moved quickly, standing before her, his hands out to assist her to her feet.

"This might all be little and nothing," he said, her hands settled in his own, worn rough with the constant writing and training he indulged in. "Don't get your hopes up, but speak to Louis about it. Determine what you both want, and need, should this be a genuine appeal for Louis' return. I believe it might be. I don't think the other potential claimants have the necessary support to try and make themselves king following the death of King Rodolphus. Not one of the West Frankish counts trusts the other."

"I'll do the same. If there's to be an embassy, we need to know any number of facts. Not least of all is just how much England would be expected to contribute to the endeavour, and how much more prestige England would gain from it. After all, your sisters are influential women, and you should be once more. Think of this in the right way. Count Hugh needs you and Louis much more than you need Count Hugh."

Fully standing, Eadgifu realised she was closer to her brother than she'd been in her entire life. She hadn't appreciated how tall and slim he was. Not for the first time, she wondered why King Athelstan had decided to never marry when he would have made a good husband.

"I'll think about it, and yes, I'll speak to Louis. Please inform me if you hear more from the embassy."

"Of course, My Lady Eadgifu, or perhaps we should revert to Queen Dowager Eadgifu now, although that might prove confusing, with our step-mother." As they neared the door, King Athelstan's relaxed stance slipped away, his courtier's poise returning to him as though he flung a cloak around his shoulders and it weighed him down with responsibilities.

Eadgifu noticed the transformation with unease. Did she, after all this time, honestly wish to shoulder such burdens once more? For all that she complained at her lack of influence and power, did she want it back? It would not be a single-edged blade. It would wound her, just as surely as she could wound others with it.

"I'll inform you of all the developments, and I'd ask you to do the same. Louis is precious to me, he always has been since the first moment I laid eyes on him, but he is a king's son, and he should rule that kingdom." Conviction laced King Athelstan's words, and Eadgifu curtsied, his hand on the door handle, waiting to expel her back into the king's hall in Winchester.

"Thank you," from somewhere deep, those words were wrenched from her mouth, and the king startled, no doubt surprised. She'd never expressed any thanks for her half-brother's care of her and Louis, even when it had been him who'd come to rescue her and Louis. Not her father, or either of her full brothers, but Athelstan, a man she'd never much cared for.

She'd always thought it King Athelstan's responsibility, inherited from her father, to assist her and Louis. But if Louis was to have his kingdom back, and the support of England was needed to accomplish the impossible, then she would truly be grateful to him.

"He is my nephew," King Athelstan reiterated, the swell of conversation from the hall almost subsuming his words as he opened the door wide, a sign that he was content for all to know of his conversation with her.

"He will always be my nephew." What went unsaid, as she walked with her head high into the maelstrom outside the king's calm sanctuary, was that she would always be his sister as well. Even if she didn't much like it, and had never done anything to enhance his kingship, other than marry a man who'd lost his sovereignty and then his life, she still shared blood with him.

Eadgifu didn't miss that curious eyes followed her steps as the king made his way to the dais. It was clear to all that the brother and sister had been deep in conversation. The rarity of such an event was worthy of discussion. If she had witnessed it, she would have whispered to the person next to her, noticing with raised eyebrows that the king was up to something once more.

But Eadgifu stepped away from the noise and chaos, keen to be alone. Even the thought of finding Louis was too much for her. Instead, she stepped beyond the king's hall, despite the chill, and made her way to the woodlands surrounding Winchester palace. So many times she'd found herself here, treading the same path, her thoughts more often than not a riot of confusion.

Trying to reason, Eadgifu considered all she knew about events in West Frankia in recent years.

While it had been Count Hugh's father who'd first claimed Charles' kingdom, King Robert had died at the Battle of Soissons, whereas Charles had lived. But Rodolphus, Robert's son by marriage, had quickly stepped in to claim the kingdom for himself. In contrast, Charles had sought out one of his firmest allies, Heribert of Vermandois, only to be imprisoned by him.

It was at that point that Eadgifu had sought the sanctuary of her birth land, with her son. Still, she'd always believed, always, that Charles would reclaim his kingdom and she would return to West Frankia when he did so.

It was evident that King Athelstan had thought the same as well. The marriage between Eadhild and Count Hugh had been contracted with that purpose foremost. After all, Count Hugh was the brother by marriage of King Rodolphus. If Hugh couldn't bring about Charles release then who could? Certainly not Count Isaac of Cambrai, although he had at least tried. The same couldn't be said for anyone else, and most definitely, not Count Hugh.

When Charles had been released, temporarily in the year of Eadhild's marriage to Count Hugh, he'd been used as a pawn between Count Vermandois and King Rodolphus over who had the right to claim the capital of Laon.

Yet, Eadgifu had been ready to return to her husband's side, only for him to be imprisoned once more, for all that King Rodolphus had returned some palaces to Charles, most fittingly Attigny, as befitted an anointed king of West Frankia. It had been too little, and Count Hugh had not once spoken in support of Charles.

Even now, Eadgifu was convinced that Charles had died from a broken heart on being reimprisoned, or that Count Heribert had arranged his murder when holding Charles had gained him nothing.

Did she really wish her son to rule over such quarrelsome men, who thought nothing of killing each other?

There had been little peace while Rodolphus was king, the nobility falling over themselves to attack each other, and undermine the potential that a united West Frankia promised.

Louis was simply not used to such bitter infighting. King Athelstan had a far firmer control over his nobility, and not just because they were often his friends as well as his firmest supporters.

It no doubt helped, that King Athelstan had not agreed to marry any of his sisters to powerful English men. In West Frankia, Heribert of Vermandois was Count Hugh's Uncle, and yet it was no assurance of loyalty. Arnulf of Flanders was her cousin, although he had allied with King Rodolphus, and taken a daughter of Count Heribert as his second wife. William Longsword of Normandy had also sworn allegiance to King Rodolphus and received one of Heribert's daughters as his wife.

It was a confusing mix of intermarriage and rivalry, and one that hurt Eadgifu's head just to consider.

Yet, it was her son's inheritance.

Charles had fathered only legitimate daughters with his first wife. Louis was all that Eadgifu had managed to birth during her brief marriage, but at least he had been the much-needed son. Now, it was up to her, and King Athelstan as well, to try and out-think Count Hugh if Louis was not to suffer the same embarrassments as King Rodolphus, or Charles before him.

Louis would need to rule, if he did rule West Frankia, with the firm command of his Uncle. And he wouldn't be able to achieve that without her help. Of that, Eadgifu was sure.

After all this time, could she return to West Frankia? It had been her home for only a few short years. She knew much would have changed in her absence, although the bitter in-fighting has remained the same.

Since Charles' had ruled, King Rodolphus had lost control of the valuable territory of Lotharingia to King Henry of East Frankia.

King Rodolphus had been forced to cede land to the Viking Raiders who'd settled around the Seine, at Bassin and Maine. Yet more land had gone to William Longsword, who'd claimed Cotentin and Avranchin.

And that was without considering the main threat to Louis. King Rodolphus had left a brother, if not any sons. Surely, she thought, Hugh the Black of Burgundy, would be keen to rule as king of West Frankia, just as his brother had before him.

The fact that, as far as she knew, Hugh the Black had no children, might deter him, but it had never stopped King Rodolphus.

Eadgifu's head span with the possibilities, problems and fears and worries.

It was one thing to want something that had seemed out of reach for so many years. It was quite another to be faced with the prospect of achieving it all.

What would Louis want? She tried to consider him in all this.

Louis might have been a rough child, no doubt suffering from never knowing his father. Still, he had grown into a handsome and intelligent young man, always keen to be seen acting as honourably as his beloved Uncle, even if he and his young uncles still occasionally fought. Louis was well-liked by all, but he'd never been truly tested.

Eadgifu had refused to allow him to ride to war in the land of the Scots, something he'd not forgiven her for. Now she wished she had allowed him to see a battle for the first time, and to know what it truly meant to kill a man. Certainly, she didn't doubt that there would be war in West Frankia in the future.

Would her son be able to command men and issue instructions that he knew would result in their potential deaths? Would he be able to stand with his warriors and face an enemy without pissing himself and crying for her?

Eadgifu shook her head.

It was not, after all, her place to decide what her son wanted, not when the prize was his birthright.

With a sigh of annoyance, Eadgifu retraced her steps through the woodland, making her way to the stables, and then the training ground behind them. She knew Louis would be there. Whenever possible, Louis liked to train with the household warriors, and she appreciated that he itched to have his own household, complete with his own men to command.

Huddling deeper into her cloak, she stood on the sidelines, not prepared to shout for her son, and content to watch him.

The weather was far from warm, the bite of the previous night's frost still holding patches of grass and mud in its icy hold. It was nearer to Easter than Christmas, but Eadgifu was sure that there was still the potential for snow to fall, especially if it stayed so cold. She shivered once more, stamping her feet to allow some feeling back into them. Perhaps it hadn't been such a good idea to spend so long outside. Not so early in the year.

Eadgifu sought out Louis easily. It was not hard to determine who was her son, even amongst the group of over fifty or so men. Louis was working hard, with his slim build, still that of a youth and not a man, his shield in one hand, while in the other, he held a wooden sword. One of the older warrior's stood by, shouting commands, as Louis attacked and defended from his young Uncle, Edmund. It was strange to think of Edmund as her half-brother, whereas Louis was her son.

But, she supposed, the same must be true for her husband's older daughters. They too had children the same age as Louis.

The two youths were not unalike in mannerisms, but Edmund had bloodied and killed. Louis had not. It leant a certain desperation to Louis' movements, which made Eadgifu purse her lips with worry. Louis needed to be more careful. He needed to learn to accept that there would always be men who had accomplished what he wanted to have achieved. After all, there was time yet, and he was still young.

Eventually, young Eadred alerted his cousin to the presence of his mother. With only a slight frown at being interrupted, Louis made his way to his mother's side.

As he did so, Eadgifu admired his chestnut hair, bound behind his neck, and yet long all the same. He wore it this way because he knew it infuriated her. In all honesty, she'd long since stopped allowing it to worry her. If Louis wanted to wear his hair long, in imitation of the Viking Raiders, then so be it.

"Lady Mother," Louis was breathless, sweat sliding down his neck and disappearing beneath his tunic. Eadgifu wrinkled her nose.

"You stink."

"I do, yes. The business of war is a sweaty one." Eadgifu nodded, not wishing to laugh at her son's dramatic turn of phrase. He could often be heard trying to make things sound far more exciting than they truly were.

"Do you have time to speak to me? I don't want to interrupt your business, but I have some important news to share with you."

Louis' face twisted at her words, only to show some interest by the end of them.

"Is this something to do with the messenger who arrived this morning?"

"Potentially," Eadgifu replied, watching Louis duck under the wooden railing that encircled the training ground. It was really for tying up the horses, but also useful for holding back the masses who wished to watch the king train.

"Then yes," Louis confirmed. "I have the time to speak with you. Come, I'll return these to the training barn." As Louis spoke, he held his shield and wooden sword aloft, and Eadgifu nodded her agreement.

As they walked back toward the stables, and then to the building to the left of it, Eadgifu stayed quiet. It was rare for her and Louis to speak outdoors, but only a few people glanced in their direction. All the same, she decided to hold her tongue. She needed to face her son when she told him of news from West Frankia. She needed to know Louis' true feelings.

Only when he returned to her, his eyes blazing with curiosity, did she consider how she would even begin the conversation.

"Should we walk, or do you want to go to the king's hall?"

"Walk, I'm too hot. I need to cool off before I dunk myself in water."

Eadgifu wrinkled her nose again but continued to walk, aimlessly worrying a path back in the general direction of the woodlands.

"King Athelstan wished to inform me of an embassy coming to York, to seek him out, from West Frankia." As she spoke, Eadgifu watched her son's face intently, waiting to see if he would immediately determine the nature of the embassy.

His forehead furrowed, and his lips replayed her words, but he refrained from speaking.

"Count Hugh directs the ambassadors. He means to offer you back your kingdom now that King Rodolphus is dead."

Louis stopped abruptly at the words, his face flushing a hectic shade of maroon, as he absorbed his mother's words.

"Count Hugh? Why would he want to help me claim West Frankia? Surely he must have a good claim in his own name. After all, his father stole the kingdom from my father," there was heat in those words that Eadgifu understood only too well, for she shared it.

"King Athelstan believes that the powerful men of West Frankia will not allow for one of their own to be king in place of King Rodolphus. You are, of course, the most obvious candidate in that respect."

"What does King Athelstan say of this?"

Eadgifu held her temper that really it should be her opinion that mattered most, and answered honestly.

"King Athelstan has always known that West Frankia was your birthright. But you are his nephew, and he cares deeply for you. I don't believe he would allow himself to negotiate with men and women who might mean you harm. But he will only act according to your wishes."

Louis' lips trembled at the words, and Eadgifu found herself reaching out to touch her son's arm, feeling it shudder beneath her fingers. For a moment she worried that he'd gone into shock.

"It's not for you to make an instant decision, just to think about it."

"Count Hugh would make me his puppet?" the words were molten and filled with fury.

"He would try to do so. He's a powerful man and one with no heir. He'll lose much if you're not king and someone else is chosen in your place who he can't hope to be so close to." Eadgifu paused then, she didn't really wish to offer the next words but knew in her heart that she had to.

"Your aunt may well be behind this move. It may be her who convinced Count Hugh that you'll make the perfect king. She has always, ever since you came to England, cared for you deeply. You might not remember, but I do, and with her failure to have children, she may well think of you as her son."

Confusion covered Louis' face at the words.

"Lady Eadhild, I hardly remember her? Do you genuinely believe that this could be her wishes?"

"I would be remiss to my sister if I didn't suggest it. I appreciate that she is a hazy shadow of your childhood, but I imagine it burns much brighter for her than it does for you."

Louis nodded at the words, absorbing them for all his face still showed his confusion.

"So you think that Count Hugh might have been convinced by your sister, that I would be the best option to be King of West Frankia?"

"I do. Aside from all the logic that dictates you should become king, there might well be a personal level as well, overriding the potential to pursue a different king."

"And what? You think I should accept Count Hugh's assistance, and then cast him aside as soon as I can?"

Eadgifu paused. She'd really gone no further than considering her sister's potential involvement. Louis, it seemed, had already accepted it and moved on, thinking of his future. Eadgifu admired him.

"We would be virtual strangers in West Frankia, and those men that I do know, and remember well, will all have been traitors to Charles. To claim back West Frankia, you would need the firm support of someone. Perhaps Count Hugh, or one of the other great men, although never Count Heribert of Vermandois. Our family must never have anything to do with that man. But you will need King

Athelstan as well. If all should fail, King Athelstan will ensure your safety. I know that, and I assure you of that."

King Athelstan was king over the most stable kingdom in Europe. If West and East Frankia should fall, consumed by the Viking Raiders, then England would remain. Of that, she had absolutely no doubt.

"Then I'll need to thank my Uncle, but I must also consider what I want. Do you believe that if you returned to West Frankia you'd be able to build your own faction of support, bring men to my side, as opposed to Hugh's?"

"We would be able to, yes. You might not need my help to do so. Count Hugh has his own enemies, but he's powerful, far more so than when your father yet lived. It might be better to rise above the factionalism Count Hugh, and the other men thrive on, to become a mighty king over them all, as Athelstan is within England."

"I would hope to do that. But first, I'd need to find my own supporters, just as King Athelstan has Ealdorman Athelstan, Lady Ælfwynn and Ealdorman Athelstan's brothers. I would need that level of support. I would want to be king over all, but know that I would need to be able to assert myself to that position through others. After all, if one count accepts me for what I truly am, then others will quickly follow suit."

"Well, you might wish to cultivate Count Arnulf then, my cousin. Yes, he's an ally of Count Hugh, but if you have the support of King Athelstan, Count Arnulf will know that you can rule as your Uncle does."

Louis fell away to silence, his forehead creased in thought. Eadgifu watched him carefully, prepared to admit that she was surprised by Louis' calm acceptance of his potential future.

She'd never lied to Louis about his place and position. She'd always told him he would be a king one day, but that his kingdom was not that of King Athelstan's. Louis had understood that well, running to her one day, fearful because someone had teased him that he'd only be king when his beloved Athelstan was dead, and Louis couldn't face the thought of that.

"I'm open to the ambassadors," Louis announced decisively, gazing into the far distance, rather than meeting his mother's eyes. "I would know all that they offer, and I would know all that I must to make a decision about West Frankia. I need to understand what is happening there, and what is likely to in the future, either when I'm king, or when I'm not. But mother," and now Louis turned to face her, his youth seeming to vanish before her eyes. "I'll be king, and rule with my own mind, not that of someone else. I will make that clear to you here and now, if not to the ambassadors. I'm no fool to be played with."

Eadgifu nodded, holding her smile of approval away from her face.

Louis would make a fine king. The time in exile had not been a waste. Louis had learned things that no man in West Frankia yet knew, and that would make him inordinately capable.

"I'll inform King Athelstan," Eadgifu offered, the thrill of the potential finally suffusing her body. It would be good to go home, after all.

AD936

York was not at all how Eadgifu imagined it would be.

In her mind, York was filled with Viking Raiders. They walked around, armed and ready to do battle at the slightest insult or provocation. The flicker of iron the most prevalent material to be seen, with everyone just waiting to shout abuse or start a fight with someone who upset them.

Eadgifu could confess that the busy markets were not at all what she'd envisaged as the king's cavalcade had made its way ever northwards, the roads never seeming to end, the horizon only slowly revealing itself.

Perhaps, after all, Eadgifu could see why King Athelstan had been so keen to add York to the kingdom of the English. And why he'd been so prepared to offer his sister as a bride for the man who'd once held York, King Sihtric, before his unfortunate, if timely, death.

Even the ripe smell of wood smoke, raw fish, cooked fish, the stench of the river, and the scent of many people living in a small space, was far from unpleasant. The king's hall, or rather the archbishop's hall, that had been made available to the king on arrival, was a stout and impressive building, at the centre of all the intense activity.

Settling to her feet, after a long day in the saddle, Eadgifu tried to keep the surprise from her face. At her side, Louis rattled off facts he'd been taught about York by the monks responsible for his education. Louis knew about the building of the walls, the men who'd claimed York as her king, and the old kings, the men of Deira who'd ruled her hundreds of years ago.

Eadgifu heard only about every other word but was impressed all the same by Louis' knowledge. It would stand him in good stead when he first saw Laon.

King Athelstan had long since jumped from his horse. Even now, he was no doubt listening to petitions from the inhabitants of York. As honoured as she'd been on the long journey north, she was merely the king's half-sister. Yes, a queen in her own right, but a queen without a kingdom. For now.

With each mile covered along Ermine Street, the spark of hope that Louis would reclaim his kingdom had continued to grow. While Eadgifu tried to contain her wild plans for the future, she also couldn't help but imagine what it would be like when she was honoured as the king's mother, and not as his widowed half-sister.

Gazing at the grand hall, Eadgifu was almost desperate for the embassy to arrive, speak to King Athelstan, and make arrangements for Louis and her to return to West Frankia. Yes, there would be battles of precedence to be won once she got there, but as the king's mother, she couldn't help but be esteemed by her son above all others. And of course, no matter what Count Hugh might think, he didn't know Louis, and certainly, Louis didn't know him.

Yet, as Eadgifu stepped unobserved into the hall, eyes peering into the recesses as one of her women moved to relieve her of her cloak and riding gloves, she couldn't help but realise that any return to West Frankia would be similar to this moment. Yes, she'd been married to the king, but only for a short time. She had no real allies in West Frankia, and she would be a stranger amongst men and women who already knew their places and functions.

The thought was sobering, dampening her growing fiery desire to return to West Frankia. Would it be worth it or was it just easier to remain in England, always overlooked, but safe, and more importantly, alive?

Not even her husband would be there to welcome her home. His death, seven years ago, while a prisoner, meant that she'd never had the chance to say goodbye to him, or even visit his gravesite. Perhaps, soon, that would be remedied, if she did go to West Frankia. Or, perhaps, even if she didn't, she might ask to be allowed to visit Charles' grave all the same.

"My Lady Eadgifu," the voice of her woman permeated her scrutiny of the archbishop's hall, and she turned, only half her attention on what was happening around her.

"The king wishes a moment of your time. On the dais."

She'd not shared a private conversation with King Athelstan again after their discussion a handful of weeks ago. It looked, as she eyed the dais with dismay, as though this was about to be a far more public affair.

Louis trailed behind her as she picked a path through the crowded hall, a servant trying to lead the way but lacking the authority to make people move aside. Annoyed, Eadgifu pulled up short, looking around for someone with authority.

Her eyes settled on Lord Æthelwine. Her cousin was held in high esteem by the king, and many other people as well. They weren't exactly allies, but he, like the king, was an honourable man. Seeing her difficulties, he made his way to her side.

"Here, let me assist you, Queen Dowager Eadgifu," the use of her title warmed her, and she inclined her head in agreement, as Lord Æthelwine took her arm, and steered her through the mass of people.

"Is it always like this?" she thought to ask, Æthelwine nodding solemnly in response.

"Men and women are always keen to have the ear of the king. They know he can be trusted to listen to them and provide what assistance is needed. King Athelstan is much loved if also feared."

Eadgifu nodded, almost unable to keep her focus on any one thing. There was so much going on. How had she never realised just how busy King Athelstan was? But then, she was either at Winchester or on one of her own properties. She didn't avoid the king's court, but all knew King Athelstan rarely stayed in one place for long. He had a restless temperament and a mind that never seemed to stop thinking.

"My Lady Eadgifu," at the foot of the dais, Lord Æthelwine flashed a smile at Eadgifu and bowed his way from her side. She watched him going, immediately regretting his absence, as people instantaneously closed in around her.

"Ah, young Louis," it was King Athelstan's voice, raised high, that finally forged a path for her and her son. Eadgifu tried to keep the annoyance from showing on her face. She should not have to rely on anyone to allow her easy access to the king. She realised that for too long, she'd hovered so much in the shadows that few here even knew who she was, although Louis was often to be found escorting the king.

Louis, a glint of triumph on his young face, bounded the last few steps and sank gracelessly into a chair before the king. Eadgifu moved swiftly to take advantage of the easy passage but paused to curtsey to the king. She might be a queen dowager, but Athelstan was assuredly a king.

King Athelstan hadn't changed from his riding clothes. Indeed, one of his gloves still covered the hand he was using to drink water from an elaborate glass goblet. Eadgifu knew it wouldn't be wine. The king refused to indulge other than during a feast. The rest of the time, he drank fresh water, from whatever river or lake they happened to be closest to.

"Come, sit," the king's voice was loud, and filled with the command, as he indicated a chair for Eadgifu.

"I would have some time alone," Athelstan further instructed. Obediently, the press of bodies evaporated, leaving the three of them, alongside ealdorman Uhtred, almost marooned at the head of the hall.

Settling herself, Eadgifu took the time to appreciate Athelstan's placement of her. She was to the left of him, in full sight of everyone within the hall. It was both a position of honour and one where her every reaction would be noted. She must keep her face as bland as possible while the king spoke to her. Whatever was said, neither joy nor fury could mar her brow, or all would know her real thoughts. Well, those that cared enough to look would.

Opposite her, Louis sat with his back to all. Eadgifu appreciated the careful placement of him. He was yet too young to be able to hide his emotions. And anyway, there had never been any need for him to do so before although he would need to learn from now on.

"The embassy arrived two days ago. They've been guests of Archbishop Wulfstan since then. And they don't come alone either." Eadgifu waited, wondering just what the king meant.

"There's an embassy from Brittany, as well as the one from Haakon. It seems our decision to travel to York has been a good one."

Frantically, Eadgifu tried to decide whether all this happening at once was a good or a bad sign.

King Athelstan toyed with his glass. Seeming to realise only then that he still wore his glove, he carefully pulled each finger loose from the leather, and then flexed his hand, pleased to be free of the constraint.

"I've happily provided shelter for two foster-sons, and my own nephew, rescued from the clutches of the West Frankish, who would have preferred him dead. Now, it seems, my support must come in terms of men and warriors, ships and coin."

"Queen Dowager Eadgifu, Lord Louis, I give you leave to meet with the legates from West Frankia. Have Bishop Oda assist you. He knows my mind on the matter. Do your best to determine what they want, what the cost will be, and more importantly if they will honour their oaths and restore Louis to his kingdom."

"I'll send no family member away without such assurances of their safety. They must know that I'll send my own men to guard Louis and my sister until I can be assured that they'll face no enemy."

As he spoke, King Athelstan's voice filled with fierce resolve.

"Remember, you are my family. All honour must be accorded to you, and reparations made for your exile from your own kingdom." Here her half-brother fixed Eadgifu with a firm stare.

"You might think that you're the weaker party in the discussions, but you're not. They want Louis. I warrant they need him to restore stability to West Frankia. None of those men there now, be it Count Hugh or Count Heribert or even Count Arnulf, as much as he is family, have the support of the others."

"They're all too mindful of one of them getting something the other doesn't have. As tedious as it is, you must use that knowledge. Remember who you are and that you are both my sister and my nephew. While East and West Frankia stumble and falter, England grows more and more settled, even York, here, falling happily under the command of my kingship."

"Ever since Queen Dowager Eadgifu married Charles, the noble families of East and West Frankia have understood that the English can provide more stability than their own nobility. Our family, the House of Wessex, is the longest surviving of all, not just in England, but within the three countries of England, West and East Frankia. We are a valuable commodity, and they should have realised that before they imprisoned Charles. Well, I imagine that Heribert of Vermandois did realise that, and that was why he also tried to take control of you, Louis, and your mother. That he failed has long been your strength. Remember that."

Louis nodded along with his uncle's words, and Eadgifu watched the interplay between the two, seeing just how much Louis revered his uncle.

"You honour me, My Lord King," Louis spoke proudly, his young face, just beginning to burgeon with an auburn beard and moustache, animated. "I will, of course, listen carefully, and inform you of all you need to know."

King Athelstan's harsh face softened, a smile toying with his lips.

"I'm sure you will. And I thank you for assisting me with this. I would sooner have committed myself fully to speaking with the ambassadors, but I must make time for all those who seek my help and assistance. I've already sent word to Winchester that Alain should journey to York. It seems that now is the time to see my nephew and foster-son restored to their kingdoms. It fills me with joy, as well as sorrow."

Only then did the king pause, a thoughtful look on his face.

"I would not wish to send my foster-sons and nephew from my court, but you all have a birthright, and I'll not deny any of you the opportunity to reclaim it. If it is within my power to help, then I will."

King Athelstan gazed at Louis as he spoke, but Eadgifu looked away from the emotion on his face. It seemed she had underestimated her half-brother. Again.

LATER THAT DAY, Eadgifu stood, waiting impatiently, to see the members of the embassy who'd been sent to treat with King Athelstan regarding her son's future.

After Athelstan's rousing speech, she'd taken some time to herself.

She could feel that momentous change was coming. For many years, she'd cursed her feelings of impotence at her half-brother's court. Still, now that the possibility of returning to West Frankia was being offered to her, she felt ill at ease, and insecure. In Winchester, she knew who she was, and what she was. The same couldn't be said for West Frankia.

Eadgifu had dressed carefully, paying particular attention to the jewels she wore.

The jewels she'd managed to bring with her to Wessex had not been worn for some time. While in her first few years of exile, she'd always insisted on wearing all of her jewels, she'd long since stopped the practice. It had been Eadhild who'd scathingly alerted her to just how desperate she'd looked, wearing the wealth of a kingdom, but without a kingdom to her name.

Now it was as though Eadgifu discovered each new gem afresh. The gold of her necklaces, the silver of her rings, and brooches, and the emeralds, diamonds, rubies and ambers of her bracelets.

Seeing each new treasure in the candlelight, from where they'd been hidden in her jewellery casket, reminded her of the gifting of each and every one of them.

Charles. She'd not thought of her husband for many years in anything but a derogatory way. She'd blamed him for what had happened. She'd hated him for being too weak to hold onto his own kingdom, for failing to protect their son, and even for dying. For leaving her alone with a young son, and no support but that of her indifferent half-brother.

Now her fingers lingered, caressing the ruby ring he'd presented her with on the birth of Louis. Soft tears filled her eyes. How happy he'd been. The man who'd been a king but had only ever fathered daughters with his wife, his sons born outside the bonds of marriage, making them illegitimate and unable to succeed their father.

An old man, unsure of his legacy, until Louis had been born.

Eadgifu thought back to Louis' birth, the horror of the pain, the fear that she'd fail, and the hope that the baby would be a boy. It had all been too much for her. But then, her only child had been all that he'd needed to be, both a son and an heir. Charles, whatever her feelings towards him, had shown the depths of his sentiments when tears had sheeted from his eyes, and he'd stumbled to his knees before the cot in which their son had slept.

She might have resented him many times over for being an old man when she was young, but in the moment of Louis' birth, she'd known genuine affection for her husband. Charles had not been an unkind lover, or a husband, or a king. Perhaps, in the end, he had been just as awkward at marrying a woman the age of his daughters, as she had been at finding her husband to be the same age as her father.

As Charles had sobbed with joy, unheeding of those who'd watched, he'd had a jewel brought forth for Eadgifu. The ring had been of such weight that she'd thought her finger would never take the strain, and yet she slipped it on now, admiring the cut of the ruby, and the delicate banding that held it in place, the flash of fire on her face.

With the ring, her husband had paid her for the safe arrival of Louis, and now she would wear it, a reminder of what she had accomplished, and of her true place within West Frankia.

It was time to become the Queen Dowager of West Frankia.

Louis, similarly, was dressed in his most elegant clothes, his tunic stiff with embroidery, his long hair, neatly braided and tied back from his youthful face. Around his neck, he wore a symbolic golden cross that King Athelstan had gifted to him, some shard of a saint, hidden beneath the clever goldwork, a sign that Louis' faith was strong if more understated than his uncle's.

Bishop Oda was also in the room with Eadgifu and Louis, where they waited to meet the ambassadors. The bishop was one of King Athelstan's most loyal advisors. Behind him, a handful of his monks and clerics waited to ply their talents, the sharp smell of ink and parchment infusing the air.

Bishop Oda was dressed to impress, and Eadgifu inclined her head to him in greeting. She had no firm opinion about Oda but knew that he was an ally of her step-mother. That might, in the past, have assured Eadgifu that Oda couldn't possibly have her best interests at heart, but now she took it as the honour it was.

Bishop Oda, high in King Athelstan's regard, as well as her step-mother's, was here to negotiate for the return of Louis' kingdom to him. Oda would have strict instructions from the king, of that she was sure, and more, he would know the king's mind better than she did.

"Queen Dowager Eadgifu," when Oda spoke, his voice was clipped with the accent of his Danish father. Still, Eadgifu knew enough to be prepared for it. Oda's skill with languages was well known, and it reminded Eadgifu that she wouldn't be alone in being able to understand the West Frankish if they chose not to speak in English.

Louis' own West Frankish had stalled, with the death of his nurse-maid. Matilde, when Louis had been old enough not to need her, had married, and sadly died in childbirth. Eadgifu had mourned for her, despite the bitter recriminations they'd once flung at each other.

"Lord Bishop," her tone was formal, and a quick nod from Oda showed his approval for her stance. It seemed that she was to play the part of the haughty queen dowager.

"My Lord Prince," for Louis it was more difficult to decide on a title for him. Bishop Oda paved the way by referring to him as 'my lord.' Not yet crowned as king, he couldn't be named as was his due. 'Prince' was a compromise. In England, he would have been given the title of ætheling, but in West Frankia, such didn't exist.

Louis' eyes flashed at the title, his shoulders tensing, before relaxing once more. It seemed that Louis had been prepared for the title, even if he was unhappy with its use.

"I've spoken with the ambassadors," Bishop Oda continued. "They are led by Count Arnulf, the brother of Count Adelolf who led the last delegation from West Frankia seven years ago. They've much to offer Prince Louis, but of course, they also seem to have some stipulations. But, I will let them speak with you first. Know that King Athelstan is keen for these talks to succeed. But not at the expense of any insurmountable costs, in terms of both men, and money, and the safety of his nephew and sister."

Eadgifu absorbed the news with interest, trying to decide just what the terms might be. Louis settled himself on a chair, close to the hearth, but far enough away that he would have the excuse of standing to warm himself, if he needed to shield his face at any point. Eadgifu chose to sit in a position of prominence, before the hearth, and close to where the monks were settling themselves. Should the need arise, Eadgifu would be able to stand and peer over the shoulders of the monks.

Bishop Oda remained standing, as did a handful of other clerics, supporting their bishop. When Ealdorman Ælfwold strode into the room as well, a greeting on his tight lips, Eadgifu was unsurprised. Ælfwold was as firm an ally of King Athelstan as Oda. It seemed that the king was prepared to put the due amount of thought and respect into this embassy, even while being unable to attend.

Bishop Oda turned then, to ensure all was as it should be within the room, his keen eyes taking in the remaining chairs. There was a table set up for whatever clerics the embassy had with them. There were seats for three men to the far end of the chamber from his own clerics. In between, there was a table laden with precious glass goblets, five jugs of wine, the smell of the spices heady against the smell of ink and parchment. A further six wooden backed chairs formed a loose circle, some close enough to the table that they could be turned without causing insult, others closer to Eadgifu and the seat that Bishop Oda seemed to be considering his own.

Ealdorman Ælfwold, festooned as a warrior, complete with ceremonial weapons belt and seax, sat amongst them in contrast to the
prince, the queen dowager, and the bishop. Eadgifu smirked softly to
herself. King Athelstan had ensured that all aspects of his kingship
were being represented.

She wondered whom Count Arnulf would have with him. No
doubt, there would be someone close to Count Hugh and her sister,
and also someone who spoke for the other nobility, and perhaps, his
own bishop or archbishop as well. But Count Hugh counted himself
as a lay bishop, that might mean he refused to invest too much of his
influence in the body of a rival bishop.

Count Hugh and Count Heribert had argued, the year before
Charles' death, over the right to be archbishop of Laon. Count Hugh
had wanted it for himself, Count Heribert for his son, a youth of no
more than fifteen. The men had made fools of themselves, and
Eadgifu knew that in the end, neither of them had gained control over
the archdiocese. She thought that a good thing.

Silence fell amongst the small grouping, all straining to hear when
their guests might arrive, as from outside, the sounds of York
intruded on the place of solitude. No matter what happened inside the
archbishop's royal hall that day, outside, regular events continued to
happen, and Eadgifu appreciated the reminder.

Whatever happened, there would be a tomorrow, and it might be
the same as yesterday, or it might be entirely different, but it would
still be happy.

A confident stride broke through Eadgifu's reverie, and she
snapped back to attention.

The door way was opened wide with the sleeve of a servant visible,
and Count Arnulf was the first to step inside the room, a beaming
smile on his face, as others trailed in behind him.

Eadgifu was standing as her cousin entered, a smile of welcome
playing around her lips. Louis too took to his feet.

"Queen Dowager, Lord Prince," Count Arnulf's greeting was as
formal as Bishop Oda's had been, and Eadgifu appreciated Oda's tact

in his use of titles. It was as nothing to hear the words glibly fall from Arnulf's mouth now.

"My Lord, Count Arnulf, Cousin." Eadgifu allowed herself to acknowledge the family relationship first. At the word, Arnulf's grin spread ever wider, and he stepped forward to embrace her, the scent that enveloped Eadgifu reminding her of West Frankia.

"I know we've never met, but I assure you, Lord Prince, that my brother often spoke of you in the years before his death, and many have been keen to know you are well and finely formed." Arnulf's words to Louis were both honourable and also laced with a hint of threat. Eadgifu was surprised that even something so simple as a greeting would be used as a power play.

"I remember him, My Lord. You look alike." Louis spoke well, grasping the forearm of his second cousin firmly, the difference in ages immediately apparent. Count Arnulf was three decades older than Louis, and yet Louis had the grace of his warrior's training. Eadgifu watched as Count Arnulf realised the difference, abruptly sucking in his belly, and holding his shoulders straighter.

"I believe Count Adelolf taught my young uncles and me a few games. Perhaps games he shouldn't have taught us." Louis' voice was high with youth, and yet it was just another reminder of the age difference between the men. Eadgifu held her amusement in place as she resettled on a chair. Louis seemed to be coping admirably on his own.

As Count Arnulf also pulled out a chair from those available, sitting closer to Eadgifu than to Louis, Eadgifu spoke again, her eyes on the bishop and the monks who had trailed in after Arnulf.

"I was sorry to hear about your brother. Cousin Adelolf was a wonderful man."

"He was, yes, he was." Arnulf's voice was bluff at being reminded of his brother's death three years ago.

"And I hear you've married once more, and are the father of two daughters." Count Arnulf seemed to enjoy that line of conversation more, for he relaxed, reaching for a glass goblet and serving himself.

"Countess Adele is a dutiful wife and a loving mother. And of course, Count Heribert is a doting grandfather." Eadgifu inclined her head at the words. The politics of family were critical to this discussion then. Count Heribert had held her husband a prisoner until his death. By taking one of Heribert's many daughters as his second wife, Arnulf had firmly enmeshed himself in the politics of West Frankia.

Somehow, it seemed, that Arnulf was an ally of Count Hugh, and yet married to Heribert's daughter. It was not uncommon.

"And I have news from your sister as well. Countess Eadhild sends her warmest regards to both you and young Louis. I have messages for you, and also some gifts."

As Arnulf spoke, one of the monks stepped forward, bowing as he went, his robes trailing along the floor, as he offered a series of rolled parchments, and also a wooden casket. Eadgifu took the offerings with a smile although she quaked to know what her sister might have sent, after all these years of silence.

Countess Eadhild. How she didn't like to hear her sister mentioned in such a way.

"I'll read them later, and my thanks for bringing them safely to me. I'll have responses for her, and some gifts as well. I take it, I can be assured that you'll be able to see she receives them promptly."

"Of course, Queen Dowager. It would be my pleasure, and of course, I must meet with Count Hugh as soon as I return to West Frankia. He's most keen for reports of a positive meeting, and to know how we'll proceed from here. West Frankia must have a king, and Prince Louis is our choice, naturally."

Eadgifu held her tongue at the end of Count Arnulf's flattering speech, although noting that Arnulf, in this at least, was in agreement with Count Hugh. It shouldn't have come as such a surprise, but still, it did.

"And your wife, she is in agreement that Louis should be restored to his kingdom."

Approval flashed in Arnulf's hooded eyes at Louis' statement.

"My lady wife is keen for peace in West Frankia. At the moment, too many men think to dictate events. As I said, West Frankia needs a king."

Eadgifu nodded at the words. There was much that Count Arnulf was not prepared to articulate, but she'd expected that.

"And now to business. I will tell you all that Count Hugh, Count Heribert and I, and the Count of Aquitaine would offer to our young king."

With a flick of his hand, one of the monks stood from his place behind the deeply polished wooden table and unfurled a parchment, the seal hanging ponderously from the bottom.

"Count Hugh, Count Heribert, Count Arnulf, and the Count of Aquitaine, pledge to Prince Louis of West Frankia, that Prince Louis would have the full support of all the nobility and churchmen of West Frankia. Further, Lord Archbishop Artoldus has pledged to officiate over Prince Louis' coronation as soon as he returns to West Frankia."

"On becoming king, Prince Louis, or King Louis as he would then be, would be accorded all the royal palaces and stronghold's once held by his father, including the royal palace of Attigny, and Laon."

"On becoming king, Prince Louis, or King Louis as he would then be, would be assisted in his onerous duties by a royal council, to include Count Hugh, Count Heribert, Count Arnulf, and the Count of Aquitaine. The royal council would assist the king until the king was sufficiently skilled to rule alone."

Here, Count Arnulf interrupted the monk's deep voice, his English accent clear and easy to understand.

"This is merely a stipulation because Prince Louis is a stranger to West Frankia. England has been his home for so many years that it will take time for Prince Louis to learn all that he must know about the West Franks. We're all assured that Prince Louis, following in the footsteps of his illustrious father, uncle and grandfather, will be a natural ruler, once he has all the information easily to hand." Count Arnulf spoke warmly, and yet there was a smugness in his voice that set Eadgifu's teeth on edge.

While she'd thought it would be a blessing to have a family member as part of this embassy from Count Hugh, she was no longer so assured of that. If Count Hugh thought to rule through Louis, then it was also abundantly clear that Count Arnulf expected to profit handsomely as well."

"Before you continue," it was Bishop Oda who spoke into the silence following Arnulf's expansive, and unnecessary explanation. It was evident to all that while Prince Louis might be restored to the kingship, it would only be if these men gained something from it.

"You must forgive my ignorance, but it seems that some names and principalities are missing from the list of those who would support Prince Louis' return to West Frankia. Most notably, if I'm correct, and please forgive me if I'm not, the Count of Normandy, Lord William, and the Count of Burgundy, brother to the previous king."

Arnulf's smile never faltered, although Eadgifu noticed that his leg twitched beneath his hand.

"Hugh, the Black of Burgundy, is unwilling to claim the kingship as his own, although, of course, he would have the right, as the brother of King Rodolphus. He is content to rule in Burgundy."

"Yet Burgundy is still subject to the king of West Frankia."

"Of course, of course," Arnulf nodded, in response to Eadgifu's words.

"There is the belief that with a little lee way, Hugh the Black will readily accept Prince Louis, but for now, Hugh grieves for his brother, King Rodolphus. He's not keen to look to any future that doesn't involve his brother. I am sure you can understand." Count Arnulf turned his gaze to Louis, and Eadgifu noticed with pride that Louis showed nothing of his true feelings on his face.

What was going unsaid, while everyone there understood it, was that Hugh the Black might not have decided to pursue his claim at this time, there was always the potential that he would, in the future.

"As to Count William. He is descended from Vikings, you know," Count Arnulf spoke as though Eadgifu would have no memory of who Count William's father was. He might think she's forgotten the arrangement reached with Charles all those years ago to cede Normandy to him. And was perhaps entirely ignorant that Count Rollo had escorted Eadgifu and Louis to safety, when they'd been forced to flee West Frankia.

"There is scope for him to agree to Prince Louis' return. He's always been loyal to King Charles, just as his father was before him."

"So, you bring the men to the table who will accept Prince Louis without further debate, and leave some who must be enticed closer, or who don't much like the men who already want Prince Louis?" Bishop Oda spoke without rancour, his hand indicating to his scribe to make a careful note of the discussion.

Count Arnulf smiled, but it was a sickly thing.

"Some men are always more stubborn when being informed of the best for their country." Count Arnulf tried to laugh at the end of his sentence, but the sound was off.

"Continue, please," Bishop Oda said, gazing at the West Frankish monk who still stood, the parchment in his hands, for all he'd not spoken for some time.

"On becoming king, Prince Louis, or King Louis as he would then be, would be protected with five hundred household warriors, with a further one hundred to be provided by the English King, and these would be paid for from the West Frankish taxes."

"On becoming king, Prince Louis, or King Louis as he would then be, would appoint his own officials to the post of arch-chancellor and other positions, although, with advice from his royal council."

"On becoming king, Prince Louis, or King Louis as he would then be, would set taxes as he saw fit, and would have the power and influence to negotiate with the enemies and allies of West Frankia, although with advice from his royal council."

Eadgifu remained still, waiting, just waiting to see what else would be offered her son. So far, everything that she heard was contingent on the support of the royal council, and it meant her son would be king, in name only, and no doubt lacking the funds and the support to bring these men who didn't wish him to become king, to his side.

It was not an unsubstantial offer, but Eadgifu was unimpressed, and she hoped that King Athelstan would be as well.

The atmosphere in the room continued to sour as the monk read on and on, citing what Louis' relationship with the church would be, and how he would be free to marry, with the support of the royal council. Only as the monk droned on, did Eadgifu hear her name spoken.

"On becoming king, Prince Louis, or King Louis as he would then be, would have it in his power to restore the royal lands once held by his mother, the Queen Dowager, and she would also be accorded all honours as befits the widow of King Charles."

Eadgifu nodded at the offer while knowing it was not enough. It would never be enough because these men, no matter what they might think, could never restore her husband to her side.

"On becoming king, Prince Louis, or King Louis as he would then be, would be advised to rely on his noblemen of West Frankia, and to arrange a time when he would no longer seek advice from King Athelstan, King of the English."

Eadgifu startled at the words, amazed at the disingenuousness of Count Hugh. It seemed he wanted Prince Louis because of his relationship with King Athelstan, but equally, he was wary of it.

This interested Eadgifu more than all the other tedious terms and restrictions, even the demand that King Athelstan fund Louis' expenses in returning to West Frankia, living there for two years at King Athelstan's expense.

But Eadgifu held her tongue, not wanting to say anything until she'd had the time to speak to Ealdorman Ælfwold, bishop Oda and her son.

Bishop Oda turned to one of his monks, and the man stood, as the West Frankish monk reclaimed his seat, his forehead sheened in sweat at being the centre of attention for so long.

"King Athelstan has made a list of his own demands. Some of them are, of course, counter to your own, but we should hear them all, and then decide how to move forward."

Count Arnulf failed to hide his surprise at his cousin's unexpected actions, so unlike when Arnulf had visited to facilitate the marriage of Eadhild to Count Hugh.

"King Athelstan has made the following requests," the monk intoned, his voice loud enough to fill the small chamber.

"The expenses of Prince Louis' return to West Frankia must be

settled by the West Frankish kingdom. King Athelstan believes a force
of five hundred English men should journey to West Frankia, to
ensure Prince Louis' coronation proceeds promptly, the date to be
decided once Prince Louis' return is agreed to. But not to be longer
than one month from his arrival. All the West Frankish nobility are to
pledge their allegiance to their new king, promising to support him,
and never apprehend him or hold him against his will."

Eadgifu's felt her eyes widen at the terms. It was as though King
Athelstan was asking to land an army in West Frankia, during peace
time. It was an audacious move, and one that would be hard for the
West Frankish nobility to disagree to, as would the demand that
Prince Louis never be imprisoned, as his father was before him.

"As soon as King Louis has been proclaimed king, Queen Dowager
Eadgifu will have her estates restored to her. There will also be
recompense for her many years in exile. The cost of which will be
reimbursed by the West Frankish kingdom, at a rate agreed before
Prince Louis returns to West Frankia. Queen Dowager Eadgifu," the
monk continued. "Is to be accorded the greatest of respect and all
honours due to her position, as agreed under the original marriage
agreement signed between King Edward of Wessex and King Charles
of West Frankia."

Even Eadgifu turned to gaze at the monk in surprise at that stipulation. Her marriage to King Charles had brought her great wealth,
and there had been a clause regarding the birth of a healthy heir that
had never been actioned in the past. It would make her an incredibly
wealthy woman if Count Hugh and his allies agreed to it.

A well of silence filled the room, as the monk continued.

"England and West Frankia will agree to a mutual treaty of
support with regards to invasions and will ensure that the two kingdoms never make war against each other, or cause others to raise
their swords in anger against the others. Additionally, West Frankia
will pledge to aid England should she come under attack, and the
same will happen for England and West Frankia."

"England and West Frankia will pledge not to treat with the
enemies of the others, or to profit at the expense of the others, and

English men and women will be as welcome in West Frankia, as the West Frankish will be in England. Trade will be advantageous between the two countries, with fewer tariffs."

Count Arnulf seemed more prepared for these terms, and he nodded, his eyes glassy as he sipped deeply from his goblet of wine. Eadgifu wished she had her own wine to sample, for her lips felt dry, and she was struggling to swallow.

The audacity of King Athelstan's plans both amazed and daunted her.

When her father had met with King Charles' embassy, concerning her own marriage, she'd been a bride of the House of Wessex, but Edward had not been king of the English. Still, the marriage terms had been advantageous to Wessex. Now King Athelstan asked for much more. Even more than when it was agreed that Eadhild should marry Count Hugh, and far, far more than when Athelstan had decided to send Ælfgifu and Eadgyth to East Frankia, on the provision that both sisters be found husbands.

The ambitions of King Athelstan astonished Eadgifu, and yet also filled her with warmth.

Despite everything, King Athelstan wasn't prepared to sell her and her son cheaply. In fact, Eadgifu worried that the demands would prove to be too high and that Count Arnulf would simply refuse. If that happened, would she still feel as valued? She wasn't sure.

The monk sat then, and there was no sound other than the breathing of the inhabitants of the room, and the crackle of the fire, as flames licked along the lengths of the thick wood.

"It seems there is much to discuss," Count Arnulf eventually managed, his eyes turning to sweep over the men who escorted him, settling on the two bishops.

"Indeed, King Athelstan is keen to ensure that as much as possible is agreed beforehand. He does not wish there to be difficulties with precedence and payments, once Prince Louis is King Louis. I believe that there were some small difficulties regarding the marriage agreement between Count Hugh and Countess Eadhild. Such mustn't happen again." Bishop Oda spoke as though he didn't insult Count Hugh, and Eadgifu found her eyes flicking between the two men.

For the first time, she thought that King Athelstan's absence from the negotiating room was probably intentional. Athelstan would never have been able to make such sly remarks, even if he'd thought them. He would have felt it beneath him.

"I can immediately assure King Athelstan that the West Frankish are happy to provide more than half of the cost of ensuring that Prince Louis is restored to West Frankia with all the ceremony and pomp to be expected for a King of West Frankia, and the English King's nephew."

"I'm also empowered to agree to a treaty of mutual benefit between West Frankia and England. It would, would it not, be difficult to imagine a future where the relationship between West Frankia and England were not even closer than it currently is?" Count Arnulf spoke as though the matter was of little importance. Yet, Countess Eadhild's marriage had not brought the desired benefits, and neither had her own wedding to the king. If anything, England had gained from the West Frankish alliances only in small ways.

Bishop Oda once more indicated to his scribe to note down the words of Count Arnulf. Behind him, Eadgifu noticed the West Frankish monks briefly talking, before one of them also quickly began to make notes.

Just how much of this, Eadgifu thought, was genuinely agreed with Count Hugh?

"The matter of the return of Queen Dowager Eadgifu's dower lands will proceed as smoothly as it can. Since the marriage took place, there's been a shifting of the lands held by the West Frankish king. Lotharingia is currently under the command of the East Frankish king."

"Then suitable alternatives would be found for the Queen Dowager? She has been many years without her properties."

"I'm sure that the West Frankish nobility would readily return possessions to Queen Dowager Eadgifu. Her presence has been much missed since she so precipitously returned to Wessex."

Bishop Oda made no reply to that, although Eadgifu felt her cheeks flame at the implied criticism. Had she stayed in West Frankia, she was sure that Louis would not have survived his childhood.

"Then I would bring this first meeting to a close. I'm sure that you, as much as we, have much to discuss and think about. King Athelstan must be appraised of the situation. Do you need the means to send word to Count Hugh and his allies, or do you act with their total assurance?"

"I have a fast ship to communicate with Count Hugh, who is making his way to Bolougne-Sur-Mer, in the hope that a quick agreement will be reached. For now, everything progresses as we expect, other than the fact I should have liked to speak directly with King Athelstan."

"Ah, yes, the king would also like to be involved. He has some other embassies to attend to but expects to appear by the end of the week. I'm instructed to keep him fully appraised, as are Prince Louis and Queen Dowager Eadgifu. Do not think that because King Athelstan is absent, he's not entirely involved with these discussions. Sadly, he's much in demand, and matters of state must sometimes take precedence over the more congenial family reunion taking place here."

Eadgifu startled at the words, delivered so smoothly that no one could doubt the sincerity behind them. Not for the first time that day, she had cause to admire her half-brother's abilities.

"Then, yes, I will bid you a good day, Prince Louis, Queen Dowager Eadgifu. I hope when we speak tomorrow, that we have more agreements than disagreements, and that Prince Louis can begin to plan his return to West Frankia."

At that, everyone in the room stood and bowed or curtsied to each other, before Bishop Oda led the West Frankish delegation from the room. Only when the door had shut, did Eadgifu allow herself to sink back into the chair. Her legs were shaking and her head pulsed with everything she'd heard and watched that day.

Louis sighed deeply at her side.

"That was not what I expected," he mumbled, and Eadgifu held out a hand to grasp Louis' forearm.

"Nor I, but come, let us see what Countess Eadhild has sent to us."

Louis nodded, but first, he drank deeply from a tankard close to hand, and Eadgifu noted that her son drank water, rather than wine, just like his uncle.

Beneath her hands, the parchments promised much, but when she opened them, she was disappointed to find little but bland comments from her sister.

Countess Eadhild had taken the time to write herself, of that Eadgifu was sure, but the words spoke only of family, of her sisters in Wilton nunnery, of her sisters in East Frankia, and of how much she looked forward to seeing Louis once more. Of politics, there was nothing to show what Eadhild thought of her husband's movement to restore Louis to the kingship of West Frankia.

Only then Louis gasped, a smile of delight on his face as he opened the wooden casket that had also been handed to them.

From deep inside the silk-lined casket, Louis pulled out a seax, shimmering in the candlelight. Eadgifu gulped on seeing it, reaching out imperiously to grab the seax from her son's limp fingers.

Louis gave up the seax, while Eadgifu held the blade up to the light, just searching, and checking, and then she smiled, and handed the knife back to her son.

"This was your father's. I gave it to him on your birth. Countess Eadhild has made it clear, by sending this to you, that she means for you to be king, that she approves of these negotiations."

Louis nodded, his eyes filled with reverence, at touching something that had once been his father's.

"We'll ensure that King Athelstan knows that you'll receive a warm welcome to West Frankia when you return. Countess Eadhild might not have managed to rescue your father, but it seems she's keen to have you restored. Perhaps, she has been working for this all these years, just waiting for you to reach manhood. Perhaps I've been wrong to doubt her, as I surely have."

Louis nodded, the sharp blade reflected in his blue eyes.

"Perhaps," he agreed, but then Louis flicked a glance at his mother.

"Or perhaps her hand has been forced. We must be wary mother, always wary."

NOT THAT EADGIFU had long to consider either her sister's message or her son's words before King Athelstan summoned her to his side.

This time, they met outside the archbishop's hall, a hubbub of activity surrounding them all as King Athelstan tended to his horse while holding court within the stables. Eadgifu considered wrinkling her nose at the fragrant aroma but held her tongue. It seemed that Athelstan was indeed busy, and his time was in short supply.

"Sister dearest," King Athelstan greeted her warmly, a kiss for her cheek, that she found unexpected, as she did Athelstan's good cheer.

"Bishop Oda has spoken to me of events today, as has Louis. It seems as though the West Frankish are keen to have Louis restored, although, tell me, what did Countess Eadhild gift to you?"

This surprised Eadgifu as she would have expected Louis to have already informed Athelstan of the contents of the letter.

"A letter, asking after our family, and a gift, for Louis, of a ceremonial seax I once gave King Charles. In fact, I gifted it to him on the birth of Louis."

King Athelstan paused in his actions of brushing down his horse and peered over the animal's back to gaze at Eadgifu.

"What does that signify?" Athelstan mused. Eadgifu paused before replying.

"I had thought it was an assurance that all was well and that Louis would be welcomed, but Louis shows more caution."

"Ah," understanding flashed in Athelstan's eyes as he flicked his gaze to Louis, who stood, as impatient as his uncle, although prepared to meet his scrutiny.

"It seems a strange gift to send?"

"It does, My Lord King. I'm wondering how it came to be in Countess Eadhild's hands. After all, my father would have had it with him when he was imprisoned. Why would it have gone to Countess

Eadhild after his death? Surely, if she had it, she could have sent it to me many years ago. I should have liked to have something that was my father's."

Athelstan still paused in his activity, furrowed his forehead in concentration.

"I've always thought Countess Eadhild free to make allies and alliances as she wanted, but much of what we know about her marriage to Count Hugh may be merely what we are led to believe."

"Certainly, it's a strange gift, and you're right to consider its true meaning. After all, it could be a warning not to consider returning to West Frankia. I would wish to know more about her true position, but it's impossible. Æthelhild and Eadflæd receive bland letters from her, Lady Eadgyth hears little about her, and Lady Ælfgifu rarely writes. I'm curious as to her true position, but it's beyond me, for now."

Eadgifu startled at the revelation of King Athelstan's network of communication from East and West Frankia. She'd not been aware that he kept in such close contact with his other sisters.

"Certainly, I'm wary merely because the gifts sent by Count Hugh and his allies lack the splendour of those they sent when Count Hugh sued for Eadhild's hand in marriage. It worries me that their offer is less honourable than it should be. But, let us see what tomorrow brings."

King Athelstan resumed his brushing of the horse, the animal pliant, no doubt used to Athelstan conducting affairs of state within his stable, and during his grooming.

"I've met with an embassy from King Haakon today. He needs my assistance, and tomorrow, I'll meet with the Abbot of Landevennec about Alain's inheritance. He may be able to tell me what I should know about Countess Eadhild."

With that, Eadgifu assumed they'd been dismissed and turned to leave, only for Athelstan to speak again.

"It would be a wonderful thing to see Haakon secure in Norway, and Alain restored to Brittany and Louis king in West Frankia. With Lady Eadgyth in East Frankia and Lady Ælfgifu in Arles, I would feel assured that all would be well. But I know it's never that simple. But, we will confer again when we all know more."

Eadgifu turned then, sure she should leave only for King Athelstan to speak her name.

"Lady Eadgifu, I would speak with you further, if you have the time?" it was a question, but more a statement and Eadgifu stayed her steps, a smile for Louis, as the other men, Bishop Oda and Ealdorman Ælfwold, left the stables. Only when all their footsteps had trailed away did Athelstan stop his actions, and turn to face Eadgifu.

"I hope you're assured of my resolve to ensure Louis is safe, no matter what happens, and that you have the honours you should always have had, restored to you."

"I am, My Lord King. I'd not expected such thought, I confess it shocked me."

Athelstan's blue eyes were level, as he held his face free from all expression.

"I know these years have been difficult, but Louis needed to be a man to face his enemies. I fear this has come too soon for him, but neither would I squander the chance for him. I'll push as much as I think I should, but I would caution you, I think Louis has the right of it concerning Countess Eadhild. I don't believe she truly sees herself as English anymore. She's become a West Frankish woman, and her concerns are those of her husband's and not her family."

"You do not think she's forced Count Hugh to offer the kingship to Louis?"

"Oh, I do believe that she has, but I also believe that there's more at stake for her than we might realise. If you return to West Frankia, she may be your enemy rather than your ally, and she might try and supplant you in Louis' affection. I think she may be desperate, to keep her husband, and her position as the countess and I think she'll use Louis just as much as her husband will. It's not a situation I'm comfortable with."

Eadgifu held her tongue, trying to decipher the words her half-brother shared with them. Was he, just as much as Countess Eadhild, warning her?

"Then we shouldn't let either of them win?" Eadgifu finally surmised, and Athelstan's normally inscrutable face lit with triumph.

"I'm pleased, sister dearest, that you've learnt a great deal, both in West Frankia and here. Now tell me, how can we ensure that Louis, when he is king, can stand independent from both his aunt, her husband, and even his second cousin? I do not foresee that Count Arnulf will have the concerns of our house at the forefront of his mind. He, too, will be keen to gain from Louis. They all will. Louis will need his own allies, and he'll have to rely on you, as his mother."

Eadgifu met Athelstan's eyes squarely and without flinching as he finally made the point that had been worrying him.

"I'm to be relied on, as always. I brought him to safety. I brought him to my father, but you rescued him, and I am forever, and as much as I wish I weren't, in your debt for your agreement with Count Rollo of Normandy and for putting yourself in such danger. You did it for my son, and I did it for my son. Surprising as it might be, I believe we both want the same thing."

"Good, that is what I expected to hear, Lady Eadgifu, I have, let me assure you, never doubted you. Not once in all these years and despite your unease around me, and distrust of what I hoped to accomplish. But, if we two are aligned, then I am unsure if others of your sisters will see it the same way."

Eadgifu shook her head then, almost incredulous and yet instantly understanding.

"Sometimes our enemy is our friend, and our friend, our enemy."

"I would sooner never have been considered your enemy, but yes, I believe you understand me."

"I do, brother," Eadgifu spoke the familiar with some surprise. "But, also realise that my sisters and I, especially Countess Eadhild, have been far from friends, ever. She has always resented me for being a queen. In the years she's been gone, she's done nothing for me. Or for Louis. But perhaps that's always been part of the plan."

Athelstan's eyes narrowed in thought, and then he sighed his annoyance.

"In England, I know who to watch, who to cajole, and who to

listen to. And who to ignore. Of the kingdoms of the Scots, of Strath-clyde, of Bamburgh, and certainly of the Welsh, I know and under-stand each and every man, even if I wish I didn't."

"But sister, well, sisters are different, and I've been surprised on too many occasions by you all to think I'm an expert. Know only this. You have my support, and Louis has my support, but you must use your wits."

"I'll not be there to interpret everything and offer my own advice. I believe you fully capable, and I believe Louis esteems you enough to listen carefully to all of your advice. But you will have to make this opportunity work for you. I will not have my nephew subjected to the same horrors as his father, and I task you with ensuring that doesn't happen."

Eadgifu nodded, absorbing her brother's commands, and accepting them for what they were.

"I will come if I need to. I'll send my fleet to West Frankia, I'll rescue you and Louis once more, and I'll hold even my cousin to account for any transgressions. Still, all of those actions will take valu-able time to happen."

"At the moment, in the heat of whatever Louis must face, you will have to make decisions, and abide by them, as I do. You'll show him how to rule the unruly West Franks, just as I've shown him how to rule the English and her neighbours."

"Louis could not have had a better teacher than in you." The words brought a lump to Eadgifu's throat, and a single tear laced down her cheek, Athelstan keeping his gaze firmly on her own.

"I'll not let you down," she eventually managed to struggle.

"It's not me you'll be letting down," Athelstan offered, not without understanding. "It is not me," he repeated slowly, ensuring each word was absorbed.

"I understand," Eadgifu spoke proudly, feeling her shoulders straighten, holding her head high.

"It's not an easy task I give you. But you're full worthy of its oner-ousness," Athelstan confirmed. In that sentence, Eadgifu felt as though she understood her brother better than she ever had, in all of their long lives to date.

Kingship was a burden, and so too was queenship.

Eadgifu nodded smartly and made to walk away, aware that the conversation had finally come to an end.

"I wish we could have reached this accord sooner," Athelstan muttered softly, but she didn't turn around to acknowledge that she'd even heard the words.

She couldn't admit, even now, that Athelstan wasn't the only one to think as such.

AD936

E adgifu had not expected to go back to Winchester when all was set in place for Louis' return to West Frankia, but abruptly, she felt the need to revisit there one final time. She had a family she'd never see again if all went well. After the unsettling revelations about Countess Eadhild, she wanted to leave her sisters in their nunnery with a better impression of her.

King Athelstan had suggested that her sisters' journey to visit her in York, but Eadgifu had shaken her head.

"I must pray, a final time, at the tomb of my father, my mother, and my grandfather, and brothers. It's fitting. Athelstan, no matter what happens, I'll never return to England. Of that, I'm sure."

While Louis complained at the delay, and Count Arnulf's face literally curdled at the thought, King Athelstan had surprised Eadgifu by smiling.

"It's only correct that you depart from our family with the requisite good wishes, and with your prayers heard by all. Count Arnulf, have the men of West Frankia ready to meet my nephew at Bolougne Sur Mer from the middle of June."

Count Arnulf had been left with no choice but to agree to the king's order. So Eadgifu found herself leaving York having bid a farewell to a settlement she'd never see again, and had only just come to enjoy, to offer goodbye to a place that had been her home almost all of her life.

She found her sisters at Wilton, both clearly aware of the news of Louis' imminent coronation.

"We thought you would have left," there was no denying the joy on Eadflæd's face when Eadgifu greeted them both outside the nunnery buildings. Unusually, Æthelhild was not so effusive in her greetings, and Eadgifu eyed her with surprise.

"She'd thought you'd gone, and forgotten all about us. Now she's been angry for a month for no reason at all," Eadflæd's explanation was hastily given, and yet it grieved Eadgifu.

"I'm sorry sister, dearest," she apologised, stepping to Æthelhild and holding out her arms to embrace her sister. Æthelhild, all rigid and angry, seemed to deflate at the touch of those arms. A tremor shivered through her body.

"I'm sorry, sister. I couldn't have left without saying goodbye, not one final time."

For a moment, Eadgifu was much younger, a bride about to depart for West Frankia, to meet her older husband, only to catch the mutinous gaze of her younger sister. She and Æthelhild had once been inseparable. It was no longer the same, and yet Eadgifu would miss her staunch support.

"Well, that is good," Æthelhild hiccupped, laughing with embarrassment. Eadflæd joined their small grouping, the three of them walking toward the church under which their mother had been buried.

Linking arms, with Eadflæd on one side, and Æthelhild on the other, Eadgifu ran her eyes from one to the other, noticing the fancy shoes that peeked beneath the robes her two sisters wore. She laughed softly, her eyebrows high with delight.

"Even sisters of the faith must-have footwear," Eadflæd admonished, clearly aware of what amused Eadgifu, and she chuckled even harder.

"Then I'll ensure that I send you a stipend each year to have the most beautiful shoes made for your royal and holy feet." Æthelhild gurgled at the words, whereas Eadflæd looked unsure whether to be pleased or outraged.

"You better make it a large one," Eadflæd finally relented. "I do like my shoes. A great deal."

With that, Eadgifu and her sisters entered the church, all levity leaving their faces as they did so. Now was not the time for giggling and laughter. Now, they would pray together, over their mother's grave, and then, well then it would be time to say goodbye. Eadgifu felt the wrench inside her as she realised what was to be given up, all over again.

She didn't feel the disdain towards her sisters that had propelled her to West Frankia half a lifetime ago. Instead, she knew the pressure she'd be under, and also the difficulties she'd face. No longer the young and beautiful wife of a king who was primarily tolerated rather than revered by his noblemen, those she'd once beguiled with a smile and a small show of favour would take much more to win round.

And more. Eadgifu would be entering an orbit that her sister had current control over, and Countess Eadhild was very much a bland unknown.

Eadgifu tried to block the worries from her mind, to concentrate on her mother, remembering what she had accomplished. Lady Ælfflæd had been a formidable woman, until her husband had cast her aside, blaming her for turning barren even after birthing a bevy of healthy children.

That had turned Ælfflæd against her husband, and against his new wife, and she'd even cautioned the young Eadgifu before she'd left for West Frankia.

Eadgifu replayed that conversation now, considering the advice her mother had given her had not been quite as unperceptive as she'd thought at the time.

Huddled before the fire in Wilton nunnery, despite the balmy weather outside, Lady Ælfflæd had gripped Eadgifu's hand too tightly, the difference between the lined hands of her mother, and her own, smooth ones, making Eadgifu want to snatch her hand back.

Lady Ælfflæd, or Sister Ælfflæd, as she'd been by then, had noticed the movement, and gripped ever tighter.

"Youth is a fickle ally," she'd taunted her daughter. "It gives you much and then month by month, or even day by day, it snatches it all back, takes what it so glibly provided, and leaves you like this, washed up and unwanted. Cast aside by a man who thinks of his dynasty but not his wives. Use your gift well, and quickly, for it will be gone too soon, I assure you."

"And think about this. You're no different from the new queen. I know you call her the bitch-mother. You've been given to an older man, to warm his bed and breed his heirs. The only advantage you have is that you offer your husband the chance of a son. The bitch-mother brought only land and influence and must live with the knowledge that Edward has many sons already, who will succeed after him. There's really no need for more children, but your father has always been a greedy man."

"You take Charles nothing but promise, and you better hope that you live up to his expectations."

"If you do then Charles will be your greatest ally, and will always protect you from others who would sooner you weren't there. I'm sure there is any number of goodly and beautiful West Frankish women who could have made a good wife for Charles. That you have no faction in West Frankia is probably your greatest asset and also your weakness."

Eadgifu had listened, her face growing flushed at all the implied criticisms her mother had levied at her. As if the marriage was of Eadgifu's devising. As if she could have changed anything!

"Make yourself wealthy in your own name, and ensure that you have men and women who'll do anything for you. You can't rely on your father. He'll sacrifice you, as he does now, if he must."

Those words had infuriated Eadgifu, and she'd taken leave of her mother with more anger than she'd ever wished to direct at her. And she'd vowed not to follow her mother's advice. The flush of youth and freedom had made her sure that her own choices would be the right ones.

Eadgifu's mouth soured at the thought. Her mother had been right. Of course, she had, and hadn't Sister Ælfflæd made a point of reminding Eadgifu when she was forced to return to England only a handful of years later.

Eadgifu had never thought to mend the unease that had characterised her relationship with her mother when she'd returned to England. In fact, Eadgifu had actively worked against her mother and had almost been pleased when she'd died. It had made life back at the Wessex court more bearable.

Now though, she felt a stray tear slide down her cheeks. Her mother had tried to advise her well, but her own anger at Edward's treatment of her had made it impossible for any sentence to be uttered that wasn't a snide rejoinder at her father or her half-brother. Eadgifu hoped she was less bitter than her mother had been.

Would she be able to, when she returned to West Frankia advise her son with the wisdom that he needed? She couldn't judge people on their past actions, and yet, equally, she needed to inform her son that Count Heribert wasn't to be trusted. In contrast, Count William might be if he could be won round.

After all, Count William's father had helped to rescue them both, all those years ago.

It was a conundrum, and as Eadgifu left the last prayer in the place of her mother's final resting place, she could only hope that she'd also learn from the lessons of her mother's actions that had so spectacularly failed.

When Eadgifu bid a final goodbye to her sisters, all three of the women were sobbing, and laughing and hugging all at the same time. By the time Eadgifu made her way back to Winchester, she knew she'd done the right thing. Still, it was impossible to deny that it would have been easier had she simply sailed for Bolougne Sur Mer and never looked back.

Now she would carry with her the memories of her sisters weeping, and of that final visit to her mother's grave, and all the thoughts that had filled her mind. It all added to her apprehension at returning to West Frankia.

Eadgifu always thought she would have accepted it as her given right, but the truth was vastly different.

The following day, Louis accompanied her to the New Minster in Winchester, there to pray at the burial place of her father, brothers and her grandfather.

Only her father and grandfather had been kings. Still, Ælfweard had been accorded a royal burial as well, because he'd been elected king, if not lived to have his coronation service. As for Edwin. Edwin had been buried there as an acceptance that he'd shared royal blood, even if he'd been executed for treason.

Louis' opinion of Eadgifu's pilgrimage was tainted with the knowledge of treason.

"King Athelstan should never have allowed Edwin to be buried here. It's wrong," Louis complained, joining his mother in praying before the high altar. The monks had left them to the peace and quiet of the large church, where even the scurrying of rats could be heard through the silence that rang out.

Eadgifu forbore from answering. It had not been her choice, at the time, and yet she knew that had Athelstan not allowed her brother's burial here, she would have been outraged. Only now, facing the prospect that she might be about to enter a treasonous atmosphere in West Frankia, did she have any sympathy for Athelstan.

"As king, it was Athelstan's choice to make," Eadgifu finally stated, when Louis refused to stop his sporadic comments. "As a king, sometimes decisions have to be made based on both more than family, and also on less. Edwin was a king's son. His burial place deserved the honour of that, even if his actions were foolhardy."

Louis's eyes blazed, and yet he held his tongue. Eadgifu returned to her prayers, her mind filled with the memory of when her father had summoned her to his side, to inform her of the marriage agreement.

Her father had not been a severe man, not with his children, or rather, not with his sons. Eadgifu had always felt as though Edward had expected more from his daughters.

"My dear daughter," even now she could hear his rasp, as she settled beside him in the king's hall at Winchester, no thought to speaking to her in private. Indeed, Eadgifu thought, she should have realised what was happening when even the bitch-mother had looked at her with sympathy in her wide eyes, belly swelling with what would be young Eadburh.

"My Lord King, Father," Eadgifu had not been unaware of rumours surrounding her future, or of the embassy that had been sent to Winchester by the West Frankish King. In all honesty, she'd been expecting to hear of her impending marriage, and she'd felt her face flush with pride when her father had bid her settle beside him.

Rough hands had reached out to grip her own, the callouses of battle still evident, for all that Eadgifu knew that Edward often left the fighting to his warriors, and commanded rather than engaged.

"I'm pleased to inform you that terms have been agreed for your marriage to King Charles of West Frankia. He's sent great gifts to me, including many holy tokens, and treasures obtained by the great king, Charlemagne. In return, I've agreed for you to travel to West Frankia, and wear your own crown. You'll become his queen, and you will birth the next generation of West Frankish kings."

Eadgifu had felt her face flush even warmer at the words her father had spoken. Thoughts of the future that awaited her had over-ridden the faint hitch of worry that had made her realise she'd be alone in West Frankia, with only a handful of her own servants to support her.

"King Charles has vowed to have you crowned in Laon, following your marriage. When you birth him a son, he'll further honour you will dower lands and riches with which to keep your own household if you should so choose to do so."

"And what will you gain?" her voice had been tight, determined to know for what her virginity had been sold. Her father had merely smiled, and squeezed her hand tighter.

"It was not a great deal, an alliance of friendship, an assurance of your safety, and the promise that, in time, West Frankish and Wessex policies will become aligned. It's rather what Charles has gained that's important, not what I've gained."

"I have many daughters, and you are my oldest, now that Æthelhild has chosen life in the nunnery with your mother. You'll bring greater legitimacy to King Charles' rule. You are a treasure, and you'll be treated as such."

And yet, while Eadgifu had thought that was all that mattered for her marriage to be a success, her father had failed to adequately protect her. Only twenty household warriors had escorted her to Boulogne Sur Mer, and then on to Laon. Then many of them had returned to Wessex immediately. Not even one of Edward's ealdormen or bishops had made the journey to Boulogne Sur Mer. Neither had her cousins, Adelolf or Arnulf, been instructed to meet her in Boulogne, or even her aunt.

While insisting on a great deal of ceremony, and pomp, Eadgifu had found herself in the days after her marriage alone and despised by Charles' daughters from his first marriage.

She knew that King Athelstan had ensured the future of his sisters far better than her father had ever done, and she also knew that he'd continue to do so.

With a final prayer for her father and grandfather, Eadgifu stood and beat at her dress, ensuring it hung correctly, before taking a last look at the New Minster.

For all the building was magnificent with its high tower, Eadgifu felt a smirk tugging at her lips.

The churches of West Frankia were more ancient, and more richly endowed, and yet, their bishops were often also secular lords. There was not a great deal of sincere devotion in West Frankia. Could she, perhaps, make a name for herself by protecting the church? She sighed. Even with all the negotiations, there were too many unknowns and too much that might never be decided to her favour.

Returning to Winchester palace, Eadgifu was unsurprised to find her step-mother waiting to greet her in the women's hall. The women's hall had long been Eadgifu's domain, only slowly ceding to her step-mother when the number of her sisters had dwindled, leaving her alone.

"Queen Dowager," Eadgifu curtsied, almost pleased that her step-mother had chosen to make her farewells here, and not in public.

"Queen Dowager," her step-mother replied, a wry smirk on her face that the two women must, if precedent was followed, be accorded the same greeting, honour and respect, even between themselves.

"I know we have not been allies," her step-mother began. "But if I can offer you some small piece of advice from my own experiences, it is only this, never consent to remarry. Your power and influence lie in what you've already accomplished, not in what might be achieved with the help of another husband."

Eadgifu, surprised by the unasked-for advice, moved to dismiss the words, and make her way to the waiting table, with its selection of wine, water and ale. Only then she paused and glanced at her step-mother.

Her step-mother had a face that showed only kindness and no sign of duplicitousness.

"Is this what you've learned?" Eadgifu demanded to know.

"It is, yes. I've never wished to remarry, other than on cold nights when my bed requires warming for me, but I know it's a whim. My sons are my future, just as Louis is your future."

Eadgifu paused, unsure why the guidance warmed her, while also chilling her. It seemed that everyone seemed to know better than she did as to what she should do.

"You never truly liked my son," Eadgifu stated, unsure why now was the time to make such a statement.

"Young Louis was a difficult child. Even you failed to control him. Only when Countess Eadhild left Wessex did Louis become a pleasing child."

The criticism, offered without malice, forced Eadgifu to consider the truth of the words.

"It was difficult for Louis, without his father, and in a strange place."

"I'm sure it was," her step-mother had the grace to agree, without mentioning that her own sons, the boys that Louis had terrorised back then, had also had no father.

"It was difficult for me," Eadgifu also admitted, wishing she could take back the words as soon as she's said then, for all her step-mother's face showed no appraisal.

"It will only get more difficult from now on," her step-mother confirmed, her eyes, usually so implacable and hard to read, devoid of all judgement.

"Yes, it will," Eadgifu confirmed, settling in a seat, pouring wine into her goblet, and noticing as she did so that her hand shook, belying her fears.

"Just remember," her step-mother turned back to say, on her way to exciting the women's hall. "You're a woman of Wessex, of England. You're the king's sister. Be like King Athelstan, and allow no one to truly know you. That way, you'll survive."

With that, her step-mother left, the door swinging gently shut on Eadgifu.

Eadgifu drank deeply from her warmed wine, trying to force some heat back into her cold body.

All her adult life, she'd dreamed of returning to West Frankia, first as the king's wife, and then, when that was no longer possible, as the king's mother.

She couldn't help thinking that she'd been wrong to do so.

Her life in Wessex might well be mundane and boring, sidelined by the king and his collection of loyal followers. But perhaps commonplace was to be preferred to the situation she'd find herself in soon.

In England, she knew who her enemies and allies were.

That would not be the case in West Frankia.

AD936 BOULOGNE-SUR-MER, WEST FRANKIA

E adgifu combed the beach before her.

It had been many years since her arrival at the same place, enroute to becoming the wife of King Charles, and fewer since she'd also escaped from the same spot, under cover of a new day.

She could detect that little had changed. In the distance smoke from hearth fires clouded over the settlement, but if she squinted, the tower of the abbey became clear.

Her attention was caught by the mass of people on the beach.

A small ship had been sent on before them, to alert those waiting to receive their young King that he was coming. Although King Athelstan had provided members of his household troop to escort them, it still came as a nasty shock to see that an equally imposing wall of flickering iron behind the nobility who'd come to receive their King.

It seemed that King Athelstan was not the only one concerned that the diplomatic accession of Louis to the kingdom of West Frankia might not be peaceful after all.

Eadgifu flicked a quick glance toward Louis.

He was too young to remember what West Frankia was like, and now his young face shone with excitement. Louis had clearly not yet seen the greeting party. But the man who led the household troop evidently had. Beornstan, the man who'd ridden through the night with her all those years ago, was now a much older man and highly respected by his warriors.

Eadgifu was pleased she'd been able to convince the King to release him to her. It had felt only right that he be involved in returning the exiles to West Frankia.

Quickly, Beornstan walked amongst the warriors on the royal ship, calling them to attention. Then he signalled to the surrounding six ships, spread out like a fan behind Louis' ship, that the men needed to be alert and armed.

Louis was oblivious of the activity until Beornstan spoke softly in his ear. Louis startled, his eyes finally lowering, to look at the immediate view before him, as opposed to the tantalising glimpse of further inland.

For one brief moment, Louis wind-roughened face paled, only then he checked his own weapons belt, and seemingly reassured by the sharpened seax his uncle had gifted him, Louis determined to look unconcerned.

Eadgifu wished she had the same to grip tightly, but then smoothed the worries from her face.

She'd been an exile for thirteen years. A guest at King Athelstan's court, often an unwanted one, throughout that time. If returning to West Frankia meant her death, then she could accept it. Better to die in the land of her marriage, than the one of her birth.

Only then, Eadgifu noticed, from beneath the gathering of flickering banners and tents, that a small collection of people had moved forward, away from the warriors. This, she assumed, would be the welcoming committee of her sister's husband. Eadgifu sought her sister amongst those few people but gave up. The ship was too far from shore, and everyone was merely a mass of colour. Her eyes had never been sharp.

The ship's captain called out a stringent order in his loud voice, and immediately, some of the oars were dragged on board, and the sail furled.

There was a small bay, cut into a rocky alcove, and it was toward that the ship headed. Eadgifu looked back at the sandier beach, trying to determine why the welcome committee waited there. Only then did she remember that the small harbour would give them no room.

Eadgifu watched as two of the English King's ships off-loaded their contingent of household warriors. They streamed out to line the path that would take her and Louis to receive the submission of Count Hugh, Count Heribert, Count Arnulf and Count William of Aquitaine.

She shivered with impatience, already believing she could taste the more pleasing air of West Frankia, as opposed to the damper stench of Wessex.

With a gentle thud, her ship docked. While ropes were thrown to secure the vessel, she waited impatiently to be helped to dry land, the splash of the water touching the stone harbour, seeming to call to her. Beornstan issued yet more instructions, his voice raised above the commotion of the activity onboard the ship as it birthed.

Just out to sea, the remaining four ships that had escorted Louis home disembarked those of their passengers who were the honour guard. The men seemed not to notice as water splashed over their knees with the swell of the tide.

Eadgifu shivered. She knew the water wouldn't be warm, even in June.

But then she had no time to think of the household warriors rusting their precious weapons in the salty water, for she'd disembarked onto the rough stone, and Count Hugh was before her.

When Eadgifu had left West Frankia, Hugh had been little older than her son was now. While she could detect the youth he had been in his bright green eyes, and broad forehead, much of him was changed.

Taking to his knee, sweeping his cloak behind him, Count Hugh greeted her and Louis. He appeared oblivious to the water that stained the stone with the influx of the tide.

A tight smile of triumph touched Eadgifu's lips at seeing Count Hugh so deferential before her.

Count Hugh's father had stolen West Frankia from her husband. But now those people who'd once supported Robert, and then after his death at the Battle of Soissons, Rodolphus, would not transfer their allegiance to Hugh. They would not make Hugh king, and so he must make her son king instead.

"My Lord King," Count Hugh's voice held the timbre of age and wisdom, but it also oozed with the charm of a seasoned courtier. Eadgifu felt her smile waver just a little.

"My Lord," Louis spoke brazenly. Eadgifu was aware that her half-brother had offered Louis a great deal of advice on how to greet his new subjects. "You may stand." The small space was rapidly becoming too cramped.

"Come, My Lord King, and Queen Dowager," Eadgifu felt Count Hugh's eyes on her, and a jolt seemed to pass through his body. That surprised her, but now was not the time to consider the implications.

"There are many who would immediately pledge their allegiance to you today. I assure you that West Frankia and her nobility are keen to welcome you as King."

Louis bowed his head in response to Hugh's words, and turning to Eadgifu, reached out his arm to escort her. This too was something that King Athelstan had insisted on. Eadgifu was pleased her son had listened so well because faced with being home once more, she was feeling overwhelmed.

Behind the small procession, headed by Beornstan, wearing his battle gear, Count Hugh led the way to the vast expanse of the beach, the sand bright beneath Eadgifu's feet. It made it difficult to walk with dignity, as it was so soft, the sea clearly not reaching so far up the beach for some time.

The collection of men and women before Louis, Eadgifu quickly tallied there were between fifty and a hundred of them, had all taken to their knee, or had dropped into a deep curtsey.

The joy of the moment thrilled through her body allowing her to stand taller, and walk over the sand without impediment.

All these years she'd dreamed of this moment, and now it was before her.

Louis was regal at her side. As soon as Count Hugh was reunited with the rest of the nobility, he dropped to his knee once more, while the English warriors formed a loose semi-circle around the gathering. In front of her, Eadgifu could see that the number of armed men of West Frankia numbered the same as the English men, as had been agreed.

All seemed to be progressing as the West Frankish ambassador had led King Athelstan to believe, but still, Eadgifu had not yet seen her sister. She needed to, to see the reassurance, or not, in her eyes.

Silence filled the air, unbroken only by the soft sound of hands clutching seaxs. Everyone waited while Eadgifu worried that Louis might have forgotten that he was to be the one to speak first.

"My Lords and Ladies," finally Louis' voice rose, heard by all provided they listened hard enough above the sound of the waves, and the gentle breeze.

"Please rise," Louis continued. The silence remained but was supplemented by the shuffle of men and women struggling to stand on the traitorous sand.

Only then did Eadgifu meet the eyes of Countess Eadhild, in the front row of attendees. What she saw there made her gasp before she could stop the sound escaping. Eadgifu could only describe Eadhild as haunted. Her face was drawn, her eyes shadowed by purple blotches, and her body so thin that there was no resemblance of the young woman she'd once pressed mint leaves on before taking ship to West Frankia.

Yet Eadhild's eyes also showed challenge, so much so that Eadgifu was forced to look away, and focus instead on her son. Louis was steadfastly being introduced to the men and women who'd come to pledge their allegiance.

Most notable, other than Count Hugh was the Archbishop of Laon, Artoldus, who would carry out the coronation ceremony in only a few days.

As he bowed to Louis, Eadgifu could see Bishop Oda eyeing up the large prelate, with his surfeit of luxurious robes, and priests hovering close to him. This then was not a man who thought himself unimportant. Eadgifu stored the information away. She might need it for later use.

Yet, while she watched Louis speak to each and every member of the party who had elected him to the kingdom of West Frankia, her mind returned time and time again to Eadhild

No, they'd not been close as children, and indeed, Eadgifu could admit that she blamed her sister for failing to bring about the release of her husband before his death. Yet, Eadhild's rare letters had never caused Eadgifu to fear for her sister's health. She'd assumed that her sister was content as Count Hugh's wife, even if she'd still never managed to give birth to a child. The gift Countess Eadhild had sent to Louis, and Louis and Athelstan's interpretation of its' meaning had made her wary.

It seemed there was much Eadgifu needed to learn, but knew that here was not the time

While Louis was not yet crowned as King, he'd been led to an elaborate chair, under one of the canvasses. He now took the acclaim of his loyal followers, while Eadgifu stood slightly to the side of him, her hand resting on the arm of the wooden chair. To the side of him, in a somewhat more deferential position stood Count Hugh. Eadgifu's lips pursed at the sight of him laying such a claim to his nephew. Yet she kept her expression blank. She focused instead on trying to remember who everyone was and seeking out any faces she'd known when the queen of West Frankia.

Eadgifu was unsurprised by how many new faces she saw. Much had happened in West Frankia in her absence. She was aware that there had been war and attrition between the more powerful noble families. Eadgifu was not unappreciative that Hugh's adoption of her son as King was a way for him to rule following the death of the previous king, his brother by marriage.

The fact that Count Heribert was also prepared to welcome Louis as the King of West Frankia highlighted just how difficult Count Hugh's position had become.

When it was the time for Count Heribert, grown old and fat, to present himself to Louis, Eadgifu felt the joyful moment turn to ash.

Count Heribert had taken her husband from her, deprived Louis of ever having a father, and still the old man smirked as he took to his knee before Louis.

Eadgifu held her face tight. She didn't want Heribert to know her true hatred toward him, but as Count Heribert turned and backed away from Louis, she realised that her breath had been held. Louis turned to her, his eyes full of understanding, for all neither of them spoke.

But, as much as she despised Count Heribert, it was Eadhild's appearance that sent a dagger into Eadgifu's heart. She'd never been one to have any sympathy for her sister and the marriage she'd consented to, despite Eadgifu's advice. For all that Eadgifu had looked forward a triumphant return ever since forced into exile, now her thoughts were consumed by worry for Eadhild.

The welcome ceremony was long, and uncomfortable after their sea voyage, and it was with a great deal of relief that the receiving committee finally moved aside and made way for their new King, and his mother to venture into Bolougne-Sur-Mer itself. Still flanked by Beornstan and his warriors, and with the West Frankish men as well, Eadgifu imagined the procession was a powerful statement of intent for those who'd come to see witness Louis' arrival.

Eadgifu was surprised by just how many called greetings to her son, waving their arms over their heads as they rode to the largest building in the vicinity, in which Count Hugh had informed them, a large feast had been arranged in their honour.

Inside the hall, huge boards had been lain out for her son and his new nobility. Count Hugh personally escorted Louis to the front of the room with much pomp and ceremony. Eadgifu watched on, her heart almost bursting with pride at the way Louis was comporting himself. Only when she was seated, did she turn to find Countess Eadhild already seated there.

"Are you well?" Eadgifu whispered beneath her hand, turning as though she simply checked her dress lay correctly while she sat.

"All is good. Why?" the whip-sharp hasp of Eadhild's voice

surprised Eadgifu so much that she turned and openly stared, immediately unsure how to proceed.

"I had not expected to find you so," frantically Eadgifu fought for a word that would not cause too much upset. "Changed," she eventually managed.

"I'm still the woman you grew up with," Eadhild snorted, her eyes looking anywhere but at her sister. "And you should know, Count Hugh is not an easy man to be the wife of, and events in West Frankia are far more complicated than you could possibly imagine. I'd suggest you take the time to learn more before you jump to any conclusions."

The words were delivered sharply, and Eadgifu picked up her wine goblet and drank deeply while she fought for composure.

No, she and Eadhild had never been the best of allies.

"Your son has grown into an attractive young man," Countess Eadhild mumbled, her hands resting on the back of a hound. Eadgifu had noted the creature earlier. There was no denying the animal was a descendant of the animal Eadhild had left young Louis when she'd married.

Eadgifu wished she could take it as a sign of Countess Eadhild's unwavering support for her son. Louis had sent the animal to his aunt a few years after her marriage. But, for all Eadgifu hoped it was a positive sign, she couldn't help worrying that it was just a hound, much favoured by her sister, but nothing else.

"I can see much of our father in him." Eadgifu nodded distractedly at Eadhild's comment. She could see Charles in her son, and also a trace of King Athelstan, but she was beginning to think that owed more to Louis' adopted mannerisms, that so closely mirrored Athelstan's. Certainly, she detected little or no trace of her father in him.

Before more could be said, the Archbishop stood and blessed the coming feast, and then Count Hugh replaced him, a beaming grin on his face as he addressed his new King, and those assembled within the hall.

"Today we welcome our King back to West Frankia. He was little more than a babe in arms when he left these shores. Now we receive him back as our King." The words were greeted with a roar of acclaim, and even Eadgifu couldn't keep the smile from her face, as the assembly toasted her son.

Yes, these men and women had forced her husband into captivity, wavering so much that the attempts to rescue Charles had fallen to nothing. But they had seen the errors of their ways. Or so she hoped.

Eadgifu looked for Count Heribert amongst the audience, to gauge his reaction, but first, she caught a glimpse of Count Arnulf, his expression pensive as he gazed at Louis.

"These people are not your allies," Countess Eadhild used the thunderous rapture to speak loudly into Eadgifu's ears.

"No one is here because they genuinely believe your son should be King. Perhaps not even me."

With a gasp of shock, Eadgifu's head swung violently to gaze at her sister, but Countess Eadhild had turned away, her hand resting on her flat stomach, her body tense, and for all that Eadgifu wished to demand an explanation from her sister, she hesitated.

Now was not the time. She knew that. Even if her sister didn't.

AD936, 19TH JUNE, LAON

E adgifu straightened her dress once more, wishing she'd chosen a lighter fabric for her son's coronation.

It had been a handful of days since their arrival on the beach at Boulogne-Sur-Mer. All of them had been spent either on horseback, making their way through her son's new kingdom, or sitting and enduring feasts held in Louis' honour by the local nobility. Eadgifu had not appreciated how many of them there would be.

While Eadgifu felt drained from the constant activity, she knew that Louis was revelling in it all, as was Count Hugh. He and Louis were barely apart, and Eadgifu couldn't help but feel a spike of jealousy, although, she knew her son had to convince Count Hugh that he was malleable.

The only moment of quiet she'd had, was when she and Louis had visited the grave site of King Charles, at the monastery of Saint-Fursy in Peronne.

It had been a sombre experience, for all Eadgifu had not cried. Charles' death seemed so long ago, and she had grieved at the time. Now, her concern was with the small grave he'd been accorded, and the lack of stonework to mark it.

Louis had assured her, his voice hushed in respect for a man he had no recollection of, that he would immediately order a new grave-stone, and endow the monastery in honour of his father.

On Charles' death, Eadgifu had sent money to the monastery. But it seemed it had not been enough, and in the intervening years, she'd not even thought to send more. She berated herself for the terrible oversight.

The abbot, deferential in his dealing with the Queen Dowager, had informed her that it had been Charles' children who had paid for the stone work Charles' grave did have, and had made some bequests to the monastery in aid of their father's soul.

Eadgifu had been touched, and also furious that Count Heribert had thought such a burial fitting for a King of West Frankia.

Eadgifu had been unable to speak with Eadhild since the welcome feast. Whenever Eadgifu saw her, Eadhild was close to her husband, a beautific look on her thin face. It seemed that despite the caution she'd offered, Eadhild was keen to see Louis, speak with Louis, and generally treat Louis as though he were her son, not her nephew.

Eadgifu often felt excluded, but had known this would happen. She needed to wait until Louis wore his crown before she demanded more.

Eadgifu fidgeted once more, wishing her head pounded less severely. It felt as though she'd been waiting for her son's arrival at the magnificent Abbey of Notre-Dame and Saint-Jean for more than half the day. Eadgifu was keen to have the ceremony concluded, to have her son wearing the imperial crown. Then, as an anointed king, Louis would be able to begin making his own allies and becoming less reliant on Count Hugh.

Eadgifu was not the only one within the vast structure, with its colossal stone pillars rising to disappear into the vastness of shadow.

Louis had been baptised here. It had been a joyous occasion, her husband accompanied by all of his loyal supporters. She shook her head to think of the treachery that had befallen him so soon afterwards.

Trying to find some semblance of serenity, Eadgifu settled herself, wishing she could close her eyes. Instead, she focused on the stunning altar before her.

Just as the abbey building itself, the altar was a statement of wealth and control. So much gold and silver shimmered from its surface, that should daylight ever seep so far inside the cavernous space it would be blinding.

Five fat candles on golden platters illuminated the surface, and along the top, Eadgifu could see priceless holy books.

Little had changed here in her absence. In fact, it could easily have been sixteen years ago.

A touch on her arm and Eadgifu startled. She'd become too engrossed in her own thoughts. Staring around, she met the gaze of Bishop Oda. His face, usually so difficult to read, appeared to be as overawed as her own, and she laughed softly.

"It is a magnificent building," Eadgifu confirmed.

"It is. I fear I'll have much to think about when I return to England."

Eadgifu startled at the realisation that she'd not always have the support of Bishop Oda. Bishop Oda had proved his worth, many times over in the last few days. King Athelstan was lucky to have such an intelligent man at his side. Oda's unique heritage allowed him to easily navigate any divide between the English and the Vikings. It would be a useful skill to possess in West Frankia where the Norsemen had settled and seemed determined to stay.

"What's causing the delay?" Eadgifu asked, assuming that this must be why Bishop Oda had sought her out.

"Ah, yes. Count Hugh is keen to ensure that everything runs smoothly. He's making the Archbishop run through the ceremony with him. And in the meantime, your sister is praying in one of the side chapels. She asked me to escort you to her."

It was a strange request, but Eadgifu nodded and stood. Her legs were numb from sitting so long, and she could feel the eyes of too many people watching her. As in Bolougne-Sur-Mer, there were faces she recognised, and also many new ones. Of those she did remember, not one was as it had been. Everyone had aged. Some imperceptibly, but others in vast swathes, sharp jawlines replaced by double chins, and eyebrows no longer neat and tidy but wild and lined with grey.

Of the women, all had rounder waistlines, thinner hair, and lips that pursed whether they wanted them to or not. Not all the jewels, or sumptuous velvets and silks in West Frankia could hide the fact. Eadgifu smoothed her own gown once more, her head high.

Having birthed no more children, Eadgifu knew she retained her youthful slenderness. If nothing else, it allowed her to feel a little superior. She might only have one son, but she had no need to hide her shape under swathes and swatches of cloth.

Bishop Oda led her to the side of the church, and in the gleam of at least a hundred candles, Eadgifu spotted a hunched figure.

With a soft thank you to Bishop Oda, she stepped forward, joining her sister in the chapel dedicated to Christ's mother.

"Sister," Eadgifu spoke quietly, not wishing to startle her sister.

Icy hands reached out and clasped her own, the tremor through them impossible to ignore.

"Please, will you walk with me to our seats at the front of the church. I meant to send word and then forgot to. This ceremony is all-consuming." The voice had lost the sharpness of their earlier meeting, and for a moment, as Countess Eadhild raised her tear-streaked face, Eadgifu thought she faced her mother, not her sister. What was this?

"Naturally, we should walk together. Will your husband not escort you?"

"The Count is accompanying young Louis as his standard-bearer."

Of course, Eadgifu thought, Count Hugh was overly keen to be closely associated with the new king.

"For Count Hugh, it is as though he crowns his son, here, today. I've worked for many years to bring this about. The death of Hugh's brother by marriage made it easier, but not inevitable."

Eadgifu listened carefully, keen to know what else her sister might divulge to her.

"I've never quickened with a child. I can never give Count Hugh the son he needs, but I have ensured he sees Louis not as the child of Charles but as a child of my family."

"Count Hugh is a proud man, from a family who've been kings for many years. But he'll not put me aside to ensure he has an heir. Despite my lack." The words were spoken with such pain, that despite it all, Eadgifu found a tear forming.

To hear her sister speak in such a way punctured Eadgifu's hard exterior.

"I know it's my fault, but still Count Hugh won't allow me to retire to a nunnery, and so I've done what I should have done when I first married him. I've forced my husband to recognise the royal line of Charles. But I warn you, Count Hugh is ambitious. He'll still use Louis, just as he would have done his own son."

Eadgifu nodded, her thoughts swirling from the revelation of her sister's trials to that of political influence. It was an awkward conversation to keep track of.

"I've not been alone either. Lady Eadgyth has ensured King Henry supports Louis' election as well."

Was it truly possible that her sisters, and her half-brother, had laboured for so long to restore Louis' kingdom? All of them were people she had at one point or another hated for their perceived failures. Could she have been so wrong about them all?

"I've tried everything to have a child for my husband. Now I've been warned that I've damaged myself. I'll never recover, but in time, I hope I'll be a great-aunt, and hold Louis' son safe in my arms. I know I'll see much of myself in him." The tone was wheedling and needy, and Eadgifu immediately realised that this was not so much a request as a prayer. Had Eadhild cause to fear her life was coming to an end? Was she truly more ill than Eadgifu had surmised?

The thought horrified Eadgifu. Her sister was so young to be thinking about her death.

"Then, we shall have to see about a wife for my son," Eadgifu tried to smile at the words although she couldn't imagine her son as the father of anyone. He was far too young, with a great deal to learn.

"All kings must have heirs," Countess Eadhild chastised, as though reading Eadgifu's thoughts. Eadgifu bowed her head low, the better to hide her true feelings on the subject.

"My ladies," the cajoling voice of Bishop Oda wrenched Eadgifu from her sister's deepest hopes and fears. "It is time. All is ready now."

Eadgifu stood fluidly but held out her hands to help her sister. Countess Eadhild felt frail, her hands still trembling. For a moment, rage sparked. What had her sister done to herself, for surely she should not be so weak and hollow when she was younger than Eadgifu?

But, with a glance at the soft glow on her sister's face, Eadgifu held her tongue.

Whatever Eadhild had done, it had led to this moment, and Eadgifu was determined to enjoy it.

They were barely in their seats when the Archbishop made his way to the front of the church. Eadgifu observed everything. Knowing Edwin, and his constant need to try and circumnavigate around any of the formal ceremonies that had underpinned her half-brother's kingship, Eadgifu was determined to ensure that everything happened as it should. The service to make her son king would be binding on all.

From this moment onwards, there would be no one able to say that her son was not the rightful king of West Frankia, even if they wished they could.

Beside her, Countess Eadhild continued to shake, and Eadgifu wished she understood her sister better but hoped there would be time for that in the future.

And, in some ways, it was reassuring to know that she was not the only one to sob as Louis was proclaimed king. He accepted the acclaim of his new subjects, attired in cloth of gold that had cost the same as ten warhorses, with jewels that weighed almost the same.

Louis sought her out with a steely look in his eye, but Eadgifu knew her son well. He might well be festooned with the accoutrements of kingship, crown, sceptre, rod, ring and sword, but beneath all that, he was her son. Eadgifu could see the emotion coursing through his young body at finally realising his birthright.

Louis had no memory of his father. Still, inevitably, Louis would be thinking of Charles. Of all his failures. And of his successes that had allowed him to rule West Frankia for two decades before his imprisonment.

Eadgifu felt her lower lip tremble, tears threatening to spill afresh from her eyes. When a fragile hand gripped her own, Eadgifu didn't even flinch.

It seemed the moment meant just as much for Countess Eadhild as it did for her.

For the first time ever, she felt genuinely united with her younger sister.

It had been too long in coming, but as Eadgifu watched the men and women of West Frankia bow to her son, and once more pledge their allegiance to him in a formal setting, she vowed to make more of an effort with Eadhild.

They'd wasted too much time already.

THE CEREMONY WAS LONG, and Eadgifu was sure that others would have found it tedious, but when it was over, King Louis was escorted from the church before all of his noblemen and women, preceded by his holy men, led by Archbishop Artoldus.

Eadgifu found the return to normality jarring. The demands of a body denied food and wine for too long made her shake, as her sister struggled to stand.

Immediately, a tall man leapt to their assistance. Gasping in shock, Eadgifu looked into the eyes of a man who could only be her husband's son.

"Rorice?" disbelief coloured her voice at the man of God who stood before her.

"My Ladies." Bishop Rorice's voice thrummed with the same textures as his father, and Eadgifu felt the room swirl around her.

"You're kind to remain behind, Bishop Rorice."

Rorice bowed again, a sombre expression on his face.

"There will be a crush outside. I thought to remain behind, and offer prayers for my half-brother to have a long reign."

Eadgifu was still struggling to find words to greet the man before her. She'd only met Rorice on a handful of occasions during her marriage. Rorice had been raised in a monastery, always destined for a life in the church.

Seeing him before her now was disorientating. When she'd thought of Rorice, on those few occasions that she had, it had always been as the youth he'd been, all gangly legs and too long chin. Now he was a well-spoken man, a hint of steel in his eyes.

Bishop Rorice courteously held out his arm for Countess Eadhild and she slipped her arm through it. It had been a long ceremony. The candles on the altar had burnt almost to nothingness, and Eadgifu felt dizzy from thirst and hunger, or so she convinced herself.

Together their small party, accompanied by a few other lingerers, made it outside, where the bright summer day was only just beginning to hint of a cooler evening to come.

The square outside the church was thronged with men and women in their finery. To the far corner, King Louis was making himself known to the men and women he now ruled as king, by distributing a unique coin struck to mark the occasion, alongside bread, to the people of Laon.

Eadgifu's eyes lingered over him, noting that his English household warriors were firm in keeping back the throng, while also ensuring the king could freely mingle with many of those come to see their new ruler.

Count Hugh stood to the side, keeping a close eye on proceedings, but Countess Eadhild and Bishop Rorice had already turned away, making their way toward the hall where the coronation feast was to take place.

Inside, Eadgifu knew that long tables had been set out, piled with fruits and gold and silver goblets, just waiting to be filled with fine wine or ale. But she directed her steps to a huge awning that had been erected just in front of the hall.

It seemed she wasn't alone in wanting to breathe some fresh air after the time spent in the church, for there were many men and women already there.

Eadgifu paused, just watching her sister for a moment, as she made her way into the hall.

Countess Eadhild seemed aged beyond all reasonable expectations, the reality even more telling under the light of the sun, rather than in the flicker of candles.

A touch on her arm and Eadgifu turned to face a woman she recognised only by the intelligent eyes that peered through the mass of golden hair that suffused her head.

"Hildegarde," Eadgifu gasped the name. She'd never been close to the daughters from her husband's first marriage, but Hildegarde, as the youngest of the girls, had yet to be married when Charles and Eadgifu had first wed.

"My Lady Mother," the title sounded old and unused on Hildegarde's tongue. Eadgifu ignored the hitch in the words, throwing her arms wide to embrace the woman she'd known as a young girl so many years ago.

In a crush of fine cloth and silks, Eadgifu inhaled the scent of exotic spices that Hildegarde used to perfume her hair. She fought to remember all she could of what had happened to Hildegarde in the intervening years.

As they stepped apart, Hildegarde sniffed delicately, just the trace of tears in her left eye.

"The king looks so like my father. I confess. I didn't expect that."

Eadgifu paused in her flurry of questions, allowing the younger woman the time to compose herself, as wine was brought to them by an attentive man she thought must be Hildegarde's husband. Eadgifu sipped deeply from the river cold wine. It was refreshingly tart.

"I'm so used to seeing Louis every day that I forget that for those who've not seen him grow to be a man, it might be a shock."

"I just hope he's learned how to be king from King Athelstan and not from his father. He'll need to be firm to deal with the rebellious nobles. There's still unease about Normandy and the other Norsemen who've settled in West Frankia. And of course, Lotharingia is always disputed."

Eadgifu heard the sadness in Hildegarde's voice. Had Hildegarde lost someone in the near-constant unease? Rather than speak and make a fool of herself, Eadgifu focused on the mention of King Athelstan.

"King Athelstan claimed the king as not just his nephew, but also his foster-son. He saw to his education, and of course, King Athelstan rules a united kingdom, where the Norsemen have both been accepted, as in the Danelaw, but also expelled, as in the Kingdom of York."

Hildegarde nodded, finally sipping her own wine. Eadgifu hadn't expected to have to comfort her, but then, Louis becoming king was a significant change for many people.

"I'm pleased to see you are well and overjoyed that my half-brother is now King of West Frankia. I'd like to meet with him, and know the man he is becoming."

"Of course. I'll see it arranged," Eadgifu assured, wanting to reach out and wipe away the troubled expression that covered Hildegarde's face.

"I would also warn him, of Count Hugh." Hildegarde's voice abruptly burned with rage. "I'll await a summons from my brother," and so spoken, Hildegarde curtsied and walked away, her shoulders rigid, her hair bouncing with each sharp step, her husband rushing to catch up.

Eadgifu felt her mouth open in shock and quickly snapped it shut again. What would those who'd been watching her make of the brief interaction between her and her husband's daughter? It hardly comforted to know that another wished to warn her son about Count Hugh.

Hastily, Eadgifu made her way to Countess Eadhild's side. Bishop Rorice remained in attendance upon her while several women fussed around Countess Eadhild. They made way for Eadgifu in a rustle of silk and linen, as they saw her approach.

Eadgifu inclined her head to all of them, sweeping a glance over them, but recognising none of them.

"Come, sister, sit, and I'll introduce you to the women of the court. This is Lady Judith, Count Hugh's niece."

Eadgifu looked into a smooth face, eyes glacial, skin pale. Count Hugh's relative, and niece, made her the daughter of the previous king.

Count Hugh was related to all of the great houses of West Frankia. His sister was married to Count Heribert, while his other sister had been queen after Eadgifu.

Eadgifu curtsied politely to the younger woman. She was little older than Louis, and already Eadgifu wished to be kind to her. But it seemed the young woman didn't feel the same. Her reciprocated curtsey was little more than a quick bob up and down, and Eadgifu heard Countess Eadhild's soft tutt of annoyance.

"Now my dear," Eadhild admonished softly, "we did discuss this, and you promised to be polite and deferential."

Fury swept across Judith's face, and yet it quickly smoothed.

"Apologies, dear aunt."

As though the initial greeting had never taken place, Judith swept into a deep curtsey, her eyes downcast so that Eadgifu had no idea of Judith's true thoughts.

"Better, my dear," was Judith's reward from Countess Eadhild, before she turned her attention to another of the women.

"And this is Adele of Vermandois, she is the wife of Arnulf, Count of Flanders." Count Heribert's children seemed determined to intrude on her enjoyment of the day..

"My Lady," Adele's voice was soft and warm, reflecting the heat of the June day. "It would seem that my small children are related to yourself and your son. As such, I think we should call ourselves family, as I do Countess Eadhild."

"It's good to make your acquaintance," Eadgifu confirmed, seeing a youthful face, filled with the joy of youth and motherhood, and tried not to notice that she shared her father's shifty eyes.

Only then a rougher voice joined their conversation, and Eadgifu felt her entire body stiffen.

For the last week, she'd tried to avoid Count Heribert. She had no true idea what to say to him, but it seemed, she would now have to think on her feet.

Countess Eadhild sent her a swift look of sympathy, and then Count Heribert stood before her.

His face glistened in the heat of the day, but other than that, he seemed entirely at ease.

"Queen Dowager," his bow was smart, as he then turned to Countess Eadhild and bowed once more.

"A fine ceremony," Count Heribert continued, his daughter coming to slip her arm through his. Eadgifu stumbled for the right words.

"Bishop Oda spent much time with Archbishop Artoldus ensuring the words of the ceremony were as close to that of King Athelstan's as possible." Athelstan's coronation ceremony had been truly magnificent, the words written by Archbishop Athelm ensuring that Athelstan's claims could never be brought into doubt.

For a moment, Count Heribert seemed lost for words.

"It's always wise for a king to have a ceremony that raises him above his fellow nobility. A divinely appointed individual is above reproach by those he rules over." Eadgifu hardly knew where the words came from or why she spoke them. The reproach of Count Heribert was far too openly spoken. Where had all her political acumen gone?

Yet, Eadgifu felt some small triumph as Count Heribert's eyes opened wide at the criticism. Charles should never have been imprisoned, not when he too had been touched by the holy oil.

A stunned silence filled the space but Eadgifu held Count Heribert's eyes with her own.

She'd never liked the man, even before his actions against Charles.

"A divinely appointed king can lose his kingship through defeat in battle," Count Heribert smirked, as though that explained the past.

"Indeed, he can," Eadgifu confirmed. "But as Charles won the Battle of Soissons, that was not the case."

Count Heribert's eyes filled with sudden fury, and Eadgifu fully expected Countess Eadhild to step in and smooth the matter over. Her silence was telling.

The atmosphere turned heavy, Eadgifu refusing to retract her words, while Count Heribert seemed perplexed.

Before more words could be exchanged, a hush in conversation alerted Eadgifu to the arrival of the king.

While the assembled were quiet, Eadgifu heard a man's voice raised high with amusement, and a lighter tone, that of her son. A spark of jealousy flattened her lips with displeasure.

Count Hugh, Count Heribert. Both men, she knew, were lethal to her son's chances of ruling well.

A light hand touched her arm, and Eadgifu turned to see Countess Eadhild cautioning her.

Eadgifu placed her hand over her sister's with a squeeze of reassurance to guarantee that all was well.

With the warnings about Count Hugh coming from two different people, including his own wife, Eadgifu didn't want her son to form a close bond with the powerful nobleman. She hoped Louis was mature enough to see beyond the honeyed words Count Hugh used.

Eadgifu sighed softly, determined not to allow her worries to spoil the pageantry of her son's coronation, for all being forced to speak to Count Heribert had dampened her happiness.

She had a celebratory feast to attend, and a week of celebrations.

Only time would tell what happened next.

AD936, SUMMER

Eadgifu was restless. A huge rainstorm had struck the night before, and outside everything was sodden and redolent with the unique tang of summer rain.

She wanted to be outside, but King Louis was soon to call together his nobility for a great meeting. Eadgifu intended on being included in it, even if she had to sneak into the room set aside for the unruly West Frankish lords.

They remained in Laon, and the meeting was to be held within the king's hall there. Countess Eadhild had advised her not to get involved, her voice rich with understanding, but since her son's coronation, two weeks before, too much had been agreed without recourse to Eadgifu. Enough was enough.

With the outcome of each meeting, Eadgifu found Count Hugh to be more overbearing, too self-important. Nothing would drag him away from Louis' side unless it was his wife.

Eadgifu was beginning to appreciate that Countess Eadhild was a skilled manipulator of her husband, but even then, there was only so much she could accomplish.

As Eadgifu paced, a messenger arrived within the great hall, eyes wide in the vast expanse of the space, his face pensive. It was evident he was looking for someone, and Eadgifu was astonished when the man strode to her. His gait was confident, and unlike most messengers she'd ever encountered, he'd bothered to wash and straighten his hair before delivering his burden.

"Queen Dowager Eadgifu," he stood smartly before her, his head bowed reverently.

"My lord?" she used the honorific because there was just something about him that made her consider that he might well be a lord or a count.

A tight smile stretched the man's face.

"Unfortunately no, but I come with a message that I've been instructed to give to no one other than yourself." Eadgifu tried to catch the lilt of the man's accent and to determine where he'd come from, but it had been too many years since she'd lived in West Frankia. For now, almost everyone sounded the same, either West Frankish or English, the regional variations were too difficult to determine.

Only then her eyes caught the seal on the rolled parchment, and her eyebrows rose high in surprise.

"You come from Saxony?" Eadgifu asked, amazed that she could no longer even detect the difference between East and West Frankia.

"My Lady," the man again inclined his head and made to move away.

"Tell me," she arrested his movement. "How fares my sister?" After the shocking surprise of finding Countess Eadhild so fragile, Eadgifu didn't wish to make the same mistake again.

"I believe you'll find the answers to your questions in the letter," the man offered, a glint of caution in his eye.

"My thanks," abruptly Eadgifu was unsure that she wanted to read whatever news the missive contained, and yet she ran her seax under the wax and spread the parchment wide.

As Eadgifu read the words, she felt the room swaying and reached out to grasp the firmness of the wall.

She reread the words, just to be sure, and then rushed to find King Louis. This was news he needed before addressing his nobility.

Eadgifu hurried outside, aware that Louis had continued his habit of training with the Wessex household warriors who'd come to West Frankia with them. She could hear the loud cries of men at war, and she smiled, never expecting to find the words of her homeland a comfort. But they were. And they would continue to be in this changed new world.

As soon as Eadgifu came upon the men, some soaked with sweat, while others had pulled their tunics from their body, all eyes looked her way.

She blushed under the intense scrutiny, as she sought out her son.

"Gentlemen," she stumbled. "I didn't mean to interrupt but only to speak with my son, the king."

At that, Louis appeared, his blond hair lank with his exertions, the words of refusal on his lips, which Eadgifu spoke over.

"A letter from your aunt, in East Frankia." Louis' eyes brightened, and he nodded, his denial dying on his lips as he walked toward her. Eadgifu watched him wipe the sweat from his brow, while a young squire ran to take his weapons belt, glinting deadly in the heat of the day, and his war axe from his hand.

King Louis raised his hand to acknowledge his warriors, for they were his and his alone, before he stood beside Eadgifu.

"What is it?" Louis asked, he was curious, not angry at being interrupted.

"Henry the Fowler is dead. Your aunt is to be the queen of East Frankia."

Louis startled at the words, whispered by Eadgifu.

"That will change a great many things," Louis immediately realised. "Does anyone else know?"

"I don't know. The messenger came directly to me. There was no mention of informing others."

"Good. I'll handle delivering the news during the council. Does my aunt make overtures of friendship?"

"Yes, she does. She's keen for the friendship of the West and East Franks to continue, despite the problems of Lotharingia, and she celebrated your coronation."

Louis grunted, thoughtful, his stance so similar to King Athelstan's, that Eadgifu wondered if she hadn't suddenly returned to England.

"It won't please my nobility to realise that I'm now related to the King of England and the Queen of East Frankia."

"Not to mention being the foster brother of the King of Norway and the Duke of Brittany."

Eadgifu nodded as Louis listed his extended family.

"You're blessed with allies, but it's the nobility of West Frankia that you must win over now."

"And I will. I assure you mother," with that, Louis bowed and strode toward the hall, sluicing water from a handy barrel down his back along the way.

Eadgifu turned to follow her son more slowly, only to be hailed by Bishop Oda.

"My Lady, Queen Dowager. I understand you've heard from your sister, in Saxony. Did she send congratulations to her nephew?" Eadgifu was always surprised by the ability of gossip to percolate so quickly through any royal court.

"Yes, she did. I assume she's also sent letters to other members of the court?"

"Then you would, I'm afraid, be wrong. Only you, and it seems you've shared the news with King Louis."

Eadgifu nodded, thinking quickly. It was evident that her sister had acted so that only she knew what had happened. Of course, the messenger himself would be aware. Eadgifu wished she'd been a bit more careful with him, only to turn and see him watching her and Bishop Oda with his alert eyes.

"I've ensured the news he carries is kept as secret as possible," Bishop Oda confirmed with a bow. "I believed it might be worthwhile having him where we can keep an eye on him."

Eadgifu nodded. She should have done the same. Owning valuable information was no longer second nature to her. She would have to relearn all the tricks she'd once employed when Charles had still lived.

"I'd meant to reward him. Perhaps I could do so now," Eadgifu announced, striding to the man's side, a warm expression on her face. The messenger returned her gaze without flinching, and she admired him afresh.

"Apologies for detaining you," Eadgifu spoke confidingly to him. "As I'm sure you can appreciate the king is keen to share the information with his council himself."

"My Lady, Queen Dowager. I assure you, I'm well aware of my duties. Your sister has paid for my silence."

"I'm sure she has. But still, I would reward you as well. I'd not have it said that the sisters of King Athelstan of England are miserly."

This made the messenger perk up, as Eadgifu considered the best gift for the man. She had many coins, but the majority of them were English. Would he appreciate them? Luckily, Bishop Oda came to her assistance."

"A horse, from the stables of the King of England," he offered. "I will have no use of the animal, not now. I intended to leave the animal in your care anyway." Oda spoke respectfully, and Eadgifu inclined her head in agreement. In this way, the messenger would know that all of King Athelstan's sisters esteemed him.

"That is surely too much," the messenger gasped, but Eadgifu could see he was pleased as well.

"Come, I'll introduce you to the animal. The Queen Dowager must attend the council." As though she needed reminding, Eadgifu felt her pulse beat faster as she saw a collection of the West Frankish nobility making their way into the king's hall.

"My apologies," she inclined her head to bishop and messenger and hurried away. She was even more desperate to see how her son handled this new information.

Unlike the night of the coronation feast, the hall was clear of all tables, apart from one needed by the scribes to record the significant decisions reached. Eadgifu peered into the room, trying to decide where to hide from the eyes of many, only to feel a hand on her arm. She turned, about to demand they leave her alone, only to be met by the eyes of Count Arnulf.

"The king has asked me to escort you to his side." Eadgifu nodded mutely and allowed Arnulf to expertly guide her through the small collections of gossiping men as she wound her way to the front of the hall. Eadgifu had thought to be unnoticed, but as she glanced at where Louis would conduct the council from, she realised that the king had a chair to either side of him. She was reasonably sure that one was for Count Hugh, but could he really expect her to sit beside him?

Straightening her back, ensuring her steps were measured, she turned to Count Arnulf.

"Tell me. How are affairs in Flanders?"

"My family are well," Arnulf spoke fondly, and before she could ask more, he gave a smart bow and left Eadgifu beside the spare chair. Eadgifu slowly made herself comfortable, ensuring her dress sat the way she wanted it to, and that her hair didn't tangle with the expanse of jewels around her neck.

Now that they had been returned to her, Eadgifu was keen to show her jewels as often as possible.

Under the gaze of so many potentially hostile faces, she felt uncomfortable. When Louis failed to quickly appear, she wished she hadn't rushed to the hall.

It had been too many years since so many people had paid any attention to her, let alone focused all of their gazes on her. Angrily, she looked down at her hands, noting as she did so, that she wore the ring her husband had gifted to her on their wedding day, the glint of the priceless emeralds, sapphires and rubies almost dazzling.

She smiled then, remembering her marriage ceremony, and the way that she was crowned as Charles' queen, despite complaints from his nobility. Charles had been adamant that any child born to their union, must be done so only when both parents had been blessed by holy oil.

The susurration of sound alerted Eadgifu that the king had finally arrived. Despite all her careful positioning, she stood, ready to curtsey.

Louis strode confidently to the front of the hall, his cloak rich with embroidery, gold and silver flickering in and out of the shadow, a firm if content expression on his young face.

Behind him, came Count Hugh. The older man looked as pleased as ever, but Eadgifu wished he would allow her son the full use of his powers, rather than trying to rule through him. Indeed, Count Hugh had asked Louis for a new title, and Louis had agreed to it, much to Eadgifu's unease. Count Hugh would soon be known as Duke Hugh of the Franks, and Eadgifu knew it would cause problems.

Eadgifu knew it had been more to make his Aunt a duchess, than her husband a duke. Still, it rankled.

As all assembled bowed, Eadgifu swept a deep curtsey, her eyes downcast, until she felt hands on her shoulders, and glanced up to see her son grinning, visible to no one but her. She allowed Louis to raise her, and only then, while Count Hugh still bowed, did Louis give the command for all to take their seats.

With a sharp look for Eadgifu, Count Hugh settled on his chair, inching ever closer to the king, despite Louis' glare of annoyance.

Eadgifu met Count Hugh's gaze without flinching. She was not her sister to manipulate a husband, but rather mother to the king. Eadgifu knew how influential her position could be. After all, she'd seen her step-mother cement her status as indispensable at King Athelstan's court.

"My lords, and ladies," Louis' voice was pitched just loud enough so that all could hear, provided everyone was silent. Another of King Athelstan's tricks.

"It pleases me to welcome you all to this council. There is still much to discuss since my coronation, but first, and this may have some bearing on what we are to debate, I must inform you all of the death of Henry, King of East Frankia. His son, Lord Otto, will hold his coronation on 4th August, and I'll be sending my mother to represent our family."

For a brief moment, silence fell, as men turned to face one another, surprise on their faces, but for Eadgifu, her eyes focused only on her son. She'd not been expecting Louis' words. Not at all.

"My Lord King," it was Count Hugh who spoke. "This should not be the work of women, but of your loyal followers. I don't believe that your mother even met King Henry while he lived."

That wasn't true, but Eadgifu felt no compunction about correcting him.

"My Aunt, Lady Eadgyth, will be crowned as well. It's a matter of family honour. I'm sure you can understand that," Louis offered by way of an explanation.

"What of Lotharingia?" a voice called out. "And the other disputed territories," another cried, as King Louis held his hands out for silence.

"I have an assurance that the close accord of the Kings of West and East Frankia will continue. And how can it not? We're bound by blood as well as our kingships." Louis spoke to appease, but Eadgifu was distracted by the furious expression on Count Hugh's face, determined to enjoy it.

"My Lord King," again, Count Hugh tried to monopolise Louis' attention. "I would not countenance sending your mother to East Frankia. There's no guarantee of her safety."

Louis looked astonished at the words.

"You think my mother's sister would allow anything to happen to her? I have my household troop, from England, I'll send them to protect my mother, along with those who know the route well. My mother will be as safe in East Frankia, as she is in West Frankia. Unless, of course, my mother is not safe in West Frankia?"

Eadgifu almost felt her eyes boggle at the way her son spoke to Count Hugh, with the authority of a man and a warrior who knew his worth. Not some small boy to be bullied.

"Your mother is safe in West Frankia," Count Hugh spoke through gritted teeth. "But the matter of the relationship between East and West Frankia is what concerns me. You, My Lord King, have been gone for many years. You can't possibly know how fraught the situation can be."

"And that is why my mother is the best choice. She has no quarrel with her sister and the new king. No one would think her capable of subterfuge." While Eadgifu didn't appreciate that comment, she understood its value to the argument.

"If you're truly unhappy with the arrangement, then I would ask you to send my aunt, Countess Eadhild, with my mother. I'm sure the royal sisters would be pleased to meet once more. And then you would be represented."

The thought of seeing so many of her sisters together surprised Eadgifu by suffusing her with warmth.

But Count Hugh looked deeply unhappy.

"No, My Lord King, Countess Eadhild is too frail to travel."

As he spoke, Count Hugh made an effort to curb his temper, his words softened by worry for his wife. Yet, Eadgifu didn't doubt that this would not be the end of the matter, even as the men of the council discussed a fitting gift to send to the new king of the East Franks and his queen. She listened with half an ear, saddened that her brief flare of delight had been so quickly squashed.

Perhaps, Eadgifu thought, it would have been better if she and Louis had discussed this matter first. But, Eadgifu could admit, she'd wanted her son to begin to exert his own power over his kingdom. If this was his first step, then she admired his audacity.

Certainly, it would give Count Hugh pause for thought. And more importantly, it would mean she got to see her sister again. Eadgifu had never thought she'd see Eadgyth once more. Not even now they were neighbours.

Eadgifu was surprised that the prospect cheered her so much.

AD936

The journey was undertaken swiftly, and Eadgifu knew that she should perhaps not thank her son for sending her to Aachen. Certainly, each night that she descended from her horse, she felt as though she'd aged.

The rush reminded her of the dash for freedom when Charles had first been imprisoned. Bringing back such twisted memories made her quiet and pensive as the journey lengthened.

Yet, the thought of seeing Eadgyth drove her onwards. Eadhild had mentioned that even Ælfgifu would probably attend as well, as her husband's brother would need to pledge his oath to the new King. Eadhild's face had shown too clearly how much she wished to make the journey as well. But it was beyond her.

Instead, Eadgifu travelled with gifts for her sisters, and the hope that there would be time, amongst all the ceremony, to speak honestly with her sisters.

With Henry dead, there was an excellent opportunity for the two kingdoms to continue their close connections. Provided Otto agreed. Certainly, Eadgifu knew that Louis hoped his mother would accomplish much to bring about more agreement between East and West Frankia, especially concerning the contested Lotharingia.

While Count Hugh had been keen that Eadgifu not make the journey, when Louis had given him permission to travel as well, Hugh had refused. In the action, Eadgifu had witnessed a man who was too fearful that even with an absence of no more than a month, Louis would realise he didn't need Hugh to rule effectively.

Eadgifu was torn. She'd not wanted to leave her son so soon after the coronation, but the opportunity was too huge to miss. Certainly, King Athelstan would have thought the decision an excellent one, if only there'd been the time to consult him.

While Eadgifu was used to the riches of West Frankia, she'd never travelled to East Frankia. But she well knew the awe that Charlemagne's royal settlement induced in all who'd seen it.

In all honesty, that was another reason she'd been content to make the journey. She would be able to visit Charlemagne's place of burial and see for herself just what he'd managed to accomplish as King of all Frankia and not just the West.

Exhausted, but excited, the road to Aachen slowly grew busier and busier the closer they came to their destination. Eadgifu thrilled to hear the variety of languages being spoken amongst her fellow travellers, as well as the vast array of goods for sale on the back of horses and carts. In places, she and her guard of English household warriors, led by Beornstan, struggled to make any headway. For a time, Eadgifu worried they would never make it in time. Only then they did.

The vista of Aachen opened up before her. Her eye focused exclusively on the huge dome, the pinnacle of Charlemagne's building ambitions in his imperial settlement.

It glittered, like nothing else she'd ever seen, and she was not alone in reining in her horse, just to gaze in wonder at the building before her.

Around her, the flow of other travellers never ceased, and she was amazed that others could carry on as though they weren't looking at something truly amazing.

At that point, Eadgifu sent on a messenger, keen for them to reach her sister, and inform of their imminent arrival. Eadgifu had no idea how Eadgyth would respond to seeing her again, after all these years.

Still, she was keen that their initial meeting be observed by as few people as possible.

When the messenger returned to her, as they neared Aachen, his face was puce with suppressed annoyance. For a moment, Eadgifu was fearful that her sister was unprepared to meet with her.

"My Lady, Queen Dowager Eadgifu, apologies for my late return. The roads are filled to capacity, and no one will let me pass." Only then did his face lose its frustration.

"The Queen of East Frankia has requested that you present yourself at the palace as soon as possible. She offered to send men to escort me. I wish I'd allowed that to happen now." Again, frustration flashed over the man's face.

"Thank you, Wulfhelm. You've done well."

"Yes, I have, but I don't know how we'll ever make it before night comes. There's no room for anyone to move either forward or backwards."

Just as his complaints reached her ear, Eadgifu became aware of a thread of silence growing outwards from in front of them. Banners could be seen moving through the crowd, and Eadgifu panicked, unsure where she could position her horse to avoid whatever was coming toward her. She was under no illusion that it was someone important from the imperial purple of the banner.

As she watched, the riders surrounded her small procession, with just the two banners, one of West Frankia, and one for England, being brandished by her household warriors. Still, Eadgifu waited, unsure who commanded the action.

Only when everyone was in place, with those who were not a part of her party moved to one side, and a small space provided for them to calm the horses, did another horse enter the enclosed area.

For just a moment, Eadgifu was unsure who had come to meet her, but then a flash of ice blue eyes from beneath an extravagant head-dress, caught her attention, and a cry of disbelief erupted from her mouth.

"My Lady Sister," the words were spoken in amazement. Eadgyth had both changed and stayed the same in all those years since they'd last met.

"My Lady Sister," was Eadgyth's reply, although Eadgifu detected a faint hesitation, and she knew why, immediately.

"My Lady Queen," Eadgifu tried to make restitution, and then Eadgyth's eyes sparkled with joy.

"My Lady, Queen Dowager," and Eadgifu grumbled, while a peal of delighted laughter poured from Eadgyth's mouth.

But then they were both jumping from their horses, and rushing to embrace, oblivious to any who watched them, aware only that it had been too long since they'd last met.

The smell of exotic spices reached Eadgifu's nose as she felt her sister firm beneath her hands, unlike poor Eadhild. The cloak Eadgyth wore was so heavily studded with jewels that Eadgyth could feel them pressing into her body, and yet she tried to ignore the unpleasant sensation, as they both spoke at the same time.

Only then did Eadgifu feel small hands trying to come between her and Eadgyth and she pulled back, surprised to see two sets of bright eyes looking her way. Both of them so reminded Eadgifu of Louis when he was young, and she knew these were her sister's children.

Eadgyth laughed once more.

"Might I introduce you to Prince Lludolf and Princess Liutgarde." The names flowed smoothly from their mother's lips, but Eadgifu paused for a moment. She was not used to the names of the East Franks, and she didn't want to upset her niece and nephew by mispronouncing them.

Not wishing to cause problems by being too familiar with the children, Eadgifu curtsied to the children. As young as they were, they reciprocated with a curtsey and then a smart bow, and Eadgifu smiled in delight.

"I'm pleased to meet you both. I'm Eadgifu, your aunt, and Queen Dowager of West Frankia."

"And our cousin, Louis, is king of West Frankia." It was Lludolf who spoke. Eadgifu could already tell that he was a beguiling child, and clearly intelligent as well.

"He is yes, and he's sent gifts for you, but I'll have to find them from my pack horses."

Young Liutgarde's eyes rounded at the thought of a present, but before she could say anything further, she stuck her thumb in her mouth and began to suck it. Eadgifu grinned to see that at least one of Eadgyth's children was still just that.

"I couldn't wait to see you, but come, come, we must return to the palace. There's much to do." As though recalled to her duties, Eadgyth shepherded her children back to their small horses, and attendant servants, before turning once more to Eadgifu.

"There's a great deal of pomp and ceremony to get through in the coming days. But no matter what you hear, and who you hear it from, know that I'm relieved Louis is restored, along with Haakon and Alain. And I'm sorry you never got to see your husband again, but you do now have your title and position, if not Charles."

As she spoke, Eadgyth gripped Eadgifu's hand tightly in her own.

"And I'm pleased that you're now a queen, even if I'm not," Eadgifu spoke the words herself, to take the sting from them.

"Ah sister, you've always been a queen," Eadgyth laughed, turning to mount her horse.

"Allow your men to ride within the guard of the East Frankish warriors. It will ensure we don't mislay anyone. It's far too busy," Eadgyth cautioned. Then they were moving forward again, Eadgyth beside Eadgifu, while the young prince and princess rode just behind them, Liutgarde safely held before a maid. The woman was well dressed, and might well have been a member of the nobility given the task of ensuring the safety of the King and queen's daughter.

While the settlement of Aachen grew ever closer, or at least what Eadgifu could see of it, surrounded as she was by so many banners flapping in the warm air, her eyes remained focused on the stunning dome before her, growing larger and larger. Beside her, Eadgyth was silent, no doubt allowing Eadgifu to absorb everything she saw.

Only when they were inside the palace grounds did Eadgyth speak again.

"I've arranged rooms for you, within the palace, and you will sit beside me tonight, while we feast. Now rest, and I'll see you later."

With that, Eadgyth left Eadgifu with her English warriors and a flurry of servants who came to help them all.

"Queen Dowager Eadgifu," one of the servants bobbed before Eadgifu, the words slurred a little by the East Frankish accent.

"I'm to be your guide while you're in Aachen. I helped Queen Eadgyth when she first came to East Frankia, and I'll ensure you have everything you need. Your men, I'm afraid, will have to sleep in canvas erected behind the palace. There's simply not enough room for everyone." She threw her hands up in mock frustration and then smiled once more.

"My name is Matilda." Eadgifu nodded, although her eyes were taken by the front of the building she stood before. Like the domed church, the palace was constructed of fine stone and was elaborately decorated. As the horses were led away, and so too her English warriors, Eadgifu caught the eye of Beornstan. He looked just as overwhelmed as she was, and they'd spent the last month in Laon, with its equally rich array of stone buildings.

"Then you have my thanks," Eadgifu inclined her head, thankful that her sister had thought of the necessity. She was sure she'd have become lost in no time at all. Matilda led her inside, and along a busy corridor, doors to the one side, while windows allowed sunlight to illuminate the stone floor.

Matilda was silent, as Eadgyth had been, and Eadgifu appreciated it. There was much to take in and many people to avoid.

The chamber she was taken to, up a set of curving stone steps, was just the right size for the fireplace to warm it thoroughly, and importantly, provided a view of the domed church.

"It's not the grandest of rooms, but it does have the best view," Matilda informed her as Eadgifu strode to the window with its leaded glass panels keeping out the cold.

"It's wonderful," Eadgifu announced, her eyes drawn to the elegant bedding and well-stocked plate of fruit that awaited her. She knew then that the decision to come to Aachen had been the correct one.

THAT EVENING, just as Eadgyth had promised, Eadgifu was seated beside her sister, but only after she'd been formally introduced to her brother by marriage.

Otto's youth and vigour immediately struck Eadgifu, as he stepped forward to warmly clasp her hand.

"My Lady, Queen Dowager Eadgifu," his voice was firm.

"My Lord, King Otto," Eadgifu spoke warmly. This was her first chance to assess her sister's husband, and she found she liked what she saw.

Eadgifu had briefly met King Henry when first married to Charles. The older man had been an ally of Charles', but the last meeting between the two had taken place just after the birth of Louis, and Eadgifu had been unable to attend. She could see now that Otto resembled his young children, the flick of his chin and the curve of his nose the most apparent signs of his parentage.

"I believe you once met my father, and I'd like to assure you that I intend to be as friendly with West Frankia as he was. I look forward to creating treaties with your son, and perhaps, being a godparent to his own children." Eadgifu nodded at the words.

"And I assure you that King Louis is as keen for friendship to mark the relationship between East and West as you are."

"If you'll excuse me, I have some small matters to deal with, but wished to make your acquaintance." As King Otto left the chamber, Eadgifu felt her sister slipping an arm through her own.

"And now, I have another who wishes to meet you."

Eadgifu turned, her mouth open in surprise, as another young woman stepped from the shadows. For a long moment, Eadgifu was unsure who it was, and then she laughed.

"Ælfgifu, is that you?"

"It is, sister, it is," Ælfgifu giggled with delight.

"I wish you could have seen your face. It was priceless."

"I was hoping you'd be here. Has your husband come as well, Lord Louis of Arles?"

"Yes, but he's busy with 'some small matters' just like King Otto. I had hoped that Countess Eadhild might have made the journey." Regret thrummed in Ælfgifu's voice.

"She's too ill, alas. She was disappointed as well."

"Ill, what ails her?"

Eadgyth's sharp question surprised Eadgifu.

"You didn't know. I assumed you were all in contact?"

"No, there's little that passes between us but some letters containing nothing but bland statements. What ails her?"

"I don't know, exactly, but it's because she can't carry a child. I believe she's tried every remedy suggested to her, but none has worked. She's as fragile as a bird. I fear to grip her hand too tightly."

The three women settled around a wooden table, the markings of a chessboard etched into its surface, although the pieces were not on display. Eadgifu would have preferred to see a tafl board.

"Eadhild should have come to bathe in the spa. The waters are recuperative."

"If she could have travelled, she would have come."

"Then we'll have some sent to her. In barrels. That way she can still bathe in the waters, and hopefully, they'll cure her of any illness she carries."

"I'm sure she would appreciate that," Eadgifu stated, although she wasn't sure at all. She honestly didn't know Eadhild well.

"Eadhild is secretive with all of us."

"Yes, but I think she still writes to our other sisters, in Wilton. No doubt they know far more than we do. But tell me, how is King Athelstan, and how does it feel to be back in West Frankia?"

Only the arrival of a fraught servant snapped the women from their conversation. Even then, it hardly stopped as they were served plate after plate of excellent food, and deep red wine when they were settled at the feast.

Eadgifu felt as much on display at the front of the hall as she had done in Laon. Yet, here she knew no one, other than her sisters, and dismissed her unease, more fascinated in talking to her sisters she'd not seen for many years. They were certainly far more forthcoming than Eadhild had been when they'd met once more.

"Tomorrow, we'll visit the shrine. You must see the octagonal basilica and cupola before it's filled with people. I've never seen anything quite so magnificent."

Beside her, Ælfgifu nodded happily in agreement, and Eadgifu chuckled. Ælfgifu, while not about to be crowned queen showed no jealousy that it had not been her Otto had chosen to marry. Of all of Edward's daughters, Eadgifu thought, it was Ælfgifu who had the warmest soul, even though she too had no children of her own, yet.

Eadgifu was delighted to see that both of her sisters were happy. On that day, seven years ago, that she'd said goodbye to them, after an assurance that both sisters would be found husbands in East Frankia, she had fretted that King Athelstan's plan might not have borne fruit.

True to her word, Eadgifu was taken to the royal chapel the following day. The palace was overwhelmed with people coming and going. Yet Eadgyth stepped through it all, surrounded by her own guard, and with her two sisters beside her. Eadgifu looked ever upwards the closer she came to the domed building. If she was this awestruck from the outside, what would she feel when she was inside the building?

Immediately, the hush of prayer greeted her ears, and it was Eadgifu's eyes that were overawed.

She'd never seen a chapel quite so bright with gold, and in so complex an arrangement. Eight arches, supported by eight priceless pillars of ancient marble, roared their way toward the sky, the one supporting the other. Above them all, eight windows allowed light to fall onto the floor of the chapel, while candles illuminated both the throne and the elaborate burial place of Charlemagne himself.

If the Vikings had ever made it to Aachen, Eadgifu thought, they'd never have needed to raid England.

She simply couldn't believe the wealth on such careless display, and when she saw the tomb of Emperor Charlemagne, Eadgifu was unable to speak. Beside her, Eadgyth was solemn in such a holy place, and yet her eyebrow quirked with amusement. Eadgifu had witnessed great wealth, many times before, but never anything on such a scale.

Tomorrow, when Otto was crowned as King, it would be an occasion that no one would ever forget.

"I will be anointed with holy oil and crowned in two days. The ceremony will be just as lavish, but tomorrow is for the King." Eadgyth beamed with joy as they made their way outside, but Eadgifu was too overcome to speak. Eadgyth slipped one arm through Eadgifu's, while Ælfgifu did the same on the other side.

Eadgifu welcomed the closeness of her sisters. It had been too long in coming, and once more, she wished that Eadhild had been well enough to attend.

THE DAY of the coronation began early as there was much to prepare. Matilda was a great help to Eadgifu, but in the end, it was Ælfgifu who came and helped her finish her hair and selecting which jewels she should wear.

As the Queen of West Frankia, Eadgifu had once possessed a considerable number of necklaces, dress brooches, rings and small crowns, but she'd fled to England with very little, desperate only to escape with her small son. As soon as Louis had been crowned as King, he'd given her a great deal of jewellery. Usually, she preferred the items that had been hers for years. Still, the coronation ceremony was all about show and power. She needed to wear some of her newer jewellery. If she were forced to wear the dress made for Louis' ceremony, few would know it.

There'd been no time to have a new dress made, although the cloak she'd selected had been further embellished. When she donned it, Eadgifu knew, it would feel heavy and cumbersome.

Ælfgifu poured over Eadgifu's jewels, gasping now and then with admiration at the selection of necklaces, bracelets, dress brooches and slides for her hair. Some of them even had onyx set into them.

Eadgifu watched her sister carefully, wanting to know that there was no jealousy from her. Ælfgifu had expected to become a queen, but instead was a lady of the kingdom of Arles, with no possibility of ever ruling it.

"Oh," Ælfgifu exclaimed, selecting a broad golden ring, studded with rubies. "This one is new."

Ælfgifu was already dressed, even her hair arranged for the ceremony. She was, like Eadgifu, not attending to swear allegiance to King Otto, but rather to witness his coronation as a royal guest, and family member.

Eadgifu envied her youngest sister her elegance and good looks, while she felt old and drab. She was the mother of a son old enough to rule in his own name already, albeit, with Count Hugh trying to dictate events

"It is beautiful, isn't it?" Eadgifu commented. "Try it on, it will bring out the red embroidery on your dress."

Ælfgifu did as she'd been told and then examined her hand in the light streaming through the glass window.

"Wear it. In fact, no, keep it, as a gift from me. I had precious little when I returned to Wessex. Keep it now. You should have had such all along."

Ælfgifu's face lit with delight, and she skipped over to kiss Eadgifu on the cheeks. The flush of her restored wealth was still strange to Eadgifu. The joy in gifting thrilled her.

"Being restored to West Frankia certainly suits you," Ælfgifu commented. She swept a comb through Eadgifu's hair before she swirled it expertly onto her head. She then pushed four elaborate silver pins through it, threaded with the wyvern symbol of the House of Wessex. Even now, Eadgifu was not beyond reminding people that she was the daughter of a king, the sister of one, as well as the mother of one, and soon to be the sister by marriage of another.

"And being married suits you," Eadgifu teased, as Ælfgifu's face light up.

"He's a caring husband. So much more amenable than our own father was. Although he's less strict than our half-brother ever was, then, he never expects to become anything more than the brother of the duke. I think it makes life easier for him. A pity Edwin never learned to be content."

The mention of Edwin surprised Eadgifu, but then she realised that Ælfgifu would never have been able to speak to anyone about him since the news of his execution. No one she knew in Arles would have ever met Edwin.

"He repented at the end," Eadgifu confirmed. "But it was impossible for King Athelstan to defer his execution. It certainly calmed things down in England. Perhaps it would have been better for our father to marry Edwin off, as he did Eadhild and me."

Ælfgifu's eyes, which had clouded as she spoke about Edwin, brightened once more.

"I know a few women in Arles who would have taken our brother to task," Ælfgifu giggled and then sobbed softly, just the once, her eyes gleaming with memories.

Eadgifu gripped her sister's hand and squeezed it.

"We can never know what life will bring to us," Eadgifu whispered. "We must just try and accept whatever comes our way. And that is not something that I've ever been good at." Eadgifu spoke wryly. She knew her own faults.

Ælfgifu giggled once more.

"Well, with age comes great wisdom," she intoned. Before Eadgifu could chastise her for the comment, a bell tolled, just the once, but enough to remind them that they had a coronation to attend.

With arms linked, Eadgifu and Ælfgifu made their way to the King's Hall, and then outside into the crowded space where many were trying to push toward the basilica.

"Will we all fit inside?" Eadgifu asked under her breath, but Ælfgifu had no time to answer, as Matilda arrived in a flurry.

"My ladies, come, there's a space reserved for you inside. I'll show you."

Eadgifu lifted her dress and followed Matilda, the press of so many people in one place a shock to her. As she was shown to a position where she could see where Otto crowned, albeit standing, Eadgifu realised she was far luckier than many others.

Yes, she might not be Otto's mother, but her sister had ensured that they could all witness her husband's elevation. For the briefest moment, Eadgifu considered that Eadgyth might have done this just so she could laud it over her sister. But then she reconsidered. There was no trace of bitterness between her and her sister, not now they'd both managed to accomplish what they'd wanted.

The events of that day were far distant in time from when none of them had known what the future would hold.

It was the Archbishop of Mainz, Hildebert who was to conduct the ceremony, and Eadgifu stilled, as did everyone else, as he made his arrival before the King's throne.

The throne, raised to the second floor of the basilica, was accessed by four or five steps, and from there, all would be able to see Otto once he was invested with his orb and sceptre.

Eadgifu was reminded not of her son's coronation, but instead of Athelstan's, as Otto made his appearance, dressed, as her sister had told her, in clothes styled after those Charlemagne might have worn. Eadgifu kept the thought to herself, that really there was little difference between Otto's clothes, and those Athelstan had worn on his own coronation.

Like Athelstan, Otto was using his coronation as a means of staking his claim to more land and more territory, to being more than just the King of the East Franks. She admired him, as she watched him anointed with holy oil, while on his knees, only to be raised up and festooned in a thick cloak. A golden sceptre followed, topped with a flashing diamond, the largest she'd ever seen and an orb, lined around its circumference with flashing rubies, as well as a ring and a sword, just like Athelstan had been.

As the final prayers died away, a shaft of sunlight poured through two of the high windows illuminating Otto in a golden glow, as though ordained by God. Eadgifu was not alone in gasping at the sight.

And then she smirked. Eadgifu could appreciate a good piece of staging by the new King and his advisors.

As King Otto was led from the church, four noblemen escorted him, holding his cloak wide behind him so that he needn't fear to trip on its extravagant length. Only then did Eadgyth and Otto's children join him, the three of them rippling as though they were golden corn in a field, illuminated by the sun.

Eadgyth's face was one of pious devotion, as all assembled either took to their knee or curtsied at their passing. Eadgifu felt a tight hand grip her own and knew that Ælfgifu was feeling just as much intense joy as she was. It was truly magnificent to watch. For the briefest of moments, Eadgifu thought of her cantankerous mother. Just how pleased would she have been to see her daughter so honoured?

TWO DAYS LATER, once more stood in the basilica, Eadgifu and Ælfgifu watched, alongside only slightly fewer people, as Eadgyth took her oaths and was touched with holy oil.

While her sister wasn't allowed to take her husband's throne, indeed King Otto watched the ceremony from its vantage, a beautiful wooden chair, made from the dark wood so common in East Frankia, had been constructed for Eadgyth to sit in and take the acclaim of the people of East Frankia.

Just like King Otto, Eadgyth seemed to glow and pulse with the power of the holy words spoken both about her and to her. With each pledge she made to serve her God, Eadgifu watched Eadgyth straighten her back until she was so rigid, it must have been uncomfortable. For all that, Eadgyth retained her stern resolve, and only much later, when the three sisters were once more able to spend time alone, did Eadgyth's expression fracture.

"My neck," Eadgyth complained, rubbing it with her newly bejewelled hand. "Why do they make crowns weigh so much?"

"It's the weight of your earthly position," Eadgifu intoned, a delighted glint in her eye to show that she only teased.

"I could sell the damn thing, and buy a duchy or two, and still have some to spare," Eadgyth laughed, but still she twisted her neck, and then turned to gaze at her sister.

"So, what now?" Eadgyth demanded to know, all traces of humour gone from her voice.

"We must work to ensure peace ensues between the two Frankish kingdoms. There's too much fighting and too much time spent trying to outfox another. The kings of the east and the West must show their followers that it's unacceptable behaviour."

Eadgyth raised an eyebrow at the words her sister spoke.

"And how will we do that?"

"We'll vow to work toward a common goal, as sisters. We have duties and responsibilities to all those who've witnessed our coronations, just as we do to our God. I would suggest a wedding, to unite East and West, to make the kings reliant on each other."

Eadgyth nodded slowly, considering the option.

"But what of Count Hugh? He's always keen to cause problems for his King."

"We must rely on Countess Eadhild to keep her husband reconciled to what must happen. As I say, we're sisters, the daughters of King Edward, sisters to King Athelstan. If Athelstan can accomplish as much as he has in unifying England, and coming to terms with England's neighbours, then we must be capable of doing the same."

"Then, as King Athelstan's sisters, we should vow to work toward this common goal, and you must have Eadhild swear the same oath. Here, I have a relic from St Oswald. We'll all take an oath, and then you must take this to Countess Eadhild and have her do the same."

As Eadgyth spoke, she turned to search through a wooden casket that sat on the side of her personal chambers. It was heavy, and the hinges protested as she opened it, and peered into the silk-lined contents.

When she pulled forth a small package and hastened to unwrap it, Eadgifu gasped.

"A piece of his cloak?"

"Yes, a small piece of home, to enable me to pray for England, and my family, while I labour to unite East Frankia."

With a glance to Ælfgifu, to ensure she was content to take the oath, Eadgifu dropped to her knees, her two sisters following suit, as they bowed before the priceless relic.

"I swear," the three women spoke together, "to work toward the goal of bringing peace to East and West Frankia." Silence fell between the three of them as they all considered what they'd said.

When Queen Eadgyth had carefully folded and then returned the package to her casket, closing the lid tightly afterwards, Eadgifu glanced at her sisters, assessing them.

They all understood the weight of the words they'd spoken, that much was evident in the firm resolve on their faces.

Only then did Queen Eadgyth call for wine and food to be brought to them. Only when they'd toasted themselves and the future, did the seriousness of their ambitions cease to haunt the face of Eadgifu and her two sisters.

AD937

As Eadgifu watched the coffin of her sister lowered into the ground, soft tears poured down her cheeks, despite her intention to show no emotion at all.

Beside her, Duke Hugh, was stoic in his grief, and Eadgifu realised at that moment just how much she truly detested him.

Her beautiful sister, gone, just like that, and with no children to her name. That the much-wanted child hadn't survived the trauma of the birth that had claimed the mother, made Eadgifu feel even more bereft.

Her sister, no matter what else she might say about her, had been overjoyed to find herself finally with child after over a decade of marriage. The spa waters from Aachen had been credited with the wonderful event, and merry letters had passed between the sisters in West and East Frankia, and the kingdom of Arles, and in Wilton nunnery, as they waited for the birth of Eadhild's child.

That it had all ended so suddenly, couldn't have been expected. Or so Eadgifu tried to reassure herself.

She should have known that the pregnancy wouldn't end well, or so she constantly berated, while the sound of the bishop's voice reverberated around the elaborate abbey, perhaps even more splendid than that in Laon. Perhaps.

As the lay abbot of the Abbey of St Germain des Pres, Duke Hugh had exerted his influence to have the abbey richly endowed, most certainly because it was the burial place of the Merovingian kings of Neustria. Duke Hugh was always too keen to be associated with the ancient rulers of the land he commanded.

When the service finally ceased, Eadgifu almost didn't notice, until Louis gently touched her shoulder, standing beside her, and she realised they were all but alone.

Louis eyed his mother with sympathy, but also frustration, as she laboured to her knees, aware of her creaking knees and cold backside. It was March, and the weather remained too cold for comfort, especially inside the abbey.

"Lady Mother," her son's voice had deepened since he'd become king, and even now, it shocked her to hear him sound so like King Athelstan.

"My Lord King," there was a hint of apology in her voice, but Louis shook his head, refusing to hear it, as he linked his arm through her own.

His voice dropped to a whisper.

"There's much to discuss," Eadgifu nodded, for all that she didn't wish to dismiss her dead sister quite so quickly. But, now was the time to act. She knew it in her heart. Certainly, Louis was desperate to remove himself from under the oppressive command of Duke Hugh.

Duke Hugh thought himself the king's father and cautioned and advised only for his gain. While content to allow the familiarity for the last nine months of his kingship, Louis was no longer keen to do so. Indeed, even King Athelstan had sent a swift messenger to advise Louis that the time was ripe for him to step aside from Duke Hugh.

Eadgifu shuddered to think of the terrible news the messenger would return to England with, and also with the realisation that King Athelstan would see the potential in this suddenly changed situation as clearly as Louis did.

Outside the abbey, Eadgifu paused, pulling her cloak tighter with her free hand, and turning to gaze at the abbey that had now become her sister's mausoleum. She only wished it had been possible to return Eadhild's mortal remains to England, to lie with her father, and brothers, grandfather and grandmother, but Eadgifu had given up the fight when fury had lit Duke Hugh's glowering face.

Eadhild had died as Duchess of Paris, and so she must remain here, even when her sister and nephew left the place.

For a moment, Eadgifu considered if she would see the abbey again, and then shrugged. It didn't matter. The memories of her sister would sustain her, just as the memories of all the others she'd loved and lost in her life, did. The death of Eadhild was no different, apart from the opportunity that now lay open for her son.

"Arrangements have been made to travel to Laon tonight, under cover of darkness, while Duke Hugh drinks himself to sleep once more."

"Tonight?" Eadgifu gasped at the speed of Louis' ambitions and then held her hand up in apology as she saw Louis' frustration with her.

"Tonight, I'll have everything ready," she confirmed instead, and Louis nodded, his posture that of a king who expected to be obeyed without question.

"When we are in Laon, we'll inform King Athelstan of our actions, and also King Otto and Queen Eadgyth. I wish it to be known that I'm the King of West Frankia and that I stand aside from Duke Hugh. I'm old enough to rule in my own name, and for myself."

Again, Eadgifu nodded. This was not a new conversation for her and Louis. It had steadily intensified over the last six months, once Louis had come to realise the scale of Hugh's intentions toward him. King Athelstan had been an uncle who'd cared for his nephew's needs. Not like Duke Hugh.

Eadgifu shivered as she picked her way through the icy puddles and around the areas that lay submerged by boggy land. It looked deceptively hard but was not at all.

The Abbey of St German-des-Pres might well be an ancient establishment, but she wished once more that the men who'd built her had considered the closeness to the river before sinking such an elaborate structure in the meadows. There was a constant, and unpleasant smell, and Eadgifu shivered as she considered her sister's cold, dead body, forever cradling her much-longed-for, but still-born son, beneath the abbey's floor.

At least, Eadgifu consoled herself, her sister wouldn't rot like so many of the other burials must have done in the abbey grounds. All those magnificent kings from centuries before, nothing but mouldering remains. The thought made her shiver, and she was pleased to step into the welcoming warmth of Duke Hugh's hall, filled with the gloom of a funeral, and well furnished with a burning hearth and warmed wine, the spices heady in the blast of hot air.

Already, Duke Hugh had settled himself around the table he claimed as his own, surrounded by his special followers, well those who'd been able to make the quick journey to Paris for the funeral of the duchess, as opposed to the celebration of the birth of Duke Hugh's long-hoped for heir.

Eadgifu felt eyes on her, as she hesitated, unsure whether to join her brother-by-marriage or not, only to decide that staying away was far better.

While Duke Hugh hunkered at the front of his hall, close to the hearth, his own allies surrounded Louis. The young men and women were sombre, as befitted the funeral feast of their king's aunt. Still, Eadgifu, attuned to those who supported Louis so firmly, could sense their excitement.

It seemed that Louis was not the only one to sense change in the air, for all that the majority of them were not aware of Louis' audacious plan for the night time.

As soon as Louis was safely in Laon, his allies would join him. Not that they knew that yet.

Eadgifu drank deeply of her warmed wine, looking to see who she might actually miss amongst those assembled to mourn her sister. She found the answer unsettling. No one.

They saw only Duke Hugh as the master here, and not the true king.

While Eadgifu was doubtful that would change, even when Louis made it to Laon, she was aware that Louis had allies elsewhere. The unease between the king and the man who ran the royal council in his name would provide opportunities for those clear-sighted enough to see them for what they were.

There was much at stake. But, there would have been more had Eadhild managed to birth her son, alive. The thought was unsettling. Eadhild's death, as traumatic as it had been, had given Louis more, not less, freedom from his uncle.

Had the much longed-for heir survived his birth, the whole dynamic in West Frankia would have shifted. While still a child, it would have been known that Duke Hugh had his own heir, and therefore, in time, wouldn't need to control his nephew.

Eadgifu swallowed down the unpalatable truth with her spiced wine, and then, without thought for proprieties, swept from Duke Hugh's hall. She had much to organise, and all of it must be done in secrecy.

Once more, she needed to flee, only this time she was heading to Laon, and not to Wessex, and her son was not a babe in arms, but King of West Frankia.

HER BREATH PLUMED before her and Eadgifu shivered, for all she wore all of her warmest clothes.

The chill of the day had turned to a freeze as she made her way to the stables. Her horse was waiting, as were the men who'd escort the royal party to Laon.

Eadgifu's women shuffled along in silence beside her, faces white with cold, but not with worry.

After all, what was the worst that Duke Hugh would do to them if they were caught? He could hardly have all of the king's loyal servants and supporters murdered.

In the cold light from the cloudless sky, the moon shone on their endeavour. It lit the path well, making the need for brands unnecessary, although it also revealed them to the warriors on guard duty. But that night, all of the men were supporters of Louis. When the king rode for Laon, they would follow on behind, leaving Duke Hugh and his household unguarded, until someone woke and realised what had happened.

Eadgifu almost wished, she could order the warriors to attack her brother-by-marriage, but for the love she'd held for her sister, as strained as it had often been, she had cautioned Louis against having Duke Hugh assassinated. It would not set the right precedent for a man who wished to rule by having the upper-hand through the honour and steadfastness that marked King Athelstan's reign in England.

Mounted on her horse, Eadgifu absorbed the warmth from the animal's back, settling herself onto the animal with a minimum of fuss. They would ride hard for Laon, but the bright moon would make their actions easier to accomplish. They could travel faster than they might have hoped and would arrive in Laon early the next day. Archbishop Artoldus, who had been readying Laon, the traditional residence of the West Frankish kings, for their use, would greet them.

Tomorrow, with Artoldus as Louis' Archchancellor, Louis' kingship would start once more, under his own name, and also under his own directives. Just the thought of that was enough to warm Eadgifu as her horse stepped clear of Duke Hugh's gated enclosure.

Tomorrow, her son would be king in more than just name.

Beside her, Louis encouraged his horse to step close to her.

"Come, Lady Mother, Queen Dowager," Louis spoke, his deep voice thrumming with excitement. "By the time the sun rises tomorrow, we'll be in Laon, and then we'll begin the work that must be done to secure West Frankia for our dynasty. I'll make Uncle Athelstan proud, and I will do it for my father's stolen legacy."

Eadgifu chuckled softly.

"Then you must lead on, My Lord King," and together they escaped the confines of Duke Hugh's tutelage.

. . .

EADGIFU DESCENDED from her horse in the forecourt of the king's palace at Laon. The night had been colder than she could have imagined, the moon, a pale ghost lighting their path. But the lack of cloud cover had turned the ground hard beneath the hooves of the horses, forcing them to travel more slowly than they might have liked.

Yet, none had followed, and while Eadgifu could admit a pitched battle with Duke Hugh, in which Duke Hugh was mortally wounded, might have made the future much easier, it also allowed Louis the time he needed to collect himself and begin planning for the future.

The death of Duke Hugh would have left a void that couldn't easily be filled.

As the sun rose in a molten haze of maroons and reds, marking the day as a fiery rebirth, Eadgifu watched as Archbishop Artoldus took to his knees before Louis, already striding about, issuing order and instructions.

Louis immediately ceased his actions and stopped before the Archbishop. Artoldus had been the man to make Louis King of the West Franks, and now, he was to be elevated by Louis to an equally grand position. Now was the time for mutual respect between the two men, and Eadgifu quickly made her way to Louis' side.

"My Lord King," Artoldus' voice carried the same timbre he'd used when conducting the coronation ceremony, and there were few in the busy forecourt who didn't stop and listen.

"Archbishop Artoldus," Louis raised his own voice to match that of his Archbishop's.

"I'm honoured by your presence here, by your trust in me, and would assure you that all is ready for you to begin governing immediately, as is your right as the King of West Frankia."

Louis paused, to allow the words to be absorbed by all those who'd already professed themselves him loyal adherents. It would assure them all that they were not alone in their desire to support Louis rather than Duke Hugh.

"Then you have the thanks of your king, for your great service, and I would have it be known from hereafter that you are my Archchancellor, that you'll have the command of my administration, and that your actions are taken with my explicit consent." Eadgifu felt the urge to restrain her son, but Louis turned to her, a twinkle in his eye, and she knew he would go no further with the powers given to Artoldus. There was no need to replace one tyrant with another.

"My Lord King," Artoldus remained on his knees, head bowed, as he absorbed the words, and only then did Louis extend his hands, and raise him back to his feet.

"Now tell me, has our guest arrived?"

"Indeed, My Lord King, a little earlier than you. He's keen to speak with you, and has, I confess, been pacing with frustration."

"Then, I shall keep him waiting no further. Come, Lady Mother, let us meet Duke Hugh the Black. I'm keen to make the acquaintance of the man whose brother stole my father's kingship, and set matters straight between us."

Eadgifu startled at the name Louis mentioned, aware of Louis' eyes on her, gauging her reaction. She allowed a smile.

It seemed her son had learned well the lesson that King Athelstan had striven to teach him.

An enemy of an enemy could easily become an ally.

If the time was right.

THE KING'S hall in Laon was precisely as she remembered it from the previous year. Hastily, she moved to remove her outer layers, the heat from the great hearth filling the room so that it was almost stifling.

Sitting as close to the fire as possible without singeing his black beard was Duke Hugh the Black. His face showed his frustration, his eyes swivelling from one side of the hall to the other, noticing all who entered and then left.

On seeing the king striding toward him, the duke stood, and hastily took to his knee before the king.

Eadgifu was surprised to see such quick and total submission to Louis.

Duke Hugh the Black was one of the few men who'd refused to

acknowledge Louis' kingship. It seemed that in the last nine months, he'd come to regret that decision.

"My Lord King," the older man's voice seemed to boom even in the rapidly filling hall, and Eadgifu felt her eyebrows rise high, her jaw locking in place, to counter her surprise.

"My Lord Duke Hugh. It's good to finally meet with you."

"It is, My Lord King," the duke stated, still on his knees. "I would pledge my allegiance now, if you would accept it."

Louis, still covered in his great cloak, and with cheeks turned pink by the sudden change from the cold of outside to the heat of his hall, seemed startled but recovered quickly.

"Of course, My Lord. Place your hand on the holy relic, and make your oath."

From somewhere, Archchancellor Artoldus had managed to produce just such a relic, a small carved box, within which Eadgifu knew a fragment of the holy crown of thorns nestled.

When Black Hugh spoke, his words were bluff and well-formed, and only then did Louis command his latest supporter to rise.

"Come, sit, and drink, there's much to discuss on this bright new day, and I would ensure that a good start is made."

Black Hugh nodded, settling on the chair Louis commanded, while Eadgifu and Artoldus followed suit.

"The rest of my supporters will arrive soon. I'll have a mint constructed in Laon, to issue coins in my own name, and with my own weights imposed on them. I'll have orders sent to all of my supporters informing them that Duke Hugh is no longer in command of the regency council and that I rule alone."

Black Hugh drank deeply from a tankard beside him, the contents of which Eadgifu couldn't determine, but she imagined it wasn't ale, not so early in the day.

"Then I'm pleased to be the first to pledge their oath to you. Together, we can ensure the future integrity of West Frankia."

"Yes, we can." Louis confirmed, his cheeks slowly starting to fade from hectic pink to their more normal shade.

With only the smallest swallow of warmed wine, Louis turned to Artoldus.

"Archchancellor, I would have messengers sent to King Athelstan, King Otto and my aunt, and also to Count William, Count Heribert and Count Arnulf. Summon them to Laon. There is much business to discuss, and I would do it with my nobility before me. Also, send for Duke Hugh. He must answer for his decisions, and it's better to have him where I can see him. Ensure he's met by a guard of my English warriors."

"My Lord King," Artoldus rose smoothly, evidently pleased to have such clear instructions so confidently given. Only then did Louis turn to Eadgifu, his face fresh with youth and vigour.

"Now the work truly begins," Louis confirmed, and Eadgifu saw not her son, but rather King Athelstan in that stern gaze.

She almost pitied Duke Hugh then.

Almost.

AD937

"My Lady, Queen Dowager," Eadgifu recognised the voice. She turned to face the man, forgiving him the impertinence of shouting from across the forecourt of Laon.

The winter had finally gone. Louis had been in total control of West Frankia for the last few months, apart from the areas under the command of Duke Hugh and Count Heribert. They threatened insurrection at every moment and resented the restraints of a reinvigorated king.

The messenger was one her sister, Lady Ælfgifu, favoured with news of a more personal nature, and Eadgifu felt a flicker of unease. What did Lady Ælfgifu need to tell her that required such discretion?

"My Lady, Queen Dowager, apologies, but Lady Ælfgifu bid me place this directly into your hands, as soon as I arrived in Laon."

Eadgifu reached out to take the rolled parchment, her eyes settling on the elaborate seal her sister insisted on using, a combination of the Wessex wyvern and the wolf of Arles, but just for a moment, the messenger held the parchment back, a concerned look in his eyes.

"You are bid to open this immediately, and with your son beside you. I'll wait to see if a reply must be sent." Only then did the parchment settle in her hands, as Eadgifu felt the weight of unease settle in her stomach.

Without hesitation, she clutched the parchment and turned to make her way to Louis' council chamber. She knew he was there, embroiled in discussions with Archchancellor Artoldus about Duke Hugh and what his next move would be.

Count Heribert taunted Louis from his own places of strength, and the two threatened to overcome all past animosity and work together to thwart Louis and his ambitions. Count Heribert's wife, Duke Hugh's sister, seemed to be the driving force bringing together the disparate men in her life.

Eadgifu could admire her resolve, but she still hoped Countess Adela of Vermandois failed.

Whatever was contained in this parchment, Eadgifu knew it would somehow impact on Louis' plans, and that Ælfgifu was uniquely placed to know much of what it was.

Trying not to consider the possibilities, Eadgifu ordered the door to the chamber opened and stepped inside, unsurprised when Louis looked at her, shock on his young face. But Louis seemed to immediately recognise the seal swaying with Eadgifu's movements and held his tongue.

Standing beside Louis, Eadgifu reached for a blade and sliced open the seal, before the watchful eyes of Archchancellor Artoldus, her eyes drinking in the sight of her sister's penmanship. Not only had this letter come by the most discrete means possible, but Ælfgifu had chosen to write the letter herself, not trusting those who might intercept her intentions.

Eadgifu gasped, as the words before her formed into a coherent sentence, rage making her hand shake.

"How fucking dare he?" she all but screeched, thrusting the letter into her son's hands so that Artoldus could see its contents as well.

Her body thrummed with the deceit of it all. With the audacity of the man, and with sheer horror at just how quickly Duke Hugh had moved to secure himself a new wife.

"Why did my Aunt allow this?" Louis thundered, but Eadgifu had no answer for her son. It was the same thought she was having. Ælfgi-fu's hasty letter to them spoke of her own desperation at just what Queen Eadgyth had consented to happen.

"I imagine she was not consulted," Artoldus tried to reason with his young king while Eadgifu tried to master her fury filled body.

"That's probably correct," Eadgifu managed to mumble, trying to think while ignoring her hatred. It enticed her to do something much worse to Duke Hugh than the news of his marriage would allow. Why, she thought, had she allowed him to live when the opportunity had presented itself to have him killed on the night Louis had fled Paris. Why?

"Is Duchess Hadwig favoured by King Otto?"

"I don't believe I've met her," Eadgifu stated, trying to remember. Otto had many sisters, she wasn't sure she'd been introduced to them all when she'd attended his coronation at Aachen. The time had been spent with her sisters.

"Not that it matters. It seems that Duke Hugh has found a new royal dynasty to ally himself with, and it's not my own, but rather that of the rival Kings of East Frankia." Contempt laced Louis' words, and Eadgifu was unsurprised. Duke Hugh had reacted to Louis' claim to rule alone with decisive and potentially damning action. The speed of the response staggered Eadgifu. As did her sister's acceptance of it. She, Eadgyth and Ælfgifu had taken an oath to bring the kingdoms closer together, not drive them further apart.

"Will King Otto support Duke Hugh to claim the West Frankish kingdom?"

"He'd better not," Eadgifu found herself all but exploding. "Queen Eadgyth might not have been able to stop the marriage, but I'm sure that she'll not allow her husband to make war against her own nephew."

Louis looked far from convinced. Eadgifu was unsurprised.

This was a damning move, and one perhaps stolen from King Athelstan's own acquisition of York through the marriage of Lady Ecgwynn and King Sihtric. Louis was right to be concerned.

"I can't believe this," Archchancellor Artoldus offered, his words expressing their own shock. "For all Duke Hugh's many faults, I can't comprehend that he'd incite another kingdom to rise against the rightful King of West Frankia."

"Duke Hugh has been thwarted by Louis. He thought Louis would be his to control, and he wasn't. Now it seems he seeks another way to enforce his command over West Frankia."

Louis' eyes met those of his mother's, and Eadgifu quickly understood the pain there.

It was Duke Hugh's father who'd first claimed Charles' crown from him. It seemed the son, despite him being the driving force in returning to Louis to West Frankia, was little different, in the end.

"We must think quickly, and ensure the other counts and lords are still loyal to Louis. Perhaps King Athelstan could be enticed to send some small force this way? The English warriors always cause fear because they're so brutal and skilled compared to the West Frankish. Perhaps, as well, an alliance could be agreed with Count Arnulf or even Count William of Normandy."

Eadgifu nodded as Artoldus spoke. He'd absorbed the news more calmly than she or her son, but then, it was not Artoldus' own family who'd turned against them. It made it easy.

"That is clear thinking," Louis recovered first. "And I'll consider an attack closer to King Otto's kingdom, alert him of my unease and that the matter will not go unpunished."

Eadgifu was nodding, and trying to think coherently, all at the same time

"An aggressive piece of warcraft will be needed," she mused softly. "We've tried peace, and that has not worked. I'd suggest a pre-emptive strike on Lotharingia. Bring the men to your side, and they'll defy King Otto if they know they have your support." Eadgifu thought of Duke Gilbert. When she'd met him, she'd sensed that all was not smooth between him and King Henry. Now, with his wife's brother as his king, he might be even more willing to change his allegiance.

Louis glanced at his mother, a look of shock on his face at what she'd suggested. Eadgifu tried to find a smile but realised it came off as less than reassuring.

"King Athelstan is a master at knowing when to attack, and when to threaten. We must do the same. Have the men ready to march on Verdun. It's a potent symbol of the East Frankish king's possession of Lotharingia."

"But what about in the king's absence? Duke Hugh and his allies will try and take advantage if he's not in West Frankia."

Eadgifu paused then, the thoughts of the battle glory that awaited her son seeming to drain away in light of Artoldus' reasoned words. Louis did not yet hold Laon and his patrimonial lands as firmly as he could. Certainly, it was not a secure holding, as Wessex and Mercia had always been for King Athelstan as he'd pushed ever northwards.

"We'll need someone to hold Laon in Louis' absence. I'll do it. Leave me with half the English warriors. Count William of Normandy might be trusted, and so might Cousin Arnulf of Flanders, although I do suspect perhaps not. It'll be a matter of putting the men in positions where they can prove their loyalty rather than embarrass the kingdom."

"In fact, no, we should have Black Hugh hold Laon for the king, a reward for his loyalty so far. I don't believe that he'll ever reconcile with Duke Hugh, not now." This was Louis' suggestion, but Eadgifu was not alone in nodding her agreement.

"And a marriage must be arranged for the king," Archchancellor Artoldus tempted fate by asking for more when Louis was only just seventeen, and yet he was right to do so.

"A suitable bride for the king can be dangled as a means of procuring the allegiance of more questionable allies. But who? Count Arnulf's daughters are too young, Count William has only a son."

Louis laughed then, the sound harsh as they discussed his future.

"In all honesty, Lady Mother, there are few daughters to go around. I'd thought to propose a union with East Frankia, but that's impossible now."

Eadgifu sighed at the words. Indeed, Louis was not alone in thinking an East Frankish wife would have been the answer. Even Duke Hugh had realised that. Eadgifu had also suggested it to Queen Eadgyth. They'd decided it would be an excellent way to secure peace between East and West Frankia. It wouldn't be. Not now. Not ever.

"For now, we'll concentrate on retaliation for the marriage. My own marriage will have to be solved in time. Have Black Hugh summoned from his lands, and my own warriors arraigned with all they need to take the war to Otto's kingdom."

Artoldus stood, bowed quickly, and understanding the words as an instruction, turned to leave the chamber.

"My Lord King, Queen Dowager," Archchancellor Artoldus paused just before he reached the door, his voice echoing over his shoulder. "The counts have always been unruly, but I'm confident that King Louis will be able to outthink them all. After all, My Lord King, you learned at the knee not of your father, who lost his kingdom, but at your Uncle, King Athelstan, who fashioned his own."

With that, Artoldus was gone, and Eadgifu turned to face her son's wild eyes, her own unease starting to settle.

"The Archchancellor is correct to remind us of your Uncle. King Athelstan does not shy away from battle. Even now, we know he's making ready to counter an attack by the Dublin Norse, the Scots and even the men of Strathclyde."

"Your Uncle will prevail, and so will you."

The words soothed Louis, and yet he was no fool, and Eadgifu could detect that in the stubborn set of his shoulders, and his clamped jaw.

This was the beginning of a war that Duke Hugh would regret instigating. The man needed to learn the limits of his own power.

WHILE PLANS WERE BEING ORGANISED, the messenger who'd travelled to Laon with news from Lady Ælfgifu was dispatched to her, his message, to thank her for the information and to determine the likely alliance of her husband's brother. Only the messenger returned much sooner than anticipated, shock on his face.

"My Lady, Queen Dowager," the bow was tight, and Eadgifu pulled unwillingly from discussions with Louis' warriors, forced the frustration from her face.

"I regret to inform you of the death of King Rudolf II of Arles." Eadgifu knew her expression blanched.

"Lady Ælfgifu's brother by marriage is dead?" she asked the question, just to be sure.

"Regrettably so, his son, Conrad, has been proclaimed as king."

"But he's a child?"

"Yes, Conrad is no more than twelve years old."

Eadgifu felt the breath leave her body in a deep sigh. Her son had only had mere months to himself, and all around her, she could feel the tide turning. Whether it was for or against him, was another matter entirely.

"There is some concern that King Conrad will fall under the spell of King Hugh of Italy or King Otto of East Frankia."

Eadgifu glanced at the man sharply.

"Did Lady Ælfgifu inform you of this?"

"Yes, she dare not commit the words to parchment, not this time."

Eadgifu nodded, surprised by her youngest sister's presence of mind.

"I'll ensure the king is made aware," Eadgifu confirmed. "Inform my sister, help will be provided if it's needed. No matter what else the king is currently dealing with."

The man nodded, his expression grim. "I imagine I'll see you soon."

"Indeed, go with my blessing and take this with you." Eadgifu slipped a ring from her finger. It was ceremonial, and not expensive, but it harboured an image of the Wessex wyvern on its surface.

"This will keep you safe, and if not, go to England. Present yourself to King Athelstan, and all will be well."

The man canted his head to one side, his hand hovering, as though unsure whether to take the ring or not.

"I have a family," he eventually admitted.

"They'll be welcomed as well," Eadgifu confirmed. She would not see a man lose his life to aid her and her sisters. That had never been her way.

"You believe it will become this desperate?" the messenger asked, his brown eyes glistening with concern.

"It's always better to be prepared," Eadgifu muttered, keen to be done with the man.

"Then you have my deepest thanks," and the messenger turned and was gone.

Eadgifu settled her expression. Louis would not take this news well. It was rife for further exploitation. As far as Lady Ælfgifu's adopted territory was from West Frankia, it was still an important kingdom. If King Otto took control of the boy, which was highly likely, he'd have an alliance with Duke Hugh, the command of Lotharingia and more than nominal control in Arles.

She found Louis seated with Archchancellor Artoldus, both of them wore expressions of purposefulness and Eadgifu was loath to spoil their confidence but knew she must.

"Lady Mother," Louis greeted her with a warm smile, that slid from his face when he saw her expression.

"What is it now?" Louis almost moaned, and Eadgifu felt sympathy for him. He was young to be dealing with a rebellion from the man who was supposed to be his greatest ally, and it was only going to get worse.

"The messenger from Lady Ælfgifu returned. I'm afraid that King Rudolf II of Arles is dead. His son is king in his place, but Conrad is only a child."

A myriad of emotions flickered over Louis' face, as he tried to comprehend what this meant for him. It was Archchancellor Artoldus who spoke first, his eyes shadowed by the realisation of these problems.

"King Otto plans to seize control of the boy?"

"It is suspected, yes."

Now Louis fully understood, and he jumped from his chair, pacing from one end of the room to the other, seemingly forgetting he was not alone.

"King Otto already thinks to have a say in the running of too many kingdoms, not his to rule. He's as ambitious as Duke Hugh."

Eadgifu held her tongue, there was no point denying that assertion. Her gaze settled on Archchancellor Artoldus as he moved parchments around the table. From the bottom of the pile, he pulled one parchment that he laid out, using water jugs and a few handy coloured stones, to weigh it down.

Eadgifu knew it to be a plan, showing the extent of West Frankia, and also her neighbours. It showed the markings of constant updating, and there were lines scratched over other lines, but all the same, it clearly showed where the Kingdom of Arles was in relation to both King Otto and Louis' domains.

"Black Hugh will be unhappy with King Otto prowling ever closer." Eadgifu spoke as she gazed at the map.

"He will yes, but he should remain our ally, if only because it will prevent him from taking orders from King Otto." Louis spoke with assurance.

"Is the kingdom also under threat from the south?"

"Yes, it will be. Arles is a new kingdom, formed only when King Rudolf ceded his claims to Italy. I'm sure King Hugh of Italy will be keen to take advantage of this unexpected event to expand his own domain." Archchancellor Artoldus spoke with his longer experience with the kingdoms under discussion.

"Yes, he will be. It feels as though young Conrad will be overrun. But, it might distract King Otto from Duke Hugh." Louis sounded hopeful.

"It might yes, or we could take our men to support Conrad, after all, he is your aunt's nephew." The thought of war worried Eadgifu, but as Louis was already determined on it, it was just a matter of where he went.

Louis grunted an agreement, his steps ceasing as he peered down at the parchment.

"King Otto thinks to profit from all this, and I'm surrounded by men who should be my allies but are my enemies."

"Then, we need to make more allies," Eadgifu offered into the silence, trying to decide the best action for her son to take.

"Lotharingia is still the answer," Artoldus advised, and Eadgifu was minded to agree with his pronouncement.

"Lotharingia is the prize that will infuriate King Otto. His own sister's husband is keen to claim you as their ally, rather than Otto. More than half the nobility still think they're ruled by West Frankia, and the other half would wish it were so."

"And, of course," and here Louis met Artoldus' eyes squarely. "As the archbishop of Rheims, you're the Archbishop of Lotharingia."

"Yes, I'd not forgotten that," Artoldus confirmed, while Eadgifu listened carefully.

"Lady Mother, you will hold Laon, as agreed, while we strike out as far as Verdun, as agreed. If we can distract King Otto from the affairs of the Kingdom of Arles, then that will assist young Conrad and Lady Ælfgifu, as well as ourselves."

Eadgifu was a breath away from agreeing when there was a thundering knock on the door of the chamber.

All three of them stood straight, staring at the door in shock before Louis found his voice and bid the servant entered.

The man who strode into the chamber was no servant, but rather a man that Eadgifu knew rather well, Duke Alain of Brittany.

Louis' eyes opened wide on seeing his fellow exile from their time together at Athelstan's court in Wessex. Louis abruptly laughed, delight bubbling from his open mouth.

"My Lord King, Queen Dowager, Archchancellor," Alain, never one to forget his courtesies, clipped a bow to them all, and then stood, a beaming smile on his face.

"Amongst all these difficulties, I bring you news from King Athelstan, emperor over all of Britain. He has secured a great victory over the Dublin Norse, the King of the Scots, and the King of Strathclyde. The battle of Brunanburh was long and bloody, and at least eight kings lost their lives on the battlefield. Still, none of them was Athelstan, although, unfortunately, Lord Ælfwine and Æthelwine lost their lives."

Eadgifu gasped at the news, her eyes sliding from Louis to Alain, waiting to see what they would do next, as her thoughts turned to her dead cousins. Ælfwine and Æthelwine had firmly been King Athelstan's allies, but it felt strange to realise these were deaths of men of her own generation. It turned her thoughts to Duchess Eadhild. Her sister, dead and gone too soon.

Louis seemed to stand a little taller at the news, seemed to grow in stature as he turned to gaze at his mother, an eyebrow quirked, a smile playing on his lips.

"My Uncle, King Athelstan, has won a great battle. And now, I will do the same." Louis' proclamation ended on a growl, and Eadgifu felt herself swept along with the heady feeling of impending success.

Louis had learned well at King Athelstan's knee. And now he would use that, and the momentum from Athelstan's own victory to secure his own.

AD938

Eadgifu listened to the messenger, a flicker of unease in her eyes, as she toyed with a wine goblet before her, although she never lifted the glass to drink from it.

King Louis and Archchancellor Artoldus were gone from Laon. They'd been for much of the previous summer and winter. Their forces had travelled to Verdun, as decided, where they'd over-wintered.

While Louis had refused to accept the oath of Duke Gilbert and Duchess Gerberga, it had been possible for Archchancellor Artoldus to have the bishops of Verdun, Toul and Metz commend themselves to King Louis. After all, they belonged to the Archbishopric of Laon, and Artoldus was subject to King Louis, and therefore, so must the bishoprics be.

It had been an intriguing way of ensuring Louis gained without declaring outright war on King Otto, but for all that, it seemed that Otto was determined to retaliate.

"Along the River Seine?" Eadgifu queried, just to be sure.

"Yes, My Lady, Queen Dowager. King Otto encamps along the banks of the Seine. Even now Duke Hugh, Count Heribert, Count Arnulf and Count William are believed to have joined him. Duke

Hugh and Count Heribert are said to have given their oath to him at Attigny."

Eadgifu absorbed the blow while managing to keep her expression calm. Attigny was her son's possession. Duke Hugh and Count Heribert had no right to be there, let alone King Otto.

Louis had returned from Lotharingia at the start of the year but had travelled to the kingdom of Arles at the behest of his aunt, to help young Conrad secure his possessions against attack. King Otto had moved quickly to take advantage of Louis' absence from West Frankia. So too had Louis' West Frankish enemies.

"So all of them have decided to put aside their oaths to King Louis," she mused. Eadgifu was aware that many eyes were watching her, some horrified at the news that there was an East Frankish king in West Frankia. In contrast, others just looked intrigued.

Eadgifu had spent much of the winter months trying to communicate with her sister, Queen Eadgyth, but her direct overtures had been largely ignored. Only encouraging news from Lady Ælfgifu, in Arles, had assured Eadgifu that Otto's queen was doing all she could to bring the continuing discord to an end.

It seemed that the task, on this occasion, had proven to be impossible.

"Does King Otto intend to attack Louis, or make a truce?"

The messenger looked blankly at Eadgifu, and she sighed softly. Why had she asked him that? He was just a messenger, sent to inform the king of the current problems.

"I'll ensure the king is made aware of the development. In the meantime, I'll summon the king's household warriors and have them at least form a barricade between King Otto's forces, and that of Louis' own."

It would be difficult, but possible. Louis needed to return from the Kingdom of Arles, but Otto was in West Frankia. It was highly likely they would meet, whether they wanted to or not.

The man bowed deeply, but he hesitated, and in the movement, Eadgifu realised there was more the man needed to tell her.

"Step closer," she commanded imperiously, and the messenger did.

"Is there more?"

"Duke Hugh has drained Paris of all her fighting men. I've seen them all, on my way here. They carry the banner of Paris with them, and there must be thousands of them."

Eadgifu nodded, surprised by the man's ingenuity in telling her this.

"Tell me again, who sent you?"

The man's face split into a wane smile.

"Duke Gilbert of Lotharingia." Eadgifu absorbed the information. Duke Gilbert was desperate to earn the respect of King Louis.

"Return to Duke Gilbert with my greatest thanks. Inform him that King Louis will reward him." The man's tongue poked through his lips, a wry grin on his face before he turned away and made his way from the king's hall in Laon.

She'd been left in Laon, to keep it safe. After all, it was the king's capital of West Frankia and was strategically vital, but it might well be threatened by King Otto's force now.

Frustrated, Eadgifu had one of her own messengers brought to her.

"Ride fast, as fast as you can while ensuring you and your horses arrive alive. Inform King Louis that King Otto has taken the oaths of his noblemen and that he's encamped on the banks of the River Seine. Inform the king that I remain in Laon, and will do for as long as possible."

The messenger, an English man who'd come to Laon when Louis had been crowned, and never returned, nodded in understanding, his eyes alert to the danger of his task.

"If King Louis sends you back to Laon, but we're surrounded by the enemy, don't attempt to get past them. Return to King Louis and inform him of the danger."

"My Lady, Queen Dowager," the man bowed and was gone quickly, but Eadgifu hardly saw him leave, so deep in thought was she.

For a moment, Eadgifu considered calling the messenger back, changing her plans. Perhaps Louis should cause further problems in the Kingdom of Arles, and even on the border with the kingdom of the East Franks? But she held her tongue.

Louis was no fool. He would quickly determine the best action to take.

Eadgifu's thoughts then turned to King Athelstan.

After the victory of Brunanburh, a swell of blood-thirsty Englishmen had come to Laon, to support King Louis in Lotharingia, the joy of their great triumph needing to be repeated. All of the men had shown their mettle, but many had returned to England now, their desire for more and greater bloodshed, seemingly exhausted. Eadgifu wished she still had the command of those men. It would have made it far easier for her to keep Laon against the pretensions of King Otto.

But, no. She must not think of war, but instead of securing peace, and with that in mind, she rose and made her way to the royal scriptorium. She needed ink and parchment to send yet another letter to her sister.

They needed to work together, to secure peace, otherwise King Otto, with the goading of King Louis' enemies, ran the risk of losing both kingdoms. Eadgifu knew that could never happen.

BUT BEFORE LOUIS could return from the Kingdom of Arles, more troubling information made its way to Eadgifu. She'd hoped with the intelligence that King Otto's force was making its slow way back toward his own kingdom, that all would be well. She'd been wrong to expect as such.

Yet another messenger stumbled before her, his face sheeted in white, his terror clear to see. Eadgifu held her jaw clenched, almost wishing she didn't have to hear what came next.

"My Lady, Queen Dowager, I come from Black Hugh. He's been forced to come to terms with King Otto to hold onto his kingdom."

Black Hugh, was Louis' most loyal supporter, now.

Eadgifu nodded.

"Where did this take place?"

"On the border. King Otto attacked Burgundy, and Black Hugh

was forced to meet him in battle, only he was captured." The outrage in the messenger's voice mirrored Eadgifu's own, and yet she held herself stony and still in the face of such terrible intelligence.

Not for the first time she wished that Louis would hurry and return from the Kingdom of Arles. What point was there in young Conrad having a kingdom if Louis lost his own?

Eadgifu wished for some good news but knew it was pointless. Her sister was ignoring her. Whether, through choice or necessity, Eadgifu was unsure. Even messages sent via Lady Ælfgifu in Arles were no longer being received. Eadgifu doubted it was because Louis was in receipt of them.

Behind the messenger, Eadgifu noticed a further disturbance, and her eyes immediately sought out what was happening, her heart hammering too loudly in her chest. What catastrophe was this?

"My Lady, Queen Dowager," this messenger was burnt ruby red by the sun, and the smell of sweat and horse reached her nostrils even from her place on the raised dais.

"King Otto has recrossed the Rhine. He's going home."

Two such contradictory pieces of news left Eadgifu at a loss as to how to reply. Instead, she indicated to one of her servants that both men should be offered food and water, or ale, or wine, or whatever they needed, before sweeping from the king's hall. She needed to be alone and away from the scrutiny of so many. She was shaking too much to be seen.

Was King Otto's retreat a real one? Did something drive him homewards? Eadgifu couldn't help but hope that Louis' involvement in the Kingdom of Arles might be the root course of Otto's actions. If it was, it meant that the disagreements between the two kingdoms were far from over.

It was her role to try and restore peace, but everything was far too complicated to even work out how that could be achieved.

Angrily, she walked into the king's chamber, inspecting the map that lay on the table. It highlighted the kingdoms of West and East Frankia, the contentious domain of Lotharingia, the Kingdom of Burgundy, the Kingdom of Arles, and of course, the smaller territories ruled by the counts of Vermandois, Normandy, Flanders and Aquitaine.

How Charlemagne had ever crafted so many personalities into one kingdom defied her understanding.

EADGIFU WAS surprised when the demand for peace came not from her sister, Queen Eadgyth, but rather from Count Arnulf. With narrowed eyes, Louis as surprised as she was, listened to the man her cousin had sent with his suggestion.

The last she'd heard, Count Arnulf had allied himself with King Otto, but now his messenger informed them that Arnulf himself would arrive in a day, two at the most, and he came under a flag of truce, at the behest of King Athelstan, and with the agreement of King Otto.

"Count Arnulf is keen to have peace between East and West Frankia," the messenger reiterated. He spoke in English and Eadgifu was convinced that he was one of Athelstan's trusted messengers.

"Why does Count Arnulf involve himself in this?" Louis asked the question, Archchancellor Artoldus behind him, his own grey eyes as interested. For a moment, Eadgifu thought the man wouldn't answer, but then he began to speak.

"King Athelstan has made overtures of friendship to Count Arnulf following the deaths of his cousins at Brunanburh. King Athelstan is keen to have peace restored amongst all of his kin."

While Artoldus looked far from believing at the lofty statement, Eadgifu, despite it all, found a smile playing around her lips. It sounded just like something that King Athelstan would have thought and found to be acceptable.

Indeed, Louis looked contemplative as well.

"Then inform Count Arnulf that he'll be welcome in Laon," Louis stated before dismissing the man.

"King Athelstan would truly have done this?" Artoldus asked, and Eadgifu found herself nodding along with Louis. It felt good to have

Louis and Artoldus back in Laon. The strains of her son's long absence had been onerous.

"My Uncle is a man of high ideals. After Brunanburh, he'll be keen to have peace restored amongst the far-flung members of the House of Wessex. It's not outside the bounds of possibility. Perhaps he's right. I personally don't like having to fight battles against family members, even when I've never met them."

"But why Count Arnulf? Why not send Duke Alain, as he did when he won at Brunanburh? He's more neutral than Count Arnulf could ever be."

Louis paused to consider his answer.

"Duke Alain hasn't been restored to his kingdom for long, and even now, I know Viking Raiders plague him. Count Arnulf is more secure in Flanders. He's held control there for over a decade and can be spared."

"And he's met King Otto," Eadgifu added. She didn't mention that it was when he'd pledged his allegiance to King Otto, as opposed to his true liege lord. "He might be best placed. Perhaps it's a good thing. Perhaps not."

"If we make peace with King Otto, he'll immediately turn his attention to young Conrad's plight. As much as I feel we didn't accomplish as much as I'd have liked, I'm at least sure that for now, the kingdom is safe in the hands of his Uncle and my Aunt. Lord Louis and Lady Ælfgifu greatly love their new, young king."

"Are you saying that King Athelstan won't get his peace?" Artoldus demanded to know, his expression showing the unease he felt at the prospect of peace talks with King Otto.

Louis shook his head, as though to deny those words, but then reconsidered.

"King Athelstan is a realist, not a dreamer, for all that this suggestion sounds far-fetched. I imagine that he's simply reminding everyone of his new status. We've relied on English warriors before. My own warriors have never left West Frankia. My Uncle will pledge more, should King Otto prove intractable."

"But it's not just King Otto, is it? It's Duke Hugh and Count Heribert. Those two men have no compunction about stirring up difficulties, and of course, Duke Hugh's wife is vastly pregnant. He could birth an heir to his kingdom any time soon."

Eadgifu felt swift fury cover her face at the reminder that Hadwig, King Otto's sister, was about to give birth. It reminded her of Duchess Eadhild, and her terrible death, and only served to reinforce the ruthlessness of Duke Hugh.

He would destroy anyone, even the women in his life, to get what he felt was his.

"Let us hear what Count Arnulf has to say, and then make a decision after that. Certainly, the wars of the last year have been difficult on the people of the kingdoms. It would work well if they could be assured of their harvests and survive the winter without the threat of starvation."

"Well said, Lady Mother," Louis agreed, only a hint of refusal in his voice.

Eadgifu mirrored her son's mixed feelings.

Did they really want peace with King Otto? Certainly, the wall of silence, using official channels between Queen Eadgyth and her, made Eadgifu think that even if peace were established, it would not last long. How could it, when neither party truly wished to make a lasting peace?

Or at least, the kings, dukes and count didn't wish to.

Eadgifu longed for Queen Eadgyth to send word of her true intentions.

COUNT ARNULF ARRIVED at Laon in a whirl of expensive cloth, mounted on an even more costly horse, and bedecked like a warrior, for all he wore no helm around his head.

Not for the first time, Eadgifu realised that where Count Arnulf was concerned, King Athelstan was blinded by family ties to his real personality.

"My Lord King," even Count Arnulf's greeting sounded forced. Yet,

Louis, somehow better at masking his emotions, was able to greet his errant second cousin, with more grace.

Eadgifu watched on, noting Countess Adele, Arnulf's wife, and Count Heribert's daughter. Already three children had been born to her and Arnulf, and Eadgifu wouldn't be surprised to find the younger woman was pregnant once more.

Count Heribert used his massive family to full advantage. The man had no compunction about hedging his bets to ensure he benefited.

Only later, after a mass and a feast in honour of their meeting, did Eadgifu feel compelled to listen to the words of Count Arnulf.

Secluded in a formal room, similar to Louis' private office, their small party came together. A handful of monks joined them to make notes as deemed necessary. Eadgifu noted that one of the monks was assuredly someone she'd seen before. How, she wondered, had King Athelstan managed to insinuate one of his most trusted men into such a position?

She held her tongue, though. If Count Arnulf hadn't drawn attention to the man, it was possible he didn't know, and Eadgifu was not about to inform him of the spy in his ranks.

"My Lord King," Count Arnulf began with a self-satisfied smirk. He exuded confidence, and Eadgifu imagined it came from the fact that Arnulf was the oldest person in the room, and therefore thought he knew better than everyone else.

"I've come to make my apologies for my actions in pledging myself to King Otto. It was, as I'm sure you can imagine, a difficult decision for me to reach. King Otto has seen fit to release me from my oath. King Athelstan has decided that because I'm known to both you and King Otto, and also his cousin, that I can smooth this terrible situation. King Athelstan's sisters must be united despite the actions of their husband and their son."

Eadgifu noted that Count Arnulf again made no mention of the Kingdom of Arles or Lady Ælfgifu. That interested her, but not enough to drag her from taking careful note of Count Arnulf's words.

"King Athelstan has proposed that a mutual accord be reached between King Otto and yourself. It will return the allegiance of all men to their actual king. It will restore the status quo to that at the time of the accession of both King Louis and King Otto."

Eadgifu tried to hear the words as opposed to the smug tone, but even so, she found herself wishing that it was Arnulf who'd died too young, and not Adelolf. Adelolf had always been less pleased with himself.

"King Athelstan suggests that such an agreement need not require hostages to be exchanged. If the peace accord is reached, neither of the kings will be losing or gaining anything at the expense of the other."

Eadgifu conceded it was a good idea, but she decried the idealistic tone of the meeting. Or she did until Arnulf continued to speak.

"King Athelstan wishes it to be known that he will personally gainsay the agreement. Should West Frankia retaliate against East Frankia, Athelstan will send his much-proven fleet to settle the matter, and vice versa. He will also send his own household warriors if it becomes necessary."

"King Athelstan did not ask me to remind anyone of this, but he has fought and won a great battle in England. The English kingdom is the most settled it has been for over half a century. King Athelstan has the reputation of a fair and just king, but one who will trample down those who rebel against him."

Whether this was an illusion to Edwin's execution or not, Eadgifu refused to be drawn on it. Edwin had been dead many years now. His passing had undoubtedly made it easier for Eadgifu to build a relationship with King Athelstan.

"And these terms have been offered to King Otto?" Archchancellor Artoldus asked the question before Louis could, but Louis seemed unoffended.

"I'll journey to East Frankia next, to visit with King Otto at Aachen, and lay before him the same terms. There is no favouritism. King Athelstan seeks only a unity of purpose."

"Then I believe that King Athelstan can have his family reunion," Louis announced, his forehead creased in thought. "I would not want my Uncle to ever think that I was dismissive of his care for my well-being and for that of my kingdom. Should the East Frankish King not wish to avail himself of this intercession by King Athelstan, then I'll call upon my Uncle to provide the support he has suggested."

A gleam of triumph entered Count Arnulf's eye, and yet Eadgifu was more admiring of her son.

Louis had taken the decision to abide by King Athelstan's desires quickly, and without asking for concessions, or less favourable terms for King Otto. Some might see it as a sign of weakness, but what Louis had done was to prove himself amenable to ending the problems caused by Duke Hugh's marriage to King Otto's sister, and to do so swiftly.

King Otto would have no room for manoeuvre, not now, and not if he didn't wish King Athelstan's fleet to come bearing down on Lotharingia.

Eadgifu watched her son carefully, seeing before her the child she had birthed, and cared for becoming the man who would rule West Frankia far better than his weak father ever had.

AD939

E adgifu moved quickly through the mass of swirling men and horses.

She had only one objective in mind. She couldn't quite understand why her son hadn't presented himself to her the moment he'd returned to Laon.

Trying to find him amongst so many others was proving difficult. No matter who she stopped and asked, each and every face showing shock at being addressed by the dowager queen, and none had yet managed to answer her demand to know where Louis was.

And his new wife.

Even now, she had to pause, take a moment and step to the side of all the horses and men, loaded carts and people. There were people everywhere, but they were not the ones she wanted.

Damn the boy.

Louis was returned from the disputed Lotharingia once more, and his campaign had been a great success. Lotharingia lay within Louis' grasp. King Otto had been out-thought once more, and Louis had taken his boldest step yet. One that Eadgifu believed she approved of. Certainly, she couldn't fault her son for thinking so quickly about how to play the situation to enhance his own prestige against Otto. Still, until Eadgifu saw her son, she refused to make a decision.

"My Lady, Queen Dowager Eadgifu," the man who bowed before her was well known to her, and she smiled. Bishop Rorice was fiercely loyal to his half-brother.

"The king is within the cathedral, with his wife. Here, I shall escort you."

Eadgifu nodded absently, taking hold of Rorice's arm. Her gaze was focused on the cathedral, shimmering in the sun before her. Now, if she squinted, she could make out the king's horse, and those of his English household warriors, close to the cathedral door. She should have realised and gone there straight away.

Content with silence, Eadgifu didn't speak to Rorice but welcomed his help in forging a clear path for her. In no time at all, Rorice was bowing to her once more, releasing her arm so that she could enter the cathedral.

She should have realised her son would be keen to show his new wife the location of his coronation, and no doubt the one he'd promised her as well.

Pausing, to catch her breath, Eadgifu cast her mind back to the time she'd spent in Aachen at Otto's coronation. Gerberga had been there, to see her brother's triumph, and yet no matter how hard she tried, Eadgifu could not see the woman in her memories. Three years ago, it had hardly mattered who Gerberga was, but now it mattered a great deal.

The warriors on guard duty close to the doors bowed respectfully as she passed. Eadgifu tried not to wrinkle her nose at the stench of horse and sweat and wondered if the men were pleased with their assignment, or if they'd rather be washing and changing.

Not that they stood alone, no, a handful of others waited. Eadgifu paused, considering who these men and women were, all dressed finely before she noticed small hands clasped the larger ones. She realised that these were Lady Gerberga's special servants. They guarded her children and had been lucky enough to be chosen to escort her from Lotharingia to West Frankia.

Eadgifu paused, unsure how to proceed, only to hear the soft murmur of voices, immediately recognising the one that belonged to her son.

Without waiting, she strode to Louis, where he stood, arm around a young woman, whose head was inclined upwards, as Louis pointed to something on the ceiling of the cathedral.

"My Lord Son," the words sounded too loud even in the vast space, and Louis' head immediately whipped around, a smile on his young face, dirtied by the sun, joy in his bright eyes.

"Ah, Lady Mother, Bishop Rorice found you. Good. I'm keen for you to meet my wife, Lady Gerberga."

As he spoke, Louis turned toward the woman, his arm staying in place as he encouraged her to turn and face the woman she would be supplanting in the king's high favour.

"My Lady, Queen Dowager," the eyes that met Eadgifu's were far from modest, and yet they held no malice either. Gerberga was used to being a woman of great importance, Eadgifu could tell. And of everyone within West Frankia, it was Eadgifu who would be Gerberga's greatest enemy or ally. It would all depend.

"My Lady Gerberga," Eadgifu was suddenly unsure if she should curtsey or not, and so chose not to. Use of her title was enough. Or so she hoped.

"I hear you've enchanted my son, and convinced him of the need for a wife."

Gerberga startled at the words, while Louis' eyebrows shot upwards. Eadgifu held her ground. It was good to shock, on occasion.

"I would welcome you to my family," Eadgifu continued, stepping forward to plant kisses on both of Gerberga's cheeks. Gerberga accepted the welcome but said nothing into the small silence that suddenly fell between them all.

Gerberga smelt of fresh air, and beneath her beautiful cloak, made of silk, and serving no purpose other than to show her vast wealth, Eadgifu could tell that for all the children she and her first husband had brought into the world, she'd retained an enviable figure.

Her face was free of lines, her cheeks flushed pink, although the spectre of the last few weeks seemed to lurk in the slight down turn of her mouth.

Only then did Lady Gerberga curtsey, a sincere show of respect. Eadgifu was as shocked as she'd made both her son and his wife.

"I thank you for such a warm welcome," Lady Gerberga offered, her words soft, and her eyes downcast, as she straightened.

"It's not easy to enter a new kingdom, with few allies, other than my husband, and I would hope to call you one. I'm more than aware that this must surprise you." As she spoke, Gerberga indicated Louis with her hand, and Eadgifu nodded, but not unkindly.

"My son is a king, he must have a wife, and children, to rule after him. Who that wife would be has long vexed me. With the decision made, I can begin to consider other problems, and of course, how to reconcile with my sister over this new one." Eadgifu spoke without heat to her voice. It was impossible to be angry with her son, no matter her personal opinions about his choice of wife.

In all honesty, Louis' marriage, to Gerberga, might just be the best piece of statecraft she'd ever witnessed. Eadgifu was sure when the difficulties of marrying the King of East Frankia's recently widowed sister without his permission had been resolved, that Gerberga would prove to be a perfect solution to the problems between West and East.

She thought back to the discussion with Queen Eadgyth when they'd pledged to try and bring about a union between East and West Frankia. It had taken three long years of war and attrition, so far.

Gerberga spoke then, as though sensing Eadgifu's thoughts.

"My brother, the king, will forgive me, in time. I've always been his favourite sister, and dearest to him, for all we have not been close for many years now. My husband, sorry, my first husband, Duke Gilbert, was keen to be respected by my brother. But I fear he also thrived on the chaos of taking up arms against Otto."

"Then your brother will settle a peace now that you're married to my son, and agree that Lotharingia is part of West Frankia."

For a moment, Eadgifu thought Gerberga was going to answer in the positive, only then she laughed, such an unexpected sound that Eadgifu jumped.

Gerberga came to Eadgifu's side, and looped an arm through Eadgifu's, only to then lean to her ear and whisper.

"My brother will be furious. I'm sure of that. But he will come to terms with it quickly, I assure you of that. But now, let us talk of family, and children, and all that must be done, and not matters of kingdoms and kings. I'm weary of the whole thing."

"I would sooner you show me around this wonderful place, and I'd introduce you to my children. Alas, I only have my daughters with me, but they are bright and beautiful, although my heart weeps for my sons. My brother Henry assures me he'll keep them safe and away from harm, but of course, they had to remain in Lotharingia, as their father's heir."

Eadgifu realised that she'd become a grandmother almost overnight. She was not sure that she'd love these children on sight, as had happened between King Athelstan and Louis.

Yet Louis still smiled, and Eadgifu knew she would try if only to keep her son happy.

With a fond look, Lady Gerberga turned from Louis and began to guide Eadgifu back toward her small collection of servants and children. Eadgifu focused on those before her, realising now that not all of the children were quite as young as she thought they were. Certainly, the eyes of one of the girls were piercing, head held high, a tremble on her lips. But for all that, Eadgifu wondered if she wouldn't like the girl.

"This is Alberade, my oldest daughter. Alberade, this is your stepfather's mother, Queen Dowager Eadgifu." The girl slithered from the sanctuary of the woman she stood beside and executed a perfect curtsey, her eyes downcast, and her movements precise and detailed.

"I'm pleased to meet you," the voice was young and yet seemed to hold the wisdom of age, although she spoke English with a strong accent.

"And I'm pleased to meet you. I hope we can be friends, and that you'll grow to like West Frankia."

"I'm sure I will," Alberade stated, the words belying neither pleasure nor pain.

"She's a good girl, and will soon make someone an excellent wife. I'm proud of her, and her father would be as well." They were hardly words Eadgifu expected from Lady Gerberga, and yet, well, they were correct. Just as she had been a daughter once, a piece of machinery for her father to play with, so to was Alberade for her mother and step-father.

"And these two are Gerberge and Wiltrude." One of the children was surely no older than two for all Wiltrude stood on her own two feet. Gerberge was older, but not by much. All three girls shared the same soft blond curls that their father had enjoyed while their mother's hair was dark and straight.

Eadgifu smiled at the children, unsure what to say to them, and saved from having to say anything by the arrival of Louis.

"My mother, Lady Eadgifu, is very strict," Louis bent down to speak to the three girls, although Alberade looked far from enamoured of him. "But, if you become friends, she is a good ally to have. She won't let anyone be mean to you, ever. And I can tell you that she gives the best gifts." There was genuine warmth in Louis' voice, and for a moment, Eadgifu was speechless. She'd never asked her son for his opinion about her. To hear it given so freely surprised and delighted her.

"I'm only strict with small boys who misbehave when they shouldn't," Eadgifu countered, amusement rippling through her voice. "I find that young ladies are much better behaved and have the added advantage of not really liking mud all that much." This earned Eadgifu a small smile from Gerberge, and even Alberade seemed to relax a little.

Louis laughed again, his voice high with delight.

"Come, I'll show you the palace, and where you'll sleep, and then you can explore, once everyone knows that you're to be treated with the respect due to the children of the wife of the king."

With that, Louis reached out his hand, and quickly the youngest children rushed to grip his hands, while Alberade stood by her foster-father. It seemed the oldest daughter was unsure of Louis, but not prepared to miss out on anything. Eadgifu smiled at the girl. She'd learned quickly, and would easily survive the recent changes to her life.

While Louis left the church, followed by Gerberga's servants and followers, Lady Gerberga remained, as did Eadgifu.

"I know you are my sister by marriage, and now my mother by marriage," Gerberga began, her voice harder, more menacing. "But the king is my husband now, and you'll find yourself less favoured by him."

Eadgifu startled at the words, her eyebrows high at the implied threat. A moment ago it had all been smiles and welcomes. That hadn't lasted long at all.

"The king is my son, and I only ever act to ensure his survival and his kingship. The affairs of others do not concern me, not at all."

Without pausing for Lady Gerberga to respond, Eadgifu swept from the cathedral, her eyes quickly picking out her son and his step-daughters making their way to the palace complex. She watched him thoughtfully.

Eadgifu couldn't help but admire Louis' actions in claiming Lady Gerberga as his wife. It seemed she was a formidable woman, unafraid to speak her mind and lay claim to her new family.

She needed to be.

EADGIFU SETTLED herself beside her son. Once more, Gerberga had claimed the position she would have preferred. Yet, Eadgifu found it impossible to feel any anger toward her daughter by marriage.

Older Gerberga might be, and a mother with five children already, but she was proving to be a good wife for Louis. Neither was it just because she'd confided in Eadgifu that she thought she already carried her first grandchild, although it was far too soon to be sure. Eadgifu didn't discount the belief. She was convinced that women who had been with child in the past must just instinctively know when they found themselves in the same condition once more.

Queen Gerberga was more than aware of her preeminent position with Louis. It was a sign of her maturity that she'd not made things awkward for Eadgifu. Knowing only too well how cruel women could be to each other, Eadgifu recognised in Gerberga a woman sure of herself, and in no need to play mind games. It was what Louis needed, some certainty. There was little of that to be found in West Frankia.

Louis had been able to rely on King Athelstan and his mother. Until Queen Gerberga had arrived that small selection of people had been swelled by few others, apart from his Archchancellor, and of course, Gerberga's first husband, until his unfortunate death only weeks before at the Battle of Aldernach, between the Lotharingian forces, and those of the East Frankish.

With King Athelstan's fleet sailing against the pretensions of Count Arnulf, once more allied with the East Frankish, and King Otto, Louis had managed to achieve a modicum of respect from the men of Lotharingia. Aside from that, Duke Hugh and Count Heribert continued to cause problems. King Otto had already sent word of his fury at Louis' claiming of his sister for his bride. All without her brother's permission. His furious letter arriving before Louis had even returned to Laon.

While a storm raged outside, Eadgifu allowed herself to relax, just a little. The weather was severe, and she reasoned the nobility couldn't be causing problems, not unless they wished to risk their own lives.

With wine in one hand, Eadgifu was settling to listen to young Alberade read her lesson to her mother. While the Latin was difficult for Eadgifu to understand, she enjoyed the sweetness of her step-granddaughter's voice.

As the hearth settled in a whoosh of wood and embers, Eadgifu heard a sound that made her curse.

"What is it?" Louis asked lethargically. The family grouping had taken the wintry weather as an opportunity to relax before the hearth, in a congenial atmosphere.

"I heard hooves. What will it be now?"

The last two years had seen one crisis after another, and Eadgifu knew that this would simply add to it. When a man forced his way into the king's hall, combatting the fierce storm that blew outside,

Eadgifu felt her annoyance drain away. She knew this man. And so did Louis. Already she quaked to know what he knew.

"My Lord King, Lady Queen, and Queen Dowager," Duke Alain was almost white with the cold, his nose shining redly in the glow of the candles, just about the only indication that he might not always be so deathly pale.

"Duke Alain," Louis found his voice, while Eadgifu pressed her own warmed wine into Alain's hand, the words of Alberade continuing. Still, the sound seemed to come from far away.

"My thanks," Duke Alain commented, slugging the wine as though he'd not drunk for days.

"Terrible tidings," Alain stated, his eyes flashing with dismay, while Eadgifu found herself sitting more rigid in her chair, the attempt to relax gone and forgotten about. Somehow, and unlikely as it sounded, she knew what Duke Alain was about to say.

"King Athelstan is dead," the words fell heavily into the near silence, Queen Gerberga gasping with shock, while Eadgifu met the bleak expression of Louis.

This was not just terrible, it was catastrophic, on a personal and a political level.

"How?" Queen Gerberga asked, and Eadgifu nodded, pleased not to have to voice the words, while Alain pressed the wine back into her own hands, even filling the drained goblet for her. She watched her hand shake, distractedly.

"A sudden illness. At Gloucester. They thought it would pass. It didn't. Edmund has been proclaimed king."

This was what had always been planned. Edmund had always been supposed to follow his brother, but not for many years yet. Eadgifu's thoughts ran wild. Two young kings, an uncle and a nephew, but truly more like brothers, for Louis was older than Edmund, if only by a year.

"England mourns," Duke Alain confirmed, his eyes shimmering with tears.

Louis had still to speak, and Eadgifu fought for the right words to offer.

"My brother," she eventually managed to gasp, unaware that she claimed him as fully her brother so distressed was she. In her mind, she thought, another brother. Why all my brothers? But she didn't say as much. If this was awful for her, it was shocking for Louis. He'd revered his Uncle, as a young boy would a father-figure. Louis had also relied on him when Duke Hugh and King Otto had incited all the nobility to abandon him. Even now, King Athelstan had known of Louis' marriage and appreciated the opportunity and difficulties it presented. A message had arrived from England concurrently with that from King Otto, filled with congratulations, warnings, and the assurance of continuing military assistance.

But Edmund was untried and untested. His name would not ring with the same authority as Athelstan's had.

"King Athelstan has been buried at Malmesbury with his cousins who perished at Brunanburh."

Eadgifu nodded, words beyond her, her throat raw with unshed tears. Alain's gaze was averted, seeking solace in the flames, and Eadgifu knew he was as profoundly affected as they all were. If not more so.

Athelstan had been a true friend, ally and safe harbour for Alain when he was younger and an exile. Just as Athelstan had been for Louis, as much as she'd once begrudged it.

"We'll need to act before everyone is aware of this," Artoldus' voice intruded into Eadgifu's thoughts. Yet, his words gave her something to grasp. King Athelstan would be dismayed if Louis suffered because of his death.

Duke Alain nodded unhappily, while Louis was still locked in shock.

Of them all, it was Artoldus and Gerberga, the two who'd never met King Athelstan who looked most able to plot, and it was Gerberga who spoke first.

"My brother will see great potential in this. He hasn't appreciated King Athelstan's attempts to interfere in East and West Frankia. For all he loves Queen Eadgyth."

"To upset my brother, you must turn your attention back to

Burgundy. Otto still has the oath of Black Hugh. Take back Burgundy, restore Black Hugh and then take the Kingdom of Arles once more. Conrad has been taken into safekeeping by King Otto."

Eadgifu's eyes gleamed at the statements, expertly made by Gerberga. She was a woman used to war and discord, and of course, she knew her brother well.

"That's an excellent idea," Archchancellor Artoldus confirmed in his commanding voice.

"The last time we went to the aid of the Kingdom of Arles, Duke Hugh and Count Heribert allowed King Otto to encamp on the Seine, and pledged him their oath," Louis spoke quietly, the grief in his voice hard to mask.

"But King Otto will not be expecting such a move. He'll think that you'll mourn for your lost Uncle and think nothing of your kingdom. And I doubt he'll wish to return to West Frankia, not now Lotharingia is unhappy under the command of my other brother. The nobility is desperate to be a part of West Frankia once more. Remember, my youngest brother has already rebelled against King Otto once. I'm sure he could be enticed to again, especially with the support of others."

"You would have to travel with me," Louis stated, his eyes seeking out those of his wife before also turning to Eadgifu. "And you should probably, as well."

But Eadgifu shook her head.

"No, we should divide again. Gain the support of others. I'll travel with Alain, back to Brittany, and seek out support from Normandy. Count Arnulf consistently tries to attack Count William. If we can turn Count William to our side, he'll be a powerful deterrent to Count Arnulf."

"And, I would further suggest that Laon be left under the command of Artoldus, both as Archbishop and Archchancellor." Eadgifu thought this the least controversial of her suggestions. Indeed, Louis nodded his agreement almost straight away, although his eyes were distant, his thoughts evidently elsewhere.

"Yes, Artoldus shall hold Laon, My Lady Mother will bring Count

William of Normandy to our side, however she must, and my Lady
Wife will travel with me, to the Kingdom of Arles. When we meet
once more, at Laon, it's to be hoped that Duke Hugh and Count
Heribert have other concerns. Hopefully, King Otto will also be
preoccupied either with his disgruntled brother, or his warrior sister."
As Louis spoke, he glanced at Queen Gerberga, a faint smile playing
around his lips.

Eadgifu was struck by just how much Gerberga reminded her of
Lady Ælfwynn. Lady Ælfwynn had made a triumph of her life since
King Edward's death. Eadgifu imagined that Queen Gerberga would
do the same.

TRAVELLING along winter roads was far from pleasant. Still, Eadgifu
simply settled deeper into her cloak and hunkered down low so that
the sharp wind couldn't chill her face any more than it already was.

She'd travelled with Alain to Brittany, and met his young family,
but now she had a meeting with Count William of Normandy to
attend, and so she travelled once more.

News from Louis was non-existent. She'd heard nothing from
England, although she'd arranged for a message to be sent to the royal
court, expressing her sorrow on King Athelstan's death, while wishing
her young brother success in his kingship.

She found it hard to believe that Edmund was now king. Her last
memories of him had been of a young man, grown into his position,
but lacking the gravitas of Athelstan. But, like Louis, she knew he had
the support required to rule well, provided he was allowed to, and
now, she thought, her step-mother would truly prove her worth.

Alain's court, during her time there, had been filled with rumours
of attacks planned on England by the Dublin Norse, in retaliation for
Brunanburh. Still, Duke Alain assured her there would be little truth
to them. In fact, he'd promised her the same rumours had begun the
very day he'd heard of the battle of Brunanburh and hadn't stopped
since. Eadgifu hoped that Alain's confidence was well placed.

But her mind was focused on Count William. William, the son of

Rollo, who her husband had reached an accord with regarding the lands in Normandy nearly a quarter of a century ago, was not the son of Rollo and his West Frankish wife, Charles' daughter, but rather had been born before that agreement had been reached. William had a fearsome reputation as a warrior, but he'd already broken his oaths to Louis once.

Count William was engaged in a war of attrition with Count Arnulf and Arnulf had made it abundantly clear that he no longer supported his young cousin's kingship. It seemed like the perfect opportunity to both make an ally and infuriate Arnulf.

Without King Athelstan to advise against the deterioration in the relationship between Count Arnulf and Louis, Eadgifu knew there was no reason to accord Arnulf any more leeway than the other counts and dukes of West Frankia. Indeed, if she thought about it carefully enough, she could determine that Louis was related in one way or another, to all of the noblemen who insisted on rising against him.

Eadgifu had arranged to meet with Count William at Montreuil-Sur-Mer, one of his strongholds.

On entering the great hall, she found Count William engaged in a heated conversation with his loyal noblemen, almost oblivious to her arrival, for all it was not a muted affair. It seemed that Count Arnulf would make it easy for her to entice William to her side, as she listened to the complaints. Even now, it was reported that Arnulf gathered his men for an attack on William's possessions, no matter that they were brothers by marriage.

While Eadgifu divested herself of her cloak, gloves, hat, and an entire layer of clothes that had both cushioned her, and kept her warm on her journey, she considered her first words to William.

Only, when William greeted her, and they were settled around a small table, wine and food before them, William started the conversation first.

"Bloody Arnulf. He's a sodding menace. What's he playing at?"

Eadgifu had no chance to reply before William continued.

"The land we have was freely given by your husband. Count Rollo stayed loyal to King Charles, even when he was imprisoned. I'd have done the same, and yet Count Arnulf flirts with any who promise him what he wants, and not what is his, by birth, to claim."

Eadgifu held her delight in place at such rage and nodded.

"I'm aware, and would also thank you, for your fierce loyalty to my husband. I wish I had met Charles once more before his death if only to learn about all who helped him while he was imprisoned. But sadly, it was never possible."

"Your husband was honourable throughout his imprisonment. He pined for his son, and for you." William commented, his eyes distant, as though he was back in time, more than a decade ago.

"Count Heribert might well be my father by marriage, but he's not to be trusted. Ever. He uses his children as though they're pieces on a board, not actual people." Count William's voice thrummed with frustration.

"Count Heribert has many children to do that with," Eadgifu commented sourly.

It was a mess to untangle the twisted loyalties of Count Heribert. Eadgifu was aware that King Otto now dallied in the same way with the lives of his sisters and his brothers.

She missed the rigid English court where such marriages between political rivals would have been forbidden for the king's daughters. Edward had been keen to keep the line of descent to the kingdom of Wessex clear from confusion. It had made him ruthless, but it had also made King Athelstan secure, and hopefully, Edmund would be as well.

"If you've come to ask me to pledge my allegiance to King Louis, then I am contemplating it if he can support me against Count Arnulf."

"The king is already determined to do so," Eadgifu confirmed, her fingers curling appreciatively around a beaker of warmed wine. Her fingertips tingled, and her chest felt tight from breathing such frigid air for so long as she had on her journey.

"Good, but the king needs to be firmer in his treatment of Duke Hugh and Count Heribert. The pair of them is a menace."

"King Louis has no intention of allowing the current situation to continue."

"Then you should know that Count Heribert plans to reclaim Laon for his son. He wishes to have the archbishopric restored to his son, and to cast Archchancellor Artoldus out."

The news was a shock, but not entirely unexpected. Count Heribert had been keen to have his son restored to the archbishopric following his removal from it for being no more than a youth, and unworthy of such an exalted position.

"King Louis has Laon secured, and the royal palace will never fall to Count Heribert."

Count William looked far from convinced but lapsed into brooding silence.

"I was sorry to hear of the death of King Athelstan. He was a man who knew the value of making alliances, and of making war. There was a time for each action, and he was not prone to make a rash decision based on his personal feelings. That's not easy for a man."

Eadgifu felt her throat constrict at the reminder of King Athelstan's death. It was still hard to speak about.

"He was a wiser man than many realised," she managed to mutter. William looked at her in surprise, his jaw locked tight, his hands, clasped around his own tankard, almost shaking. She didn't know whether he realised she included herself in that statement.

"It's all to play for now," Count William muttered, and Eadgifu couldn't help but agree with the less than optimistic outlook on the future.

ANGLO SAXON CHRONICLE
ENTRY FOR AD939

This year king Athelstan died at Gloucester on the 6th before the Kalends of November, about forty-one years, except one day, after king Alfred died. And Edmund the ætheling, his brother, succeeded to the kingdom, and he was then eighteen years of age; and king Athelstan reigned fourteen years and ten weeks.

AD940

Eadgifu reined in her horse, gazing at the view before her. It was not what she'd hoped to see, and it made her uneasy.

While there was no outward sign of the change in who held Laon, Archchancellor Artoldus had managed to have word sent to her that despite her assurance to Count William, Laon had been attacked by Duke Hugh and Count Heribert. Artoldus had been forced to flee. Now the centre of Louis' kingship was in the hands of his enemies, while Louis was slowly making his way back from the Kingdom of Arles.

Of all the players in this terrible game, it was King Otto who had stayed the quietest. He'd not rushed to try and take full command in the Kingdom of Arles, although he sheltered her young king at his court. Neither was Otto supporting Duke Hugh and Count Heribert in their fresh treason.

All she'd managed to do was to bring Count William to Louis side, and in the face of Duke Hugh and Count Heribert colluding against Louis, it was but a small thing.

Yet, she refused to despair and instead allowed her fury to keep her senses sharp, her desire to help her son succeed paramount in her mind.

Once more, she had resolved to try and contact her sister, Queen Eadgyth.

Queen Eadgyth had been all but silent for many months now, but the death of King Athelstan was a common concern for them. Eadgifu was sure that this time, Eadgyth could be convinced to communicate with her sister. They could share their sorrow then, for Eadgifu could admit that she still grieved for her lost brother.

Added to which, now that Duke Hugh had both a son and a daughter with his East Frankish wife, that son could attempt to claim the kingdom of the East Franks just as he could that of the West Franks. Eadgifu was going to make sure that Eadgyth fully understood the danger her husband faced.

Retreating to Attigny, close to the border with East Frankia, Eadgifu settled to write to her sister. It was difficult to know where to start, and so she began with King Athelstan. In that regard, it was almost too easy to speak from the heart.

Eschewing the help of Archchancellor Artoldus monks, Eadgifu clasped the quill tightly in her hand.

She'd been given the finest of parchment to write on, but now she almost feared to make her mark on it. She was not the most skilled of writers, most probably, she realised, because she didn't practise enough. As a child, she'd resented being forced to learn how to wield a quill, but now she knew how unusual it had been, she felt grateful thanks to her father, or rather her grandfather. It was King Alfred who'd compelled her father to educate all of his children.

"Dearest sister," the words sprang clear from the page, the quill sliding smoothly over the almost priceless parchment.

'I write to share my grief with you. Our dear brother is gone too soon, the greatest of kings, the first king of England, and it feels strange to know for sure that I will never see him again. Not in this life.'

Eadgifu paused, worried about how to phrase the next part of her letter.

'As King Athelstan's sisters, I hope we can continue his legacy of trusting peace enough not to go to war with those who are enemies, but could be our allies if only common ground could be found."

Eadgifu liked the words, as she reread them. She hoped her sister would not immediately see in them a criticism, or even a threat that Louis intended war against his uncle by marriage, and brother by marriage both.

'Families can hold kingdoms together and also force them apart. As family, I pray for an accord between West and East Frankia, for my son's marriage to be legitimised in the eyes of your husband, and for the children of both your marriage, and the children of my son's marriage, to show the same respect, and unity of purpose that King Athelstan was able to live his life by.'

Eadgifu sighed once more. This was more difficult than she could have imagined. It had been years since she'd last seen Queen Eadgyth, and in that time Eadgyth's letters had slowed in frequency and then stopped altogether.

'I would hope to meet with you soon, to honour our brother, and to consider the future.'

Here she stopped, squinting at the words. Is this truly what she wanted? Was it even possible?

Impulsively, Eadgifu signed her name, before she could reconsider, and had the letter sealed with her royal seal, and handed to Archchancellor Artoldus, for a messenger to take to Aachen.

Eadgifu didn't believe this poorly worded letter would solve all of Louis' problems, or that it would even elicit an immediate response from Eadgyth. None of the previous letters had.

But she had to start somewhere, and if she had to write every week for a decade, she would do so, and in every letter, she would share her sorrow for King Athelstan's death, and her hope that peace could be restored between the two kingdoms.

She would write a letter to her sister, each and every week, for as long as it took Eadgyth to respond. And in not one of those letters, would she remind Queen Eadgyth of the oath they'd made in Aachen. The affirmation that had promised peace and not war.

AD942

E adgifu strode from one side of the room to the other, trying to still her rapidly beating heart, but unable to do so.

It had been too many years since she'd last seen Eadgyth, and too much had happened in that time. Knowing that Eadgyth was close by was making these last moments apart stretch on interminably.

Eadgifu forced herself to stop, to stand still and to think about what this meeting would be like.

It had been six years since she'd seen her sister. Since then war and unease had run counter to the relationship between East and West Frankia, all of it oiled by the ambitions of three men; her son, King Otto and of course, bloody Duke Hugh. Although Count Heribert could not be discounted.

Eadgifu found herself pacing once more.

Duke Hugh.

It was on his shoulders that much of the blame for past actions must rest.

"Lady Sister, Queen Dowager," so caught up in her pacing, Eadgifu had failed to hear the wooden doors opening, and her sister being admitted into this hall, chosen as their place of peace weaving.

Eadgifu had never wanted to think of herself as a weaver of peace, as so often was the case for royal women, but now it was her primary task, and for all the warmth in Queen Eadgyth's voice, Eadgifu swallowed heavily, before turning to greet her sister.

"Lady Sister, Queen Eadgyth," the words felt strange on Eadgifu's lips. They earned her an arched eyebrow. Eadgifu hoped that sign meant Eadgyth approved.

Eadgyth seemed to glimmer with jewels, from her hair to her shoes, and Eadgifu bit back a smirk of derision. Eadgyth had never been one to stint.

"I pity the horse," Eadgifu stated dryly, walking to stand before her sister, her arms outstretched, although she was unsure whether an embrace would be welcomed.

"I don't," was Eadgyth's reply as she stepped into the half-offered embrace. Strong arms wound around Eadgifu's back as she reciprocated, inhaling the scent of her sister, finding nothing there that was at all familiar.

It had been six long years. It seemed Eadgyth was truly the queen of the East Frankish kingdom. She had adopted many of their customs, for all King Otto had once been at pains to remind everyone he was a Saxon by birth.

"I see the light doesn't favour your hair," Eadgyth stated, stepping smoothly from the embrace, her tone cool. Eadgyth moved to walk the path that Eadgifu had been pacing. It ran from the hearth to a table almost bowed with the weight of fruits and wines on offer.

"I see you've chosen to bring your own light," Eadgifu retorted, stung but refusing to pat down the grey of her hair, where it showed beneath the jewels she covered it with. Now she wished she'd decided to wear the wimple. She'd discarded it as something her mother would have worn, but it would have stopped her sister from appreciating just how much damage time had done to the blond hair of her youth.

"Majesty should always shine," Eadgyth stated blandly, the bait in her tone clear to hear. Eadgifu looked down at her hands, the twin rings that gleamed on fingers grown thin and weak, and smiled at the memory of her marriage, and her son's birth. It seemed that before they could make peace for their countries, they would need to make one between the pair of them.

"Wine?" Eadgifu asked her sister, prepared to serve her, an acknowledgement, without being one, that Eadgyth was the queen. In contrast, Eadgifu had merely been one, many years ago.

"Yes, warm, thank you." Eadgyth swept back toward her, the rustle of her silk dresses an indication of how close she stood to the table. The goblet was gaudy, the gold a mocking yellow, the gems a glitter of rainbows, but it was worthy of a queen, even if Eadgifu wished for something simpler, perhaps coloured glass and none of the fuss.

With the wine in her hand, Eadgyth took a small sip, and then a deeper one, a look of appreciation in her blue eyes, slightly thawed under the influence of a good vintage.

"So, we've been given a task that no one else wants. As the grand-daughters of King Alfred, and the half-sisters of King Athelstan, we can accomplish what everyone believes is impossible, peace between my husband, your son, and our sister's widowed husband, not to mention our other sister's kingdom."

"It would seem that way, yes." Eadgifu agreed softly, settling on a warm chair, the back carved with mythical sea creatures, the wood dark and mysterious.

"Yes, when all else fails, put down the shields and swords, and let two sisters battle it out with words, and see what happens."

As much as Eadgifu had fought for the idea of a peace accord her and her sister, suddenly it seemed too much. Too much rested on her shoulders, and it appeared her sister was not happy either at being tied to something upon which so much depended.

"I'm the Queen of East Frankia, the land of my birth is but a distant memory, and the people I once knew, even more so."

Eadgifu inclined her head, acknowledging the words.

"So we've failed even before we've begun, then?" Eadgifu meant it as a question, but also, a statement. When Eadgyth made no reply, Eadgifu continued.

"Why even come here, then?"

"I couldn't let you have all the glory for the suggestion, and then refuse to honour it. I've come because you made it impossible for me not to come, with your suggestion that we could right what the men cannot. And you've been so damn persistent."

"So now it's my fault that our countries fight?"

"He is your son."

Eadgifu felt her calmness ebb away. The damn bitch. She ignored the complaint about persistence. Two long years of tedious letters had brought about this meeting.

"And he is your husband, and he uses his relationship with either Duke Hugh, or my son, as though it were a child's toy. East and West Frankia were once united, whole. It's good that there are now two kingdoms to accommodate our family unless your husband means to unite it. I wish him luck bringing Duke Hugh under his command." Eadgifu spoke as she found, all traces of political needling forgotten about in the face of her sister's complaints.

Eadgyth's body slowly stilled with Eadgifu's words, the fury seeming to transfer from one sister to another, before Eadgifu took a final deep breath, and exhaled loudly.

"We are sisters. We can do this, or we can allow them to continue to fight. I would sooner have peace, and Duke Hugh brought to heel, if only for the sake of our dead sister, and her lost hopes for Louis."

"You would use Eadhild against me?' Eadgyth rounded, blue eyes blazing, her hand shaking where the goblet was clasped too tightly.

"I would do no such thing. But your husband allowed Duke Hugh to wed one of his sisters when our own was barely cold in her grave. And now the bastard has his precious heir, and he means to do nothing but cause carnage."

"That child is my nephew."

"Not by blood, not like Louis."

"Well Louis has his own wife now as well, and his son is also my nephew, as well as my great-nephew."

Eadgifu laughed. She couldn't help it.

"So either way, your husband can lay claim to West Frankia in the future."

"Of course," the soft answer infuriated Eadgifu. "Anyway, King Otto and Queen Gerberga might well be brother and sister, but they're far from reconciled. I expected her to be here with you." The criticism was too barbed, the look on her sister's face too delighted.

"I thought it best to practise some level of diplomacy," Eadgifu countered.

"There is a first time for everything," Eadgyth's reply was laced with venom. Rather than respond, in a manner that would bring this peace conference to an immediate end, Eadgifu held her tongue. She'd learned much throughout her life. It was time to see if her sister had, as well.

The silence between them was long enough that Eadgifu became aware of noises outside, the tread of the warriors in their boots, the clatter of horse hooves. In the distance, a raucous argument, no doubt about a man, or a woman, certainly, the two voices were spiteful and vindictive. Not unlike Eadgifu and her sister.

"Do you remember when our father put our mother aside?" the question was so unexpected that Eadgifu startled. What a time to be reminded of that.

"I do, yes."

"I always thought she went quietly, and without argument." Eadgyth's eyes were filled with longing for the past, if not that past.

"Our mother called our father a bastard and told him his cock would shrivel and drop off," Eadgifu provided the information. "There was nothing quiet about our mother. Or indeed, any of us."

"No, I imagine that you're right. Apart from Eadhild. She was the best of us all."

"She was the most biddable, and father knew it."

Silence fell once more. Eadgifu fought for something to say. It seemed her sister was keen to build walls, if not the ones they had been sent here for.

"How do you think our young brother fares as King of the English?"

It still felt strange to realise that King Athelstan was dead, and

Edmund king in his place. Edmund was younger than Louis, and yet to Eadgifu, he would always be a child.

"He has much to learn, as do all the younger generation," Queen Eadgyth offered. "He'll have to make a name for himself, but I'm sure he will. Just like Athelstan. He certainly had the upbringing for it. We might not have liked our half-brother for much of his life, but he did know how to raise boys to be king."

Eadgifu felt her head swivel at the tart reply. What was her sister implying?

"Louis, my dear," Eadgyth stated, her eyes showing surprise at Eadgifu's immediate reaction. "I spoke of Louis and Alain and Haakon. King Athelstan taught them all how to rule, how to fight outspoken men and Viking bastards."

"Haakon is a Viking bastard," Eadgifu muttered.

"No, he's King of Norway. He just happens to rule Viking bastards."

"He rules well, or so I hear. I pity him his half-brother."

"As we must pity all who have half-brothers?"

Eadgifu shook her head, irritated with her sister's reasoning.

"Maybe all relatives," Eadgifu complained. She'd not come here to speak of her half-brothers, but perhaps it was inevitable that their thoughts would be of family.

"My husband is still angry with his sister," Eadgyth announced, eyes steady.

"My son is still angry with your husband for allowing Duke Hugh to marry one of the King of East Frankia's sisters. It was too high an honour for him."

"My husband did not consult me about his intentions concerning Hadwig."

"So you didn't approve either then?"

"It little matters. But as you say, Duke Hugh's third marriage was conducted with indecent haste. About as indecent as Gerberga's. Her husband was barely even dead."

"He drowned. How much more dead can you get?" Eadgifu felt a faint hint of amusement touching her face. There was no one at her son's court that she could genuinely tangle with, and in all honesty, Gerberga had supplanted her now. Everyone looked to the king's wife for favours, not his mother. It felt good to be able to bicker, for Eadgifu knew this for what it was.

"But my brother loved Gerberga. He was only tolerably fond of Hadwig."

Eadgifu chuckled. She couldn't help it.

"Tolerably fond?"

"She's a snappy sort of woman. Have you not discovered this?"

"I assumed it was her husband that made her so. He's an old man, and she's very young."

"Yes, and now that Duke Hugh knows he can father children, he's keen to have many. I pity her and blame her brother for the situation. I'm sure my husband will live to rue the day he set the old badger on his younger sister. I don't even like to consider it. But she is a snappy sort of woman, all the same. Anyway, you're now a grandmother as well, with a young prince in the cradle."

"Yes, but I'm a grandmother, not the mother. Hugh is the father when he should be a grandfather."

"Maybe he'll wear himself out and do us all a favour," Eadgyth's comment was spoken with a sparkle in her eyes. Eadgifu laughed at the deliciousness of the thought conjured in her mind.

"We can but hope."

"And in the meantime, we must make peace between the two kings, my husband and your son?"

"We must, or Duke Hugh will have everything, and we wouldn't want that. He has had more than enough."

Eadgyth leaned forward now, one elbow on the arm of the chair, her head resting on her upturned hand. Eadgifu noticed how regal it made her look. No doubt, she'd been practising the movement as well as her barbs.

"The King of East Frankia demands the return of Lotharingia."

Eadgifu settled herself as well. It seemed the time for negotiation, real negotiation, had finally arrived.

"Queen Gerberga holds Lotharingia for the sons of her first

marriage. And by that right, Louis holds them, as Gerberga's husband, and Henry rules in place of all of them."

"I'm well aware, but I tell you the terms that the king has ordered me to ask for."

"So, he would take his nephews inheritance from them?"

"No, he would raise them as his own sons, and allow them to command Lotharingia when they're old enough."

"So he would take their kingdom, and give it to who?"

Eadgyth sighed heavily, waving her hand as though it was of little importance.

"Henry can still have the command. He is their uncle. King Otto will not allow Lotharingia to just 'fall' into the hands of Louis. Louis would be foolish to think he would."

"And what of Duke Hugh?" She knew that Louis would have been keen to keep Lotharingia. Still, even Queen Gerberga had informed her husband the fight was not worth having. Not if Louis wanted Otto as an ally and not an enemy.

"What of Duke Hugh?"

Eadgifu held her smirk in place at her sister's adopted disinterest.

"Duke Hugh is your brother by marriage, and as such, I'm sure he would expect to rely on his kingly brother for support, should he ever be attacked, by King Louis."

"No doubt, yes. I'm not sure of the exact arrangements between my twice-brother by marriage, and my husband."

"King Louis would want an assurance that no help would be given. Not to a man rebelling against his rightful king and lord."

"King Otto would not wish to endanger his beloved sister."

"You just said that Hadwig was King Otto's least favourite sister," Eadgifu countered quickly.

"Yes, she might be. But sometimes liking someone is the least of it. She *is* his sister."

"So King Otto will give no reassurance on this matter then?"

"Yes, he will. King Otto will assist his sister, and her children, if the need should arise."

"But not Duke Hugh?"

"I don't believe I mentioned Duke Hugh's name," Eadgyth spoke breezily.

Eadgifu nodded. This was a victory, and one she'd thought would be harder to extract. But then it seemed Eadgyth had about as much love for Duke Hugh as Eadgifu.

While Duchess Eadhild had lived, Duke Hugh had been difficult. Since Eadhild's untimely death, Hugh had become more and more unmanageable. His marriage to Hadwig had caused no end of heartache. And not just because he seemed to have thought so little of Eadhild, but because of the potential difficulties the marriage would cause if it proved fruitful, as it now was.

Hugh's new ambitions had quickly become apparent as soon as his first child had been born. The relationship with Louis, the boy he'd thought to adopt as his son, had deteriorated ever since.

"But how will King Louis handle Duke Hugh? King Otto would wish a guarantee that his nieces and nephews will be safe."

"King Louis would gladly give the assurance, provided King Otto accepts that the royal line runs in Louis' blood, and not that of Duke Hugh."

"King Otto will agree to that, provided King Louis accepts the children of Duchess Hadwig have no legitimate claim to the East Frankish kingdom."

"The children will only inherit the land claimed by Duke Hugh, nothing more, and nothing less. The county of Neustria is enough for one man to rule."

Eadgifu nodded. It was the only possible solution to the problem.

"Duke Hugh's children will be excluded from the succession of East and West Frankia, as will their descendants."

"Agreed."

Eadgifu gently expelled her breath as Eadgyth gave her acceptance to another part of the terms of the agreement they'd been tasked with reaching.

The problem of Lotharingia hadn't yet been resolved as Louis would want it, but the suggestion that the kingdom continued in the hands of Otto's brother, his allegiance restored to King Otto, was not a bad compromise.

The man in charge would not change. Just the king. Louis would still be able to work with Henry in ensuring his step-sons future.

It still left scope there for Louis to work with, and certainly, Queen Gerberga would be happy that her children with her first husband wouldn't lose the expectation of ruling Lotharingia. Louis' suggestion that he retained control of Lotharingia would never have been acceptable to Otto, and Louis was aware of that. All the same, he'd insisted that the suggestion be made.

"And what of the rest of the fickle men who routinely run to King Otto? Count Heribert, Count Arnulf, Count William of Aquitaine, will King Otto refuse to treat with them in the future as well?"

"King Otto will pledge not to meddle with King Louis' subjects provided King Louis extends the same to King Otto. It's not good that these men believe they can simply choose their own king when the one they have displeased them. The borders need to be secure, and the way to provide secure borders is to hold these men to task."

Eadgifu nodded. She wasn't about to argue with her sister when she whole-heartedly agreed. In England, King Athelstan, and now King Edmund, didn't suffer this problem of disloyalty. No Englishman would dare approach another king to support them against the king. But it was a problem routinely encountered by the men who ruled in East and West Frankia. All the land borders made it too tempting to simply offer a pledge to another.

Eadgifu could see many bonuses to the way King Athelstan had chosen to rule England. In time she hoped that the counts and dukes would be brought more firmly under the control of Louis' kingship.

"King Otto would happily seal this agreement if it meets with the approval of King Louis by sealing it with marriage. Only, as the marriage has already taken place, he would instead bestow his blessings onto the marriage, lifting all restrictions on Queen Gerberga."

"The two brother kings should preside over a great feast, held in honour of the agreement reached here," Eadgifu suggested, keen to see Eadgyth's reaction.

"Somewhere significant, on the borders, perhaps King Otto could sit on the West Frankish side, and King Louis the East Frankish side, a sign of true trust, friendship and agreement between the two brothers?"

Eadgyth gave little away, although her lips twitched, just a little, and Eadgifu knew her sister too little now to understand if that was a good or a bad sign.

"The border would be that of Lotharingia, to the west."

"I think to the east would be better."

"Or perhaps no border at all, but rather in the centre of Lotharingia. Perhaps in Verdun?"

"Perhaps the kings need not meet after all," Eadgifu stated too quickly, aware her son would not approve of these suggestions. He had given her permission to try if she felt it a possibility, but certainly, the conclusion of the settlement did not rest on this final stipulation.

"Perhaps it should be just you and I who conclude this treaty, add our agreement to the legal document drawn up. Then Queen Gerberga can act as our intermediary when she and her brother are fully reconciled."

Eadgyth's lips curled at the thought.

"A fine compromise," she confirmed, and then they lapsed to silence. Eadgifu considered both what had been said, and unsaid. She deliberated her sister's power and influence with her husband, and her own, with her son.

As much as they both wished to rule, Eadgifu could admit that she and her sister were entirely reliant on their sons and husbands for the honours they currently held. Without Otto and Louis, what would either of them be?

The same could never be said of Duke Hugh.

Without Eadhild, he'd simply remarried and finally become a father.

If anything, Eadhild's death had made Hugh more influential, not less.

Exactly the opposite would happen to them. Indeed, it had occurred to Eadgifu on the death of Charles. She'd been left with no kingdom, no allies, and no one to fight for her, apart from her, at the time, despised half-brother.

"A deep sigh, sister. Our discussion is unsatisfactory?"

"No, it's deeply satisfying. I was merely deliberating how we came to be here at all."

"Well, your father arranged for you to marry a king. Then you had a child together. Only then your king was overthrown. You were forced to flee your kingdom, with your child, and seek sanctuary in Wessex, under our half-brother."

"Our half-brother then wed your sister to your husband's enemy, and then he wed me to the son of the King of East Frankia and Ælfgifu to the brother of the King of Arles."

"And then your sister convinced her husband to adopt your son as his own, to make him king on the death of the previous king."

"Your son became king, and my husband became king, and all should have been well. Only, your sister then died, leaving her husband grieving, although, not a great deal, or so it seems."

"Free from the influence of Eadhild, her husband stirred up a hornet's nest of difficulties and still does. Luckily, you and I remember Eadhild and her hopes and dreams that she invested in King Louis."

"Then King Louis wed my husband's sister, without permission, and all seemed as though it were on fire."

"Luckily, there are wise heads amongst us."

Eadgifu gazed at her sister with interest, before she spoke. "And it is that simple for you?"

"Of course, it's that simple. Take away all but the bare bones of the story, and we are here today because our father was an ambitious man, whereas our brother was left with his legacy, and his daughters, and did what he could for us."

"We might never have liked King Athelstan, until it was too late, but he saw us as people, not like our father."

"You say that even though you were sent as one of two suitable brides for your husband to choose."

"I say that even thinking I never wished to marry Otto. All I knew was that I didn't wish to be a nun and that my brother didn't expect me to become one. He never made you take vows either, or marry again."

"Our brother, for all it galls me to say as much, was not an unkind man. Far from it. And more, he was proud of his family, and we should be pleased to have served him as well as we have."

"England might be struggling without him, but I believe King Edmund will resolve any problems. King Athelstan made his kingdom too strong. It will survive, and it will endure. Its borders will not change as often as those of East and West Frankia. I believe the 'England' that Athelstan forged will long endure. King Edmund has a wife now, and a son, and of course, his mother supports him."

Eadgifu held her tongue. Her opinion of her step-mother was well-known, and yet she too knew that she had been unfair to his father's third wife.

Time had shown her that step-daughters were cruel monsters, on occasion.

"You have a daughter suitable for this new child of England?"

Eadgyth laughed at that, the sound a soft warble of delight.

"I've not considered that, but no. I'll not wed one of my daughters to their cousin. My daughters will need to look elsewhere for husbands. They cannot wed your step-daughters, or our nephew."

Eadgifu startled at the thought, and then she leaned toward her sister, gripped her hand.

"And so the next generation absorbs our attention."

"Yes, they do. As always. The future and continuity guides the hands of all kings."

Eadgyth didn't remove her hand from Eadgifu's but instead gripped it.

"We are not done yet, dear sister. In fact, we could say that our influence is only at its beginning."

Eadgifu laughed with delight.

"Then, we should conclude this damn peace accord and get on with more important meddling."

"Indeed, we should," Eadgyth replied, her blue eyes alight with conspiracy.

"There is much for us sisters to accomplish."

"Then, let us undertake it."

Together, Eadgifu and Eadgyth stood, each mirroring the movements of the other, more united than they had ever been before. Their exquisite dresses draped over their legs, showing shoes festooned with gems, covered by dresses edged with meticulous embroidery. Ceremonial belts wound around their waists, holding keys to the homes they ruled over. As well as more elaborate ones, carved in the images of West and East Frankia. They were a potent symbol that they ruled over them as well, even if through their husband and their son.

Crowns of gold covered their hair, once blond, and now turning to grey, gems flickering in their settings as the candlelight seemed to bathe them in the first flushes of youth when they'd been young, and newlywed.

Much had changed, a great deal, and yet Eadgifu smiled, gazing at her sister, the expression returned, for they were both queens, and they both had kingdoms to command.

Just as King Athelstan had always intended.

HISTORICAL NOTES

Edward the Elder had many daughters. In fact, it is not actually known with accuracy how many daughters he had. I've opted for the more conservative number of eight, others number it at nine, but it's believed there is some confusion regarding the final daughter, from either his second or third marriage, who may have been 'double-counted.'

These daughters have no mention in the Anglo-Saxon Chronicle, apart from the daughter married to Sihtric of York (Lady Ecgwynn). The Anglo-Saxon Chronicle was written by monks/holy men. It's often only the kings who are mentioned, as well as the bishops and archbishops.

While the story of the more famous of Edward's sons are reasonably well known – that of Ælfweard, Athelstan, Edmund and Eadred – (this just misses out Edwin, who is said to have drowned, possibly as a punishment for treason, or just in the normal run of things, it's impossible to say – this does get a mention in the Anglo-Saxon Chronicle under AD933) But the daughters. Well, what varied lives they had, mostly far from England.

Of those daughters who did marry, as opposed to living life either as a nun, or a lay sister, all of them married into one or other of the dynasties dominant in East and West Frankia, apart from Ecgwynn, who had a Viking for a husband. While many would argue this was a sign of the influence of the Wessex royal family in Europe, it also made perfect sense. The kingdom of England was newly made, and would become 'unmade' a few more times yet. The thought of a rival royal claim to the throne was not a palatable one, and the early years of King Edward the Elder's reign had been made difficult by the rival claim of his cousin, son of Alfred's older brother, Lord Æthelwine, until his death in AD902. Sooner to marry these daughters and sisters far from England's shores.

To Edward goes the initiative of marrying Eadgifu to Charles of West Frankia, and he is also credited with Eadhild's marriage to Hugh, Count, and later Duke, of the Franks. It's interesting to think what he would have done with the remainder of his daughters had he lived longer.

Three of his daughters spent their lives in nunneries – two at Wilton, a royal establishment, while young Eadburh joined the Nunnaminster, founded by her paternal grandmother, Alfred's wife. Lady Ecgwynn may also have founded Polesworth nunnery after her failed marriage.

Writers of the period will make much of this working for the Wessex dynasty – it was always good to have royal women praying for the soul of the king and his family – but there was little other choice for royal women, regardless of their convictions, if they decided not to marry, for whatever reason. Somehow it was better to marry and become a widow, than live without the protection of a husband or the Church.

Athelstan was, it seems, at the height of his powers in AD936. He was able to 'interfere' in the rule of at least two other countries, and potentially three countries (West Frankia, Brittany and Norway), ensuring his foster-sons received their birthrights. The role that his sisters played in the negotiations for Louis's return to West Frankia, if they had any, have not been recorded, but it cannot be a coincidence that Louis was about 16 years old, and his aunt married to Count

Hugh, who was childless at the time. Louis was young enough to need a regent if he was proclaimed as king by the West Frankish nobility.

Hugh came from an incredibly powerful and influential family. The thought of losing his control over the West Frankish if a rival claimant had been made king might have made him susceptible to Eadhild's suggestion that Louis could be the son they never had – although this is my own invention.

AD936 could have been the culmination of all of Athelstan's plans, which was only reinforced in AD937 and the great victory at Brunanburh against the Dublin Norse, the kingdom of the Scots, and Strathclyde. His death in AD939, unexpected as he was only in his forties, made his young half-brother king, and might well have added to the destabilisation between East and West Frankia at the time. Without Athelstan to sort out the bickering, the bickering was going to continue.

It is not possible to reconstruct an accurate timeline of events in AD929/930, AD936/7 and certainly not from AD939/42. The causality of events can only be inferred – did Athelstan marry his sisters off to counter the death of King Charles? Or had the marriages been arranged? Did the death of Eadhild turn Duke Hugh against Louis? And whatever the nobility of West Frankia was up to in 939-42, had the untimely death of Athelstan incited them to discard their young king?

I am not, yet, an expert on Frankish history, far from it in fact. Any errors in my portrayal of either West or East Frankia are my own. The infighting and fighting seems to have been on a wholly new level compared to the more 'placid' account of events in England, where the problem of 'overmighty' subjects is either ignored in sources from the period, or didn't occur at all until the later eleventh century. And I also confess that I have substantially simplified the events of AD940/942. Almost everyone changed allegiance at least once, and probably twice.

Here, I confess, I have birthed the Kingdom of Arles four years early to avoid confusion with the Kingdom of Burgundy and the

County of Burgundy. I felt no one else needed to undergo my utter confusion with people who are all named 'of Burgundy'.

There is, alas, no proof that the three sisters met at Aachen in AD936, but it could certainly provide a credible explanation as to why East and West Frankia worked hard to forge a peace when Louis and Otto were newly come to their kingdoms.

The events of AD942 likewise, make no mention of the involvement of Eadgifu and Eadgyth, but the desire of East Frankia to become a true friend to West Frankia is certainly much easier to understand if it's seen as the labours of two sisters, coming together, to ensure their families didn't rip each other apart, because of their association with the ambitious Duke Hugh.

Any children born to the union of Louis and Gerberga would have been Eadgifu's grandchildren, as well as Eadgyth's nieces and nephews. Surrounded as they were by warring, powerful factions, I imagine they would have preferred unity to discord.

What happened to Edward the Elder's daughters after AD942 lies outside the scope of this novel, and for good reason. The deaths of the sisters who became nuns at Wilton is not known, although young Eadburh, the daughter of Edward and his third wife, does have her death recorded in AD952, after which she was revered as a saint. Lady Ecgwynn, the sister who married Sihtric of York, is difficult to track down with any great deal of accuracy, but was also potentially a nun, at Polesworth. Her date of death is not recorded.

Queen Eadgifu of West Frankia died in AD951, and Queen Eadgyth would die, seemingly suddenly in AD946, and so would not live to see her husband become Holy Roman Emperor. It would take a devastated King Otto five years to remarry. Of Ælfgifu it is difficult to say because there is so much confusion about her actual identity in the sources.

Through his daughters, Edward the Elder's family extended into both East and West Frankia. In time, his grandson, great grandson and great great grandson wore the crown of West Frankia (descended from Queen Eadgifu – Louis IV, Lothar and Louis V), while a great grandchild through Queen Eadgyth's line became the the pope (Pope

Gregory V (AD996-999)) and another became Holy Roman Emperor (Conrad II).

But none of his daughters birthed a dynasty that ruled for centuries. This is their tragedy and the reason their story is so little known.

Through his sons, 'England' was 'eventually' 'born,' and his grandsons, great grandsons, and great great grandsons would become king of England. Only with the death of Edward the Confessor in January AD1066 did his family cease to hold the kingdom of England.

In writing this book I have made use of the Anglo-Saxon Chronicle, Sarah Foot's book on Athelstan, and the academic book on Edward the Elder edited by D Scragg, as well as Claire Downham's work on the Viking dynasty of Ivarr. These books are all accessible to the non-specialist, although Edward the Elder is a series of essays, and may not be quite as enjoyable, focusing as it does on aspects of his reign, and containing some papers which contradict each other.

I have also accessed many papers on Academia Reader. I would like to thank all those who have made the papers so readily available. For events in Frankia, I have found R McItterick's The Frankish Kingdoms Under the Carolingians, which has many lovely genealogies and maps.

Much of this story is fiction – there is simply not enough known about these women to truly know them. A pity.

CAST OF CHARACTERS

King Edward, son of **King Alfred**, King of Wessex, and his wife, **Ealhswith**. King of Wessex from 899-924, also King of Mercia by the time of his death.

    m.1 Lady Ecgwynn
    b.Athelstan
    b.Ecgwynn
    m.2 Lady Ælfflæd
    b.Ælfweard
    b.Edwin
    b.Eadgifu
    b.Æthelhild
    b.Eadflæd
    b.Eadgyth
    b.Eadhild
    b.Ælfgifu
    m.3 Lady Eadgifu
    b.Eadburh
    b.Edmund
    b.Eadred

Lady Æthelflæd, Edward's sister

m. Æthelred of Mercia

b.Ælfwynn

m. Athelstan, known as the Half King in later life

Lord Æthelweard, Edward's brother

m. unknown

b.Æthelwine

b.Ælfwine

Lady Ælthryth, Edward's sister

m. Count Baldwin of Flanders

b.Adelolf

b.Arnulf

Edward the Elder's daughters

Lady Eadgifu, Queen of West Frankia, daughter of Edward the Elder and his second wife, **Lady Ælfflæd.**

m. **Charles III**, King of West Frankia in AD919

b.**Louis** September AD920

Æthelhild, daughter of Edward the Elder and his second wife, a nun at Wilton

Eadflæd, daughter of Edward the Elder and his second wife, a nun (or lay sister) at Wilton

Eadhild, Countess/Duchess of Paris, daughter of Edward the Elder and his second wife

m. Hugh, Count/Duke of the Franks, in cAD926 – the union appears to have been childless

Eadgyth, daughter of Edward the Elder and his second wife

m. **Otto of Saxony**, son of King Henry of East Frankia

Liutgarde born c.932

Lludolf born c.930

Ælfgifu, daughter of Edward the Elder and his second wife

m. **Louis of Burgundy**, although the kingdom was by this date known as the Kingdom of Arles

Lady Ecgwynn, daughter of Edward the Elder and his first wife, also called Ecgwynn

m. **Sihtric of York in c.AD926**. Sihtric repudiated/divorced his wife.

Eadburh, daughter of Edward the Elder and his third wife, a nun from a young age, at the Nunnaminster, dies AD952

Edward the Elder's sons

Athelstan, son of Edward the Elder and his first wife.

King of Mercia in AD924, and then of Wessex after the death of Ælfweard, although his coronation service made him King of the English.

Ælfweard, son of Edward the Elder and his second wife.

King of Wessex in AD924 following his father's death, but only for a handful of days until he too died.

Edwin, son of Edward the Elder and his second wife.

Drowned/died in AD933

Edmund, son of Edward the Elder and his third wife.

Eadred, son of Edward the Elder and his third wife.

The Royal Court of England

Lady Eadgifu, queen of the Anglo-Saxons – referred to as 'step-mother' to prevent confusion with Queen Eadgifu of West Frankia.

Third wife of **Edward the Elder**, and mother of **Eadburh, Edmund and Eadred.**

Lord Osferth, an ealdorman, and also relative of the Wessex royal family – either a relative of King Alfred's wife, or perhaps an illegitimate son of Alfred.

Ealdorman Ordgar, ealdorman at the beginning of King Athelstan's reign.

Ealdorman Wulfgar, ealdorman at the beginning of King Athelstan's reign.

Lord Ælfstan, supporter of Athelstan, would become ealdorman of Mercia during his reign. The brother of Athelstan, known as the Half-King, married to Lady Ælfwynn, King Athelstan's cousin.

Bishop Cenwald, of Worcester, one of Athelstan's household priests until promoted in AD929 to Worcester. Travelled to Saxony with the royal sisters in AD929.

Bishop Frithestan, of Winchester to AD932 died in AD933

Ealdorman Uhtred, ealdorman under Athelstan

Archbishop Wulfstan of York

Bishop Oda

Ealdorman Ælfwold, ealdorman under Athelstan

West Frankia

Charlemagne, much revered former ruler of the Franks from AD768

Charles III, ruler of West Frankia from AD893, imprisoned by **Heribert II of Vermandois** from AD923 (after the Battle of Soissons) until AD929, although briefly restored to power in AD927-928. He also had a number of acknowledged illegitimate children.

m. (first wife) **Frederuna** (from AD907-917)

b. **Ermentrude, Frederuna, Adelaide, Gisela, Rotrude and Hildegarde**

m. (second wife) **Eadgifu,** daughter of Edward the Elder and his second wife in cAD919

b. **Louis** b.10th September AD920. Would be crowned as Louis IV, King of West Frankia on 19th June AD936.

m. **Gerberga**, sister of King Otto

b. AD941 **Lothar**

m.Concubine/unknown

b. AD unknown, **Bishop Rorice**

King Robert I, claimed the throne from Charles III, killed at the Battle of Soissons.

Count Hugh of the Franks/Paris, the son of King Robert and the brother by marriage of King Rodolphus

m. (1) **Judith,** of Maine

m. (2) **Eadhild**, daughter of Edward the Elder and his second wife.

m. (3) **Hadwig**, daughter of Henry the Fowler and Matilda

b.938 Beatrice

b.940 Hugh

Artoldus, Archbishop of Rheims and Archchancellor, conducted Louis IV's coronation in AD936

Count Heribert II of Vermandois, Charles III's gaoler

m. **Adela**, sister of **Count/Duke Hugh** (seven children, including)

b.AD910 **Adele**, married **Arnulf of Flanders**

b.AD915/20 **Liutgarde** married **William of Normandy**

b.AD920 **Hugh, Bishop of Rheims** (925-932) and (940-945)

King Rodolphus of Burgundy, became King of the West Franks after the death of his father by marriage, **Robert**, the father of **Hugh the Great**. Married to Hugh's sister, **Queen Emma**.

b. **Judith**

Count Rollo of Normandy, Norseman who in signing a treaty with Charles the Simple in AD911 created Normandy. Charles' son by marriage as he married his daughter **Gisela**.

Count William, known as Longsword, ruler of Normandy after Rollo (Rollo's son from a previous relationship to Gisela). He was the Count of Normandy – it did not become a dukedom until later.

Count Arnulf of Flanders, son of Baldwin II of Flanders and Lady Ælfthryth (Alfred's sister)

m.2 **Adele**, daughter of Count Heribert

Count Adelolf, brother of **Arnulf**, and son of **Baldwin II of Flanders** and **Lady Ælfthryth**. Died AD934

Duke Alain II of Brittany, lived in exile at Athelstan's court, until fully reclaiming his kingdom in AD936-9.

Abbot of Landevennec

Hugh the Black, Duke of Burgundy, brother of King Robert I of West Frankia

King Rudolf II, of the Kingdom of Arles (confusingly sometimes also called Burgundy)

b. **Conrad**

Lord Louis, brother of **King Rudolf II** of the Kingdom of Arles

m. **Ælfgifu**

Count William III of Aquitaine

Hugh, King of Italy, in contention with the Kingdom of Arles after the death of King Rudolf II

East Frankia

Henry the Fowler, king of East Frankia until his death on 2nd July AD936

    m.(2) **Matilda**

    b.**Otto**, king of East Frankia after his father's death

    m.**Eadgyth** of England

    b.**Lludolf** b.AD930

    b.**Liutgarde** b.AD932

    b.**Gerbega,**

        m. (1) **Gilbert of Lotharingia** (dies in AD939)

        m. (2) **Louis IV of West Frankia** (in AD939)

    b. **Lothar**

    b.**Hadwig**

    m. **Count Hugh of West Frankia**

    b. **Beatrice**

    sb **Hugh Capet**

    b. **Henry**

    b. **Bruno**

Duke Gilbert of Lotharingia, contested land between East and West Frankia.

    m. Gerberga, King Henry's daughter in AD928

    b.Alberade

    b.Gerberge

    b.Wiltrude

Hildebert, Archbishop of Mainz, conducts King Otto's coronation service

British Kings

    Constantin of the Scots

    Hywel Dda of Wales

Idwal of Wales
Owain of Wales

Misc (fictional)

Matilde, Louis' West Frankish nursemaid
Beornstan, Wessex warrior who supports Eadgifu in West Frankia
Mond, Louis' hound when a child
Wulfhelm, Eadgifu's warrior
Matilda, East Frankish servant

Places mentioned

Aachen, in East Frankia, where King Otto is crowned, burial place of Charlemagne

Flanders, a county in West Frankia

Wilton Nunnery, where two of Edward's daughters live as nuns. Their mother also lived there after her marriage was dissolved.

Tamworth, ancient capital of Mercia, in England

Attigny, royal palace in West Frankia

Abbey of Notre Dame and Sain Jean, in Laon, where King Louis is crowned

Peronne, where King Charles III was held in captivity

Monastery of Saint-Fursy, West Frankia.

Abbey of St Germain Des Pres, near Paris

Verdun, in contested Lotharinigia

Metz, in contested Lotharinigia

Toul, in contested Lotharinigia

Saxony, in East Frankia

Montreiul-Sur-Mer, in Normandy

Gloucester, in England.

Malmesbury, abbey in England.

Battles

Battle of Soissons, in West Frankia, between King Charles and King Robert in AD923. King Robert dies in the battle, but it is not a conclusive victory for King Charles.

Battle of Brunanburh, in England (exact location unknown) in AD937, between King Athelstan and all the British kings at that time, as well as the Dublin Norse.

Battle of Aldernach, in Lotharingia, in AD939 Duke Gilbert dies during the battle

ABOUT THE AUTHOR

I'm an author of historical fiction (Early English/Saxon, Vikings and the British Isles as a whole before the Norman Conquest, as well as three 20th-century mysteries) and fantasy (Viking age/dragon-themed).

I was born in the old Mercian kingdom at some point since 1066. Raised in the shadow of a strange little building, told from a very young age that it housed the bones of long-dead kings of Mercia and that our garden was littered with old pieces of pottery from a long-ago battle, it's little wonder that my curiosity in Early England ran riot. I can only blame my parents!

I like to write. You've been warned!

Find me at www.mjporterauthor.com and @coloursofunison on Twitter. https://linktr.ee/MJPorterauthor

facebook.com/mjporterauthor
twitter.com/coloursofunison
instagram.com/m_j_porterauthor
amazon.com/author/mj-porter
goodreads.com/M_J_Porter

ALSO BY MJ PORTER

The King's Daughters

Fantasy

<u>The Dragon of Unison (fantasy based on Viking Age Iceland)</u>

Hidden Dragon

Dragon Gone

Dragon Alone

Dragon Ally

Dragon Lost

Dragon Bond

<u>As JE Porter</u>

The Innkeeper

Twentieth Century Mysteries

<u>The Erdington Mysteries</u>

The Custard Corpses

The Automobile Assassination

Cragside - a 1930s mystery

Printed in Great Britain
by Amazon

32387768R00198